SF Books by Va

DOOM STAR SERIES
Star Soldier
Bio Weapon
Battle Pod
Cyborg Assault
Planet Wrecker
Star Fortress

EXTINCTION WARS SERIES
Assault Troopers
Planet Strike

INVASION AMERICA SERIES
Invasion: Alaska
Invasion: California
Invasion: Colorado
Invasion: New York

OTHER SF NOVELS
Alien Honor
Accelerated
Strotium-90
I, Weapon

Visit www.Vaughnheppner.com for more information.

Battle Pod

(Doom Star 3)

by
Vaughn Heppner

ISBN-13: 978-1496145765
ISBN-10: 1496145763
BISAC: Fiction / Science Fiction / Military

Prologue

It was dark in the shuttle as Marten crept to the medical unit. The ship was under one-G of acceleration. Using the glow of the life-support monitor, he examined Omi lying in the clear cylinder. Tubes were attached to the Korean's flesh. His chest rose and fell with each breath.

Marten studied the cylinder. It was airtight. He pressed a switch, and there was a beep as a small red light blinked several times. Clamps appeared, securing the medical unit for emergency ship maneuvers.

Marten exited the chamber. His features were stern, and his heart hammered. Any number of things could go wrong. He knew Highborn arrogance had given him this chance. Surely, they couldn't believe they were in danger from a lone preman.

The hatch to Lycon's sleep cubicle was open. This evening, all the hatches were open. Marten had been busy and had made sure.

He eased onto his stomach and slithered past the hatch. Soon on his feet again and in another section of the shuttle, he used a stolen electronic key, opening the suit locker. With practiced speed he donned his old vacc-suit. He tried to be quiet, but there were clunks and clatters. Finally, he sealed his helmet and shuffled to the airlock.

A fierce grin spread across his face. The Highborn had been careless. He was only a preman. What could he do to them?

Marten produced an override unit, one he'd tampered with the past few hours. He licked his lips and entered his code.

1

Then he engaged the manual override. Numbers flashed on the unit. A klaxon should have sounded, but Marten had overridden it with his stolen unit.

There was a hiss as the inner hatch slid open. Marten worked feverishly, applying clamps, making sure it was impossible for the inner hatch to close. With the last clamp in place, he stepped into the airlock. He switched on the vacc-suit's magnetic hooks to full power, securing himself to the wall. Then he manually opened the outer hatch.

Immediately air hissed past as it rushed out into the vacuum of space. Then the airlock was open all the way, and the sound became a gale-force shriek.

A stylus with a purple tip shot past Marten. Then cups and cutlery flew past as they tumbled into space.

Marten heard screaming. Almost too fast to notice, the Highborn pilot flew past him. Marten resisted the impulse to lean out and watch. Instead, he remembered how shock troopers had tumbled off the *Bangladesh's* particle shields. Now their arrogant, uncaring commanders would pay.

The medical Highborn flew outside next.

Then Lycon the Training Master appeared. The seven-foot Highborn managed to latch his fingers onto the hatch clamps. He strained to hang on, his massive body inches from Marten. In a feat of amazing strength, Lycon tore off a clamp. With desperate will, he began to work on the second.

Then the rapidly dropping air pressure began to tell on Lycon. His body and face began to bloat as his blood and other bodily fluids began to turn into water vapor and form in his soft tissues. The ebullism occurred even more strongly in his lungs. The escaping water vapor cooled around his open mouth and nostrils, creating frost.

Then, as he was magnetically secured, Marten began raining body blows against Lycon's horizontal and now grotesquely swollen torso.

With the last of the ship's air shrieking past his bloated face and whipping his hair, Lycon peered blindly at Marten. The Highborn must have realized he was dying. Maybe he wanted to take Marten with him. His clothes had torn off and blown into space. Bare Highborn fingers reached for Marten. Marten desperately slapped away the freakishly large hand. Lycon's frost-covered lips moved soundlessly. Then the huge Highborn lost his grip, and he shot out into space. Marten leaned out and watched the Training Master tumble away into the void.

Marten closed the outer hatch. Next, while breathing hard, he turned off his magnetic hooks. Then he removed the clamps and let the inner hatch hiss shut. The shuttle immediately began to pressurize.

A terrible laugh escaped Marten as he removed his helmet. He owned a spaceship and he was free. Free! Now he had to decide what he was going to do with his hard-won freedom.

Clones

-1-

The first thing Marten Kluge did with his freedom was shut off the shuttle's engines. Then he sat in the pilot's chair before a bank of color-coded controls. He eyed the vidscreen and the single polarized window that showed him the awesome beauty of the stars. The moment the engines cut out acceleration died and weightlessness returned to the shuttle.

Marten grinned harshly. He was a lean ex-shock trooper with a blond crewcut and angular cheeks. He had survived horrible ordeals, and it may have been that full sanity hadn't yet returned to him. Sitting there staring into space was his first moment of relaxation in….

Marten frowned, a frown that stayed with him until later when he found he was still staring at the stars. He shook his head. He had to concentrate, to try to become a normal human being again.

From the control panel Marten began to run diagnostic tests on the engines, the life-support system, and the ship's radar and teleoptic scopes. He was free, which meant he had to rely upon himself now. He owned a shuttle, a spaceship that could possibly take him anywhere in the Solar System.

He laughed. It was a strange sound in the endless silence of the shuttle. He cocked his head. Why would his laugh sound strange? He rubbed his face, feeling oddly disconnected.

He was free. He owned a spaceship. He—

A klaxon began to wail. It startled Marten. For a wild moment he thought that Lycon had survived and somehow was trying to gain admittance back into the shuttle.

Marten studied the controls and froze in shock. He turned off the klaxon, knowing now why his laugh had sounded strange. The carbon-scrubbers were turned off; his CO2 levels had been too high.

He adjusted the life-support controls as he berated himself for making such an elementary mistake. He couldn't afford any mistakes out here and hope to keep his freedom. He had a spaceship, but if the Highborn found him, if Social Unity found him, they would take away both his ship and his freedom.

How was he going to remain free? The space between Mercury, Venus, Earth and Mars—the Inner Planets—swarmed with the warships of both sides. His shuttle was effectively defenseless against any of them. He had to tiptoe. He had to remain hidden. He had to make clever choices if he was going to remain free.

For the next half hour Marten's fingers moved across the controls as he accessed information. He was in the void between Mercury and Venus, with a heading that would bring him to Earth if he initiated one-G acceleration and let the engines burn for…eleven more hours. The journey would take several weeks. During his computer search he also discovered the whereabouts of three Doom Stars. He didn't use the shuttle's radar or teleoptic scopes, but had referenced computer data on all known locations. After fifteen more minutes of computer exploration he discovered the location and vectors of several SU spacecraft, the majority of them war vessels. Neither the Doom Stars nor the SU craft were in position to affect him presently.

That eased some of his tension. Yet he wondered how long it would be before Highborn command sent him a message. Somewhere in their computers, they must be tracking him. Probably, the ship was sending a friend-or-foe signal. He had to find it, and then decide whether to shut if off or to leave it on.

Before Marten did that, he had to decide what to do with

5

his freedom. He couldn't just drift out here. He needed a plan, a master plan, and make his moves accordingly.

He had no desire to go to Earth. Nothing good awaited him there. As all Free Earth Corps *volunteers* had learned, Social Unity received updates on the FEC battle-rosters. In other words, if Political Harmony Corps captured him, he would be treated as a traitor to Social Unity. Likely the thought police would shoot him in the back of the head and dump his corpse in a mass grave.

Factoring in his present heading and velocity, it would take massive amounts of fuel to brake and redirect his spaceship to Venus. The majority of Venus was still in Social Unity's hands, but the Highborn had bombarded and laid siege to the planet with a Doom Star, space platforms and orbital fighters. Even if he had the fuel to redirect his flight to Venus, there was little incentive to do so. What held true for Venus in terms of fuel was even truer for Mercury. Besides, the Highborn controlled Mercury. The planet and the Sun-Works Factory that circled it comprised the bastion of Highborn power.

Marten stretched his lower back. He had to sit on the edge of the pilot's chair to use the control panel, because like everything else in the shuttle, it was sized for a Highborn. It made him feel childlike, and he found that annoying.

He continued to study the data. It was possible he might dock at one of the many *open* habitats orbiting Earth. Because of the open policy concerning the farm habitats, it might be possible for him to slip into obscurity there.

The situation there was tenuous, however. At the various Lagrange-points were massive farm habitats that helped feed Earth's billions. The Highborn could storm each habitat and cut off some of the planet's food supply. Or they could beam the laser-launch sites on Earth that propelled the food ships into orbit. Maybe they hadn't tried yet because it would prove too costly in Highborn casualties storming the habitats. Maybe the Highborn wanted the Earth intact, to use it later as a base for the further conquest of the Solar System. Mass starvation might cause catastrophic destruction of a future industrial basin.

Marten checked on the shuttle's air-mixture as he considered the possibility.

Slipping onto one of the farm habitats could benefit Omi. Omi might need better medical attention. Their present heading would take them to Earth orbit, and that rather quickly. Marten knew Earth customs and could probably blend in more easily there than anywhere else in the Solar System.

Marten studied the fuel situation as he plotted possible course headings to Mars and then to Jupiter. It wasn't simply a matter of distance. It was where in their orbit around the Sun each planet would be when his shuttle reached the needed distance. It soon became clear that Jupiter was too far. He couldn't actually land on Jupiter, but could head for one of the many moon colonies or the gas giant's atmospheric cloud cities.

Dejected, Marten slouched in his seat. It had always been his long-term plan to escape to the Jupiter Confederation. He wondered if Nadia Pravda had made it to the emergency pod. If so, her destination would be Jupiter.

Marten grinned at the prospect of holding Nadia again, of kissing her. He wanted to go to Jupiter. He wanted Nadia. Maybe he even needed her. But Jupiter was out presently as a reasonable possibility. That left Mars. He remembered rumors about a rebellion there.

There was a red light blinking on the control panel. Marten's heart sped up as he tapped keys. Something was wrong in the medical unit.

Marten unbuckled and leapt for the hatch. He sailed too fast and bumped his head. Muttering, practicing greater control, he floated through the hatch and pushed toward the medical chamber. A light was blinking on the life-support monitor.

Marten felt queasy. He wasn't a doctor. In the clear cylinder Omi twitched, and his features had become blue.

"Don't die," Marten whispered. He checked the monitor. It was the air-mixture. There was far too much carbon dioxide in the cylinder. He realized that he'd adjusted for the ship, but the controls on Omi's system were still cycling the wrong mix.

Marten used the emergency release handle. The hatch hissed. Marten swung the hatch open.

His friend stopped twitching, and the blueness faded from his skin. After a minute, Marten slid Omi back into the cylinder. He stood and watched for a half-hour.

Then he returned to the oversized pilot's chair. He had to decide where to go. Before he could he needed to know more about Mars. He studied the computer files until he found and read HB intelligence reports on the Red Planet. The information surprised him.

Mars had rebelled against its Social Unity garrisons. A single Doom Star had orbited Mars as the Highborn exterminated SU military personnel on the habitats and on its two moons. According to what Marten read, many SU personnel had escaped onto the surface. In other words, part of Mars belonged to Social Unity and the rest was in Rebel hands. The Doom Star had then departed the Mars Gravitational System. As their last act, they'd installed the Rebels in the surviving orbital military installations.

Marten tapped at the console. The Highborn had left the Rebels, the Mars Planetary Union as they called themselves, in control of near orbital space. The Martians were separate from the Highborn and separate from Social Unity. Might the Mars Planetary Union welcome an ex-military man? Might they greet with open arms an independent captain owning a shuttle?

Marten rechecked the computer. An hour later he hooked a line to the latch outside the airlock. Marten wore a vacc-suit with a toolkit on his belt. He floated as stars shined all around him. Behind him the Sun blazed. Marten magnetized his boots and clanked along the shuttle's hull. Soon he reached the friend-or-foe device. He knelt and extracted a wrench from his kit. For the next twenty minutes he loosened bolts. It brought back fond memories of working with Nadia on the repair pod.

Finally he detached the unit. He pulled so it floated upward. Then he crouched under it and heaved with all his strength. The friend-or-foe device sailed away into the void.

Let the Highborn monitor that on their computers.

Grinning within his vacc-suit, Marten began clanking back to the airlock. He coiled the safety line as he did so. Once at the airlock he pressed the switch. But nothing happened. The outer hatch remained shut.

Marten frowned, and tried again. Again, nothing happened. He blinked in growing concerning. Then it hit him. He'd never operated Highborn-built spaceships before. Was this a different design from the vessels he'd used while growing up around the Mercury Factory? Maybe it was a Highborn security device, an airlock that couldn't be opened from the outside.

Marten banged on the hatch. After several blows he realized that would do nothing at all. Omi was in the medical unit. He was stuck out here in space with a limited air supply. He'd better think of something else fast.

2

"General Hawthorne, sir, this is highly irregular. I must insist you return to headquarters. I can't possibly guarantee your safety."

General James Hawthorne was a tall man with gray along his temples. He wore camouflaged body-armor and held his helmet in the crook of his arm. He was the de-facto dictator of Social Unity, a military genius and one of the key reasons the Highborn conquest of Earth had slowed to a crawl.

The speaker was Colonel Diego of the Tenth Battalion of the Sixth Division, Third Army, in South America. It was the hot spot of the war, at the southwestern edge of the mighty Amazon River Basin. The Highborn had just captured La Paz of Bolivia Sector as they continued their push north through the heart of the continent.

General Hawthorne was here because he was tired of watching video-feeds. He wanted to see the real thing, to gain the pulse of his troops, and see how the new tactics worked. Thus he had risked leaving New Baghdad to come here to the jungle warzone.

"An orbital strike occurred yesterday about this time, sir," Colonel Diego said. He was a slim, stern-featured man, with a slender mustache. He glanced uneasily at Captain Mune and the rest of Hawthorne's security team.

Everyone stood under the canopy of giant rubber trees. Monkeys screamed in the upper branches. Soldiers waited by heavy artillery tubes. General Hawthorne had just arrived in four tracked infantry carriers packed with his bionic bodyguards.

All the bionic men were like Captain Mune. Specialists had torn these men down and rebuilt them with synthetic muscles, titanium-reinforced bones and sheath-protected nerves. Like Hawthorne, Captain Mune and the others wore camouflage gear. Mune had heavy features that were a little too wide and which hinted at plasti-flesh. He wore a peaked cap, and a barely audible whine emanated from him when he moved. Special enhancement glands had been grafted into him. If the need arose they would squirt drugs into his bloodstream and dull any pain he might receive, or stimulate him to even greater strength and speed. He wore a holstered gyroc pistol. Captain Mune was Hawthorne's personal bodyguard, and had saved his life more than once.

"Carry on, Colonel," Hawthorne said.

"But, sir, the Highborn battleoids—"

"Are one of the reasons I'm here," Hawthorne said.

Colonel Diego blinked with incomprehension.

"The Field Marshal has the same concerns you do," Hawthorne said. "As I told him, I'll take care of myself."

"But General—"

"Those are my orders," Hawthorne said quietly.

Colonel Diego hesitated a moment longer and then turned back to his communications team. They had set up a data-net under a camouflaged tent.

"Our presence has made him nervous," Hawthorne shortly whispered to Captain Mune.

"You're making me nervous, sir," Captain Mune said.

"Nonsense," Hawthorne said. He put on the helmet and lowered the visor. Then he purposefully strode into the jungle, toward enemy lines.

Captain Mune motioned the security team. Several bionic men took off running ahead of Hawthorne. They were much heavier than normal troops, and their boots sank deeper into the moist soil. The bionic men held gyroc pistols and were conditioned to give their lives for General Hawthorne's safety.

Listening to his labored breathing as he climbed over a giant root, Hawthorne understood why everyone was so uneasy. If he died out here, Captain Mune, Colonel Diego and even Field Marshal Santiago would take the blame. It was unfair, but it was how politics worked in Social Unity. Hawthorne knew he shouldn't be here. But he absolutely needed to know firsthand how the war was progressing.

It had been a political risk coming here as it left New Baghdad to the Directors, giving them greater freedom to plot against him. In that sense, being here was unwise.

The real political danger for him was the fact that the Highborn were winning the war. Unless he could achieve a real victory against the Highborn, Social Unity was doomed. The strike on the Sun-Works Factory had hurt the Highborn, but not badly enough. It had cost Social Unity too much to do the damage. They had even lost the experimental beamship.

He needed to know if this was the place to attempt a critical defeat against the Highborn. He needed to know if it was even possible. So he took this risk, and he risked the lives of others.

An hour later, after they'd traveled several kilometers deep into the jungle, they finally made contact with the enemy.

"Get down, sir!" Captain Mune shouted. He shoved Hawthorne from behind.

The bionic captain's strength was irresistible. Hawthorne found himself hurled against a mossy rise. He grunted, his body-armor rattled and his faceplate mashed against the damp soil. For a second Hawthorne's lungs locked as harsh whooshing sounds streaked over him.

Explosions lifted him from the mossy hummock, and his armor rattled again as he slammed back down. Hawthorne grunted as weights fell on him. It took several seconds before he realized two bionic soldiers were shielding his body with their own.

More explosions occurred. Then something fast and powerful boomed overhead. Were those the new magnetic lifters?

"Get off," Hawthorne whispered. "I must witness this." He squirmed free, wiped muck from his visor and blinked to get rid of the spots before his eyes.

Captain Mune lay beside him. "Sir, we must retreat."

Hawthorne raised himself higher and peered down into a jungle valley. He used his chin to select one of his helmet's special features: telescopic sighting.

He witnessed a Hawk Team. They were Free Earth Corps, traitorous humans who fought for the Highborn. They used a rugged, fuel-efficient battlefield jetpack. Two of them lifted into the air, armed with portable missile-launchers. A burning SU infantry carrier lay on its side two hundred meters ahead of the fliers. Three SU soldiers tumbled out of the wreckage. Two missiles streaked from the Hawk Team. There was an explosion, and then no one moved on the burning carrier.

"The bastards," Hawthorne said through gritted teeth. Before he could order his bionic men to take aim, one of the newer bio-tanks raced out of the jungle growth.

Bio-tanks were smaller than cybertanks, and were built upon different principles. The bio-tank was low to the ground and had a single silver dome atop its tracked body. A portal opened along the silver dome, and a chaingun poked through. The chaingun whirled into life, shredding the two jetpack infantry. Other FEC infantry hidden in the trees opened fire with their portable missiles. As the flaming streaks closed upon the bio-tank, the vehicle activated its defensive armament. It deployed beehive-shaped charges. The shrapnel took out all but one missile. That missile cracked the silver dome, and it appeared to have angered the bio-tank. The engine revved and the tracks churned, causing grass and dirt to fly behind it. The bio-tank roared for the trees, its chaingun shredding leaves, branches, bark and FEC soldiers.

"Excellent," Hawthorne said.

"Sir," Captain Mune warned.

Hawthorne saw it; a great, bounding humanoid, a Highborn battleoid. With exoskeleton strength, a battleoid could make fifty-meter leaps.

A second and a third bio-tank appeared. They must have tracked the battleoid. Their chainguns poured rounds at the armored Highborn.

Stricken, the first battleoid sprawled onto the ground. Then enemy lasers struck, stabbing down from the heavens. The giant beams melted one of the bio-tanks' silver domes, and the vehicle exploded. More lasers stabbed down, striking the other bio-tanks.

Hawthorne's visor polarized and saved his eyes. The lasers were striking uncomfortably near.

Before Hawthorne could stop him with a command, Captain Mune hefted the general onto his shoulder and ran. The other bionic men followed. As they ran SU artillery began to pound the area with high explosives, no doubt seeking other battleoids. High command desperately sought Highborn casualties. Due to Hawthorne's orders they were not aware of his presence in this combat zone.

The giant lasers stabbed down again, beaming to Earth from the Highborn orbital laser platforms. Hawthorne and his strategy staff had yet to find a battlefield answer to that tactic. Knocking them down was the only real solution. The cost in merculite missiles was always too high, as the Highborn savagely defended the orbital platforms.

"Set me down," Hawthorne ordered.

"Respectfully, sir," Captain Mune said, "I must decline. I just heard over Colonel Diego's data-net that more battleoids are coming. I think the Highborn know you're here. I think this is a trap to capture you, sir."

Hawthorne endured the indignity of being carried until Captain Mune reached a tracked infantry carrier.

After setting him down, Captain Mune said, "It's time we left the battle zone, sir."

Hawthorne counted his bionic men. About half were missing. Had they died so he might live? Was seeing the jetpack infantry killed worth half his security team?

"We must defeat the Highborn," Hawthorne said.

Captain Mune hustled him toward the infantry carrier.

"There has to be a way to stop them," Hawthorne said.

"Right now, sir," Captain Mune said, "I'd just worry about surviving the afternoon."

The hatch clanged shut, and the engine fired into life. As it roared for Colonel Diego's headquarters, General Hawthorne was sunk deep in gloomy thought.

3

Time ticked away for Marten as he sweated outside the shuttle, and the inside of his vacc-suit smelled like fear.

He was magnetically adhered to the hull. At its present velocity, the shuttle sailed serenely for the Earth Gravitational System. The stars shined their beauty, but Marten had no interest in them now. He'd worked hard the past half-hour to remove the final plate and gain access to the sensor system.

He checked his air supply. He had another twenty minutes left. The vacc-suit's tanks hadn't been fully charged before he'd gone outside. Marten shook his head. He couldn't believe the mistakes he'd made these last few hours. For years, he'd dreamed of freedom. For years, he'd labored under rules set by others. With freedom, came responsibility. He could no longer afford the luxury of thinking *some* of the time. He needed to engage his wits all of the time.

If he survived this, he vowed to plan each move with care. Maybe he had spent too many dreadful weeks lost in space. Maybe that had played havoc with his senses and dulled his mind. He would now sharpen his mind.

There, he finally had it. Marten licked his lips, clipped the tools back onto his belt, and pried the plate loose. He used a magnetic bolt to keep the plate fixed against another part of the hull.

Now came the tricky part. He hooked his suit to the sensor net so he could use the ship's computer. In five minutes, he'd established a link. If there were some Highborn code—

No, no code was needed. That was a mistake on the part of

the Highborn, an oversight in their security details. They had probably never envisioned someone else gaining control of their shuttle with the killer locked outside.

Blinking sweat out of his eyes, Marten used voice activation. He wasn't used to this and he had little time left, but he managed to override the airlock controls.

The computer told him the outer hatch was open. Marten swallowed hard and clanked along the shuttle's hull, hurrying now. Time was running out.

He made it to the hatch with five minutes of air left. He closed the outer hatch, pressurized the chamber, and opened the inner one. He only had two minutes left as he cracked the seal and twisted off his helmet inside the shuttle. He stood staring at the wall. That had been far too close.

Taking a deep breath, Marten began to open the vacc-suit. He needed to go outside later and reattach the sensor plate. But he couldn't go now. He was too paranoid to go now. He had to first figure out why the outer hatch hadn't opened properly. Maybe Lycon had done something to it as he'd fought to remain aboard.

There was a lot to do to make this shuttle his, and to make sure it was shipshape for a longer voyage to Mars. Marten floated to the oversized pilot's chair, and he reconfigured the flight path.

"Think," he whispered to himself.

Once he changed heading…would that bring him to the notice of any Doom Stars or to SU warships? A spaceship was difficult to spot. It was such a tiny mote compared to the vastness of space. A shuttle was even harder to see than a warship. Once he fired up the engines all changed. In the void an engine's heat signature stood out like a beacon. The trick was to be out of range of any warship's weaponry. A Doom Star had the longest range, and any warship could launch a missile.

"You have to tiptoe, Marten," he said.

For the next hour Marten studied his radar and teleoptic scopes, and all known positions of all warships. The time came when he had to choose. He was nervous. He wondered what he had forgotten. This was the moment. Once he engaged the engines and used up precious fuel he wasn't going to be able to change his mind. What he decided now would affect what happened to him months from now.

He first floated to Omi and rechecked everything. Then he returned to the pilot's chair, reconfiguring his course yet again. His stomach was queasy. This was crazy. He was free and that meant he had to be brave.

Finally he reached out and engaged the thrusters. The one-G of acceleration returned. It brought back gravity, or pseudo-gravity. Marten laughed. He couldn't believe it, but he laughed with relief. He had made his decision, his biggest yet as a free man.

Now his destination was Mars.

-4-

General James Hawthorne paced with his thin hands clasped behind his back. He was in a magnetic bullet train, riding in a railcar speeding in excess of five hundred kilometers per hour. He was crossing through Peru Sector he believed, the northeastern corner of it. It was dark outside his window as the train barreled through tunnels most of the way. Because the Highborn owned the air and owned space, this was the safest and presently the fastest transportation on Earth.

He had left the battle zone some time ago. His ribs were still sore where Captain Mune had thrown him onto the ground.

Hawthorne paced before a desk. On the desk was the gun Ulrich had used to murder so many good people. It was made of nickel-plated steel, and shone like a polished mirror. Hawthorne bent close and saw himself in the shiny barrel. He kept the gun as a reminder of the treachery that lurked around him.

He believed himself cagier these days. He'd learned from his political mistakes, and he'd vowed never to be taken unaware again; there had been several attempts on his life. He now knew that more assassins would likely come for him.

It was the message that lay on the table beside the slivery pistol that made him paranoid. Madam Director Blanche-Aster had requested an emergency session with him. She was in Central American Sector, waiting for him. That was strange. She should be safely in New Baghdad, not in Central America. Had she engineered a coup in his absence?

Officially, Madam Director Blanche-Aster ran Social

18

Unity. In reality, she was his figurehead. It suited them both. He needed the pretense of her rule to pacify Political Harmony Corps and thirty-eight billion citizens. She needed his skill and military muscle to survive the other scheming directors, and to survive Chief Yezhov of PHC.

Why had she come to Central America?

Hawthorne checked his chronometer. Soon, he would find out.

***

Two hours and fifteen minutes later there was a heavy rap at the door of General Hawthorne's railcar.

"Come in," Hawthorne said. He sat at his desk, reading Julius Caesar's *Commentaries on the Gallic War*. He felt as if the Highborn were like Caesar's Roman Legions and the SU Military like the many Gallic warbands that had suffered endless butchery. Hawthorne kept wondering how the Gauls could have defeated Caesar's crack legionaries. If he could discover the answer, it might help him against the Highborn.

Captain Mune entered, and said, "Madam Director Blanche-Aster is ready to see you, sir."

"Did she bring her security clone?"

"I took the precaution of having the clone wait in the detention car, sir."

"Did you disarm the clone?"

"No, sir."

Hawthorne nodded, glad for Mune's discretion. It was wise to hide the steel fist of his rule. Lord Director Enkov had never understood that. It made people more comfortable to pretend they had power, even when they knew better. He wondered why that was, and then dismissed it from his thoughts.

"I'll go to her," Hawthorne said, rising.

Captain Mune allowed himself a small smile. "I took the liberty of anticipating you, sir. If you'll follow me…"

***

General Hawthorne entered a plush railcar with red carpeting, hanging ferns, famous portraits and fans gentling wafting the odor of roses. Those odors couldn't hide the medicinal smells emanating from Blanche-Aster's special chair.

The Madam Director was one hundred and sixty-two years old. Longevity treatments had controlled the encroachments of age; her chair kept her breathing. It was a bulky gleaming-white unit with magnetic repulsors, floating an inch off the carpet. Tubes snaked from it into her, fluids surging through the plastic.

Hawthorne nodded a greeting, took a seat across a white cube from her, crossed his legs and idly smoothed a crease in his trousers.

Her vibrantly alive eyes tightened. Tubes rustled as the Madam Director leaned forward. "You're no doubt curious as to why I've traveled this far for a simple conversion," she said in a conspiratorial whisper.

"You have my attention, Madam."

She gasped at the effort of leaning forward and sank back against her chair. Her withered fingers twitched over armrest buttons, and the floating chair backed away from the cube and turned toward a window. Sunlamps burned brightly in the tunnel outside, showing the granite walls.

Hawthorne waited. The gurgles from her chair were the only sounds in the room. Then a slight whine occurred as she faced him.

"I understand you will think my worry part of a subtle plot to remove you from office," she began. "It is exactly the opposite. I have learned to fear Chief Yezhov." Her unnaturally smooth features twisted with distaste. "I fear your Captain Mune almost as much. He is inhuman, the wrong direction for humanity to have taken."

"You may be right about that. However, Captain Mune's *inhumanity* has saved my life more than once." Hawthorne refrained from rubbing his sore ribs.

The Madam Director cackled like a holovid capitalist. Maybe she knew it was a mad sound; she stopped almost the moment she made it. Then her chair floated nearer to the white cube.

"Do you realize that our own arrogance has created this intolerable situation?" she asked.

Hawthorne waited. He had learned that holding his tongue,

20

combined with unruffled patience, awarded him many advantages. It often made others nervous, and it usually caused them to speak their mind without his having to reveal his position. There was an ancient proverb concerning the matter: *Even a fool is thought wise if he keeps silent.*

The Madam Director hissed through her teeth. "Our eugenicists created the Highborn in their labs. They spliced genes and tampered with DNA. We wanted the perfect soldiers in order to bring harmony to the Solar System. The capitalists in the Outer Planets recklessly hoarded the limited resources of our system. Billions lived harshly on Earth. With those resources equitably shared under Social Unity, we could have achieved an era of peace and plenty."

"Ambition often leads to disaster," Hawthorne said, thinking about the ancient Athenian Empire and its Sicilian Expedition in 415 B.C.

"If we had never created the Highborn," she said, "we could have averted this war."

"The past is always more clearly seen than the future."

The Madam Director scowled. "Aphorisms won't avert the coming disaster."

Hawthorne kept his face bland, but she had his interest. She was seldom this agitated.

"We should have understood that altered humans would view reality through altered eyes and that superior intellect breeds superior ambition," she said. "How could these supermen join us in social harmony? Man is a communal being. In many ways, massed men are like a herd of sheep. It isn't a complete analogy, but I think you can understand my meaning."

Hawthorne waited stoically. This lengthy preamble was undoubtedly leading to something momentous. She likely believed he would find her proposition repugnant, so she buttressed it with this speech.

"These words are not heretical to Social Unity theory," she said. "They are plain facts, if stated in an uncomplimentary fashion. I hope I may speak frankly with you?"

"Our task is to face uncomplimentary facts head-on, in the interest of serving the people," he said.

"Yes, yes," she said. "That is well-spoken. Chief Yezhov hints that you possess anti-socialist tendencies. Your statement just now belies Yezhov's words. I have come to understand the steel of your spine. You eye intolerable facts with unwavering resolve. Perhaps a taint or two touches you and infests your thinking. But those are wounds gained in service to Social Unity."

Hawthorne allowed himself a small twist of the lips.

"General, you should not belittle the importance that the other directors place on Social Unity theory. There are whispers that you attempt to sully the purity of the movement. Your monomaniacal insistence that all cybertanks and bionic soldiers remain under your command has led to strange rumors."

Was this the thrust of her argument? Was she actually going to try to get him to relinquish command of the pillars of his power? If that was true, it meant she had become his enemy. Hawthorne felt tired then. He didn't want to order her death. But he couldn't allow her free rein if she worked this openly against him. Mentally, he began to cast about for her replacement.

"I'm not impugning the bionic soldiers," she said. "Because of the Highborn, we need them. They are a lesser evil. For all their machinery, the bionic soldiers are still Homo sapiens. The Highborn are not Homo sapiens. They are like…"

"Wolves," Hawthorne suggested.

Blanche-Aster gave him a blank look.

"You spoke about sheep before," he said, "so I assumed you knew about wolves."

"In my younger days, I worked in the farming habitat of *Taping Five*," she said.

"It bred sheep?"

"Yes," she said.

"Wolves were predatory animals like dogs that lived in the wild in the ancient times."

"Ah," she said. "I understand the allusion now. Yes, the Highborn are like the pit-fighting dogs that the slum dwellers breed."

"Sheep and wolves can't mingle without the wolves

devouring the sheep," Hawthorne said.

"As the Highborn try to devour us," she said. "That is my point. We are engaged in a death struggle. Either we must exterminate the Highborn, or they will replace humanity. Should they win they won't slaughter Homo sapiens immediately. But given several hundred years..." She paused as the color of the fluids in her tubes changed from blue to a reddish tinge. Then a clot of deeper red tumbled and wavered like jelly as it surged through the tube and disappeared into the chair.

"I'm not sure I completely agree with you," Hawthorne said, keeping his face impassive. Her chair—he suppressed a shudder. "History shows that master races desire slaves or inferiors. I believe that Homo sapiens shall become a permanent slave race to the Highborn."

"I have also studied the prehistoric files. What became of the Neanderthals?"

"I concede you your point," Hawthorne said. "But it is all academic. Social Unity shall defeat the Highborn."

"With bionic soldiers and cybertanks?" she asked.

A crease appeared in Hawthorne's broad forehead. "Are you forgetting the cyborgs, Madam Director?"

Her eyes shined with a weird intensity as she leaned toward him.

General Hawthorne understood before she began to speak that here was the reason she'd wanted to meet with him. Here was why she'd left New Baghdad and crossed the ocean.

"I have not forgotten the cyborgs, sir. Consider what has occurred. Our eugenicists labored intensively for many years to mold the Highborn. They are biologically altered men. They were created to become a soldier race. Meanwhile, other scientists funded by us were hard at work in the Neptune System. They labored to create the perfect machine-man." The Madam Director cackled. "I have taken to calling them genus *Cyborgus*."

"An apt name," Hawthorne said.

"More apt than you realize," she said. "As I was saying, our biological creation has rebelled against us. They captured the Doom Stars, and with them seized control of the orbital space of Mercury, Venus, Earth and Mars."

"They have retreated from Mars," Hawthorne said.

"Please bear with me. The Highborn have also seized the Sun-Works Factory, the greatest industrial plant in the Solar System. They have conquered Antarctica and the islands of Earth, and are in the process of conquering South America. Now we seek the help of the second creation, the machine men, to oust the biological error. But do we realize that the machine-men will be even worse than the altered biological men are? Instead of pit dogs among us, we will have automated killers."

Hawthorne uncrossed his legs. "Madam, we already have machine men, the bionic soldiers."

"No!" she said. "The bionic men are still human. The cyborgs are something completely different."

"I have read the files. What you're—"

"The files," she sneered. "The files. Ha! Have you seen the cyborgs? Have you spoken with someone who lived through an encounter with them?"

"Have you?"

"Yes! Yes, I have. And I realize that we have sent for annihilation to save us from subjugation."

Her fervor surprised Hawthorne. "Would you care to share this information with me?"

"May I use the holograph in the cube?" she asked.

"By all means," he said.

The Madam Director pressed buttons on her armrest.

The top of the white cube between them flickered with life, projecting a holographic image. It showed a man-shaped being, bald with plasti-flesh and dead shark-like eyes. He moved with uncanny speed. It was a combat video, jerky, sometimes showing nothing but blasted buildings or falling men. There were occasional glimpses of the cyborg.

"Where did you get this?" Hawthorne asked.

The Madam Director twitched her withered fingers. "I have connections with PHC Outer Planets Intelligence."

"Yezhov gave it to you?"

Madam Director Blanche-Aster gave another of her unnerving cackles. "No, no, Yezhov has no idea I have this. He awaits the cyborgs with great relish."

"Why?"

The old woman bit her lower lip, and the grim vibrancy in her eyes become hooded, perhaps for the first time showing fear.

"Not all the experimentation occurred in the Neptune System," she said. "Yezhov has access to the scientists who labored in secret here on Earth."

"I've heard nothing of this."

"No, no, I should have been surprised if you had. You know about Yezhov's brain-wiped agents, the ones he plans to use to assassinate Highborn."

"I'm familiar with the project."

"General, there is a process…" She tapped a button and a mechanical arm extended from her medical unit with a small fan on the end. The fan whirred to life, gently blowing air into her perspiring face. "I've debated a long time about this. For I've come to understand that your position is weaker than Chief Yezhov's position. He waits for an unbeatable addition to his power base. He could use my secret help, and it would cement my place in the new order. Even so, I have decided to risk everything and unreservedly throw in my lot with yours. Yezhov doesn't understand the horror he wishes to use. All he knows is that he desires to rule Social Unity. The cyborgs have created an assembly line, a ghastly thing that tears down a human and recreates him or her into a cyborg."

"Tears down? As Captain Mune has been torn down?"

"No," Blanche-Aster whispered. "Can't you understand what I'm trying to say? The Highborn have shattered Inner Planets. They have torn much of Earth from our control. They own Mercury. They have allowed the Planetary Union rebels to regroup on Mars. Venus is under constant bombardment. The biologically altered Highborn have pushed us into a corner, but we're battling hard to remain free. Imagine how much worse our situation will be once a true race of machine-men has escaped our control. The cyborgs have the means to expand like a virus among us. We cannot allow them to land on Earth. If that happens, our demise shall be swift."

"Your holographic image was unsettling, but hardly—"

"I have another clone," Blanche-Aster whispered.

Hawthorne sat very still, and he noticed movement on the farthest wall, a tiny spider slowly crawling toward the ceiling. For a moment he wondered if it was a mechanical listening device, a new type of spy-stick. Another clone was news, and he realized how difficult it must have been for the Madam Director to tell him this.

"My second clone arrived from the Neptune System three weeks ago," Blanche-Aster said. "The holovid was brought by her. I request that you speak with her."

"That can be arranged."

"If you let the cyborgs land on Earth, General, we are doomed. I assure you that neither you nor your bionic men will be able to control them. They will quickly see that Yezhov will give them the freedom of operation they want. They will help engineer Yezhov's rise to power. That rise can only occur over your corpse."

"What do you suggest I do?"

Madam Director Blanche-Aster grimaced. "What I would now do if I were in charge. Blast the cyborgs in their pods before they can unload."

"Murder them?"

"Yes!"

"Because you fear them?"

"Because we've created our own aliens, General. Because they will supplant us in ways that would make the Highborn seem benevolent."

Hawthorne stood up and strode to the window. The harsh lights showed the granite cracks in the tunnel. Water dripped there. They lived like moles because of the Highborn. Cyborgs—he recalled the bio-tanks. Programmed human brain mass ran the bio-tanks. Why should these cyborgs be any different? What was the real reason behind the Madam Director's request?

"When can I speak with your second clone?" he asked.

"In an hour, if you desire it. I brought her along with me to Central American Sector. She's waiting in the city."

Hawthorne regarded the Madam Director. "I'll speak with Captain Mune. Let us say, two hours from now."

"Wonderful."

"You will remain my guest during that time. Hmm. To make it easy, I'll have you stay here on my bullet train."

The Madam Director smiled grimly. "That you're so suspicious raises my hopes that you'll understand the danger. We must not compound our errors."

General Hawthorne thought about that. Then he inclined his head and took his leave.

"I don't recommend this, sir," Captain Mune said.

General Hawthorne and the bionic soldier stood outside the cell where Blanche-Aster's second clone waited. A vidscreen showed the clone sitting at a table. She was young, with short brunette hair, a thin face and a long, supple body. She wore the brown uniform of a habitat farm-worker. Unlike the Madam Director's other clone who had been a bodyguard, this one had a fervent manner. She tried to maintain indifference, but her gaze slid about the cell. She seemed nervous. She either twitched fingers or her shoulders, or blinked too rapidly.

"This clone is a PHC Outer Planet's Intelligence Operative," Hawthorne said.

Captain Mune adjusted the controls of the vidscreen. It showed a modified x-ray image of her body. He zoomed to the base of her skull, to a tiny black dot there.

"It's artificial," Captain Mune said.

"Did the Madam Director send you the clone's medical specs?"

Captain Mune nodded. "According to them, the implant was fused in her skull before she spaced out to Neptune. It's a neural-charged explosive."

Hawthorne recalled the neural inhibitor Ulrich had once stuck in him.

"Its purpose is what?" Hawthorne asked.

"The specs say the clone can will the device to explode. The Madam Director has gone to great lengths to ensure that no one can turn her clones against her."

"Has the explosive been tampered with?" Hawthorne asked.

"We haven't been able to establish that," Captain Mune said.

"You think it has?"

"It's my job to be paranoid, sir. I suggest you talk to her via vidscreen."

"Would the explosive be enough to take out both of us?"

"No, sir."

"Where is the danger then?"

"She could attack you physically, sir."

"I am combat-trained," Hawthorne said.

"Begging your pardon, sir, but you're an older man."

"And I am a man and she's a woman."

"If the Madam Director is correct concerning the devious nature of the cyborgs, who knows what other surprises have been modified into her."

"Enhancement drugs?" asked Hawthorne.

"She may also have been trained in special fighting techniques."

Hawthorne clasped his hands behind his back and scowled at the clone. For months now he had awaited the cyborgs' arrival. He desperately needed shock troops superior to the Highborn. The war in South America went against them in a slow and bitter grind of attrition.

Hawthorne unclipped his holster and withdrew his sidearm, a Gauss needler that fired heavy steel needles. It had a rubber-coated grip so it wouldn't slip, and it felt good in his hand. He checked the gun, flipped the safety so it was ready for immediate fire, and shoved it back into the holster.

"Even an old man can draw a needler," Hawthorne said.

"Her reflexes may have been enhanced."

"Paranoia is a good attribute in a bodyguard. For the Supreme Commander of Social Unity it can lead to paralysis. I must weigh the risks versus the benefits, play the odds, and then strike boldly if that is called for. Deciding what to do with the cyborgs could be the most critical decision of my life. If she's been tampered with so she'll attack me I want to know that. I suspect the only way to learn the truth is to present

29

myself as a target."

"If she makes it past your needler and is killing you, sir, do we have permission to gas the chamber?"

Hawthorne nodded curtly. Then he adjusted his holster and strode for the entrance to the cell.

**

Hawthorne sat across the table from the clone. The clone's name was Rita Tan. It felt odd, because Rita Tan used the Madam Director's voice and had many of her mannerisms. He shook his head. What Rita lacked was the Madam Director's confidence.

Here was a person who had seen too many horrors up close. She acted like a person who believed the world was imminently doomed, and that no one else understood the nature of the peril. Rita Tan blinked much too rapidly. Her head jerked at the oddest moments, and she had the annoying habit of smiling too much, as if she feared Hawthorne would attack unless she pacified him. Rita Tan put her elbows on the table and leaned forward too far. Her facial skin was stretched, and she spoke in a hushed tone.

"He showed me the assembly line, the process." Rita shuddered. "It removed the skin and incinerated it. The stench was horrible. The saws, the artificial attachments—it removed the brain and put it in a sheathed braincase, and connected a new spinal column."

"Why did this…"

"Toll Seven," she whispered.

"Why did Toll Seven show you the assembly line?"

"They calculate their actions using logic parameters. The trouble is I had no idea of their ideal outcome and what weights they put to each action. I found their speech either incomprehensible or frighteningly naive."

"Did Toll Seven or the others give any indication they planned—"

"I escaped that night," whispered Rita. "I knew they planned to alter me, to strip away my flesh, my humanity, and implant my brain into a cyborg body. I used sleep enhancers and shot to Earth using full thrust. I had to beat them here. I had to warn my mother. You can stop them, can't you? You

30

can order their destruction? You have the authority, I hope?"

Hawthorne gave her a small nod.

Rita Tan sat back and sagged in her chair. "Then I'm not too late. Please tell me you have the authority to order the pods blasted out of space. I have to speak—"

"Calm yourself," Hawthorne said, as below the table he secretly wrapped his hand on the butt of his needler. Rita Tan wanted too much assurance he had the authority.

She blinked rapidly.

"I am the Supreme Commander of Social Unity," Hawthorne said. "All final authority rests with me. Yes, I will destroy the pods."

Rita Tan's head jerked to the left. She gave him a weird smile, and she opened her mouth. Then she surged with manic speed, flinging the table at him.

Hawthorne had expected such an obvious tactic. Despite his age and lanky frame he rolled out of the chair, and kept rolling as he drew the needler. The altered clone was fast, maybe even faster than what Captain Mune had suggested. Rita twitched her head with insect-like rapidity, pivoted even as she lunged the wrong way, and changed direction to fly at him.

The Gauss needler was a deadly weapon against unarmored opponents. It used a magnetic impulse to shoot a heavy steel needle, and it fired a great number of needles in a matter seconds.

Firing from the hip Hawthorne sprayed needles at Rita Tan. The needler made its signature crackling noise. The first few missed. They smashed against the steel wall behind her and disintegrated, flinging sliver-like shards. From the floor, Hawthorne aimed. Rita Tan screamed wildly, a battle cry meant to frighten her opponent or to increase her chi as she attacked. The needles riddled her torso, ten in less than a second. Twitching in agony, she thudded onto Hawthorne and knocked the needler from his grasp. He shouted as the door swished open.

Hawthorne flung Rita Tan away as Captain Mune charged into the room, his gyroc pistol ready. She flopped onto the floor as Mune snapped off a single shot. Because of the short distance, the rocket-packet in his gyroc round never ignited.

31

The rocket-bullet smashed against the middle of her back, however. With a grunt she sagged to the floor. She had been rising to attack anew. She twisted her head to glare at Hawthorne. Her lips writhed. Hawthorne groped for his needler. Then the back of her head exploded, raining blood, bone and gray matter.

Shocked, Hawthorne stared at Captain Mune. The bionic soldier moved fast as he knelt beside the twitching corpse. He slid it across the room, away from Hawthorne.

"Never mind that," Hawthorne said in a hoarse voice. He was breathing hard. The clone had attacked him. The implications might be far-reaching. "Leave her!" Hawthorne shouted.

Captain Mune looked up.

"This could be the beginning of a coup attempt," Hawthorne said. "Chief Yezhov and the Madam Director might be working in concert."

Captain Mune's features hardened. He surged to his feet, whirled around, and aimed his gyroc at the open door in one incredibly fast motion. His gun-hand was rock steady, and the muscles in it were rigid and stood out in stark relief.

Hawthorne pulled out his communicator as it crackled with life, and he began to issue instructions to his security team.

That's when an even heavier explosion occurred outside, rocking the railcar. Hopefully, it lacked the power to bring the tunnel down on them.

-6-

Three shiny jets streaked across the Atlantic Ocean one hundred meters above sea level. They were the latest in military technology, built with laser reflectors. A powerful headwind blew against them, causing the steel-colored ocean below to seethe with white-capped waves.

In the second jet, General Hawthorne stared out of the polarized canopy. He stared at the dark clouds in the sky. High above the clouds lurked Highborn orbital laser platforms and orbital launch stations. Heavy orbital fighters often swooped down from those stations. It was a terrible risk flying across the Atlantic like this. Lasers or orbital fighters could easily take out these three jets. Using a fast submarine would have been wiser.

Hawthorne shook his head. It might have been wiser for his personal security while crossing the ocean, but foolish for a different reason.

In the first jet sat the late Madam Director's prime clone, the former bodyguard. The second clone was dead, her head a gory ruin. The Madam Director was also dead. The remains of Hawthorne's security team had poked through the wreckage of the bullet train. The blast that had nearly killed everyone in the tunnel had come from her bulky chair.

Hawthorne brooded about that. If she had wanted to kill him and had been willing to die to do it, why hadn't she exploded her chair during their meeting? The prime clone, the former bodyguard, had provided a possible answer. It was the reason why the prime clone made the emergency trip to New

33

Baghdad with him and with Captain Mune in the last jet.

Captain Mune's people had questioned the prime clone, the surviving bodyguard named Lisa Aster. They had pumped her with interrogation drugs. What they'd learned troubled Hawthorne. The late Madam Director had feared the cyborgs, had talked about it ever since the second clone had returned from the Neptune System. According to the prime clone, the bodyguard, the second clone from the Neptune System had spent several hours alone with the Madam Director. That was highly unusual, according to the bodyguard clone. Afterward, the Madam Director had seemed disoriented.

As the jet continued to flash across the Atlantic Ocean, Hawthorne came to a decision. The clone from the Neptune System, the one whose head had exploded, had been tampered with by the cyborgs. That clone must have inserted the bomb in the Madam Director's chair. That the bomb had passed Captain Mune's security x-rays, likely meant the Neptune-tampered clone had used advanced technology. By the compromised clone's actions, the cyborgs had sent her back here in order to assassinate him, the head of Social Unity.

The conclusion was obvious: the cyborgs were his enemies. Hawthorne didn't know why the cyborgs had rebelled, but that didn't matter now. Getting back to New Baghdad before word of the assassination attempt leaked out was what mattered.

Hawthorne leaned toward the polarized canopy, staring down at the waves. It was intolerable that the head of Social Unity had to scurry across Earth. They were losing the war, and now a needed ally had become a liability. Hawthorne pressed his forehead against the pilot's seat ahead of him. He closed his eyes and began to do some deep thinking.

***

General Hawthorne survived the trip and landed at New Baghdad. Captain Mune immediately led the city's security teams through the vast underground megalopolis. An hour later Hawthorne received a call from Chief Yezhov of Political Harmony Corps.

"General Hawthorne," Chief Yezhov said over a vidscreen. "I'm getting reports you're back in the city."

Hawthorne sat at his desk with a computer stylus in hand,

as if he was hard at work on a project. He stared into the vidscreen, attempting to appear impatient because he was so busy. It was a ploy to confuse Yezhov.

"Yes, I'm back," said Hawthorne.

The head of Political Harmony Corps wore a scarlet uniform, and a black plastic helmet held in place by a chinstrap. He had pale skin, washed-out blue eyes and a ridiculous little mustache, twin dots under his nose. He was short and thin and possessed an almost nonexistent chin.

"How—" Chief Yezhov frowned. "I thought you were in South America."

"Yes."

Chief Yezhov blinked like a reptile. "...I've heard rumors that the Madam Director is dead."

"You are amazingly well-informed. I'd hoped to keep her heart attack secret a little while longer."

"...I see. A heart attack," Yezhov mused. "That is most unfortunate. We shall mourn the great lady."

"Orders for a temporary blackout of communications are about to go in effect," Hawthorne said. "Any unauthorized back-channel use will be severely punished."

"You of course do not mean Political Harmony Corps."

"The delicate nature of yet another Director-in-Chief dying so soon after Enkov's accident means we must proceed with extreme caution. While I applaud your devotion to duty, I must insist on your cooperation in the coming investigation. There is a possibility that some of your deputies have exceeded their authority."

"It is with the greatest reluctance that I must disagree with you, General."

"The possibility occurred to me," Hawthorne said. "If you will look out your window, I imagine you'll see a squad of cybertanks patrolling the premises. It might seem highhanded or excessively militant, but a breach of the emergency blackout orders will result in a cybertank assault on PHC Headquarters."

"...you take heavy responsibilities upon yourself, General."

"That may be true. Since we shall be working so closely together in the future, Chief Yezhov, I feel you should be the first to hear about my promotion."

"You're stepping into the Directorate?"

"I hold the maxims of Social Unity too highly for such a move," Hawthorne said. "Instead, the remaining directors have just ratified a new rank for me. For the duration of the emergency I am the Supreme Commander of Inner Planets."

"The directors voted on this?" Yezhov asked with obvious disbelief.

"The surviving directors," Hawthorne said.

Yezhov's pale reptilian eyes narrowed. "Did more than one director have a heart-attack?"

"Including the Madam Director, there were three."

"…I see."

"I dearly hope you do, Chief Yezhov, as I need your cooperation for the coming fight. I may count on it, yes?"

"PHC will never cease struggling for ultimate victory."

"I am a military man and am used to something a little less ambiguous."

"…I shall cooperate with you, General. Excuse me, Supreme Commander. May I be the first to congratulate you on your elevation in status."

"Thank you, Chief. If you would be kind enough to arrive at my headquarters in the next half-hour, I will outline my revised policies. And please, no clones this time." Hawthorne referred to Yezhov's use of a clone during the initial coup that had gained him, Hawthorne, control of Social Unity.

Chief Yezhov pursed his lips. "May I be indelicate enough to ask for assurances?"

"That will be one of my newest principles," Hawthorne said. "Social Unity will only survive this ongoing crisis with the highest display of trust between its members."

"I must trust you?"

"Either that, Chief Yezhov, or trust my cybertanks to do their duty."

"I agree. A new era of trust will help stiffen resolve. There has been far too much distrust lately."

"If it's any consolation, Chief, I need men like you if we're going to defeat the Highborn."

"Men like me, Supreme Commander?"

"Cunning infighters with a gift for assassination,"

Hawthorne said.

"You give me too much credit."

"We shall see. A half-hour, Chief. Then—"

"I understand. I'm on my way."

Grand Admiral Cassius, the leader of the Highborn, stood in a viewing port of the *Hannibal Barca*. It was the nearest of the Doom Stars to Earth. The Grand Admiral admired the blue planet. South America was in sight, with heavy cloud cover over the Amazon River Basin.

Cassius had iron-colored hair and gray eyes. He stood like a granite statue, but there was a terrible intensity in his stare. He wore his admiral's uniform, complete with a Stellar Cross pinned to his chest, above it a Platinum Nebula. He had won the Platinum Nebula, the highest medal in the Social Unity Space Force, for his brilliant victory of the Second Battle of Deep Mars Orbit in 2339. That had been before the Highborn Rebellion. There, twelve years ago, he had broken the combined space fleets of the Mars Rebels and the Allied forces of the Jupiter Confederation.

The Grand Admiral heard a door open behind him. There was rustling and shuffling. The *Hannibal Barca* was presently under pseudo-gravity caused by rotation. With the shuffling sounds came a heavy odor. There were also low, angry mutterings.

Cassius frowned for a moment. Then understanding lit his gray eyes. Rock-still, a terrible change came over him. His was a fierce intensity. He held every muscle rigid to prevent them from trembling in anticipation of a swift death.

From the strange smell and the muttering it was clear that neutraloids were behind him, altered humans. They were blue-skinned, and each had been castrated. They were the Praetor's invention. The Praetor was presently in the Earth System, and the Praetor was his greatest enemy among the Highborn.

It was possible this was a crude ploy of assassination on the Praetor's part. Either that or one of the Praetor's supporters hoped to present the Praetor with an amazing victory.

Cassius used the viewing port. But he no longer watched the blue planet, the jewel of the Solar System. Instead, he used the faint reflection of the viewing port glass. He watched the neutraloids shuffle into the chamber behind him.

They were muscular to an intense degree. Some held stunners. Others gripped vibroknives. Each wore a harness around his blue-tattooed torso. The Grand Admiral had read the reports on the neutraloids. They were dangerous, certainly, but their conditioned rage made it difficult for them to use anything but their hands in combat.

Cassius nodded to himself. This assassination attempt was due to insufficient external danger. The Highborn needed deadly goals to concentrate their thinking. When they lacked deadly goals, the infighting began. The trouble was that Cassius was waiting for the premen of Social Unity to make their grand move. He had studied the files concerning their directors and this General Hawthorne. Cassius thought South America might be the location of the big push on the premen's part. Until that push occurred, he kept most of his Highborn out of combat there. Let the premen bleed each other. The FEC armies had their uses.

Ah, the neutraloids hesitated. That hesitation might allow one or two of them time to use their wits.

"Come on then," said Cassius. "If you're going to do it, do it!"

Behind him, the neutraloids snarled. They were so easily enraged. An enraged foe usually made critical blunders. He would have to enrage the Praetor in a subtle way. Yet the Praetor had a following, and the Praetor possessed powerful friends in high command. He would have to handle that delicately.

Behind him, one of the neutraloids hurled his stunner.

Grand Admiral Cassius shifted. The stunner flew past him and cracked against the viewing port. He allowed himself a low, taunting chuckle.

The snarling intensified. The small creatures shuffled nearer. One of them actually lifted his stunner as if to aim.

Had the Praetor's Training Masters made a breakthrough among the neutraloids? Cassius decided he would have to change that. These neutraloids, he despised the entire angle of them. Castration—it was disgusting.

Grand Admiral Cassius whirled around as a leaner neutraloid lifted his stunner and fired. The charge took Cassius in the gut, caused him to stagger backward. A numb sensation spread across his stomach.

The seven neutraloids howled and gnashed their teeth. Stunners and vibroblades hit the deck, but not all of them. Another stunner numbed the Grand Admiral's left thigh. Then the neutraloids charged in a pack, screaming in their high-pitched voices, taunting him with obscenities. They shouted what they would do to his corpse.

Grand Admiral Cassius was a nine-foot giant with impossible strength and abnormal reflexes. He used his fists like sledgehammers and waded among the berserk creatures. He took a deep gash in the side, and another in his numbed thigh. Neutraloids bounced off the walls, hit the deck with broken bones, and fell with crushed skulls.

The survivors screamed wild cries. Cassius roared with joy, with battle-madness. He tore the last neutraloids apart as a shredding machine might pulp wood. Combat, he loved it. To win, to crush, it was the joy of life.

He lifted the last neutraloid above his head and heaved the creature against the bulkhead. The sound of breaking bones was beautiful. In such a manner he would break the Praetor, and break the premen who sought to survive against their genetic superiors, the new lords of the Solar System.

-8-

Twelve days after taking the title of Supreme Commander, Hawthorne sat at his desk. His eyes ached from reading endless reports.

He turned off the vidscreen and leaned back, rubbing his temples. Then he opened a drawer, took out a bottle and twisted the cap, dumping three white capsules onto his palm. He popped them into his mouth and chewed. The pills were dry, with a bitter taste. He swallowed several times, wishing he had a glass of water.

His security team lacked Political Harmony Corps' subtlety. If only he could trust Yezhov. Then they could pull Earth's resources together and aim them all solely at the Highborn. The deadly infighting between directors and between the various governmental agencies sapped too much energy, stole too much time, and misdirected the focus of too many powerful personalities. That this power-struggle was part of man's inherent nature didn't make it any easier to accept. One would have thought that with such a frightening enemy as the Highborn, everyone's focus would be on the survival of the species.

A blue light blinked on his vidscreen. He pressed the communication's button, and Captain Mune's harsh features appeared.

"I have a priority message from Commodore Blackstone of the *Vladimir Lenin*," said Mune.

"How did to it come to route through you?"

"It has a Security Gold clearance."

Hawthorne massaged his forehead, bewildered. Then he realized that Security Gold was from the old days, before the Highborn attack that had taken out Geneva.

Hawthorne split the vidscreen and typed in *Vladimir Lenin*. Ah, it was a *Zhukov*-class battleship. They had too few of those. It was stationed in a far-Mars orbit.

"A priority message?" Hawthorne asked.

"Shall I patch it through, sir?"

"Please."

Hawthorne sat up as he became aware of what he was reading from Commodore Blackstone. The *Vladimir Lenin* had been in far-Mars orbit for a singular reason. That a *Zhukov*-class battleship had been used instead of a picket ship was incredible and almost criminally wasteful of space combat resources. Through powerful teleoptic scopes the battleship had monitored the nearly invisible cyborg battle pods. The only reason the *Vladimir Lenin* had been able to do that was that the tracking officer there had been given the exact coordinates to watch.

The critical part of the Security Gold message read: *The battle pods have begun deceleration. According to estimates, that will bring them into near-Mars orbit in fifty-seven days.*

According to Hawthorne's information the cyborgs were supposed to head directly to Earth. Why then had they begun deceleration for Mars? Hawthorne lurched to his feet and began to pace. He strode back and forth along the worn lane in his carpet. He ignored a call on his communicator. Captain Mune knocked on the door several minutes later.

"Handle it!" Hawthorne shouted through the door. "I'm thinking." There was no second knock and no further communication interruptions.

Hawthorne clasped his bony hands behind his back. His head tilted forward to what many of his officers would have recognized as his "deep thinking" pose. As he churned his way back and forth across his carpet the headache receded and then disappeared altogether. He examined many apparently disparate facts. Then he began to think about Doom Stars, the bedrock of Highborn power.

When he was like this Hawthorne had likened his mind to a

computer that pulled up one file and examined it with complete concentration. He brought up the next file and gave his complete concentration to it in turn. He halted once and looked up in wonder. He had been so consumed with cyborgs, directors, and maintaining political power that strategy for the war had fallen into second place.

Whoever had convinced the cyborgs to go to Mars must have done it to hurt him. It might now be possible to use the cyborgs there for Social Unity's good. Who had alerted them? Chief Yezhov seemed like the logical villain.

Hawthorne savagely shook his head. That wasn't the important point now. He hurried to the computer. For the next nine hours he used his computer stylus on the touchboard and voice-activated the keyboard. He sped-read through report after report concerning Mars. He laughed twice. It was a predatory sound. He began to outline a classic Hawthorne strategy. He had come to understand Highborn mentality and now used that to his fullest advantage.

At the end of the nine hours he threw himself back against his chair so hard it creaked ominously. His eyes were red-rimmed, and his features haggard.

He lurched to his feet and strode to the door, shouting for Captain Mune the minute it opened. He would sleep for several hours and take a special cocktail of stimulants when he awoke. Then he would meet with Chief Yezhov and afterward summon his military staff. A strategy had finally revealed itself, one that could give him the lever Social Unity desperately needed to turn the tide of the war.

He would send a reinforcement convoy from Earth filled with desperately needed supplies to Mars. The trick would be to slip the convoy past the Doom Stars that besieged the planet. Many SU warships were already headed there. He would order all the others there as well. The SU Battlefleet would be the bait for the Highborn to draw Doom Stars to Mars. With the cyborgs' help, he could destroy Doom Stars and change the course of the war. Why would the cyborgs help him? The answer was easy. They would help him to confuse him. Through Chief Yezhov, he would let the cyborgs understand that he didn't suspect them. To keep themselves from being suspected the cyborgs would have to help him win the battle for Mars.

"You're a clever bastard," Hawthorne whispered. Then he hurried for the first of many meetings.

Nine long, frantic days passed. Hawthorne functioned with the aid of stimulants as he prepared for the Mars campaign. He seldom slept as he raced to a hundred different locations, pushing officers and lashing others into a frenzy of effort. During that time the Strategy Staff turned his idea into a detailed set of operational orders.

Nine days was too short a time to write the operational orders from scratch, however. Fortunately, the Strategy Staff had long studied and planned for a hundred different operations. Many of those operations were wildly exotic in military terms, perfect now for Hawthorne's needs. Code Valkyrie, Code Vida Blue, Operational Plan XVII, and Skyhook Thirteen each had enough similarities to different aspects of Hawthorne's idea to be useful. Thus various members of the Strategy Staff lifted entire sections of those plans, changing details and incorporating them into the Campaign for Mars.

The governmental machinery of Social Unity was ponderous; the military found it difficult to race at Hawthorne's speed. The highest levels of Political Harmony Corps grew concerned, and then alarmed, once it realized the scope of the initial steps in Hawthorne's plan. Despite Hawthorne's dictatorial powers, key members in PHC, the Army, and the Directorate coalesced into stubborn blocs. They pointed out the dangers of Hawthorne's plan, and there were many.

Finally on Day Seven, Hawthorne called an emergency

meeting with Chief Yezhov of Political Harmony Corps, Director Danzig of Eurasia, Director Juba-Ryder of Africa, Air Marshal Crowfoot of Earth-Air Defense, and Commander Sargon of Orbital Sector.

The meeting began at 7:17 PM around a large conference table. It was in the basement of Hawthorne's emergency command center in Kazakhstan Underground Launch Site 10. Captain Mune attended, sitting in the back like a statue with his gyroc pistol resting on his lap.

***

From the Supreme Commander's biocomp transcriptions, File #9:

HAWTHORNE: Gentleman, madam (speaker nods to Director Juba-Ryder of Africa) time presses with its inexorable weight. The Highborn gained the advantage over Inner Planets with their precision first strikes. They commandeered the Doom Stars, captured the Sun Works Ring, and obliterated the old Directorate and Social Unity's governmental agencies when they destroyed Geneva on the first day of the rebellion. That paralyzed Inner Planets for too many weeks in the opening stages of the war.

YEZHOV: I hope the Supreme Commander forgives me for interrupting.

HAWTHORNE: That is the purpose for this emergency session. Tonight, you are free to air your grievances.

YEZHOV: I assure you, sir, I have no grievances. Rather, they are qualms.

DANZIG: Let's not quibble, Chief. (To Hawthorne) Instead of grievances, Excellency, I have stark fear concerning this coming assault against the Highborn.

HAWTHORNE: Fear is reasonable. Before you air your fears, however, I want you to realize the nature of the war.

YEZHOV: If I might interrupt again, sir. We know the history of the war. A recap—

HAWTHORNE: Is necessary, Chief. If you would indulge me?

YEZHOV: (nods reluctantly.)

HAWTHORNE: (looks around the table.) The Highborn have unusual abilities. It is part of their genetic heritage. They

46

gained the initiative at the commencement of the rebellion, and they have never released it. Fortunately, Social Unity retains many of its spaceships, although these vessels have scattered into the deepness of space.

DANZIG: What good do these spaceships do us then? The Highborn gobble up chunks of landmass here on Earth. Soon only Eurasia and Africa will be left to us.

HAWTHORNE: Exactly.

DANZIG: (pounds the table with his fist.) Then why are you endangering Eurasia? Your madness—

YEZHOV: No! You are wrong to slur the Supreme Commander.

DANZIG: He gave us permission to speak our mind.

HAWTHORNE: I am a man of my word.

YEZHOV: But to call your plan madness. Will you allow that, sir?

HAWTHORNE: I desire to understand the Director's logic for use of such a word.

DANZIG: Madness was the wrong word, sir. I beg your pardon.

HAWTHORNE: Granted.

DANZIG: You know I'm an emotional man. My heart seethes with hatred against those genetic abominations. The madmen of the old Directorate— as you say, Chief Yezhov, that is old history. I fear for Eurasia. Sir, you staked your reputation and dared to expend much political prestige pushing for increased proton beam construction and a quadrupling of the merculite missile production. Because of that, we have greatly increased the depth of our defenses. Isn't that right?

CROWFOOT (Air Marshal of Earth-Air Defense): Our coverage has increased one hundred and sixteen percent.

DANZIG: Does that include the anti-air batteries?

CROWFOOT: Our production levels there have given us a three hundred percent increase.

DANZIG: There's my point, sir. You've pushed for massive increases against space-borne attacks. Now you wish to fire our merculite missiles to cover the launching of your space fleet. With the depletion of our stocks of merculites it will make us vulnerable again. Eurasia is the heart of Inner

47

Planets. If it goes, the war is over. We know that. The Highborn must know it too.

HAWTHORNE: My plan is a gamble. You are quite correct in pointing that out.

YEZHOV: Supreme Commander, have I heard correctly? Are you admitting that Director Danzig is right?

HAWTHORNE: Only in that Eurasia will soon be more vulnerable to attack.

DANZIG: Am I missing something, sir?

YEZHOV: I cannot fathom why you would disarm us. I hope you do not take offense, but this seems criminally negligent.

SARGON (Commander of Orbital Sector): I didn't want to say this. In lieu of what I've heard here, however, I feel I must. Supreme Commander, Code Valkyrie will threaten the Earth with mass starvation. You must realize this. The open habitat policy between the Highborn and us is of a very delicate nature. Your gross violation of the understanding will doom millions, perhaps billions, to a slow and painful death.

JUBA-RYDER (Director of Africa): This is unseemly. You gentlemen are openly accusing the Supreme Commander of sabotage. I protest in the strongest manner possible.

YEZHOV: If it's any help in understanding the situation, Political Harmony Corps' psychology profile shows the Supreme Commander to have a greater leaning toward the Highborn than to Social Unity.

CAPTAIN MUNE: (stands up.)

HAWTHORNE: (motioning Captain Mune to sit down) Would you clarify that statement, please, Chief Yezhov?

YEZHOV: I mean no disrespect, sir, but your thought patterns are nearer those of Highborn soldiers than a grounded practitioner of Social Unity.

HAWTHORNE: If a man came at you with a gun, Chief, would you fight with your bare hands?

YEZHOV: You are Social Unity's gun, sir?

HAWTHORNE: I detest false modesty and bragging. So let me put it this way. Social Unity has hurt the Highborn twice, and only twice. Each of those times, the idea that propelled the action that harmed the Highborn was mine.

JUBA-RYDER: Chief Yezhov is your enemy, sir. I suggest your captain take him outside and have him shot.

HAWTHORNE: The Chief is a deadly opponent, of that there is no doubt. He is also a master of the secret ploy. Today, as he has been doing the past few days, he has sown discord. Few can match him in that regard. Director Juba-Ryder, you are correct in pointing out that Chief Yezhov is a danger to me. The safest course is to kill him. However it is not in my nature to throw away powerful weapons. Chief, I dearly hope you will employ your skills to kill Highborn rather than engaging in intrigue against me.

YEZHOV: I support you one hundred percent, sir. You wound me with these allegations.

HAWTHORNE: Your vote of confidence fills me with resolve, I assure you. Gentlemen, and madam, Director Danzig is correct in stating that our present plan will deplete our defenses. Commander Sargon is equally correct in stating that implementation of Code Valkyrie will cause mass hardship on Earth.

DANZIG: Then why are you sending this convoy?

HAWTHORNE: Because we're losing the war. The Highborn have the initiative, and we have not been able to wrest it from them. As long as they own space, we cannot win. Perhaps we can stave off defeat, but even that is unlikely. Because they control space they can pin down one planet and concentrate on another. If we hope to win, we must win space control.

YEZHOV: Against five Doom Stars?

HAWTHORNE: You have hit the mark, Chief. The Doom Stars are the bedrock of Highborn power, because those ships give them space-superiority. The Mars Campaign has a single goal; we must destroy Doom Stars.

DANZIG: You told the Directorate that you hoped to gain control of the planet.

HAWTHORNE: I do.

DANZIG: But you just said—

HAWTHORNE: We must accept terrible risks in the calculated hope that we can destroy Doom Stars. I predict that the critical campaign for us is this one. We failed to destroy the operational capacity of the Sun Works Ring. Now as has been pointed out, the Highborn are gobbling landmasses on Earth. Soon, they will control more of Earth than we do.

DANZIG: How can we win on Mars?

HAWTHORNE: The exact nature of the operational plan will remain unknown to those present. I have calculated, however, that in eight out of ten times we shall achieve victory.

YEZHOV: We must trust your military genius?

HAWTHORNE: What else do you suggest we trust?

YEZHOV: (to the others) Do I stand alone in my qualms?

DANZIG: I tremble at the depletion of our defensive stocks. But I can see the Supreme Commander's logic. We must take the terrible risk if we are to stave off bitter defeat in two or three years.

HAWTHORNE: Well-spoken, Director Danzig.

SARGON: Is the implementation of Code Valkyrie absolutely necessary?

HAWTHORNE: I tremble when I think of initiating it, Commander. Believe me, this is a difficult decision. Yet it is not a one hundred percent certainty. I will hold Code Valkyrie in reserve.

SARGON: I strongly suggest it stay in reserve, sir, unless its implementation can guarantee total victory.

HAWTHORNE: I will repeat it: Those are my sentiments also.

SARGON: (nods slowly) Then with the greatest reluctance I agree to your logic, although I am unfamiliar with the exact merits of your plan.

HAWTHORNE: Does anyone else have any other comments? …Chief Yezhov?

YEZHOV: As a faithful son of Social Unity, I concur with the majority, suppressing my will in the interest of solidarity.

HAWTHORNE: (rising) Social Unity shall overcome. That is my pledge, my dedication, and my most fervent dream. This meeting is adjourned.

10

Two days later Supreme Commander Hawthorne stood in the Space Command Center deep in the Joho Mountains of China Sector. These ancient coalmines had been converted into a headquarters and fortress.

It was intense but quiet in the command center. Many uniformed personnel sat at their consoles, staring up into blue-colored vidscreens. The screens showed many different facets of the war. There were enemy laser platforms, orbital launch stations, orbiting farm habitats, asteroids and a giant Doom Star at far-Earth orbit. The single purpose of their planned attack was to create a hole in the Highborn blockade of Earth, and to screen outbound supply vessels for Mars. The position of the two Doom Stars—one in far-Earth orbit and one in lunar orbit—had been carefully calculated.

Hawthorne brushed his moist palms against his trousers. He stared at a screen showing him a merculite launch site in Kazakhstan Sector. It was a barren plain with steel doors covering the blast pans.

"Ten seconds," a woman down the row said.

Hawthorne stared at those steel doors in Kazakhstan Sector. Slowly, they began to move. Soon, they were open and giant merculite missiles roared out of the earth. The exhaust burned hot, but the giant missiles moved so slowly. Tensely, Hawthorne waited for Highborn lasers to begin shooting them down.

A deadly red beam lanced out of the heavens and struck a merculite. The missile was heavily shielded, but three seconds later, it exploded. The others were moving faster now. More lasers struck from the orbital platforms that ringed the planet.

Targeting the laser platforms and the orbital-fighter launch stations, Social Unity fired thousands of merculite missiles from sites located in a seven-hundred kilometer diameter. Six proton beams also lashed the heavens. It was the heaviest space attack since 10 May 2350 and the wounding of the Doom Star *Genghis Khan.*

The silence in the underground command center was ominous. Along with Hawthorne, the military personnel stared at the vidscreens. Hundreds of merculite missiles were burned out of the sky, and hundreds more were going to die.

The proton beams struck, however. The one from Stalingrad obliterated the Highborn laser platform known as LP-23. As the space platform broke apart on the many screens, a ragged cheer arose in the Joho Command Center.

"Strike one!" a colonel shouted.

Hawthorne smiled grimly.

Then other Highborn platforms died: LP-16, LP-40, LP-41, and OLS-10 and OLS-11. OLS was an acronym for Orbital Launch Station.

As always, the Highborn response was swift. From other orbital launch stations heavy fighters dropped down from space. The sonic-booming orbitals attacked the proton beam installations. Anti-air flak-guns opened up. They fired depleted uranium shells and sabot missiles, and another blizzard-salvo of merculite missiles lofted. Heavy orbital fighters disappeared to growing cheers in the underground command center. Other fighters survived, firing missiles or dropping bombs. In five places multiple nuclear mushroom clouds appeared.

In the command center a chair scraped back as a major stood, shaking her fists at the screen and cursing the Highborn.

Hawthorne sympathized. He hated the Highborn. He hated being on the defensive. But today they attacked. As he studied the figures, over thirty-four percent of the orbital fighters were destroyed. Against the Highborn, those were fantastic numbers.

The loss of so many orbital fighters and the space platforms must have stung the so-called Master Race. A Doom Star engaged its engines and began to move from its position behind

Luna. The Doom Star at far-Earth orbit also began to accelerate. There were two Doom Stars in the Earth System, each far enough away so they were out of range of the merculite missiles and proton beams.

Before the first Doom Star could leave its lunar orbit, however, the Social Unity attack slackened. In this brief window of time Hawthorne had expended a third of the Eurasian merculite missile reserve and burned out two of the proton beam cannons. It was the unprecedented scale of the attack that had won them the destruction of Highborn space targets.

To use more merculites would leave the heart of Social Unity on Earth dangerously exposed to another strike. Military Intelligence had discovered ten asteroids circling in far-Earth orbit. It was a grim reminder of Highborn power. Also the very scale of the merculite missiles launched had resulted in a twenty-three percent degradation of launch capacity. That meant many of the blast pans used for the missile launches had been worn down and would require maintenance to function again.

The merculite missiles and the proton beams were meant as defensive weapons, primarily against any asteroids and the close approach of Doom Stars. The use of the carefully built-up stocks of missiles and the burning out of two proton beams weighed heavily on Hawthorne, and on the men and women dedicated to the space defense of Earth. Despite the conference two days ago, it also cost Supreme Commander Hawthorne in perhaps the most critical area, his power base. Highly ranked military men and women questioned his decision. This was a gamble. The Highborn might very well use the depletion of defensive stocks to launch an all-out space attack on the Eurasian landmass.

Hawthorne shook his head. Now wasn't the time to worry about that. Now was the critical moment. Now a small window was open to launch the supply convoy to Mars.

"Launch the Orion ships," Hawthorne said.

The orders went out from the Joho Command Center, and then the military personnel waited. The probable success or failure of the Mars Campaign rested on what happened in these next few hours. The Orion ships had to get into space and past the Doom Stars before they could close the gap in their blockade around Earth.

***

Waiting in one of the many convoy vessels was the prime clone of the late Madam Blanche-Aster. This clone had been the bodyguard who had survived the detonation of Mother aboard Hawthorne's bullet train.

The clone's name was Lisa Aster. As a former bodyguard, she knew guns, knives, unarmed combat and security arrangements. She was a master at kinetics and reading body language, trained to note the subtle signs of those readying themselves to kill. The late Madam Director's death infuriated Lisa. She attributed it to the Neptune clone, the one tampered with by the cyborgs. Thus, Lisa hated the cyborgs and wanted to see them destroyed.

The clone Lisa Aster waited with thousands of other people aboard the Orion ships because Supreme Commander Hawthorne had given her a mission. Once the supply convoy reached Mars she was supposed to study the cyborgs and discover their weaknesses.

Lisa Aster lay on an acceleration couch. Like stout General Fromm on the other couch, she wore a vacc-suit and a helmet. She had a buzz cut of pale hair and a narrow face with intelligent features.

Words sounded in her ears, something about four, three, two, one—

Then Lisa Aster's world dramatically changed. The first nuclear bomb exploded with a mighty sound.

BANG!

It shoved her hard against the acceleration couch and made everything rattle around her. She clenched the bars beside her and then clenched her teeth.

BANG!

BANG!

The gigantic Orion ship lifted from an underground launch-bunker in Kazakhstan Sector.

It was a crude booster and one of the most powerful propulsion systems known. Weapons-grade U-235 was the

54

fuel, nuclear bombs. A bomb detonated under each booster. An immensely thick metal plate absorbed the blast as it was blown spaceward. It looked like a city block with tall buildings, lifting out of the Earth and heading for the clouds. Those "buildings" were supply spaceships. Lisa Aster peered at a screen in her ship and saw the clouds jump nearer at each bone-crushing *BANG!* After the Orion ship's thick metal plate were tons of hardened ablative foam. The foam's single purpose was to cushion the shock to the riding spaceships clustered and perched at the front.

Each nuclear blast poured x-rays, heat and neutrons onto the planet. It had been a hard decision, a terrible choice, but the Orion ships had several key advantages. The weapons-grade U-235 moved the boosters fast. Each exploding warhead tremendously increased velocity. If the convoy fleet was to get past the waiting Doom Stars, it would need velocity. The other gift the Orion ships gave was the ability to lift tons of mass. No other propulsion system in the Solar System provided as much quick lift out of the Earth's gravity well as nuclear bombs.

In the center spaceship of the second Orion ship, the first created clone of the late Madam Director endured the explosions that hurled her closer to the waiting Doom Stars.

***

On many of the screens in the Joho Command Center the Orion ships exited the stratosphere and headed into the space of near-Earth orbit.

"Your gamble is paying off, sir," Captain Mune whispered.

Hawthorne wasn't ready yet to accept that.

"They're attacking," someone said.

Hawthorne and Captain Mune walked to a different vidscreen. It showed a kilometers wide Doom Star, a spherical spaceship of outlandish size. Its primary lasers stabbed into the darkness of space. They could fire to a million kilometers accurately. No other surviving warship had such range. Once, Social Unity had possessed the experimental *Bangladesh*. Its range with its single weapon had been 30-million kilometers, a breakthrough in space combat technology.

The Orion ships had two protections against the deadly lasers. The first were packets of prismatic crystals. The normal procedure was to accelerate and then shut off the engines and drift toward the enemy. Only then would spaceships spew the prismatic crystals in their tanks to form a cloud of shiny particles that floated before, beside, and behind at the same velocity as the spaceship. Unfortunately, because the Orion ships still accelerated, any prismatic crystals spewed out were soon left behind. In such a situation combat procedures called for the spewing at carefully timed intervals. The second defense against the lasers was the massive metal plate of each booster and the hardened ablative foam behind it. For those to come into play however, the Orion ships had to be flying *away* from the Doom Stars, not toward them. At this point, the supply ships clustered on the boosters were in the direct-line of laser fire.

"Estimates?" Hawthorne demanded.

The uniformed captain at the console tapped computer keys. "At this rate, sir, it seems like seventy to eighty-five percent destruction of the convoy."

Hawthorne kept his features stoic. He could accept thirty percent destruction, could endure thirty-five, and grudgingly go with forty percent. This was the only supply convoy he was going to be able to launch from Earth. The scattered SU warships in the voids had been operating on their own for far too long. They needed re-supply. They needed these munitions.

Hawthorne glanced at Captain Mune. The bulky bionic soldier watched the staff, not the screens. Mune was more interested in the personnel than the battle. His hand was on the butt of his gyroc pistol. If anyone thought to assassinate the Supreme Commander, that potential assassin would die.

Hawthorne took a deep breath, and then another. His insides seethed. He could not accept a seventy percent destruction of the supply convoy. There was only one way they might be able to defeat the Doom Star that was sure to join the battle. The risks, however, were terrible. It was not a present risk, but a future one. This was a dreadful moment. Hawthorne's shoulders slumped. A trickle of sweat ran down his back. He waited, unwilling to give the order. He risked billions of lives. He risked his position as Supreme Commander. He risked even his own life giving the order. Did he believe his own rhetoric? Had it all been a sham? He desperately wanted to ask someone else his or her opinion. His stomach seethed. He realized that no one else on Earth could help him. The terrible command decision was his alone. He would never be able to shift the blame onto someone else. How would history regard this decision?

No. He couldn't worry about that. The great captains in the past had taken awful risks. Hannibal had lost the war against Rome because he'd been afraid to risk his splendid cavalry on a hell-ride to the gates of Rome after the annihilating Battle of Cannae.

Seventy percent of the convoy destroyed.

Supreme Commander Hawthorne lifted a trembling hand. He willed it still. Then he put his hand on the captain's shoulder at the vidscreen. The woman looked up at him in alarm. "Issue Code Valkyrie." Hawthorne was grateful his voice remained firm.

"Sir?" she whispered.

"Now, captain."

The woman leaned toward her microphone. She opened her mouth but nothing came out. She cleared her throat and spoke harshly. "Initiate Code Valkyrie," she said, and then she added a string of alphanumeric variables to verify the command.

The Space Command Center grew deathly quiet as others realized the dreaded order had been given.

The order went out via radio. The seconds ticked by. Then select personnel on gigantic farm habitats at far-Earth orbit began to initiate desperate code sequences. Over a period of many months they had emplaced heavy lasers onto the habitats. Social Unity had been able to achieve this feat because of the open farm habitat policy of both sides. That policy would no doubt change very soon because of Hawthorne's order. The lasers were only supposed to be used if Earth was in imminent danger of being overrun.

There would be starvation in parts of Earth if the Highborn destroyed or captured the many habitats. Many would question the order. Hawthorne knew that. Some would believe him mad, but the full impact of his decision would not occur until months from now.

Maybe by that time he could give Earth the news of a stunning victory at Mars. This entire campaign was a terrible gamble. Hawthorne had recognized that from the start, and it had only weighed more heavily on him as the days passed. One thought gave him the strength to continue. Social Unity was losing. If they couldn't turn the tide of the war soon, nothing would help.

Displayed on countless vidscreens deep in the Space Command Center in the Joho Mountains, lasers from many farm habitats began to chew into the thick hull of the *Hannibal Barca*. The vast warship had massive particle shields composed of asteroid rock. Lasers chewed into that rock so dust, stones and even boulder-sized pieces began to slag off.

"Enemy lasers have changed targeting," the captain said at her console.

The minutes ticked by as the Orion ships accelerated hard. The needed bombs dribbled one after another under the metal blast pans. The gigantic boosters gained velocity and freedom from the fierce gravity well that was the Earth.

Then, "*Taping* Habitat is under attack."

Several minutes later: "*Chicago Seven* Habitat has taken a direct hit to its fusion core."

"*Caesar Chavez* Habitat is breaking up!" someone else shouted.

Supreme Commander James Hawthorne closed his eyes. He was consigning millions to their deaths. Millions more on Earth might come to curse his name.

"There is a burn-through in *Taping* Hab."

"Sir, *Tel Aviv* Hab has fifty percent greater firepower. They hotshotted their lasers, sir."

Supreme Commander Hawthorne opened his eyes. He should have thought of that. Someone else should have thought of that. Next time—

Hawthorne swallowed. There would be no next time with these habitats. He stared at the vidscreen, at the lasers pouring from the many habitats, and at the nearly impregnable Doom Star. He had ordered this. He would watch the grim consequences and remember. He deserved nightmares in his sleep for the rest of his life. Why did he feel so dreadfully alone?

-11-

For a brief time the orbiting farm habitats poured laser fire into the *Hannibal Barca's* heavy particle shields. Normally, the Doom Star would never have gotten close enough to have any laser hit so hard, but the habs had the element of surprise on their side. The *Hannibal Barca* was close indeed. Those lasers were hot and on target.

More than the massive merculite launch, more than the six proton beams, even more than the gigantic Orion ships, the heavy lasers on the farm habitats took the Highborn by surprise.

Grand Admiral Cassius roared for more speed. He sat in his command chair aboard the *Julius Caesar* at lunar orbit. The clever premen had timed their attack well. Luna was presently on the opposite side of the Earth as compared to the launching Orion ships. Many of the farm habitats also used the Earth as a shield against the *Julius Caesar's* lasers.

"Faster!" Cassius shouted.

Highborn could take greater G-forces than premen could, about twice as many before blacking out. The Doom Star already accelerated to six gravities. The super-ship surged through far-orbital space, moving to gain a clear line-of-fire.

"Sir, it is Commander Scipio."

Cassius could see the holoimage of Scipio before him, a Highborn with a jutting nose.

"Destroy the farm habitats!" Cassius shouted. "Above all, keep your Doom Star intact and unharmed."

The holoimage nodded curtly before fading out.

Cassius studied the other hologram image before him. It showed the massive Orion ships. Most of them had made it off Earth and into space. They headed for Mars. First, he would save the *Hannibal Barca*. Then the premen would see what long-range heavy lasers could do to the fleet heading for the Red Planet.

***

Three days after the battle Grand Admiral Cassius hardened himself to demote Commander Scipio of the *Hannibal Barca*. It was a painful decision, as Scipio was one of his most ardent supporters. This humiliation might well cause Scipio to commit suicide.

Cassius piloted a shuttle to the Doom Star, using the quiet of the ship to think.

Scipio had targeted the Orion ships for too long before engaging the farm habitats. The *Hannibal Barca* had taken more damage than the *Genghis Khan* had on 10 May 2350. Better that Scipio had let more of the Orion ships survive than allow his ship to be damaged.

Cassius was going to need the *Hannibal Barca* soon, and thus he could not send it to the Sun-Works Factory for repair. They would have to repair it here in the little time left them.

After a brief glance at the Earth above Cassius studied reports. Long-range laser fire had destroyed forty-five percent of the Orion ships and the spaceships they carried. The surviving boosters spread prismatic crystals, shielding the SU spaceships headed for Mars from the long-range lasers of the two Doom Stars.

Fifty-five percent of the Earth Fleet had survived.

Cassius shook his head. The premen had fought harder than he had expected. Because of that he was going to lose his good friend, Scipio. The Praetor's people would expect him to give the Praetor the open command slot.

Cassius crackled his knuckles and began to make plans.

-12-

The former Praetor of the Sun-Works Factory walked with a lesser Highborn, a Lot 6 creature. The Praetor believed it was his dire luck to find himself forever saddled with inferior Highborn.

The two of them strode through a utilitarian steel corridor on a combat training station in near-lunar orbit. The station was torus-shaped and rotated to simulate one hundred and thirty percent Earth gravity. The extra thirty percent helped to harden the training soldiers.

The Praetor towered over the Lot Sixer, an earlier subset from the *vats* and many years his senior in age. The Praetor possessed broader shoulders, a deeper chest, and a more sharply angled face. They both had short cut thick hair reminiscent of panther's pelts. The Praetor's eyes were pink, intense and perhaps possessed more than the usual Highborn ferocity. Each officer had abnormal vitality, at least when compared to sluggish Homo sapiens.

The Praetor's hands were massive and strong. He clutched an ivory baton, a symbol of the successful destruction of the experimental beamship *Bangladesh*. No other SU warship had so impressed the Highborn with its deadliness.

The Lot Sixer wore the green uniform of an infantry specialist, and he had pitted features. He'd earned those scars in South America destroying his twentieth bio-tank. He was the Praetor's new training master of the subhumans. The last one had died after the failed neutraloid "accident" concerning the Grand Admiral.

Grand Admiral Cassius had no doubt secretly engineered the foisting of yet another Lot 6 upon him. The Grand Admiral was First. He, the Praetor, was Fourth in the strictly graded hierarchy. The Grand Admiral was wise to fear him, wise to try to sabotage him with inferior officer material.

"I've read Training Master Lycon's paper concerning shock troopers," the Lot Sixer was saying. "He has many credible points."

The Praetor stopped and stared down at the Lot Sixer. "Training Master Lycon has fled Highborn service. He is a traitor."

"Perhaps he was killed and the premen—"

"Do not strain logic, Training Master. Do you seriously suggest that half a dozen shock troopers could overpower a Highborn?"

"I've read his reports. Lycon trained them to the razor's edge of premen lethality."

"That begs the question. Could half a dozen premen defeat you?"

"If I was unarmed and they possessed high technology, it would certainly be possible."

"Let me rephrase the question. If you possessed a shuttle and picked them up, and *then* they overpowered you, would that be possible?"

"I stand corrected, Praetor."

The Praetor nodded and began striding down the corridor. The new Training Master hurried to catch up.

"Lycon's shock troopers did capture the *Bangladesh*," the new Training Master said.

"All the shock troopers are dead or converted."

"Praetor?"

The Praetor allowed himself a small smile. "After Lycon's departure, I took the liberty and assumed leadership of the shock trooper regiment. Those that remained on the Sun-Works Factory were gelded and converted into neutraloids."

"You castrated high-quality premen?"

"Your statement is illogical. I turned questionable premen into trustworthy neutraloids."

"I admit that your neutraloids have unique fighting

63

qualities, at least in a primitive setting. But their rage, Praetor—"

"I have already successfully altered three platoons of neutraloids. They are now undergoing space combat training. Incidentally, that is why you've been assigned to me."

"You wish me to attempt to train these neutraloids?"

"To space combat efficiency. Yes, Training Master."

"…I've read your reports, Praetor. You hand me a daunting task."

"Do you feel it is beyond your capabilities?"

The Praetor watched the other sidelong. The Training Master had a harsh face with muscles in odd places. They tightened and bulged at his jaws and near his temples. A vein across his forehead grew and throbbed with blood. Oh, how this Lot Sixer wished to challenge him. The Praetor hoped he would. He would break this one in single combat and force the Grand Admiral to send him a real Highborn as Training Master.

The Praetor's communicator beeped, temporarily breaking the tension.

"Yes," he said, speaking into a wrist communicator. Ah, he spoke with the Grand Admiral.

"Praetor, I have sent a shuttle to pick you up. You will bring your retinue with you."

"At once, sir." The communicator winked off. The Praetor's pink eyes seemed to glitter.

The Lot Sixer lost his truculent manner as he seemed to notice the change come over the Praetor.

"You heard him," the Praetor said, his voice rougher than before. He slapped the baton into his open palm, enraged that as Fourth he had been bypassed twice for command of a Doom Star. This time, it would be different. Commander Scipio had committed suicide. Now there was no excuse for the Grand Admiral. That cagy old soldier would *have* to give him command of the *Hannibal Barca*.

***

The Praetor and Grand Admiral Cassius sat in a lounge aboard the *Julius Caesar*. Each hulking Highborn was bent before a three dimensional chessboard.

64

The Grand Admiral's skill was legendary. He had three of the Praetor's pawns and a knight. The Praetor had four enemy pawns, each carefully lined up in a row beside his ivory baton.

The Highborn likened the Grand Admiral to the great captains of the premen, those uncanny soldiers of history: Alexander the Great, Hannibal Barca, Julius Caesar, Genghis Khan, Napoleon and others. Instead of a premen genius, however, Grand Admiral Cassius was a *Highborn* genius. That meant he was superior by a probable factor of ten than when compared to the greatest warlord ever born to Homo sapiens.

That genius radiated from the iron-haired admiral. It was a palpable force, as the Grand Admiral exuded a fierce presence.

The Praetor felt that force, just as he felt the Grand Admiral's merciless attack on the three dimensional chessboard. The Praetor refused to succumb to a legend, however. He silently berated himself and jeered at his own nervousness. He was the Praetor. He was a superior Highborn. He was Fourth in the unbelievably competitive world of the genetic super-soldiers. He would ignore the stories about Cassius's legendary chess assault. He would play his own highly aggressive game and catch the Grand Admiral in a long-term trap.

The room possessed bronze busts of generals of the past and various famous battle paintings. A subtle vibration told the Praetor that the *Julius Caesar* was under acceleration. It approached Earth, linking with the second Doom Star in the Earth System.

Grand Admiral Cassius decisively moved a pawn, clicking the metal piece onto the glass tile. He then stared at the Praetor across the three dimensional board.

"I do not approve of the gelding of fighting troops."

The Praetor nodded crisply. "I have sent your office a recording of the battle files of the Storm Assault Missiles. A percentage of the shock troopers sent against the beamship spoke treason against us."

"Those were words, Praetor. The shock troopers' action spoke loudly enough about their ultimate loyalty."

"In the storming of the *Bangladesh* you are correct. What occurred afterward?"

"You have files concerning that?"

"The Grand Admiral knows I do not. The experimental beamship was destroyed."

"It's your move."

The Praetor studied the chessboard. After a moment, he looked up. "My neutraloids are superior to the shock troopers."

"In a primitive setting, you may be right. The shock troopers were high-tech soldiers. We will need a four hundred percent increase in space combat premen to help secure the remaining farm habitats in Earth orbit. If the neutraloids could function as police, they could perform some useful task. They are, however, too savage to be policemen."

"I have taken steps to modify their savagery."

The Grand Admiral grunted in a noncommittal manner.

The Praetor shifted in his chair and resumed studying the chessboard. He willed his thoughts onto the game and spent the next five minutes mentally moving the chess-pieces five, six and then seven moves ahead. Finally, he dropped his bishop two levels and captured another pawn. This piece he lined up precisely with his other captured pawns.

"If—" the Praetor began to say.

Grand Admiral Cassius held up a big hand, signaling for silence. He then clasped his left wrist again and leaned forward like a statue. After three minutes he captured the bishop with a castle.

The Praetor nodded, trying to hide his smile.

"I appreciate your dedication to solving the space combat dilemma," the Grand Admiral rumbled. "We have too few Highborn and need additional population if we're to conquer the Solar System."

The Praetor yearned to hold up his hand and halt the Grand Admiral's words. He recognized the tactic of only talking during his turns. The Grand Admiral used his position of strength, of possessing the higher rank. The Praetor did not think that was unfair. A position of strength should be exploited for all the advantages it could give. He simply wished he had the high ground, not the Grand Admiral.

"It is a pressing dilemma," the Praetor agreed.

"This training of premen space-combat soldiers fails to

engage your talents to the full benefit of the Highborn."

The Praetor blinked slowly, the game forgotten now. He trembled with seething vitality, his rage only held in check by his will. He yearned to flex his big hands. He wanted to lunge across the chessboard, wrap his fingers around the Grand Admiral's throat, and *squeeze* the life from him. Surely, the Grand Admiral had to offer him the command of the *Hannibal Barca*.

"The premen of Social Unity have moved more quickly than I'd foreseen."

"They surprised you?" the Praetor asked.

The Grand Admiral shook his iron-haired head. "Surprise is the wrong word. I have set a trap for them. It is a delicate trap, however. I have debated with myself whether their side had a commander worthy enough to see the possibility, and thereby find himself lured by my bait."

The Praetor waited as he wondered what the Grand Admiral was talking about. He was too proud to admit that he didn't know.

"Five days ago, Social Unity launched a surprise assault."

"I'm obviously well aware of that," the Praetor said.

"You are probably also aware that we probed the Earth's defenses with the *Hannibal Barca*."

"You're bringing the *Julius Caesar* into near-Earth orbit to help?"

"The premen expect it, so it's best to comply and keep them from thinking too deeply," the Grand Admiral said.

The Praetor's nostrils flared. He wished the Grand Admiral would get to the point and offer him command of the *Hannibal Barca*.

"Consider the problem, Praetor. We possess five Doom Stars. There are four planets in the inner system. We could pin down each planet with a Doom Star and have one extra warship for duty wherever the primary objective happens to be. That extra warship, however, took damage. Fortunately the *Genghis Khan* nears completion of its repairs. The problem still remains, however, especially with the damage sustained by the *Hannibal Barca*."

"Our Doom Star left Mars for just that reason," the Praetor

said. "Mars is now in Rebel hands, so it's out of Social Unity's hands. That means we have five Doom Stars for three planets."

"The *Bangladesh* highlighted our dilemma," the Grand Admiral said, as if he hadn't heard the Praetor.

"Guerilla attacks?" the Praetor asked.

"Would you call the pounding your Sun-Works Factory took a guerilla attack?"

"We destroyed the *Bangladesh*," the Praetor said.

"But we have not yet solved the situation. Mind you, it could become worse if the other planets came to Social Unity's aid."

"The Outer Planets?" the Praetor asked in jest.

"The Jupiter Confederation once came to the aid of the Mars Rebels."

"Those Rebels now control Mars."

"I will frame the situation exactly, Praetor. We own Mercury, but must guard it with at least one Doom Star to insure its safety. We pin down Venus with a Doom Star and thereby cut it off from the rest of Inner Planets. Soon, we will have three Doom Stars in Earth orbit. Yet if we wish to travel anywhere else in the Solar System we must leave at least one Doom Star on guard duty here, and preferably two."

"Go on," the Praetor said.

"As I'm sure you understand the problem is the Social Unity space fleet. As long as it exists, we must scatter our Doom Stars in this inefficient manner. The longer the war progresses, the longer the Outer Planets have to come to their senses and join their fellow premen against us. Premen are slow-witted, and often foolish to an amazing degree. They still do, however, have overwhelming numbers."

"Has the Intelligence Service discovered communications between Inner and Outer Planets?"

The Grand Admiral nodded.

The idea made the Praetor uncomfortable. There were two million Highborn, more or less. The training schools graduated just enough young Highborn to make up for combat losses. Earth System alone still contained over thirty-eight billion premen. If the entire Solar System of premen should unite against the Highborn—

68

"You spoke about a trap," the Praetor said.

"I believe the director of the premen war effort possesses elementary cunning. The *Bangladesh* affair proves that. The stiffening of their war effort on Earth also points to it. Our days of easy victories are over for the present. I therefore withdrew the Doom Star from Mars in order to give him a golden opportunity."

"You left the Rebels in charge of the orbital defenses."

"Yes. Now you're beginning to see. Our exit from Mars seemed reasonable from their limited view. The SU premen will think we believe we've garrisoned the planet against them."

"But we have not done so sufficiently?" the Praetor asked.

"No. I say this for two reasons. One, Social Unity still possesses many powerful warships, a more than credible force if combined. Two, that force will have another surprise for us."

"Of what nature?" the Praetor asked.

The Grand Admiral chuckled. "This is nothing the Intelligence Services have discovered. It is something I have logically deduced."

The Praetor frowned.

"We are superior, Praetor, but we are not infallible. The premen have among them intelligent scientists and able tacticians. They will have a surprise, maybe even two surprises, that we have not foreseen. I accept that and plan accordingly. The trick is to use their surprises against them."

The Praetor waited, having expended his willingness to ask questions.

"I have enticed Social Unity to gather their scattered warships into one place," the Grand Admiral said. "This place is Mars. Using their trick they will likely capture the Rebel orbital defenses in short order. If it is bloody for them that will be even better for us. The point is they will set their space forces and orbital defenses to face us. They will no doubt believe they're setting a trap for us."

The Praetor's frown deepened, putting creases in his broad forehead.

"I see your doubts concerning my plan, and I accept it. I am blessed with superior sight. I will tell you a secret, Praetor.

Sometimes it is a curse to see farther and more clearly than anyone else. Too often in the past others I hold dear have doubted me. I would like to say that I've become inured to it, but that would be a lie. However, I can give you evidence that even you can comprehend, Praetor."

The Praetor stiffened.

"The Social Unity space attack five days ago occurred in order to send a flotilla of vessels to Mars."

"So their high command could escape the coming disaster?" the Praetor asked.

The Grand Admiral shook his head. "I've heard those rumors, and they're absurd. If nothing else, these socialists are stubborn. They've been in control of human destiny too long to simply give up and flee to the Outer Planets. No. That was a supply convoy, and the majority of it now hides behind a growing prismatic crystal shield. I have ordered a cessation of laser attacks against it."

"I see," the Praetor said slowly. "The premen gather their fleet into one force and will capture Mars. We then send... two Doom Stars to smash their fleet and retake Mars."

"You are almost correct."

The Praetor's cheek twitched. When was the Grand Admiral going to offer him command of the *Hannibal Barca*? "This fleet that lifted from Earth," he said. "You called it a supply convoy. They will refit their warships?"

"Exactly," the Grand Admiral said. "They will have surprises that we cannot yet foresee. But we too shall have a surprise."

The Praetor blinked, waiting.

"It's your move," the Grand Admiral said.

It took the Praetor a moment to understand that the Grand Admiral meant the chessboard. He tried to concentrate on the game. The Praetor pondered for only a minute and then swept the Grand Admiral's castle with his queen. He neatly placed the captured castle in a new, second line of pieces, one behind the smaller pawns.

The Grand Admiral moved immediately, seeming to make a blunder. He took a pawn, but left the Praetor's queen open to maneuver.

70

As the Praetor bent forward to examine the possibilities, the Grand Admiral spoke.

"I know you've desired a field command in space. Until now, I've needed you in charge of supplies at the Sun-Works Factory. It was critical that we kept ourselves well-supplied."

The Praetor looked up. Here it was, at last. "I am to head the expedition against Mars in the *Hannibal Barca*?"

"No. That position belongs to Admiral Brutus. He will command the *Hannibal Barca*. Nor are there any available positions in the other Doom Stars. But if you are agreeable, Praetor, I wish to award you the captainship of our secret weapon."

Rage washed through the Praetor. He found it hard to speak. "If you would explain the weapon—"

"The beamship *Bangladesh* gave me the idea," the Grand Admiral said. "Even as we speak, a special weapons team is converting a captured missile-ship. They are rapidly adding stealth technology and installing our new drones. Your task, Praetor, will be to take the stealth ship and circle the Sun. The technicians are adding booster pods. As you build velocity, you will shed those pods. It will be a highly uncomfortable time as you circle the Sun, mostly spent on the acceleration couches. At a precise time you will sling yourself out of the Sun's orbit and head for Mars. Then you will shut off the engines and coast for the Red Planet. I will tell you now, Praetor, that your ship neither carries particle shields nor will it employ a prismatic crystal cloud, nor aerosol gels with lead additives."

"I will be defenseless?" the Praetor asked.

"You will effectively be invisible, a black object hurtling through the empty void of space. Your close approach to Mars will be timed so it coincides with the hard deceleration of the Doom Stars. You will attack with stealth drones dropped from your ship. Your second objective will occur once you've passed their positions behind the moons, the planet itself, or their prismatic fields. You will then beam critical information concerning their formation to the Doom Stars."

"They will fire at me once I beam these messages."

"Their window of opportunity to do you damage will be small. Your speed will be great, and the technicians will have

71

supplied your ship with many escape pods."

"Escape pods and the ship together will drift at high velocity toward the Outer Planets."

"Shuttles will already be on their way to pick you up, if that proves necessary."

"The timing would need to be exquisite for the flyby."

"I have computed the numbers," the Grand Admiral said. "It is well within Highborn capacity. Praetor, it is a dangerous mission. It calls for iron nerves and a will to conquer. I know you possess each of those qualities. You will also be in possession of the spaceship that tilts victory hard toward the Highborn. Needless to say, you will be a hero."

"If I survive," the Praetor said.

"Glory inherently demands risks."

"Excellence brings rank," the Praetor recited.

"Then you accept the assignment?"

"What about my neutraloids?"

"They will train until such time as the Doom Stars leave Earth orbit. I have plans to use them to retake Rebel strongholds on Mars."

The Praetor wanted to examine the captaincy in detail. Yet he feared hesitating lest the Grand Admiral offer the chance at field command to someone else.

The Praetor forced himself to mutter, "I would be honored, Grand Admiral."

"I knew it would be so," the Grand Admiral said. "Now, it's your move."

The Praetor examined the chessboard and captured another piece, a bishop. He pressed his fingertips against the top knob of the bishop and ran the edge of his thumbnail through the bishop's crease. Then he clunked the piece down into his growing row of captures.

"Hm," the Grand Admiral said. He made another seemingly strange move.

The Praetor captured a pawn.

The Grand Admiral moved his queen and said, "Checkmate in three moves."

Stunned and disbelieving, the Praetor examined the chessboard. He saw it then. He looked up into the Grand

Admiral's face. It was at that moment a cold icicle of fear stabbed the Praetor's heart.

The Grand Admiral had outmaneuvered him all down the line. Could the old man be that much more cunning than he was? The thought made the Praetor wonder if this field command was a suicide mission intended to get rid of him, his reward for the failed neutraloid "accident."

Cyborgs

-1-

Marten Kluge sat in the pilot's chair of the *Mayflower*. He had renamed the shuttle after a mythical ship of freedom seekers. His mother had told him the story many times. The ancient Pilgrims had left the tyranny of one land, seeking a new country where they could breathe the air and practice their beliefs as their consciences dictated.

Marten considered himself a new pilgrim in a Solar System seething with tyrants. Social Unity had slain his mother and father. It had forced him to flee to Earth. Then Social Unity had stolen Molly and Ah Chen from him. Day and night, hall leaders, the holoset, the sheep-like philosophies spouted during the hum-a-longs had all tried to grind him down. Social Unity had tried to turn him into a cog to fit into the machine of State. Major Orlov had sent him to the slime pits and later the punishment tube. Every aspect had been calculated to break his spirit and his will.

Marten had refused. He would always refuse. He had learned about freedom and truth from his parents. His mother and father had trumped the State. His first allegiance was to God and to his conscience, then to his family and friends, and lastly to the State.

Marten grinned as he stared at the stars. He had beaten Hall Leader Quirn. He had beaten Major Orlov. He had slain mad

Colonel Sigmir, the Highborn who had made his life hell during the Japan Campaign. Now he had beaten Training Master Lycon and owned a spaceship, the *Mayflower*.

It was a small spaceship, a shuttle. But it *was* a spaceship just the same. It gave him liberty and freedom of movement. If he calculated it right, if he used his wits at Mars, he could reach the Jupiter Confederation yet. He could escape the Social Unity fanatics and the bigoted Highborn Supremacists.

A klaxon wailed. It shattered the quiet peace that Marten had known for weeks. He whirled around and blinked five times before he realized the significance of the noise.

"Omi!" he shouted.

Marten fumbled at his buckles. He took a deep breath and told himself to calm down. With greater concentration, he unsnapped the last buckle and pushed himself toward the hatch. He floated through the *Mayflower* to the medical unit.

Omi looked up through the clear cylinder.

Marten grinned like a maniac. With practiced speed, he opened the cylinder and slid Omi out.

"Take it easy," Marten said.

Omi frowned and opened his mouth, but no words came out. He was dreadfully thin compared to the muscled shock trooper he had been eight weeks ago.

Daily, Marten had slid the unconscious Korean from the cylinder and massaged his muscles with a specially designed machine. The machine had worked on similar principles as their acceleration suits aboard the Storm Assault Missiles. It had massaged and moved the muscles so they wouldn't deteriorate too much, wouldn't atrophy altogether.

"Where are we?" Omi finally whispered.

"You're aboard my spaceship," Marten said proudly.

Omi's frown deepened. With methodical slowness he turned his head, looking around.

"Where..." Omi wet his lips. "Where are the Highborn?" His voice was hoarse and hard to understand.

"Let's get you set up first," Marten said.

Marten found him clothes, a one-piece jumper. He let Omi sip concentrates and had him float throughout the shuttle with him.

"We're alone," Omi said at last.

Nodding, Marten laughed.

"I don't understand," Omi said.

Marten pointed at the heavily polarized window in the pilot compartment. "Training Master Lycon is floating with the stars."

Omi's eyes narrowed.

With barely restrained glee, Marten told Omi how he'd spaced the three Highborn. A part of Marten scolded himself for his enthusiasm. He had killed three humans in cold blood. It was true the Highborn had treated him like an animal. They had caused the death of all his friends. Yet there was something too bloodthirsty about taking such inordinate joy in having spaced three of the Master Race.

Omi stared at him, with that cold hard smile playing along his lips. "I would like to have seen them die." Then Omi closed his eyes and fell asleep.

2

Commodore Joseph Blackstone's body ached most of the time from radiation poisoning. He sat before his vidscreen in his tiny wardroom aboard the *Vladimir Lenin*. It was a *Zhukov*-class battleship in far-Mars orbit.

The *Vladimir Lenin* had taken hits from a Doom Star. The super-ship had previously been orbiting Mars. They had finally repaired the engine damage and stopped the radiation leakage, but his crew and he had been weakened by the ordeal. Now everyone took anti-radiation tablets and tissue regeneration drugs.

Commodore Blackstone was a short man, noted for his decathlon victories in his younger years. Once, he had been vigorous, a dynamo of energy and self-confidence. Unfortunately he had seen better days. He had seen better years. The war, the extended voyage and the grim encounter with the Doom Star had caught him at the worst possible moment in his life.

He had dearly loved his wife, had always looked forward to their time together during his shore leave. Then his wife had sent him a divorce decree through official channels. He'd discovered that she'd had a string of lovers for years. Worst of all, she had kept a careful dossier on his sarcastic comments regarding Political Harmony Corps and the Directorate of Inner Planets. Learning those things had been horrible enough. The fourth blow had arrived a month before the beginning of the Highborn Rebellion. His only daughter had been horribly mutilated in a flyer accident on Venus. For some inexplicable reason she hadn't taken to regeneration therapy. He desperately wanted to see her, to hold and comfort her as he had when she'd been a little girl after her hoverpad accident that had chipped her two front teeth.

His once smooth features had become slack as he lost weight. He had bags under his eyes and too often forgot to shave. He was listless and thin, never smiled, and lived far too much in his memories of happier days.

Blackstone doubted that Supreme Commander Hawthorne was aware of any of his personal problems. Hawthorne had been an old friend from academy days. Blackstone suspected that he knew nothing of the attributes of the political officer assigned to the *Vladimir Lenin*. Because of his ex-wife's files the political officer had boarded the battleship with a company of PHC enforcers and with extra-military authority. She was a three-star commissar, a daunting woman with a bruising personality and heavy-handed attention to protocol.

Commodore Blackstone lifted a shaking hand and turned on the vidscreen. The *Vladimir Lenin* had a task to perform. He'd never failed before. He studied the Supreme Commander's operational plan for the reduction of the Rebel Mars Planetary Union orbital defenses.

"Destroy Doom Stars," Commodore Blackstone whispered later. He was supposed to take Mars in order to lure Doom Stars here. The ache in his bones told of the danger of attempting any engagement with the super-ships.

Blackstone tapped at his desk screen. A simulation of the Mars System appeared. Mars' average distance from the Sun was 1.52 AU (an AU was an Astronomical Unit, the average distance of the Earth from the Sun). The Earth and Mars were on the same side of the Sun presently, so it should have been a short journey for the convoy fleet. The closest the Earth ever came to Mars was 56 million kilometers. Now however, Mars was nearing its farthest orbital distance from the Sun. It was also 100 million kilometers from Earth and made the convoy fleet's journey nearly twice as long.

Commodore Blackstone rubbed his bristly chin. He needed a shave. He had forgotten that daily ritual for two mornings now.

He began to read the bulletins and study spaceship velocities. He read deceleration schedules and reports concerning the structure and position of the battle pods these *cyborgs* from the Neptune System came in. Blackstone had seen bionic soldiers before and assumed the cyborgs must have advanced prosthetics. How the cyborgs could benefit the coming assault, he had little idea. Hawthorne's plans for them were patently absurd.

The scattered units gathered here in far-Mars orbit simply couldn't do what the Supreme Commander fantasized they could do. Blackstone had toured a missile-ship yesterday that had escaped the Venus System. He had been appalled at the sloppy uniforms, the lackluster salutes and the depleted ship's supplies. If the other warships were in similar shape he doubted there would be enough firepower left in his growing fleet to give the Highborn much worry.

How was a commander supposed to gather a dispirited fleet in the far orbit of any planet? Then he was supposed to re-supply them, ship-to-ship, without any base facilities. Then he was supposed to effect repairs, erasing previous battle-damage.

James Hawthorne had always been far too prone to try risky endeavors. It meant that if his plans worked, they were brilliant. But if they failed, they were disasters. Who would be blamed for the disaster this time? Not Supreme Commander Hawthorne. No, it would be Blackstone, Hawthorne's old comrade from the academy days.

The thought brought a spark of anger to Commodore Blackstone. The spark showed in his eyes, replacing the sadness that usually dwelled there. It momentarily tightened the sagging flesh on his face.

A loud rap against the wardroom door startled Blackstone out of his anger. He flinched as he looked up. The rapping sound came again, and there was a muffled voice that demanded he unlock the door immediately.

The Commodore was hardly aware that he had locked it. He realized belatedly that the Commissar had ordered every door aboard the *Vladimir Lenin* remain unlocked. Comrade soldiers of Social Unity had nothing to hide from each other. Locked doors implied privacy, and that hinted at property and capitalist possessions.

"Enter," Blackstone said.

The door automatically unlocked itself and swished open. Three-star Commissar Kursk strode in. She was a fierce woman in an overly tight brown uniform. She had severe Slavic features that would have appealed to those who lusted after a latex-fetish dominatrix. She wore her cap so the brim was low over her eyes. Those eyes were black, intense and demanding. Surprisingly, she had a flat chest. The rest of her was lean, with just enough curvature to her hips so men turned to watch her walk away. She wore her Order of Solidarity Badge, Second Class. It was big, shiny and pinned on her chest. She'd won it several years ago suppressing *individualist mania* among the space-welders of the Sun-Works Factory.

Behind her followed two enforcers in red PHC uniforms, natural sadists with agonizers clipped to their belts. Their long-fingered hands never strayed far from their stun guns. These two had strange stares.

Blackstone suspected their stares were from post-hypnotic commands and an over-indulgence of *glaze*. Blackstone had heard rumors that some Political Harmony Corps enforcers and slime pit operators developed strange psychosis after eliminating too many enemies of the State. Many of them turned to *glaze*, which helped for a time but eventually made most users paranoid.

"Your door was locked," Commissar Kursk complained. There was a hint of the agonizer in her voice. It made Blackstone wince.

"Having you been taking your tablets?" Commissar Kursk asked.

The Commodore nodded his bald head.

"You are not above discipline." Kursk unclipped a keypad and typed until a warning beep sounded. "I have added a mark to your profile. I am also duty-bound to inform you that another three marks will result in a half-minute of agony."

Blackstone blinked at her. Could she be so rash? With Supreme Commander Hawthorne's rise to power the authority of the political officers had dwindled. It was true that Commissar Kursk commanded an abnormal number of enforcers. She also had a formidable personality. But to use an agonizer on him as the commanding officer of the assault....

Blackstone opened his mouth to protest.

Commissar Kursk planted herself before his desk, putting her hands on her hips. "Forget about that for now. I have something more important to discuss. I have toured three of the newest warships and have spoken with their political officers. What I found amazed me. I know you've also toured two vessels. Surely, you have seen the same thing."

"Everyone needs shore leave," Blackstone said.

Kursk scowled. "Social Unity is fighting for its life! Shore leave is the least of anyone's concern. This fleet represents one of the most potent forces left to us. Yet what do I find? There is a sullen quality to shipboard ideological fervor. For too many months now these warships have sulked like isolationists in dark corners. Instead of yearning to come to grips with our bigoted enemies they plot how to survive what they see as a catastrophe."

"The Highborn aren't a catastrophe?" Blackstone asked.

"Your tone is defeatist. I'm tempted to add another mark against your profile. You are the chief officer of this endeavor. You must exude confidence in order to pour it into your underlings. They in turn must motivate the crews with fierce ideological certainty of our coming victory. Anti-cooperative supremacists cannot defeat a socially aware humanity. I demand that you hold immediate court-martial proceedings and weed out the defeatists. You must stiffen everyone's spine, Commodore."

"Yes," Blackstone said listlessly.

Commissar Kursk's features turned glacial. "I have been timing the extended periods that you spend alone in here. Your personal misfortunes can no longer be allowed to interfere with your responsibility to Social Unity. The Directorate of Inner Planets has thought fit to use your martial abilities for the betterment of humanity. I recognize that human frailty sometimes worms into our responsibilities. At this critical juncture, however, I will not allow that to happen to you. Commodore Blackstone, the Directorate sent me to instill socially responsible behavior into you. I would be derelict in my duty if I failed to prod you to maximum efficiency in this grave hour."

"If it's any consolation," Blackstone said, "I have been studying the attack plan." He turned the vidscreen to show her the orbital positions of moons and satellites.

Kursk scowled. "You surprise me, Commodore. You molder in here like an isolationist, thinking that some revelation will elevate you above the rest of us and give you military insights. You should be with your staff, debating ideas and formulas, obtaining a group consensus."

"No doubt you're right," Blackstone mumbled.

Commissar Kursk made an explosive sound as she blew out her cheeks. She leaned toward him, putting her hands on his desk. Her black fingernail polish seemed to suck the light from the room like mini-black holes.

"What is wrong with you? The cyborg battle pods are near, the supply convoy is less than four weeks away, and twelve major warships have matched orbital velocity with the *Vladimir Lenin*. You should have visited each ship, counted supplies and demoted the inefficient. Your malaise is close to criminal sentimentality."

A flicker of annoyance entered the Commodore's sad eyes. He sat up, jerked once on his uniform to straighten it, and almost lurched to his feet. "You overstep your bounds, Commissar."

"I'll trample well outside my bounds to save Social Unity," she said. "My allegiance is to humanity's future greatness. That can only be achieved through realizing the perfection of equality, the core of the human spirit."

She unclipped her keypad and began to type. "You will join the scheduled hum-a-long at 1400 hours and tomorrow at 2600 hours."

Commodore Blackstone frowned, and he opened his mouth to protest.

"Your malaise increases in direct proportion to your time spent in isolation," she said. "You must mingle with the soldiers and derive your solace from unity. That will charge you with renewed zeal for victory. I am adamant on this and I will brook no disobedience. Have I made myself clear?"

Blackstone barely nodded.

"I demand an audible affirmation."

"This is really too much," he said.

"Commodore, it will pain me to apply it, but I will order my enforcers to use the agonizer on you. You are not alone, either in your pain or in exclusion from punishment. I am your conscience, and I refuse to fail in my duty to you and to Social Unity."

"Very well," Blackstone said. "I will join the hum-a-longs."

"Excellent!" Kursk turned to go, but paused and looked back. "I think you shall be surprised at the hum-a-longs' efficiency in soothing your pains."

"No doubt true," he muttered.

Commissar Kursk snapped her fingers and pointed at one of the enforcers. "See that the Commodore remains here no longer than another twenty minutes. Then call me and we shall implement the punishment."

Commissar Kursk thereupon marched out of the wardroom in the company of her second enforcer. Despite her severity, Blackstone watched her hips sway and knew a stab of longing. He would like to run his hands over her butt, and give it a good squeeze. As the door swished shut the second enforcer moved around the desk so that he stood behind the Commodore and could see what he looked at on the vidscreen.

If Commissar Kursk had planned to irritate the Commodore until he exited his wardroom, she was successful. Blackstone remained in his wardroom only long enough to turn off the vidscreen. Without acknowledging the enforcer's presence, he left to go to his sleep cubicle and shave.

3

Transcript #17 of SU Directorate-Mars Planetary Union talks: An exchange of messages between Director Danzig representing Inner Planets and Secretary-General Chavez representing the Martian Rebels. Dates: February 7 to February 11, 2351.

Note: The messages were exchanged via the Larson-Rodriguez Lightguide System, with an approximately five and half minute time lag between the sending and receiving of the priority messages.

February 7
From Secretary-General Chavez:
Our core memories store pleasant and unpleasant data with equal facility. We have therefore not forgotten Social Unity's trickery prior to the 2339 sneak attack. Then as now, Mars had to be ever vigilant to maintain its freedom from the tyranny of Social Unity. We were foolish enough to believe the Directorate's stated policy of joint peace between our sovereign entities then and sent our representatives to Earth. After twelve years their flesh still rots in the slime pits of your injustice and insincerity. I ask the Director to forgive me my passion, but such savagery and double-dealing is difficult to expunge from our collective hearts.

It will thus surely not surprise you to realize our qualms concerning the continued rendezvous of SU warships in far-Mars orbit. The numbers exceed reason, and we can only conclude that after twelve years Social Unity plans another assault against our native planet.

February 7
From Director Danzig:
Need I remind the honored Secretary-General of the true historical record? More than thirteen years ago the mass Martian assaults against SU Peacekeeping personnel brought a wave of terror and butchery to thousands of innocent people. The notorious 2334 assassinations of SU fleet personnel in Martian jurisdiction left a scar that still poisons relations between us. Now the recent Martian wave of planetary terror-attacks on SU space-defense facilities has left us shocked at your perfidy. Worse, your joint tactical campaign with the Highborn supremacists has deeply wounded our belief that you possess any social consciousness worthy of the name.

The SU fleet units in far-Mars orbit are entirely peaceful in intention and defensive in orientation. We have agreed to the Secession Accords and have sent an emergency convoy fleet to begin evacuation of SU personnel that you presently hold captive.

We demand, however, as a sign of your good faith, that you immediately halt your ground assaults on the North Polar Region. Furthermore, we demand that you cease space-borne laser attacks on the Valles Marineris Canyon.

May I also point out that what you call excessive numbers of fleet units in far-Mars orbit is simply an example of our caution? We have come to appreciate when dealing with Mars the need for an appeal to strength. Therefore, we have concentrated our fleet units to assure a peaceful exchange of prisoners as per the Secession Accords and to assure the safety of our emergency convoy fleet.

February 8
From Secretary-General Chavez:
The hard acceleration of your so-called *emergency convoy fleet* has led our military analysts to conclude it is an attack fleet meant to augment the continued gathering of your spaceships in far-Mars orbit.

I will refrain from further recrimination concerning past

Social Unity lies, misinformation, intimidation tactics, murder sprees, and mass repression of human dignity. However, I cannot help but inform you that the manufactured outrage of the oppressor at finally feeling the sting of retribution from the oppressed left me nauseated. The inhumanly oppressed are justified using any means necessary to tear off the cruel yoke of tyranny. What cannot be tolerated is the breakage of inter-planetary protocols painfully hammered out through the centuries. To wit: when two sovereign entities engage in political discourse, honesty is an assumed prerequisite. Past Social Unity dishonesty toward the original Martian Planetary Union has led to our present suspicion.

We shall warm the primary lasers on Phobos and Deimos for instant beaming. However, as per your request, we shall turn the orbital platforms away from the Valles Marineris Canyon—from which Social Unity launches daily air raids—and toward your far- orbital gathering.

Mars shall meet any further additions to the gathered far-orbital fleet with missile and laser attacks.

February 8
From Director Danzig:
Any attacks on SU space vessels will result in an immediate repudiation of the Secession Accords!

Think well on what this would mean, Secretary-General. Mars and Inner Planets would engage in needless war while the Highborn supremacists solidify a repressive regime based on a master-slave relationship. We would both weaken ourselves in a time of planetary and solar-wide crisis. In a year, two years, or even three, the genetic bigots might well sweep aside whatever remnants Mars retains in space defense capabilities and conquer your union.

I realize the Martian Rebels believe they have many outstanding grievances against Social Unity. The lack of high social consciousness among the citizens of the Red Planet has long been noted. Now isn't the time to address such a failing in you or such a failing you think to perceive in us. I have studied the situation and have begun to wonder if in the past Political Harmony Corps failed the citizens of Mars by applying insufficient rigor.

What I wish to point out, Mr. Secretary-General, is that the Directorate of Inner Planets never pre-sanctioned the harsh Highborn retaliation during the Second Battle of Far-Mars orbit in 2339. Why is that important now in 2351? Because twelve years ago the Highborn slaughtered Martian personnel in that regrettable incident. What the genetic supremacists did once, they will likely attempt again.

Let me reiterate. Any attack on SU space vessels will result in an immediate repudiation of the Secession Accords. To show our good will the Directorate has issued an immediate halt to the air assaults from the Valles Marineris Canyon. We ask in return that you halt the North Polar Region attacks.

February 9
From Secretary-General Chavez:
We are not the *Martian Rebels*, but the sovereign Mars Planetary Union.

We have noted that no new SU air assaults have originated from the Valles Marineris Canyon. Consequently we have halted the North Polar Region attacks.

I wish to point out however that our orbital defenses are on high alert. Any movement toward the planet from the spaceships in far-Mars orbit will be met with fierce resolve.

Your comments concerning the Highborn have been noted. We also note that Social Unity geneticists engineered the Highborn. And we note that Highborn atrocities in 2339 were committed while they wore Social Unity uniforms, as they fought under your control.

We demand full planetary sovereignty and an exit of all military space-capable vessels from the Martian System. The continued Social Unity military presence on the planet can only result in the eventual resumption of hostilities in space.

If the gathered war vessels in far-Mars orbit are not directed against us, what is their military objective? How does the Directorate suggest we end all hostilities so both sovereign governments can plan against future Highborn aggression?

February 10

From Director Danzig:

After an emergency meeting with the full Directorate, I am authorized to offer a fully accredited envoy to Mars to discuss peace talks and possible defensive treaties.

February 11
From Secretary-General Chavez:

We welcome an accredited envoy and wish to guarantee his or her safety. However, as unpleasant as this may sound, I must reiterate the Mars Planetary Union warning. Any SU military vessel that enters near-Mars orbit will be targeted and destroyed.

As much as we agree that ultimate Highborn objectives remain unknown, we also acknowledge past Social Unity actions and must react accordingly.

I hope this clarifies our position.

February 11
From Director Danzig:

As the spokesman for the Directorate of Inner Planets, I applaud the Martian Planetary Union's good sense. Our convoy fleet shall join the gathered military vessels and thus stay out of near-Mars orbit. All prisoner exchanges shall occur by shuttle.

On all accounts, we must refrain from mutual destruction while the genetic supremacists expand their master-slave regime.

4

General-Secretary Chavez smoked a stimstick as he listened to the last lightguide message in his office deep underground Olympus Mons. The bite of the smoke felt good in the back of his throat, comforting and steadying him. Chavez was a thin man with a long head and delicate fingers. He had a goatee and wavy dark hair that surrounded a worn face.

The Social Unity bosses on Mars had been ruthless. The Martian Unionists had been cleverer and had lived in hiding and through secrecy for many years before the present Martian self-liberation.

Chavez replayed the last message, studying Director Danzig the entire time, as if he could probe the director's thoughts.

"He's lying," Chavez told his secretary. The secretary was an even thinner man with gaunt cheeks. He wore a dark tunic and held a computer stylus and a blue slate on his lap.

Chavez clicked off the vidscreen. With a trembling hand he put the stimstick between his lips and puffed. Red smoke trickled from the glowing end. The smell of the stimulant permeated the room, a sweet odor.

"They're buying time until the convoy reaches their military vessels." Chavez dragged deeply on the stimstick before mashing it out in an overflowing ashtray. Then, like some delicate dragon, he blew red smoke out of his nostrils. "If only the Highborn had left us warships. Our orbital defenses can't match the SU fleet, not in our present state of disrepair."

Chavez's fingers brushed his goatee as he stared at some

unseen point. "Take this down: The technicians have two months. Then the proton beam must be ready."

General-Secretary Chavez referred to the proton beam installation on Olympus Mons. It had been badly damaged during the recent Mars Rebel liberation and had been taken offline. Technicians worked day and night attempting repairs. Whether it would be ready in two months was highly questionable.

"At least they stopped their air attacks out of the Valles Marineris Canyon," Chavez said. "So we can begin to use the Harrington Launch Sites. Take that down. We must ferry more missiles and repair each laser focusing system in turn on the orbital stations. Social Unity will try to swamp us. We have to make it too costly for them. We have two months at the most. I fear, however, it will be less than four weeks. It's simply not enough time."

Chavez opened a drawer and shook another stimstick out of a half-crumpled pack. He put it between his lips and inhaled it into life. "Are you ready for more?"

The secretary nodded.

Chavez continued dictating, "To the Shop Steward of the Phobos Local, I send these emergency instructions…"

***

As he swam laps in an indoor pool in New Baghdad, Supreme Commander James Hawthorne listened to Director Danzig. Captain Mune stood farther off near the diving board.

Hawthorne swam strongly, and despite his lankiness, with grace. Director Danzig walked along the side of the pool, reiterating his conversations with Secretary-General Chavez.

"I doubt we convinced him," Hawthorne said as he flipped onto his back, doing a long-limbed backstroke. A small amount of chlorine-tasting water trickled into his mouth.

"They're trying to buy time," Danzig said.

"Obviously, and so are we. The question for us is: What do they need the time for? …have we intercepted any Rebel messages to the Highborn?"

"Just that the Rebels have appealed to them, not the nature of the queries."

Hawthorne stopped and stood up in the pool so water

sloshed around his waist. There was too much chlorine in it. The harsh odor stung his nostrils. He'd have to have a word with the manager. The man must know that he took a swim at this time every day.

"The important thing is they're not molesting our individual warships as they decelerate and match orbital speeds with Blackstone," Hawthorne said. "It must mean Martian orbital defenses are weaker than we suspected. That's both good and bad."

"General?" Director Danzig asked.

"It's a phony peace as we both prepare for war." Hawthorne laughed. "We caught them flat-footed with the convoy fleet. That must be the truth of it. They didn't expect us to appear at the Mars System so soon. Yes, they must be using the time for emergency repairs and re-supply. Let's just hope the Highborn are as surprised."

"Do you really think they are?"

Hawthorne examined the middle-aged director. The air was humid, and Danzig's suit was damp. The director looked tired. The man probably needed to exercise more. Hmm. The Highborn had a plan. They always did. For a moment Hawthorne had the chills as he wondered if the Highborn had already outthought him.

No. Such thinking was debilitating. He had to believe it was possible to outwit the super-soldiers.

"Of course the Highborn are surprised," Hawthorne said. "The savagery of their space-borne attacks these last weeks on Eurasia prove it, as does their storming of half the habitats. We've enraged them, and that's the best sign there is that we've gained a step on them."

Director Danzig grinned. "That's good to hear, sir. We need this victory."

"We do at that," Hawthorne said, and he began to wade toward the steps. The chlorine bothered his eyes. He was going to find the manager and have a word with him.

-5-

The long weeks passed in worry and hard deceleration for the clone Lisa Aster. She was in the safest central cargo-ship of the Earth convoy fleet, the *Alger Hiss*. She thus had the highest probability of surviving the grueling journey. The oppressive G-forces caused by the deceleration stopped. During the half-hour intervals of weightlessness Lisa could float to the facilities, eat and flex her limbs without the bone-crushing pressure. She complained to stout General Fromm, Mars Supplies, with whom she shared the acceleration/deceleration area.

The general sat on his couch eating salted herring, a delicacy he ate regularly. It left a horrible fishy odor in the module. In the interest of politeness, Lisa kept her intense dislike of the smell to herself. However she floated near the ceiling, as far away from the offensive odor as she could go.

"This trip has nothing to do with our sensibilities," said General Fromm. Despite the relish with which he ate his herring, he had been losing weight. He'd become increasingly pale and somber. "The trip has everything to do with speed. We have accelerated and now decelerate near the acceptable limits of human endurance. Battlefleet Mars desperately needs these supplies."

"The journey is killing us," Lisa said.

"...yes," General Fromm said after he'd torn off another length of dried herring with his teeth. He chewed thoroughly and swallowed. "...but eighty-five percent of us should survive. You're healthy and young, so you should recover

92

quickly from any debilitating effects."

"Killing ourselves is foolish," Lisa said.

General Fromm checked his chronometer. "Five minutes to continued deceleration. You'd better strap yourself in." He slid the remaining herring into a container, sealing it. Then he lay back on the couching, strapping himself in and settling down for another six hours of pain and torment.

Lisa continued to float near the ceiling and waved her hand before her nose as the general occupied himself with his straps.

"We're not killing ourselves to set speed records," Fromm said, finally looking up. "We're trying to outwit the Highborn. Our window of opportunity to defeat the Mars Rebels and reorganize the orbital defenses in time to face and destroy Doom Stars is narrow indeed. Our supplies are critical to the refitting of our united fleet." He checked his chronometer again. "You really should strap-in."

Lisa grinned tightly. General Fromm meant well. He was a brooder and deep-thinker. He never took risks if he could help it, but carefully thought out the best way to do everything. She hated lying on the couch, and she was unbelievably bored. Timing her landing on the couch and strapping in to the exact second of the re-igniting thrusters had become one of her sole games. Having a brooder to scold her only made the game more enjoyable.

"Ms. Aster," the general said, "your risk of debilitating injury far outweighs any juvenile pleasure you might gain in waiting so long. You must strap yourself in now."

At least the general had learned not to try to order her. She *was* the Blanche-Aster now, even if she was the only one to acknowledge it. Despite the handicap of being a clone, she would climb the ranks of Social Unity into the rarified heights of leadership.

"Thirty seconds to deceleration," General Fromm said testily.

Lisa grinned at him, and she shuddered at the idea of another six hours of labored breathing and straining just to scratch her nose. Her face itched abominably during deceleration. What made it even worse was that she would have liked to study the files on the cyborgs and study the

Supreme Commander's attack plan. She had tried quizzing the general, but extended conversations soon become too tiring under the high Gs pressing against their bodies.

"Ten seconds," General Fromm said.

Lisa yawned as if bored.

"Ms. Aster, this is absurd. I demand you strap in now."

"I didn't hear you say please."

"Seven seconds," he said. "Please, hurry."

"Very well," she said. Now her pulse pounded. Now it was almost too late. If she pushed off wrong and missed her acceleration couch she could break bones. If a rib punctured a lung, she would quickly bleed to death.

Lisa smoothly shoved off the ceiling, sailed to her couch, and hit so she grunted. She spun around fast and made the fabric squeak. She barely managed to settle into position. Then the mighty thrusters switched on. A horrible grinding weight slammed against her, shoving her down into the padding of the acceleration couch. It was a strained effort to bring the straps across her body. Buckling them left her wheezing at the exertion.

"Was—that—worth—it?" General Fromm wheezed.

Lisa tried to make herself more comfortable. Someday, she was going to kill cyborgs. Originally, her motives were vengeful, as the cyborgs had engineered her mother's death. Now, it was for this brutal journey. Lisa closed her eyes, already longing for the next half-hour of weightlessness.

***

As Lisa Aster and the convoy fleet decelerated into far-Mars orbit the many months journey aboard the *Mayflower* were ending for Marten Kluge and Omi.

They decelerated, but at a fraction of the convoy fleet's rate. They had been traveling at a much slower speed.

Omi had given Marten a haircut. Marten's hair was short and his manner was alert. He felt as he had during his best times as a shock trooper. Marten's muscles were hard again, and his stamina had built back up from endless exercises on the machines.

Omi had gained weight, and he was no longer so dreadfully thin. He hadn't regained his original muscle-mass, but this last week had seen him hit the machines much more vigorously than before. Unfortunately it had become stale throughout the shuttle. To conserve water, they had long ago stopped taking showers. Before leaving the shuttle they would each shower thoroughly. Until such time, each endured the other.

The *Mayflower* was a shuttle, hardly big enough for extended flights between the inner planets. To the distant outer planets, it would have almost been impossible.

The shuttle lacked a warship's detection equipment and the accompanying squads of trained personnel using such equipment around the clock. Still, the *Mayflower* possessed limited radar gear and teleoptics. Using the teleoptics Marten easily discovered the hard-decelerating convoy fleet. The constant burn and plethora of fusion engines created a discernible image against the cold backdrop of space. The number and size of the war-vessels impressed Marten.

It was more difficult for Marten to spot the growing Social Unity Battlefleet. Those warships possessed greater ECM, Electronic Counter Measures, than his relatively tiny spaceship. A few were stealth ships with low signature hulls. Most, however, had large particle shields, the largest of those were 600-meter thick slabs of asteroid-rock. The reason Marten failed to detect them was simple. They were hidden behind Mars. The majority of the Battlefleet had already assembled in far-Mars orbit. Marten therefore spotted the few remaining warships that decelerated to help Mars' gravitational field catch them.

With the convoy fleet a mere two weeks out of Mars orbit, and with the sightings of major Social Unity war-vessels, Marten knew they were in serious trouble. He had worried about it for some time. The worst part was he lacked fuel to do anything else other than continue the deceleration.

"Social Unity is going to retake Mars," Omi said after Marten told him about the situation.

"They're certainly going to try," Marten said. "Yet we've both served under the Highborn. They gave Mars to the Rebels."

"The Martian Planetary Union?" asked Omi.

"That's what the Rebels call themselves," Marten said,

nodding. "I doubt the Highborn gave the Rebels Mars if the Highborn thought the Rebels were going to lose it right away. It's not reasonable to think the Highborn ran from Mars out of fear. So that leads me to the conclusion that the Highborn gave the Rebels enough war supplies to fight off any Social Unity attacks."

"If we see those warships," Omi said, "those warships must see us."

Marten tapped a red light on the lower part of the vidscreen. "Correct. This means radar is bouncing off us."

"From where?" Omi asked.

Marten fiddled with the controls. "From that approaching fleet there," he said, pointing out the blaze that signified the convoy fleet. "And from that warship there."

"Why doesn't the warship call us?" Omi asked.

Marten shrugged.

"Why don't they launch a missile and blow us up?" Omi asked.

"They might already have launched a missile."

"The radar doesn't show that," Omi said.

"Sometimes warships release a drone, leaving it behind like a mine. If we see a sudden bloom of engine-burn we'll know we're in trouble. But the more likely explanation is that we're a shuttle, so we're nothing to them. Besides, maybe they believe that our radio is out. If they're worried enough, they'll try to capture us later once we're in near orbit."

"Let's head out to Jupiter," Omi suggested.

Marten stared at the vidscreen, at the controls. He wished his ship were sized for men, not for Highborn. If he could move the pilot's chair closer and raise it a little higher, that would be great.

Jupiter System, Marten nodded. Going there had been one of his thoughts, too. They had enough fuel to change headings, but hardly enough to increase their velocity to anything like the needed speed. That meant a trip to Jupiter would take several more years than it would have if he'd started for there originally. Marten had little desire to spend six years in this cramped shuttle alone with Omi.

"We need to refuel first," Marten said.

"What do we use for currency?"

"Passage out of the war."

Omi nodded. "How many people do you think you can pack into our shuttle?"

"A few rich ones would be best," Marten said, "although I wish we could take more."

"How do we keep Social Unity from firing on our shuttle? A single missile kills us. So all they have to do is tell us to stop or we're dead."

"Ideally we need to modify the shuttle, attaching anti-missile pods."

"We lack currency," Omi said.

"I call that: Problem number one."

"Would the Rebels be willing to part with war supplies?"

"That's problem number two," Marten said.

Omi stared out of the polarized window. "Does the shuttle have reflectors to bounce laser-fire?"

"Reflectors would make us easier to spot, and reflectors won't bounce a military laser. But the short answer is no, our shuttle lacks reflectors. That would be our next purchase, a warfare pod filled with prismatic crystals."

"What else do we need?" Omi asked.

"Luck," Marten said.

The radio crackled, which startled Omi. Marten adjusted the controls, but there was too much static for the speakers. So he put on headphones and listened carefully.

"Mars Defense is calling," he soon told Omi. "They're asking us to identify ourselves. I'd tell them, but then the SU ship might fire a missile as you've been suggesting."

Marten tapped at the console as he studied the vidscreen and studied the satellites and habitats in near-Mars orbit. "It would be a shame to have escaped the Highborn, only to have the Martian Rebels kill us."

"Can you send them a tight-beam message?"

Instead of answering, Marten slapped a switch. The engines cut out, bringing weightlessness to the *Mayflower*.

"We're going to drift in faster and decelerate harder nearer the planet," Marten explained. "We'll have to take to the couches for that. Hopefully that will make whoever is scanning and calling us think we're damaged. That seems like the best way to buy us an arrival without any missiles."

"Will Social Unity warships be in range by that time?" Omi asked.

Marten studied the headings. "Frankly, I'm surprised the SU warships and Rebel moons aren't trading missiles or laser fire."

"Do you know why not?"

"It must have something to do with this being a three-way situation. It's not just the Rebels versus Social Unity. The Highborn change everything. Why fight if you don't have to?"

"You said before that the Highborn helped the Rebels."

"They did," Marten said, "but that doesn't make them friends."

"It should make them allies."

"Temporary allies," Marten said. "The Rebels aren't fools, and they probably have long memories. The Highborn crushed the Martian Rebels and the Jupiter Confederation Fleet back in 2339."

"Maybe if we're lucky, we can slip in and slip out before the shooting starts."

Marten grinned. "Now you're talking." He pushed out of the pilot's chair.

"Where are you headed?"

"All this thinking is making me edgy. I'm going to do some rowing. See you in an hour."

Omi nodded and then continued to stare out of the heavily polarized window.

6

The cyborg battle pods traveled silently through the stellar void. Each pod had begun its journey almost a year ago in the Neptune System. Neptune was 30 times the distance from the Sun as Earth, or about 4,486,100,000 kilometers away. It took sunlight traveling 300,000 kilometers per second four hours and fifteen minutes to reach Neptune.

The pods had long ago accelerated, and now decelerated much harder than anything a human could have survived. Each was an ultra-stealth pod, with a ceramic hull that gave the lowest sensor signature of any vessel in human space. Each pod was also crammed with the latest Onoshi ECM equipment and decoys.

All the pods were spherical and as black as night. Within all the pods but one lay a cyborg platoon in cryogenic stillness. The cyborg known as OD12 was in pod B3.

The designation OD12 referred to her lost humanity and machine code number. OD had once been Osadar Di, the female pilot with the perennial bad luck of being in the wrong place at the wrong time.

As the battle pods decelerated an electrical impulse surged through OD12's frozen body. At the same time, cryogenic heaters began the painful defrosting of the cyborg cargo.

OD12 awakened, but her mental facilities were kept offline. Instead she was hooked into the Web-Mind. There, Osadar Di practiced a hundred combat evolutions. It was similar to a human playing intense hologames while wearing a virtual imaging suit. The difference was that her reflexes gained one hundred percent conditioning, as if she physically participated in each action. These Web-Mind combat drops, bunker assaults, storm attacks, and sniper targeting took place at an accelerated rate. She thus gained "years" of practice.

There was a glitch, however, in six out of every one hundred simulations. The Web-Mind noted this malfunction in OD12. Accepted anomalies were one tenth of a percent, not six percent. Because of the extreme distance to the Master Web-Mind in the Neptune System, the Web-Mind in Toll Seven's command pod initiated a phase two diagnostic.

In the simulator, OD12 bounded across a moon in the Saturn System. She wore a vacuum suit churning at full heat. She knelt in frozen ammonia, lifted her laser carbine, and hesitated instead of firing the two-kilometer distance to pick off the retreating battleoids. OD12 glanced around her and then scooped a handful of the orange ammonia in her gloved hand.

The diagnostic program froze the image. Then it confronted OD12's personality.

Why did you hesitate?

"The expanse of orange snow struck me as beautiful. I had to feel it."

Explain beauty.

"The sight filled me with longing, with pleasant memories."

Describe these memories.

"...I'd rather not."

Computer.

Something in OD12 clicked into life. It was the computer inserted into her and connected with her brain.

Administer level three pain sensations.

In battle pod B3, OD12's online cyborg body jerked as she opened her mouth and metallically screamed.

A Web-Mind code caused the pain to cease, and OD12's body was taken offline with the others.

Describe these memories.

"...why did you do that?"

In a nanosecond the Web-Mind ran through a possibility of options, the primary of which was to delete OD12. It decided on option two instead, as the supply of cyborgs for this campaign was limited.

The Web-Mind resumed running OD12's combat simulations until it came to another anomaly. This time OD12 used a thruster pack as white particles of hydrogen spray propelled her toward a slowly rotating torus. Behind her followed the rest of the cyborgs in vacuum suits. They assaulted a Jupiter Confederation Habitat, with the vast gas giant beyond the torus.

OD12 twisted her head and looked back at the other suited cyborgs. Each used white particles of hydrogen spray. Each had breach bombs and rocket carbines. Each fixated on its targeted landing location. The only cyborg body movement was the occasional twitch of their fingers as they adjusted their flight paths to perfection. Only OD12 looked back. Only she saw the awesome spectacle of individual cyborgs "jetting" through cold space to the human habitat.

The Web-Mind froze the scene. It caused OD12's dark visor to turn clear. Within the helmet, the solid black metallic-seeming eyes stared with infinite sadness as tears streamed down the plastic cheeks.

Why are you crying?

OD12 answered with a blunt profanity.

This time, the Web-Mind issued level seven pain sensations.

OD12 thrashed in the eerily dark battle pod. Beside her lay the perfectly motionless cyborgs, each mentally engaged in combat simulations. None of the other cyborgs had experienced more than one tenth of one percent anomalies.

Cyborgs do not cry. You were crying. Explain what caused emotions to override your programming.

"...I remembered how we tried to escape the alien."

The answered confused the Web-Mind for two seconds. Then it understood OD12 meant Toll Seven.

"We wanted to live."

You are alive.

"Live, not just breathe."

Computer.

The computer in OD12 awaited further instructions.

You will monitor your host's emotions. If category two

emotions are employed, you will initiate immediate shutdown procedures and pulse me a report of the situation.

The computer logged the order in its command override logic core.

You must suppress these emotive anomalies, OD12, if you wish to continue functioning. Noncompliance will result in your termination.

"I want to function."

Then proceed within the guidelines.

"Affirmative."

The Web-Mind wasn't certain. It thought it might have detected sarcasm. It was impossible, however, for a slaved cyborg to exhibit sarcasm at a deeper level than the emotion sensors could detect. So it marked the observation and sent a lightguide message to the Master Web-Mind in the Neptune System. Then it proceeded to link with Toll Seven as they continued to refine the subterfuge plan of the conquest of Inner Planets.

7

In the *Mayflower* Marten and Omi braked hard for Deimos, Mars' smallest and most distant moon. The radio crackled with strident messages from the Planetary Union Space Force. The messages had been ongoing for the past five hours. Red Mars had grown before them until the planet dominated the heavily polarized window.

"We are now targeting your shuttle with Laser Port Seven," the radio crackled. There was a *ping-ping* from the controls as it alerted them of a radar lock-on.

Marten licked his lips, scooted forward, and reached up, pressing the comm button. "Mars Union, this is the free ship *Mayflower* requesting permission to dock."

"Why haven't you answered until now, *Mayflower*?"

"We've noticed the military situation and feared a missile attack from either you or Social Unity, depending on who we answered. So we waited until we were too close to you for Social Unity to fire without causing an incident."

"...*Mayflower*, your code registers as a Highborn vessel. Are you Highborn?"

"Negative, Mars Union. We are the free ship *Mayflower*."

"Are you a Social Unity vessel, *Mayflower*?"

Marten glanced at Omi before he said, "Negative, we're a free ship, requesting permission to dock, to buy fuel, and then to be on our way."

"What is your ultimate destination, *Mayflower*?"

Marten hesitated before he said, "The Jupiter Confederation."

"…where did you originate, *Mayflower?*"

"We request permission to dock and speak with the commanding officer of the Deimos Moon Station," Marten said.

The radio fell silent.

Omi said, "We should have told them we were Highborn and demanded the fuel."

"It would never have worked."

"*Mayflower*," the radio crackled. "You have permission to dock. Follow these coordinates…"

***

Marten slowly eased the shuttle against a docking module and then shut off the fusion engine. He soon heard the clank from a docking tube attaching to the outer airlock.

"Now it gets tricky," Marten said. "Do you remember what to do?"

Omi nodded, and he slapped the sidearm attached to his belt.

Marten formally shook hands with Omi before entering the airlock. The inner hatch swished shut behind him. Marten recalled the struggled he'd had with Training Master Lycon in this very airlock. He recalled the reflection of Lycon's eyes as they bulged, and the disbelieving look as Lycon shot into space.

Eager to be out of the airlock, Marten squeezed through the outer hatch as it swished open. Because Deimos was smaller than many asteroids, it had a negligible mass. It was hardly different from weightlessness as Marten float-walked through the docking tube.

His skin tingled from his shower a half-hour ago. His clothes smelled clean, and nervousness boiled in his gut. He was about to face the big question. Omi and he had escaped Social Unity, and they had escaped the Highborn. Now he had to interact with people again, this time with the Martian Rebels. Would the Martians try to steal his shuttle? If so, he had to outwit the Deimos commander. Marten heaved a deep sigh. He had to keep his wits about him, and he had to be ready to act decisively.

In all the Inner Planets there was probably no one in his

situation. Three governments struggled for existence. Everyone had to belong to one side or another. Now he and Omi were their own side, free agents who were much more common in the Outer Planets. He had to get fuel. He had to purchase warfare pods if he could. He had to keep the *Mayflower* out of the hands of desperate people.

Marten reached the hatch that led into the docking bay. The door opened, and Marten glided out of the tube to see three thin soldiers with drawn weapons aimed at his chest. The pitted gun-barrels pointed at him looked dark and deadly, but the soldiers holding them seemed too slender to be military men. The fourth person was a woman, an officer by her shoulder boards. She was as thin as the others.

"I'm sorry for the guns, Mr. Kluge. But you must give us your weapon and then come with us."

Marten nodded curtly. He'd expected this. It's why Omi had remained onboard. He'd expected this, but he'd hoped for something better. He had reentered the struggle for life.

"This way, Mr. Kluge," the officer said.

***

A Martian Unionist with pinched features glared at Marten. The man was tall and slender, with a beak of a nose. He was also pale and had oiled his dark hair into ringlets. Marten judged the man to be in his mid-forties.

The female officer remained in the office. It overlooked a hanger stacked with metal boxes, a shuttle under repair, and arc-welders flashing their blue glows as men fixed a multitude of articles. The office itself seemed more like a shed, with masses of equipment shoved into the corners and piled on top of each other. There was a vacuum pump, a magnetic lifter and a wrist communicator with a tiny flashing red light lying on the desk.

The Chief Unionist at the desk stood behind a vidscreen. He hadn't offered Marten a chair, but in this almost nonexistent gravity, it didn't matter.

"I demand that you declare who you're spying for," the Unionist said. "I would assume Social Unity. But you have a Highborn shuttle. This leaves me wondering."

"How can you tell it's a Highborn shuttle?" Marten asked.

105

The Chief Unionist drew himself straighter, which had seemed impossible. "You could have simply painted the Highborn symbols onto it. I understand. Why would a PHC officer do that, however?"

Marten glanced back at the Planetary Union military officer. She wasn't taking chances, and had a needler trained on him. It was smaller than the Gauss needlers used on Earth. Hers was compact, with a short and very thin barrel, and it was shiny, likely meaning it was newly unpackaged. He hoped she knew how to use it and didn't accidentally shoot him.

"Okay," Marten said, "I'll tell you what happened. But I suspect you won't believe me."

"Why bother lying?" the Chief Unionist asked.

"I haven't said anything yet," Marten said.

"I'm a university professor by occupation," the Chief Unionist said. "Because I understand physics, they put me out here. They're hoping I can perform a miracle and make Deimos useful again. My point, Mr. Kluge, is that my students always tell me I'm not going to believe something when they're getting ready to lie."

"Have it your way," Marten said, and he shut his mouth.

"...well?" the Chief Unionist asked. "Let's hear it."

"I hate being called a liar," Marten said.

The man lofted thin eyebrows. "A bit touchy, are we?"

"I think you're the liar. I think you're a sanitation scrubber, not some scholar."

The man's lips tightened. "Explain the situation then. How did you come to possess a Highborn shuttle?"

"I earned it," Marten said. "I paid for it through my sweat and blood. It's mine."

"For the moment, you're here in my office, Mr. Kluge. And my patience is wearing thin."

"The Highborn used me," Marten said. "They used my friends. We were shock troopers."

"I never heard of them."

"How about Free Earth Corps, you ever heard of them?"

"The Earth traitors who fight with the Highborn?" the Chief Unionist asked.

"You Mars Rebels helped the Highborn," Marten said,

106

knowing he was becoming too angry. But he couldn't help it.

The Chief Unionist lightly placed his fingertips on the desk. "We are the Planetary Union, not *the Rebels*. We did what we had to in order to rid ourselves of Social Unity."

Marten nodded curtly. "If you'd lived in Australian Sector when the Highborn conquered it, you'd realize that most Free Earth Corps volunteers joined at the point of a gun. I fought in the Japan Campaign. Afterward, the Highborn pinned medals on my friends and me. They called us heroes. Then they said they could use good soldiers like us. So they took us into space and retrained us into shock troopers. Our specialty was storming habitats or spaceships and taking control."

"That doesn't explain the shuttle," the Chief Unionist said.

"Our masters packed us into Storm Assault Missiles and fired us at the X-ship *Bangladesh*. It was a new type of warship, able to fire its beam many millions of kilometers."

"That's impossible!" the Chief Unionist declared. "Everyone knows the Doom Stars have the longest-range lasers of any military vessel."

"That's why the Highborn wanted the *Bangladesh*. That's why they fired us at it. We took it. But SU missile-ships destroyed our hard-won prize. A few of us escaped the destruction. Later, Highborn picked us up in the shuttle."

"If true, that's highly interesting. It still doesn't explain how you came to possess the shuttle."

"I killed the Highborn and took their shuttle for my own," Marten said.

In frank disbelief, the Chief Unionist stared at Marten. The officer behind Marten snorted in derision.

"You don't expect us to believe that?" the officer asked Marten.

Marten shrugged. "That's the trouble with you soft-timers. You fear the Highborn too much. If you'd been a shock trooper, you'd know that everyone has weak points, even super-soldiers. They made a mistake and thought me a mere preman. Well, this preman spaced them. Now I'm here. Now I want to buy fuel, a spare-warfare pod if you have it, and I'll be on my way."

"You're mad!" the Chief Unionist shouted.

"Then you explain to me how I'm in possession of a shuttle."

The Chief Unionist blinked at Marten with incomprehension. "*You* killed Highborn?"

"Three of them," Marten said.

"You pirated the shuttle," the Chief Unionist said. "I understand that."

"Just as you pirated Deimos," Marten said.

"He has a point," the officer said.

The Chief Unionist shot her a dirty look. "The Planetary Union is confiscating the shuttle, Mr. Kluge."

"I don't think so," Marten said.

The Chief Unionist lofted his eyebrows. "You're here, Mr. Kluge, as you pointed out earlier. Officer Dugan has a needler pointed at your back. You are in no position to stop me."

"You have a gun pointed at my back. I have a bomb attached to your docking bay."

"Are you threatening me?" the Chief Unionist demanded.

"With certain death," Marten said.

"You would die, too."

Marten shrugged.

"He's bluffing," the Chief Unionist told Officer Dugan.

"Maybe," the woman said.

"You're bluffing," the Chief Unionist told Marten, although a faint sheen of perspiration had appeared on the man's forehead.

"I rode a Storm Assault Missile at 25-Gs to the *Bangladesh*," Marten said. "I spaced three Highborn. If you think I did all that to meekly hand over my shuttle to some piss-whelp of a university professor, then you're mad."

Outraged, the Chief Unionist groped for words.

"I'm finished playing by other people's rules," Marten declared. "I'm finished being a slave. I'm a free man now. I'm going to remain free or die trying. If that means blowing the *Mayflower* and taking you and me down, okay. I'm fine with that."

"He's not bluffing," Officer Dugan said.

The Chief Unionist blushed as anger washed over his features. "Just what are you suggesting then?"

"Let me buy fuel," Marten said.

"Buy how?"

"With my services," Marten said.

The Chief Unionist blinked at Marten. "That's out of the question. You will order the remaining people on the shuttle to come—"

"I'd reconsider that," Officer Dugan told the Chief Unionist.

"You be quiet," the Chief Unionist said, pointing a long finger at her. The finger quivered, and its ring reflected the lights overhead.

"He's like us," Officer Dugan said. "He fought free, and now he plans to keep free, even dying for it if he has to. We can't steal his shuttle without fighting to the death for it, just as Social Unity can't have our planet back without a death struggle. If nothing else, sir, call the Secretary-General and ask his advice."

"I can't call about this," the Chief Unionist said.

"Then give this man fuel."

"*Give* it to him?" the Chief Unionist asked.

"You've been talking about getting the sick personnel off station and back to Mars," Officer Dugan said. "Here's your chance."

The pinched features to the Chief Unionist's mouth tightened so his lips began to whiten. He made a sweeping motion with his arm. "Go! Take this madman outside. I have a call to make."

***

Ten hours later, Marten and Omi left the tiny Martian moon of Deimos. A warfare pod had been welded to the *Mayflower's* underbelly. It contained five anti-missile missiles, Wasp 2000s. Aboard ship were twenty injured and ailing personnel. Like the other Martians he'd seen, they were thin and under-muscled. In spite of that Marten had frisked each and had helped them to various sleep cubicles or into the medical facility. Then he had closed each hatch and secured the hatches with emergency clamps.

Marten had received only a miniscule amount of fuel, however. It was enough to allow them system maneuvering as

109

they headed for an orbital launch station. Apparently Secretary-General Chavez was intrigued with them. The ruler of the Planetary Union wanted to speak in person with Marten.

As Marten and Omi sat in the control module, they planned.

"It's a trap," Omi said.

Marten had just told him how Chavez couldn't take time from his busy schedule to go to the orbital station. Thus Marten would have to go down to Mars, to Olympus Mons to be exact, and meet the Secretary-General there.

"It could be," Marten admitted. "That still leaves you in control of the *Mayflower*."

"How long must I stay here?"

"How long can you last?"

"Several more months if I have to," Omi said grimly.

"Social Unity will attack before that. I doubt, however, it's a trap."

"Why not?" asked Omi.

"Would the Secretary-General of an entire planet stoop to lying just to get us out of the shuttle?"

"It depends on how badly they need the shuttle."

"No," Marten said. "If they need it that badly, then they've lost already to Social Unity, and they would know it. He wants something else."

"What?"

"What can I offer him?" Marten asked. "Information. He's curious. Why he's curious, I don't know. But I need to use his curiosity to buy us fuel and more warfare pods."

"You won't be able to bluff him like you did the Deimos Unionist."

"Omi, do you realize who we are?"

The Korean gave him a blank look.

"We're the shock troopers. There's no one tougher than us. There's no one who could have done what we did. I don't mean for that to sound arrogant, but I do mean to recognize what we have. Think about it. We're the toughest military men on Mars and the toughest in all Social Unity. Yeah, there are only two of us. But we survived the Storm Assault Missiles, and we survived the *Bangladesh*. If that doesn't give us something powerful, I don't know what would."

"What's your point?" Omi asked.

Marten studied the flight path and made a small course correction. "We can't let anyone or anything overawe us. After slamming into the *Bangladesh's* particle-shield and storming onto the beamship, I don't know of anything else more frightening. My point is that maybe I can intimidate the Secretary-General. How many of them could have slain Highborn?"

Omi let a tight smile slide onto his face. "You're saying that all we have left are our balls. So we might as well maximize that. Yeah. You're right. Go see the Secretary-General. But remember that even Highborn can die. We're not invincible."

"We are hungry, though," Marten said. "Hungry to taste our freedom. Hungry to live and act like free men."

"Free," Omi said. "I like the sound of that."

Marten made another small course correction. Then he tried to envision why a planetary leader in the midst of a looming war would want to speak face-to-face with an ex-shock trooper.

8

As they journeyed toward Mars Marten debated with himself about trusting Secretary-General Chavez. The man had guaranteed their shuttle, quite a concession from a planetary leader.

Besides, Marten could seal the shuttle and make it difficult for the Martians to enter. His father had taught him about explosives, and his mother had taught him about computer codes and overrides. Her computer cunning had kept her, Marten and his father alive and out of PHC hands for three years in the Sun-Works Factory.

Omi might go stir-crazy waiting in the *Mayflower*. There were psychological tricks the Unionists could try if they wanted the shuttle badly enough. The bomb threat against the Chief Unionist on Deimos likely wouldn't work a second time. The Unionists could just have him dock at an armored area and call his bluff.

Instead of Omi staying onboard Marten could set up a complex entrance code. If anyone tampered with it, he'd set the shuttle to explode. The trouble was that given time, a tech-cracker could break the computer code.

He asked Omi about it.

"You're only going to be gone a few hours," Omi replied.

They neared the orbital launch site. It was torus-shaped and rotated, creating artificial gravity for those within. The station had heavy particle-shields, but it hadn't deployed any prismatic crystals or aerosol gels. There were a few visible shuttles docked. One of the shuttles was open, and a small pod with a mechanical arm placed a long tube into the waiting spacecraft.

"We hope it's only going to be a few hours," Marten said. "I'm going down there." He pointed at the rust-colored planet. "If something bad happens it's a long way to get back up here."

"What are you worried about?" Omi asked.

"Getting tricked for one thing. Remember what the Highborn used to tell us? Two guns are greater than one plus one. Meaning it's easier for a soldier to act cowardly when he's by himself, but much harder with another person he knows watching."

"You want me to come along?" Omi asked.

"It would be the smarter move," Marten said.

"We risk losing the shuttle then," Omi said. "It's our ticket out of the Inner Planets. With it, we have bargaining power. Without it, we're just two grunts."

Marten's chest tightened as they inched toward the orbital launch station. He'd spoken with Officer Dugan before they'd left Deimos. She'd let slip some critical information; for one thing, the size of the SU Battlefleet hiding on the other side of Mars. It was at far orbit, about the distance the moon was from Earth, about 384,000 kilometers. It was obvious Social Unity was planning an attack on Mars. Social Unity was losing the war against the Highborn, so they had to do something. Yet if they were losing to the Highborn, why bother attacking Mars and adding to their enemies? It would make more sense making allies of the Mars Rebels if they could.

Whatever the case, the important thing for Marten was the presence of the SU Battlefleet. According to Officer Dugan the convoy fleet was two days from rendezvousing with it. That made Marten wonder. Suppose the Rebels granted them fuel. Would the Battlefleet ignore them as they headed for the Jupiter Confederation? It seemed highly unlikely. So until the SU Battlefleet left Mars orbit the shuttle wasn't going to help them escape Inner Planets. That meant it was wiser to keep together. Every Horror Holovid he'd watched in Sydney with Molly had the actors splitting up so the individualist villains could pick them off one at a time.

"We should definitely both go," Marten said.

"What about the *Mayflower*?"

Marten began to type control keys. During the long journey here he'd set up several coded defenses. Now it was a matter of choosing the best one and engaging it with the fusion engine.

***

As Omi and he exited the shuttle-tube no one tried to take their sidearms. The space-station commander nodded curtly when Marten explained about the coded lock and what would happen if anyone triggered it by trying to enter the shuttle.

The space-station leader, Commander Zapata, was lean, but he wasn't too thin like the other Martians. He wore a crisp uniform and had a badly burned face. He had an eye-patch over the left eye. Why he didn't have a skin graft and a glass eye or an optical implant seemed strange. Maybe PHC had put him on a blacklist when the accident had occurred. That seemed likely the more Marten considered it. Commander Zapata had likely once been an agitator, at least according to Political Harmony Corps' view when it ran Mars. Marten assumed it because now Zapata ran this important orbital launch satellite. So that logically meant Zapata had already been highly placed in the Rebel movement. The Rebels had only controlled Mars for less than two years.

Commander Zapata escorted them down narrow steel corridors to a hanger with a dozen orbital fighters on the main deck. The orbitals were atmospheric attack-craft from a Doom Star, the one that had been here six months ago. The black-painted orbitals had stubby wings and armored plating with harsh red numbers on the sides. They were squat, ugly and deadly when flown by Highborn, who could take higher G-forces than regular humans could.

"Why's everyone staring at us?" Omi asked out of the side of his mouth.

The hanger wasn't as cluttered as the one on Deimos. It still had arc-welders flashing, personnel pushing trolleys, and personnel creating bangs, clacks and other metallic noises. There were also deck sergeants shouting instructions. The Planetary Union uniform everyone wore was gunmetal gray with a single red star and two crescent moons. Most of the personnel had longer hair than Marten was used to, making them look like civilians in military garb. Like Zapata, each was

114

lean without being as anorexic as those on Deimos.

As Omi and Marten marched to the farthest orbital people stopped what they were doing, straightened, and turned toward them. Some pointed. Most grew quiet. The stillness was like a wave in a pond, and soon the booms, bangs and the shouts all stopped.

Commander Zapata gave them a hideous grin. "You're already famous. That's why they're staring."

"Famous for what?" Marten asked.

"You killed Highborn, didn't you?"

Marten nodded sourly, wondering if it had been a mistake bragging about that. In time the Highborn would hear about him. That kind of information always leaked out to the wrong ears. The Highborn wouldn't like the idea of premen running around bragging about fragging Highborn officers. If nothing else, the Highborn would put a bounty on his head.

"We've seen the Highborn," Zapata was saying. "We've seen what they can do."

"They helped you against Social Unity," Marten said.

Commander Zapata snorted. "Didn't you hear me? We've seen Highborn. I've spoken to several. I've never met people that were more arrogant in my life. They're not really people. I would call them scary giants on the edge of going berserk. I always got the feeling the Highborn wanted to rip my head off. It's like they were juiced."

"Juiced?" Marten asked.

"It's a Martian term. The deep planetary crews drink too much vodka and get in fights. They're juiced."

"You sound as if you don't approve of your allies," Marten said.

Lean Zapata with the eye-patch glanced sharply at Marten. "We're not *allies*. The Highborn used us. We know that. Even while helping us they treated us with contempt. The funny thing is I don't think they understood how we felt about it. They simply know they're a superior form of humanity and expected us to recognize our inferiority."

"That's the Highborn," Omi muttered.

"I can't imagine having them in charge," Zapata said. "My point is that I sympathize with you. I can visualize them

115

training humans as humans might train animals. And I can see them inserting soldiers into a missile and shooting you at a spaceship as if you were worth no more than a bullet."

"Word gets around," Marten said dryly.

Commander Zapata stared at Marten. His single good eye was brown, with flecks of gold in the iris. There was something very determined about Zapata. "When Secretary-General Chavez sends a priority message to ready an orbital and tells us to honor your request that no one enter your shuttle, yes, word gets around. Many of the people here worked with the Highborn for several weeks. None can imagine trying to tackle the super-soldiers. Now two men are here who survived that insane—what did you call the missile?"

"The Storm Assault," Marten said.

"Yes. Your story is incredible. That you also slew Highborn is amazing. That's why everyone is staring."

Marten wanted to halt and motion the hanger personnel near. He wanted to tell them that fighting for freedom was the greatest privilege and duty that any person could have.

Marten stopped walking. Commander Zapata stopped and so did Omi, who looked about warily.

Marten thrust out his hand. Zapata didn't seem to comprehend. Then he gave Marten a quizzical glance. Slowly, the Commander held out his hand.

Marten grabbed it and shook heartily. He clapped Zapata on the shoulder. "I respect what you're doing. You're fighting for freedom. You're standing up. It's a pleasure to have reached the Mars System and see that there are others doing exactly what Omi and I did. I wish you Godspeed."

Zapata grinned crookedly, the only way he could, it seemed. "We could use a soldier like you, Mr. Kluge. We've lived under the heel of Social Unity all our lives. Political Harmony Corps has hunted us for years and killed many of our best people. Now we're trying to understand how to fight in the open. We failed twelve years ago. We want to win this time. That's why we endured the sneers from the Highborn and swallowed our pride."

Marten's grin slipped. He knew he had to tell this man the obvious. "Social Unity is going to attack Mars soon."

"Believe me, we know. That's why we need all the help we can get. We're trying to fix everything we can and make it too hot for them when they make their attempt. But time is running out on the Planetary Union before it really had a chance to find its feet."

Marten looked around, and he realized that most of these people were going to die soon. Maybe they knew it. The convoy fleet must be bringing supplies for the SU Battlefleet waiting out there. The Mars Rebels should have been firing at the individual SU warships, not waiting for a slugfest against the united fleet.

"Social Unity is insane to fight you now," Marten said. "They need their fleet to battle against the Highborn."

"It's our sole hope," Zapata admitted. "It's the Secretary-General's reason for waiting."

"Why does he want to see me?"

Zapata became somber. "Perhaps to ask you the same thing I did. Perhaps there is another purpose. Well—here we are."

They stood before the orbital fighter, the squat craft that towered over them. A ladder led up to the cockpit where the pilot adjusted his helmet. He looked painfully young.

"It's a double-seater," Zapata said. "Fortunately for you, it's built to hold Highborn. It will still be awkward for the two of you in the back seat, but you'll manage."

"Is he a rated pilot?" Marten asked. "He looks so young."

"Ortiz is our best."

Marten didn't think that was too reassuring. "Can I ask you a question?"

"Of course."

"On Deimos, everyone was so painfully thin. Here, everyone is lean but looks normal. Is there a reason for that?"

Zapata laughed. "I'm sorry. I'm not laughing at you. The laser and launch orbitals are considered hardship duty for anyone from Mars."

"Why?"

"You've never been to Mars before?" asked Zapata.

Marten shook his head.

"Our planet only has eleven percent of Earth's mass," Zapata said. "That makes everyone on Mars much lighter than they would be on Earth. People born on Mars live on a world with weak gravity. You have big muscles because Earth's gravity demands it of your body so you can function. A Martian doesn't develop those heavy muscles because he never needed them. Correspondingly, Martians don't need as much food. You'd starve to death on a Martian's diet. It also means we have less trouble feeding our millions."

"So why is working here a hardship?" Marten asked.

"Haven't you noticed? Our orbital launch station has Earth normal gravity."

Marten frowned.

"We fly the orbitals and thus need to be stronger to use them to full capacity. Everyone here takes growth hormones and has finished an accelerated weightlifting regimen. Compared to regular Martians, we're abnormally muscled supermen, if you will. That has always been one of Social Unity's advantages. It rotated peacekeepers on a constant basis so the Earthmen here were wickedly powerful compared to us."

Marten understood. Eleven percent mass… it left the Martians at a constant disadvantage. Well, maybe it was an advantage because the population could live on less food. Yet even a starvation-dieted population desired freedom. So it proved they were still human.

Marten shook Commander Zapata's hand again, careful not to squeeze too hard. Then he and Omi began to climb the ladder to their place in the cockpit.

***

It was an exciting ride down as young Ortiz plunged the orbital Mars-ward like a rock. The atmosphere was visible at the edge of Mars as a whitish rim. Then they entered the atmosphere. The orbital soon began to shake and a faint screeching sounded from outside.

Aboard the *Mayflower* Marten had been studying the Red Planet. Because of the weak gravity Mars had negligible air pressure, roughly one-half of one percent of the Earth's surface pressure. A jet pilot would have to travel forty kilometers up into Earth's stratosphere to reach the same air pressure as found on Mars' surface. That meant it never rained on Mars' surface. It could only rain in the deepest canyons where the air

118

pressure was heavy enough. It also meant parachutes were next to useless for braking aircraft or capsule-launched drop-troops.

"There!" Ortiz shouted over his shoulder and breaking Marten's reverie. "That's where we're headed."

The pilot pointed at a rough circular shape, a deeper red color than the planet around it. White ice-clouds like guardians were at its western curve. Just slightly off center in the middle was another ring, even deeper red, its huge cone crater.

Olympus Mons was the Solar System's largest shield volcano and largest mountain. The base of the volcano was 600 kilometers, making it about the distance from the San Francisco Crater on Earth to the Los Angeles slag fields. The Martian volcano was 2.5 times taller than Mount Everest. The volcano's cone was 25 kilometers higher than the plain surrounding it and was large enough to contain Manhattan Island.

One of the reasons why Olympus Mons was the tallest volcano was that Mars had no continental drift. That allowed the volcano to continue growing. On Earth, a volcano eventually moved off its underground source of magma and thus stopped growing.

"Does Mars have much of an air defense?" Marten shouted.

The pilot turned around to stare at Marten. "Good enough," the pilot said. As he faced forward again, the pilot curved the orbital sharply left and then nosed them straight down. Burners roared into life and pressed Marten back against Omi.

"This baby can kill anything the Earthers have!" the pilot shouted. He soon eased the craft to a gentler descent. When he switched off the burners the shaking all but vanished.

So the air defense was weak, Marten told himself. Why had the Highborn given the Planetary Union the launch and laser stations but no capable air defense? And why not give the Martians viable military spaceships? Maybe the Highborn hadn't foreseen Social Unity gathering the bulk of its space fleet here. The Planetary Union had enough to fight off a small force of ships—maybe. No more than that.

It was unlike the Highborn to miscalculate such an obvious military deficiency.

"You're lucky," the pilot shouted.

"Why's that?"

"No dust storms this time of year. They're a bitch. Then again, it would make it harder for Social Unity to think about space drops. The storms cover entire swaths of the planet then."

Marten nodded. He remembered reading about that. The sands of Mars contained ferric oxide, something akin to rust. It was the reason for the planet's red color. Those sands were also finer than any found on Earth's beaches. At certain times of the Martian year—which was 687 Earth-days long—global dust storms were generated. Greater than 100-kilometers an hour, the storms whipped the fine sands to more than 50 kilometers into the atmosphere and often shrouded the entire planet. For about a month a yellowish haze covered Mars. Only many months later did the last of the dust drift back onto the planet's surface. The storms sandblasted the surface and anything found on the surface. The storms, however, occurred when the planet was at its closest to the Sun. The Red Planet was now at its farthest distance from Sol, and it would be for many, many more months.

That seemed like another miscalculation on the part of the Highborn.

While he admired the Rebels' fight for freedom, Marten was beginning to become anxious about being caught in the Mars System once hostilities started. What was the Martian plan? Maybe they would arm everyone and make it impossible for Social Unity to control them.

He knew that most Martians lived in great underground cities as the people did on Earth. He'd read that the planetary crust under Olympus Mons was much thicker than the crust anywhere on Earth. City-planning technicians had discovered that although Mars was only a little more than half the size of Earth, its crust in most places had the same depth. Apparently, vast farming domes covered portions of Mars. They acted like hothouses on Earth. What did most Martian's eat? Marten suspected it was algae just like on Earth.

No Highborn ate algae-bread or algae anything. Lot 6 Colonel Sigmir had spit out algae-bread the one time he'd tried it in Marten's presence. Marten remembered Sigmir saying it was cattle-food, meant for weaklings and inferior premen.

Marten stared out of the cockpit. Olympus Mons had grown until it dominated the scene. Whitish clouds circled the lower slopes.

Why did the planet's secretary-general wish to speak with him? Did the man want to hire the shuttle? The more Marten thought about it, the more he realized these Unionists had to be desperate. The idea of being stranded on Mars was unappealing. Trapped on a world of anorexic people who ate starvation diets—

Marten shuddered at the idea of becoming as rail thin as the Martians on Deimos. Omi and he had to escape Mars and get past the Battlefleet before Social Unity re-conquered this place.

-9-

It reassured Marten when tough security honchos escorted them from the sealed hanger in the crater to a large elevator. The security people were lean like the soldiers on the launch station. They wore segmented battle-vests and helmets with black visors, although it left their mouths visible. Each held a needler, which so far seemed like the preferred weapon among Martians.

Did slug-throwers kick too hard for Martian wrists? That wasn't reassuring. How had the Mars Rebels fought off Social Unity a little more than a decade ago? The allied military of the Jupiter Confederation had helped then, but it had to be more than that. Despite being rail-thin, the Martians had always given PHC a harder time than anyone else had, except maybe for the Unionists on the Sun-Works Factory. Martians were known as clever people. Maybe that was the answer.

What clever trick would they perform to defeat the SU Battlefleet?

The elevator door closed, and the packed car dropped with gut-wrenching speed. It made Omi lurch, and two of the security people nearest him grinned at each other.

"You'll have to hand over your sidearms before you speak with the Secretary-General," a man beside Marten said.

Marten turned to face the man. The security honchos had needlers aimed at him. He couldn't see the man's eyes, just his mouth. It was a firm line. It was a gut feeling, but Marten decided this was a test. He cleared his throat. Omi looked over.

"Ready?" Marten asked Omi.

122

Omi nodded coolly as he used to as a gunman in the Sydney gangs.

After that, Marten said nothing else. He waited. He didn't try to stare the security men down, but he did attempt to appear bored.

"...I have my orders," the security chief said.

Marten faked a yawn.

Around him, the security people tightened the grips on their needlers.

"We can shoot you down," the security chief said.

"Either show me you can do it or shut up about it," Marten said. "But if you shoot, shoot to kill. Because I'll kill you if you try and fail."

A different security man pressed a needler against Marten's side. Marten chopped hard, striking the man's wrist. The man's needler clattered onto the elevator floor.

The others grew tense.

"Wait!" the security chief said. "Don't fire." He faced Marten. "We know you're tough. Our brief said ex-shock trooper. But this is the Secretary-General of Mars you're going to meet."

"I didn't ask to see him," Marten said. "He asked to see me. You see what I mean?"

The security chief swallowed uncomfortably. "We can—"

Marten held up his hand, and it made one security man hurriedly step back. That told Marten all he needed to know. "We're here to help Mars, not assassinate its leader. If you insist we disarm, however, then call the Secretary-General and explain to him that we're heading back up to the launch station."

"What?"

"You heard me. Now make your choice."

Omi gave Marten a cool glance.

Marten recognized the look. Omi thought he was overdoing the tough-guy act. Marten said nothing. He waited, letting their reputation do the work. It would tell him what the Martians really thought about them.

The security chief turned away and whispered into a wrist-link. After a time, he whispered more. Finally, he turned back to Marten. "You can keep your sidearms. But any wrong moves—"

"Yeah," Marten said, interrupting. Then he folded his arms. He was beginning to suspect that killing Highborn had given him a serious aura with these Martians. How could that help them here? That was the question.

***

Marten met Secretary-General Chavez in a work lounge of the proton beam station.

The spacious room held ten tables with chairs, with square dispensaries along a wall. Posters with various slogans hung on the walls. *The State gave you this job. Now give the State your best.* Or: *Protect our joint investment and wear your safety equipment at all times.*

Secretary-General Chavez spoke to the seated people. By their green coveralls and the yellow hardhats on the tables, Marten assumed they were proton-beam technicians.

Chavez was painfully thin with a long head. His youthfully colored hair and goatee didn't match the look of his aged face. He gestured as he spoke and had delicate fingers, with a slender silver ring on his middle finger.

A few of the seated technicians glanced back as the security team and Marten lined up against the wall. Then the thin technicians gave their attention back to the speaker.

Despite his gaunt appearance, Secretary-General Chavez had a deep voice and spoke well. He urged the technicians to accept calculated risks bringing the proton beam back online. It would be better that it fired at half-power in three weeks than at full power after the SU Battlefleet swept into near orbit. Chavez added a few Rebel slogans and told those seated that victory hinged upon their efforts.

The technicians rose as one and clapped heartily. Then they approached the Secretary-General, shook his hand, and asked questions. Soon an even thinner man declared the meeting was over. Reluctantly, the technicians filed out of the lounge.

When the last green-suited technician left, Chavez's shoulders slumped as he shuffled to the nearest table and collapsed onto a chair. In a tired way he withdrew a small package from his coat and shook out a red stimstick. He

124

inhaled it into life.

The security chief glanced once at Marten before he hurried to the Secretary-General. There the man stood deferentially, waiting. At last Chavez looked up and mumbled a question. The security chief pointed at Marten.

Chavez immediately straightened, took the stimstick from his lips and glared at it. He dropped the glowing stick onto the floor and crushed it with the toe of his shoe. He lurched upright, smiled, and strode toward Marten.

"The two shock troopers," Secretary-General Chavez said.

Marten saw Chavez glance at their guns. A crease in the Secretary-General's forehead almost immediately smoothed away. Chavez held out his hand. Gently, Marten shook the thin-boned hand and then so did Omi.

"Welcome, welcome," Chavez said. "Would you like refreshments?"

"A glass of water would be good," Marten said.

"A sandwich," Omi said.

The security personnel lined the walls, while the skinny man who had declared the former meeting ended went to the dispensaries. He pushed a button here and another there. Slots opened and he brought Marten a cup of water and Omi a pale green sandwich.

Chavez sat across the table from Marten and Omi as if he was in his office. He grinned as Marten sipped water.

The Secretary-General had tired features and lines on his forehead, and his dark eyes were too shiny. The hint of sweet stimstick in the air told the story. He surely relied too many hours of the day on the mild stimulants. In Marten's estimation the man had likely been doing that for quite a while.

Chavez spoke platitudes as Marten nodded from time to time. As the Secretary-General made sweeping gestures he spoke about Martian courage and determination. The gestures continued and his wedding ring flashed as it caught the lights at times. He spoke about the perfidy of Social Unity, and he spoke about how the Martians had struggled for years for this glorious day of self-government. Mars was for the Martians!

"What about yourselves?" Chavez asked, as he rested his hands on the table. "Please, tell me how you acquired a

Highborn shuttle."

Marten spoke tersely about the Storm Assault Missile, the experimental beamship and Training Master Lycon's pickup.

"Incredible," Chavez declared. "And now you own a shuttle and plan to do what with it?"

"Fulfill my parents' dream of freedom," Marten said, "and reach the Jupiter Confederation."

"Parents?"

Marten spoke briefly about the Unionist attempt on the Sun-Works Factory many years ago.

Chavez glanced with surprise at the sticklike man standing behind him, a personal aide, no doubt. Then the Secretary-General concentrated on Marten again. There was new vigor in Chavez's voice.

"You're a Unionist then?"

"My parents were," Marten said.

Chavez gave a delighted chuckle. "That's wonderful, just wonderful. You must surely be sympathetic to our cause."

"I applaud anyone's desire for freedom."

"An excellent attitude, Mr. Kluge." Chavez frowned, and he studied the table. Then he looked up with a diffident smile. "I realize you must have seen horrendous combat. The storm assault onto that beamship, it's an amazing tale. You are obviously elite soldiers."

Marten remained silent, as he realized here was the Secretary-General's reason for wanting to talk to him face-to-face.

Chavez glanced back at the sticklike man. That man set a computer scroll before Chavez. The Secretary-General scanned it.

"Yes," Chavez said, looking up, "you spoke earlier about buying fuel and warfare pods. We... sold you a pod already with five anti-missile missiles. For it, you ferried some of our sick from Deimos to the launch station. It was a good bargain for you, I believe."

"I have no complaints," Marten said.

"Let us save time, Mr. Kluge. Do you mind if I speak bluntly?"

"Be my guest."

"Thank you." Chavez cleared his throat. "I would like to hire you. I would like to hire your expertise."

"I'm listening."

"For it, Mars will supply you with several more warfare pods and a shuttle full of fuel. Does that sound agreeable?"

"First, I'd have to know what you want us to do."

"Only what you've been trained at, Mr. Kluge. I want you to develop a storm assault group of our own. I'm not talking about blasting you at the enemy in a missile. What Mars needs is space-capable marines."

"You don't have an enemy with habitats orbiting Mars," Marten said.

"No, no, I'm thinking—"

"Nor do you have the capacity to storm aboard SU warships," Marten said. "So what is it that you're really asking, sir?"

Secretary-General Chavez stared at Marten before he turned away. He bit his lip, and finally he reached into his coat and pulled out the crumpled pack of stimsticks. "Do you mind?"

Marten shrugged.

Chavez pulled out a stimstick and began smoking. "It's a foul habit," he muttered.

"You're the most important man on Mars," Marten said. "That's a crushing burden. A few tokes certainly seems like a small price to pay in order to maintain a semblance of normalcy."

Chavez took a deep drag before turning away and blowing red smoke into the air. He coughed afterward, and he turned a red-rimmed eye at Marten.

"Are you familiar with the Valles Marineris?" Chavez asked.

Marten shook his head.

Chavez typed along the bottom of the computer scroll. Then he turned it toward Marten. The words had vanished and a map of a portion of Mars appeared. It showed an incredible chasm like a scar across the planet.

"It's 5000 kilometers long," Chavez was saying. He tapped his finger on a large red dot to the chasm's northern left.

"That's Olympus Mons, where we're at now."

"Got it," Marten said.

"This—" Chavez ran his finger along the chasm "—is Valles Marineris. Social Unity still owns it. In some places, it is 80 kilometers wide. Its cliffs are 8 kilometers high."

"I hope you're not expecting me to lead an army into there, conquering it for you."

Secretary-General Chavez shook his head. "Nothing so grandiose. For the moment, Social Unity has halted its air strikes out of the chasm. Because of that, we can use the Harrington Launch Sites situated here to ferry equipment into space. We've moved tons of supplies to the sites and are about to begin accelerated liftoffs. We must get those supplies to the moons and to the laser platforms. My fear is that Social Unity will recognize the importance of the Harrington fields and begin immediate air strikes against them as they did before the ceasefire."

"What does that have to do with me?" Marten asked.

"We have a few orbital fighters, but not enough to fight past their aircraft and bomb those airfields out of existence. The angle is wrong for our laser platforms to reach the bottom of the canyon. Yes, we could move the platforms. But that would move them out of their optimum location against the Battlefleet, which we expect at any time."

"You want to use Special Forces to destroy aircraft?" Marten asked.

"Yes," Chavez said.

Marten leaned over the computer scroll, studying the 5000-kilometer chasm with its 8-kilometer walls. "It looks like it would take suicide teams."

"Not for elite soldiers," Chavez said. "We have skimmers. One hundred good soldiers knowing what they're doing could do fierce havoc against the airfields. You've been trained for exactly that kind of mission."

"Once you attack those fields, Social Unity would likely begin air strikes again."

"Not necessarily," Chavez said. He gave Marten a tight smile. It had a hint of cunning, perhaps of desperation. "If we beamed it with lasers, yes, you're right. But we can say that

128

partisans beyond our control are making the attacks."

"Meaning that if we're caught," Marten said, "you would make no attempt to regain our freedom."

Chavez's eyes slid away so he gazed elsewhere. "That doesn't necessarily hold true."

"Right," Marten said.

Secretary-General Chavez took another drag on the stimstick. "The critical thing is that none of you get captured."

"I don't see why you need me," Marten said. "I don't know Mars like—"

"Mr. Kluge, please. Don't insult my intelligence. You're Highborn trained, which means to a higher pitch than anything Social Unity or the Planetary Union could achieve. This is precisely the type of attack in which you excel. We have an elite troop, but we desperately need even a few perfectly trained soldiers to show us what we're doing wrong, and what we need to do right. You have arrived here as a gift for Mars, Mr. Kluge. After the battle, we will gratefully supply you with the needed fuel and pods. Then you can be off to the Jupiter System or perhaps, if you wish, you can remain here as an officer in our military."

Marten sat back as he tapped his fingers on the table. He glanced at Omi, who betrayed nothing. "Let us talk it over."

"By all means," Chavez said. "But—"

"No," Marten said. "Don't add any threats. We've had a bellyful of them from the Highborn. Just tell us what you'll give us, not what you'll do to screw us if we refuse."

Chavez blew smoke through his nose as he stood up. "Yes. I understand. Think it over and give me your decision..." he checked his chronometer. "In ten minutes."

"Sure," Marten said. "Ten minutes it is."

Commodore Blackstone waited with Three-star Commissar Kursk in the cramped hanger terminal of the *Vladimir Lenin*.

The Commodore had shaven, and he wore a pressed uniform. The lost quality to his eyes had dwindled since he'd joined the hum-a-longs. The pain still lingered in his heart regarding his ex-wife. And if he thought about it too long, the *bad-thoughts* came. The desire to return to Earth, hunt down her lovers, and splatter their flesh and blood with aimed fire from a heavy-duty gyroc. That was better than moping, however. It was better because he transferred his hatred against her lovers and toward the damned Mars Rebels. It would be a joy to obliterate their space stations and capture the moon bases.

Commodore Blackstone rubbed his jaw, and he glanced sidelong at Commissar Kursk. She had taken to eating with him in his wardroom. She said it was because it was wrong for him to brood alone with his thoughts. She had always brought food with her, a tray for her and a tray for him. A terrible thought now surged through Blackstone, and he wondered how he could have missed it.

Had she put mood-altering drugs into his food? He'd never felt hatred toward the Martians before. And he'd never considered blowing away his ex-wife's lovers so their brains rained globules of gray matter against the side of her house. He grinned at the image. He grinned thinking how his ex-wife would scream and scream. She might even melt in remorse and crawl to him on her hands and knees. Maybe right there out in the open, with blood dripping down the side of the house, he would take her and—

"You put something in my food," Blackstone said.

Three-star Commissar Kursk was taller by a few inches than he was. She wore her cap's brim low over her eyes. Her uniform was tight against her hips, and her hands were firmly clasped behind her back. The way she stood at attention, if she'd had any kind of breasts at all, they would have jutted against her uniform. Instead, her badge shined in the harsh glare of the terminal's lighting.

"This is hardly the place to discuss it," she whispered.

Three red-suited PHC enforcers waited behind her. Five of the Commodore's deck police waited along another wall. They all anticipated the first meeting with the cyborgs from Neptune. The cyborg command pod had docked with the *Vladimir Lenin*. Beyond the terminal door were clangs and the hissing of returning atmospheric pressure.

"That is against all regulations," Blackstone hissed at her.

She gave him a stern glance. "Don't be sentimental. Look at you now. You have rage in your veins, as a military man should. You wish to kill. That is good."

"You're drugging me," he whispered.

"Nonsense, I've re-balanced you to what you were, a fighter and a warrior. These past weeks have seen a marked improvement in the Battlefleet. Morale has been boosted and fighting vigor almost returned to acceptable norms."

"I forbid you to administer any more drugs."

"You should fall on your knees and clasp me in gratitude for what I've done." She gave him a vicious grin. "I always achieve results. It is why I am a three-star commissar, and why PHC sends me to the hotspots. Rid yourself of weakness. The cyborgs arrive. We must present a united front against them."

Blackstone had read Hawthorne's secret report about Blanche-Aster's clone, the one that had gone to Neptune System. Hawthorne had clearly stated the danger that the cyborgs possessed a chemical or mechanical way of altering a human's loyalty. It's why Blackstone had issued an order that no one board any cyborg battle pod.

"Against the cyborgs?" Blackstone asked. "What haven't

you told me about them?"

Commissar Kursk's eyes narrowed as she faced the terminal entrance. "This is a critical juncture in Social Unity's existence. The Highborn run amok. Now we have summoned the cyborgs to help us defeat our scientists' genetic folly. There are some in PHC…"

She scowled.

Commodore Blackstone tugged his uniform straighter. He had noticed Commissar Kursk more, the shape of her hips, the tight fit of her boots and the way her butt swayed when she marched. It was as if she understood he watched her and secretly enticed him. She had stern features, but those features had appeal. If his ex-wife had taken lovers, why couldn't he indulge in sins of the flesh with this arrogant PHC officer? He would make her whimper. Yes, he would show her the kind of officer he used to be in the old days. Even now as she scowled at the terminal entrance—

Blackstone shook his head. These weren't his normal thoughts. She had drugged him. It had masked his malaise. It had heightened his anger and likely heightened his sexual desires. Wouldn't she be surprised if he—

"No," he whispered.

"What is wrong now?" she whispered.

A new clang told Blackstone that an inner hatch had opened. The cyborgs were almost inside the *Vladimir Lenin's* pressurized quarters.

Commissar Kursk had just hinted at PHC rumors. Supreme Commander Hawthorne had warned him that Political Harmony Corps likely had a hidden method of communication with the cyborgs. Hawthorne believed it's why the cyborgs had decelerated for the Mars System instead of for Earth as originally planned. Perhaps as importantly, Hawthorne suspected that PHC and the cyborgs had a hidden understanding between them. Hawthorne had warned him to be careful of the cyborgs and to use critical judgment in dealing with them.

Blackstone snorted quietly. Now the commissar had drugged him. The jackboot-wearing commissar he'd like to drag into his wardroom and—

The terminal entrance began to slide open. The cyborgs from Neptune were here.

Commodore Blackstone stood at attention, curious at what he'd see. Beside him, Three-star Commissar Kursk clicked her jackbooted heels together.

The terminal entrance slid open, and an abomination strode onto the *Vladimir Lenin*. He, or perhaps *it*, wore a blue uniform like a large human, but he looked like a robot with polished metal parts and plastic flesh. His face seemed capable of only minimal expressions. His eyes were shiny silver-metal orbs that moved smoothly in black plastic sockets. He was bald like Blackstone, and he was taller than Commissar Kursk. There was a sense of great weight about him, as if he was solid metal, and yet he moved with a predator's grace.

Behind the chief cyborg were three taller, elongated monstrosities of flesh and graphite-bones. They were too long-limbed, and with every motion they made faint *whirring* sounds of motorized joints. They had armored bodies and had dead faces that they wore like masks. Their incurious eyes held inhumanity and something worse. They seemed like quickened mechanical zombies, with tiny hints of their lost humanity. Blackstone had never felt such a chill in his heart. Those hints of humanity looked out of the cyborg pupils as a screaming prisoner might, trapped in Hell.

Commissar Kursk gasped, and she might have staggered back. Blackstone grabbed her elbow, steadying her. Then he stepped forward and saluted crisply. He wanted to order the deck police to draw and fire until nothing but smoldering electronics and twisted metal parts lay before him. He doubted, however, that his five MPs and the three PHC enforcers would win a gun-battle with these things. The Highborn were out there, conquering Inner Planets. Now Social Unity had called for deadly allies to help tip the balance. Blackstone suppressed a shudder of horror. Sweet bones of Marx, was Hawthorne mad? Social Unity should unite with the Highborn to exterminate every infestation of these mechanical terrors.

"Welcome aboard the *Vladimir Lenin*. I am Commodore Blackstone, the commanding officer of the Social Unity Battlefleet Mars."

"I am Toll Seven," the chief cyborg said in a modulated voice. It only hinted at machinery, but it lacked emotive inflection. There was power in the voice, but a coldly logical power that would likely ignore any appeals to love, hope or mercy.

Blackstone hated the voice as a new dread formed in him of this Toll Seven. Humanity had searched its nightmares and foolishly manufactured this thing. It was inhuman, nonhuman. It was an alien. This was madness.

Blackstone had to concentrate to listen, as Toll Seven was still speaking.

"We have arrived to achieve victory for Social Unity. Therefore, it is imperative that we commence with the battle plan."

Blackstone felt as if he was floating outside his body. He was looking at the other cyborgs, the elongated things with whiplash limbs, limbs that seemed abnormally strong. Who would have ever agreed to let technicians tear away their humanity to be rebuilt as that? How had the scientists in Neptune found volunteers? It was incomprehensible.

The Commodore was surprised to hear he was saying, "It has been an incredibly long journey for you. Would you like to rest first?"

"Logic dictates an immediate attack," Toll Seven said. "...mingling to initiate friendship can commence upon final victory." The chief cyborg thereupon smiled, revealing evil steel-colored teeth.

Certainly, Toll Seven must have meant the smile as a friendly gesture. To Commodore Blackstone it seemed like a grin from a ghoul about to feast on the living.

-11-

A day after meeting, Secretary-General Chavez, Marten and Omi went on an inspection tour of the Special Forces equipment and personnel. Both were located on Olympus Mons.

The giant volcano housed hundreds of thousands of people and some of Mars' most critical military assets. The proton beam was the most important and was located near the volcano's crater. The volcano's great height pushed its cone well up into the weak Martian atmosphere. With less gas to burn through the beam had greater space-destructive capability than the proton beams on Earth. Those on Earth had to fire through dense atmosphere. Massive friction weakened the Earth proton beams and thus limited their range. The Mars proton beam had correspondingly greater outer-space range due to almost negligible atmospheric friction. Unfortunately, the targeting problems were immense.

The Red Planet rotated and moved through space, both in its orbital path around the Sun and in the Sun's orbit around the center of the Milky Way Galaxy. Secondly, as negligible as the Martian atmosphere was, it still caused minute diffraction. A man looking at his foot in a pool of water would notice that his limb didn't seem to be exactly where he knew it should be. The same problem occurred with the targeting system on Olympus Mons. Unfortunately, long-range beam-fire called for intensely accurate shooting. Thus, the Mars proton beam wasn't used for truly long-distance fire, which in this case meant anything over 10,000 kilometers.

The SU Battlefleet was in far orbit, at a distance of 350,000-kilometers from the surface. That was well out of the proton beam's range. The closer moon Phobos was within the proton beam's range, but Deimos was well out of reach.

There was only one deep-core mine on Mars, and it was situated under the mighty volcano. It powered everything on Olympus Mons and it would power the proton beam.

There were several merculite missile sites here. But the Martians lacked anything like the barrage of missiles that could fire from the Eurasian landmass on Earth.

Marten asked the security chief about that.

The security chief, Major Diaz, was lanky, but had more muscles than most Martians. He'd admitted to heavy growth hormonal use and an equally heavy addiction to weight training. Major Diaz scowled most of the time and was darker-skinned than the rest of his men. His face was sharp and angular, with his dark hair was swept back hard. He had a beak of a nose and suspicious brown eyes. He'd muttered something earlier about being almost full Aztec, but Marten hadn't any idea what he'd meant by that.

It turned out that the elite Special Forces team was made up of Chavez's security people. There were about fifty picked men from five hundred or so gunmen. They were able fighters, but Marten was less than impressed.

Diaz spoke about Mars' planetary defense as he walked with Marten and Omi around an open-topped skimmer in a vast underground garage. The lights in the underground facility were at low power, and the air was cool. Marten could see his breath, and the air here tasted strange.

The skimmer was rectangular. Its open area in the center could hold four men and their backpacks. It was silver, had triangular wings and possessed jet power to give it VTOL abilities.

Marten didn't like the open tops. He would have preferred enclosed pressurized hovercraft. But this was Mars, and the Planetary Union was poor. Marten rapped his knuckles against the skimmer and was surprised at the aluminum sound. "It isn't armored."

Major Diaz shook his head.

"We need armored skimmers," Marten said.

"Don't have them," Diaz said.

"I don't get this. You hardly have any defensive missiles, almost no attack aircraft, and now you lack armored skimmers."

"PHC has them," Diaz said.

"You'd better explain that."

Diaz told Marten, and his story made sense. After the suppression of the first Mars rebellion twelve years ago, PHC had made certain Mars lacked military equipment. There were a few laser platforms, a few launch stations, and the two moons. But there were no planetary defenses other than the proton beam, a small scattering of merculite missile sites, and some point-defense guns. If the Jupiter Confederation attacked again, the stated plan had called for the SU Battlefleet to arrive and destroy the invaders in space.

"In other words," Marten said, "Mars was left open to attack."

Major Diaz nodded.

Marten rapped the skimmer again and kept walking. He'd been surprised to learn that Political Harmony Corps had supplied the peacekeeping occupation force. It should have been the military.

Later in the day, Omi and Marten inspected the fifty elite soldiers they were supposed to lead to the Valles Marineris. They were Major Diaz's people, security-trained these past six months. Before that, they had been the chief Rebel enforcers and gunmen.

The fifty security people were lined up in an underground gym. They were lean and tough-looking, and to a man wore needlers.

Marten nodded slowly, asked a few questions and then took Diaz aside. "Where do you keep the heavy weapons?"

"Meaning what?" asked Diaz.

"Mortars, plasma cannons and heavy gyroc rifles," Marten said.

Major Diaz shook his head.

"You haven't been trained with them?" Marten asked, incredulous.

Diaz said nothing, just frowned in an uglier manner.

"You have those weapons, right?" Marten asked.

"The grunts use them."

"You're not grunts?"

"We're Special Ops."

"You'd better tell me what that means," Marten said.

It took time and more questions, but Marten finally extracted the truth from Major Diaz. His security people had been the assassin squads that had murdered PHC personnel during the long years of simmering rebellion. They were experts at city ambush. They knew how to draw their needlers, spray surprised cops and governors, and then disappear into alleys or safe houses. They'd killed squealers, had planted bombs, and had enforced union discipline on the wavering or against traitors.

"You didn't beat back the occupation police using assassins," Marten said.

"We are the elite," Major Diaz said stubbornly.

It was beginning to dawn on Marten that he didn't understand the complete situation. He was beginning to suspect that the Mars Rebels only possessed a few true military men. Those few were likely in strategic locations, in space guarding the planet. From the sounds of it, the Martian military had personal weapons but not much more than that.

"How did you Rebels ever take over?" Marten asked.

"We killed the police. In the past, more police always arrived. After the Highborn attacked Earth, however, Social Unity couldn't send any more police to take the place of the dead ones."

"Right," Marten said. "Wait here." He grabbed Omi's arm and pulled him away from Major Diaz. He walked Omi to a large net for some sports activity he'd never heard about. The net hung limply, and the knots in it seemed ragged. Here they were out of earshot of the waiting security people. The selected fifty mingled in groups, glancing at him and then looking at a frowning Major Diaz.

"What do you think?" Marten whispered.

"Where's the army?"

"Political Harmony Corps' army?"

138

"PHC's and the Planetary Union's," Omi said.

"Do you know what I think?"

Omi shook his head.

"I think there never was an army," Marten said. "It was a vast police force pressing down the masses, with SWAT to congregate and slaughter anyone who resisted too well. The Martians fought back the same way."

"It's like a planetary cop-gang war," Omi said.

"There you are. So it makes sense why the Highborn could leave the Martian so few orbitals, a few space platforms, and expect them to hold onto what they have. The surface is a barren red desert. You need pressurized suits or Environmental Combat Vehicles to move in the open. By the sounds of it, the war—if you want to call it that—took place in the underground cities."

"Just like Stick, Turbo, you and me in Sydney," Omi said.

"It was mostly small-arms fighting, remember?"

"By what these people have here, I'd say the Martians mainly fight with needlers."

"There should still be some plasma cannons and heavy gyroc rifles," Marten said.

Omi shook his bullet-shaped head. "Those are stand-up weapons. Major Diaz and his security detail were assassins and enforcers. Those types hate trading gyroc-rounds with the enemy."

"The enemy has pilots and aircraft. I bet the Rebels also have some true soldiers guarding those fields."

"Maybe," Omi said.

Marten scratched his jaw. "There must be a few real Martian ground-pounders. I'm beginning to think Chavez wants his security detail trained into something more deadly than what he already has. I think that's why he has us here, not to raid airfields in the giant canyon."

"Why not tell us that?" Omi asked.

"Wherever there are people, there are power struggles." Marten grunted. "Or maybe I'm wrong about a tougher security detail. Maybe Chavez wants to gain points by having his men knock out those airfields."

"What does it matter to us why Chavez does anything?"

Omi asked. "Let's train these killers and get our fuel."

"It matters, because it tells us how likely the Martians are to win. If they lose, they're not going to give us anything."

"So what are you saying?" Omi asked.

"That I wish I'd chosen to head straight to Jupiter," Marten said. "It would have been better to sit out a few years in the shuttle and finally get out of Inner Planets. We're in a bind now, and our shuttle is up there, with a Battlefleet in our way once we try for Jupiter."

"Tell Chavez we've changed our mind."

"You know what they say about Martians," Marten said. "They're clever. Chavez is on top so he's likely trickier than the rest. Maybe the reason everyone thinks we're so deadly is that Mars hardly has any real soldiers."

"Vip wasn't much of a soldier to start with," Omi said. "But the Highborn turned him into a standup fighter."

Marten grinned. "There you are. That's the answer."

"What'd I say?"

"We're going to take... ten of these assassins. Yeah, I'm going to weed them carefully. Then I'll use the ten on a practice strike into the giant chasm."

"And?" Omi asked.

"And I'm going to fashion me a small combat team that's fought under fire and survived together. You know how everything changes once you live through a firefight."

"These are Chavez's chosen people. They're here because they're loyal."

"I understand," Marten said. "They're loyal. But we're going to build a different loyalty, one forged in battle. I'm not looking to shift all of them, just a handful."

"Why?"

"Because I'm recruiting," Marten said. "I'm recruiting for a small combat team so we can take a lift up to the launch station, storm it, grab our fuel and get the heck out of this system before that Battlefleet decides to move in."

Omi slowly shook his head. "That's a wild long-shot."

"You have a better idea to get us out of here?"

"...no."

"Then that's our plan," Marten said. He was thinking about

140

Nadia Pravda as he turned around and hailed Major Diaz, asking the Aztec Martian to have the men line up again for a second inspection.

Several days after Marten spoke with Omi in the gym and 350,000 kilometers away, the clone Lisa Aster leaned back and massaged her eyes.

She had a small cubicle aboard the supply ship that had brought her to Mars orbit. It was cluttered with computer equipment, tactical body-armor, vibroknives and various guns. For the past few hours she had been studying screenshots of the cyborgs and processing known data. The Toll Seven cyborg was different from the others.

Lisa had been trying to figure out the differences. It was the meld, she decided. Toll Seven was heavy like a robot, more like a cybertank with two legs than flesh melded with machine. The elongated cyborgs—Lisa shuddered as she examined a screenshot. Their limbs were skeletal, and their frozen faces a mockery of their former humanity. It seemed obvious the cyborg masters must have converted criminals into these horrible machine-things. Lisa had used Bioram computers before, the thin sheets of human brain tissue surrounded by programming gel and aided by processors. The brain tissue came from incoercible criminals against the State, those who insisted on committing antisocial acts. Such criminals died justly, giving their body parts to the State they had insisted on robbing during their lives.

What crimes had the elongated cyborgs committed? Lisa knew little about the conditions in Outer Planets. Yes, she'd watched the reality shows, but she'd always suspected they had overplayed those strange capitalist notions. If everyone spent their money as they wished, chaos would ensue. That was so logically obvious that Lisa couldn't accept that free capitalism existed in the Outer Planets.

Lisa leaned forward in concentration, switching screenshots, studying them closely. Maybe the cyborgs were built-up like a Bioram, the organic parts *shaved* from various criminals and melded with machines.

Lisa adjusted the controls on her vidscreen until the battle pods appeared. She zoomed in. They were shaped like bullets, and they had dark ceramic hulls with a blizzard of antennas on the front and the back. They seemed unbelievable small. General Fromm had suggested the cyborgs had been switched off for the journey. Lisa doubted that. You couldn't just switch off flesh. Maybe they had been frozen. That struck Lisa as gruesome and made the battle pods seem like flying coffins.

There was one larger battle pod. Toll Seven had exited it and no one else. Its greater mass indicated it was loaded with cyborg devices. Lisa had also discovered that it sent and received lightguide messages to and from the Neptune System. It was impossible to snoop on a lightguide message, as it was a communications laser shot to an exact receiver. It was also incredible the cyborgs could fire a laser that distance and hit the receiver. It was so amazing it seemed supernatural.

Lisa's narrow face tightened as she ran her fingers across her buzz-cut hair. The cyborgs had done something to Rita Tan, the Blanche-Aster clone sent to the Neptune System. That something had cost the clones their Mother. Had the Neptune cyborgs implanted obedience devices into Rita Tan?

Lisa stared at the larger battle pod, Toll Seven's ship. Supreme Commander Hawthorne suspected that PHC on Earth had communicated with the battle pod. Hawthorne suspected the cyborgs had an agenda all their own. He wanted to confirm that, or he wished to gain hints about them the cyborgs didn't want known.

There were various plans, all much too dangerous in Lisa's opinion. One plan called for her secretly contacting the chief cyborg as she pretended to be Rita Tan. Lisa had already ruled that out. She dreaded being alone with Toll Seven. Maybe the cyborg could inject her with cyborg converters or with

143

obedience drugs. No, she wouldn't take any foolish chances. Another plan called for her spacewalking to the battle pods in a chameleon-suit and planting listening devices on the vessels.

Oh yes, she was going to do that, and find herself face-to-face with a suited cyborg who would drag her into a battle pod to convert her into one of those. No, Lisa rejected such dangerous plans. She would watch, study, and wait for a chance when a safe one came. If a safe chance never came her way, well, then she would return to Earth having failed, but still very much alive as the clone Lisa Aster.

***

A day later Commodore Blackstone listened to Toll Seven. He, the cyborg, Commissar Kursk, and stout General Fromm from the supply convoy stood around a holographic map-module.

The *Vladimir Lenin's* command center was cramped, red-lit, and circularly-shaped. A dozen officers sat around them behind vidscreens. The officers passed orders and information between the Battlefleet's warships and monitored Mars.

Powerful probes and detection satellites watched the voids of space, those most likely to contain enemy Doom Stars on secret maneuvers. They also watched Mars for new Rebel satellites trying to spy on the Battlefleet. As quickly as the Rebels sent up new probes, the Battlefleet launched drones. With stealth technology those drones crept upon the satellites, eliminating them and hopefully keeping the Martians ignorant about exact fleet dispositions.

The holographic map-module showed a large burnt-orange image of Mars, with a dotted line around the planet placing the Battlefleet in far orbit. The green dots near the planet were the known Martian space-defenses.

Toll Seven had clumsily adjusted the controls the first few seconds. Now he worked them flawlessly, making the blue Battlefleet symbol dance for him as he outlined possible adjustments to Supreme Commander Hawthorne's operational plan.

Once, General Fromm looked up from the holographic map and stared at Toll Seven. "That's brilliant," the stout Earther said hoarsely.

"Your approval is noted," Toll Seven murmured. "Further adjusts might be made here…"

As he listened to Toll Seven, Blackstone silently agreed with Fromm. The big cyborg was frighteningly brilliant.

Yet Blackstone currently wondered about something else. Why was this cyborg so different from the long-limbed ones that made metallic purring sounds when they moved? Those cyborgs never spoke. Those cyborgs radiated menace, and they managed to emanate a terrible sadness.

Who would ever volunteer to become a cyborg?

Blackstone shuddered. The idea was mind-numbing. He noticed as Toll Seven talked that Commissar Kursk never looked at the cyborg. She stared fixedly at the holographic map. She never agreed with anything Toll Seven said, and she never spoke up in praise of Social Unity. That was unlike her and odd.

"Further, if we modify the attack vector…" Toll Seven said in his alien way.

With his twitching features stout General Fromm avidly noted each new detail of Toll Seven's refinements. The man kept muttering in amazement. "Yes, yes, that's masterful." Fromm frowned later, absorbed, his nods quick little twitches. "That's diabolically clever. The Rebels will never notice."

"The probability that they will notice is five point sixty-two percent," Toll Seven murmured.

Commodore Blackstone wondered how the cyborg could make such a precise, mathematical judgment. The variables needed to be cataloged, correctly analyzed, and then weighted against other elements… it was too daunting to think the cyborg had given the right percentage.

Blackstone tore his gaze from the holograph. Did the cyborg hypnotize them with his words? He studied Toll Seven. The silver eyes moved like machine parts. The steel-colored teeth seemed as if they should have shredded the cyborg's plastic lips. Were those lips truly plastic, or were they some weird synthetic flesh? Who had ever conceived the need to build Toll Seven? And why had Social Unity done so in the Neptune System? Surely it would have made more sense to make the cyborgs on Earth or on the Sun-Works Factory.

Blackstone's head twitched as what the cyborg suggested sank in. The Commodore became alarmed. "No," he said. "I don't agree with that."

General Fromm looked up in wonder. With his fleshy neck and his bulging eyes he seemed like a frog, and he seemed dazed. "What possible objection could you have, sir?"

Blackstone shook his head. "I object for several reasons. Firstly, command and control must always remain under my authority. Secondly—"

"No, no," General Fromm said. "That's not the issue here at all. This is a stunning example of Sun Tzu's dictum of pretending to be weak where you are strong. It's—"

Blackstone cleared his throat and glanced sharply at Commissar Kursk.

She raised haunted eyes from the holographic map and only briefly met the Commodore's gaze. She shivered, and the muscles hinging her jaws tightened. "You will agree with the Commodore," she whispered.

Fromm frowned at her. "I fail to see—"

Kursk's head whipped about as she snarled, "You will agree or face the agonizer, General!"

There was silence on the bridge. No officer pressed a button. No one coughed, moved so his or her chair squeaked, or said anything. Then an alerting beep from someone's comm unit broke the silence, and the officers around them began to whisper.

Fromm's fleshy features had sagged. Now he nodded.

Blackstone noticed that Toll Seven had watched the interplay with computer-like detachment. Now the cyborg resumed talking.

Blackstone had the terrible feeling that the cyborg had cataloged everything and given an insane number of variables precise mathematical weights. Maybe later, while he was alone in his command pod, Toll Seven would plug himself into a cyber-computer. The two machines would then analyze this new data. The small argument would enter the data-stream of the program for whatever the cyborgs ultimately wanted. *What did this alien really want?* The longer Blackstone spent with Toll Seven, the more he concluded that the cyborgs' ultimate objective, by definition, must be harmful for humanity.

***

With a sharp tug, OD12 detached the last plug from her head and rose from the crèche in the battle pod. Other cyborgs rose from their womblike electronic crèches. A dim green glow bathed their skeletal bodies. They moved jerkily these first few seconds, advancing in a line toward a cylindrical chamber.

The chamber rotated, revealing an opening to the first cyborg in line. Purring motors sounded as the former commander of Ice Hauler 49 stepped into the chamber. It rotated so the entrance and the cyborg disappeared. Harsh chemicals immediately sprayed into the unseen chamber.

OD12 heard the spray, and she heard the cyborg in the chamber thrash and utter metallic groans. It was an odd sound. It triggered a distant memory in OD12.

She alone of all the cyborgs awaiting their turn for the obviously painful chemical shower showed a different pose. OD12 cocked her elongated head. She cocked her head, and her mask-like face betrayed little of the horror the memory slammed home into her controlled thoughts.

She remembered laying on a conveyor. A hellish shock had awoken her, and she had torn a muscle causing horrendous pain. A chemical mist had drifted onto her face, and she'd heard harsh klaxons shrieking. Despite extreme lethargy, she'd moved her head to the side and had screamed as she'd stared at the dead face of the commander of IH-49. Others had lain beyond the commander, others on the moving conveyer and sprayed with the fine, orange mist.

Cyborg OD12 remembered the moment. It had burned into her because her worst fear had been played out. Life was rigged against her. The extreme paranoia that had told her she could never win was one hundred percent accurate. She'd tried to move off the conveyor. A long mechanical arm with a needle attached to the end had descended toward her. It had been descending doom. She'd tried to thrash away from it. Instead, the hypo had touched her flesh and hissed, pumping something into her. She'd fought to keep her eyes open and had horribly failed as her eyelids drooped.

As she stood in line with the other cyborgs, OD12's head

147

cocked a bit more. She recalled many years of combat training. She had been to a hundred planets in a thousand varied situations. At least, the combat simulations inside the Web-Mind had seemed like real years.

Her nearly lifeless eyes tightened—that tightening was close to being an anomaly. It triggered the programming in her internal computer.

Warning, OD12!

The computer warning caused her to blink. Her self-awareness might have curled up and died the death of inertia and terror. This deep part was the "I" of OD12... of Osadar Di, her true name.

Warning! Your emotions have increased adrenal secretions. Emotive responses above the accepted norms will result in an immediate shutdown and a possible personality scrub.

Osadar Di understood perfectly. She was screwed. She'd never had a chance, really. It wasn't fair. But then life was a crapshoot where all the odds were stacked against you. It was the norm for her. She'd always known it. Look at her. She was a monster, a mechanical thing with a slave driver to control not only her actions, but also her thoughts. If that wasn't the ultimate screw-job, she didn't know what was.

Emergency procedure twenty-seven: select from tempo, highdrox *and* nullity-4.

Osadar was faintly aware she heard more from her computer than she should. It was choosing from certain drugs to inject into her bloodstream. Yes, as the drugs began to work the grim horror gripping her began to fade. Unfortunately, the memory also began to recede with the lessening terror.

Osadar—no, she was OD12. She belonged to the Web-Mind. She was a component of the grand scheme of Solar System conquest. This was part of Step Nine, whatever that meant.

A tiny twitch of her cyborg lips escaped the notice of the computer's censor program.

She was screwed. She knew it. She had always known this was going to happen. She hadn't known she'd become a cyborg or a part of Web-Mind, but she had known that eventually she'd become immersed into something vile and irresistible.

Yet that was the thing, her quirk. Despite the odds, she'd always resisted. Did that make her foolish? Sometimes she had thought so. The deep "I" of OD12 decided to play along for now. She believed she could have resisted enough to enter shutdown and maybe even gotten herself personality scrubbed. But she didn't want to be scrubbed. She wanted to survive. She wanted to screw the thing that had screwed her. It was part of who OD12 was, just as it was part of her to know she ultimately couldn't win.

Maybe the hardened understanding of the futility of life gave her the needed mental resources to kick against the perfected cyborg reconditioning. Maybe it was just a quirk of fate. Maybe even the Web-Mind and precise cyborg superiority failed sometimes. It was possible and might even have a probability that Web-Mind had given an exact score. Maybe the score was 0.001 percent. All the maybes could have been the answer.

The reality was that OD12 stepped toward the chemical shower with the rest of the line of cyborgs. She entered the cubicle in turn and felt the chemical spray sear her skin and make her scalp prickle as if sprayed with jets of flame. She was enslaved like all the other cyborgs. She would perform her tasks. But she would also plot in the deepness of her half-mechanical heart to throw a laser calibrator into Step Nine of the Web-Mind's plan of conquest.

***

After the preparatory shower OD12 entered another shutdown sequence. So did the many cyborgs of her battle pod. After her delivery to an SU ship and under Toll Seven's guidance SU military personnel lifted her stiff form and inserted it into a battlesuit. The personnel used lifters and inserted her and the suit into an attack pod loaded with weapons. Other lifters set the pod into an ice machine. The ice machine sprayed water around the pod, hardened the water into ice and sprayed more water. In a layered onion manner the ice machine built a large ice chunk to a precise size. Once done, the ice machine secreted the frozen chunk onto another lifter.

149

An SU sergeant drove the blackened ice chunk to an encasing processor. There, a thin steel coat encased the ice with the frozen cyborg in its exact center. The steel-jacketed ice-chunk was shipped to a select vessel that possessed a single cannon.

The cannon was a mass driver. It used magnetic coils to accelerate metal to high speeds. Normally this was a mine-laying warship, or a mine-spewing warship. It shot mines. Those mines possessed radar capability, electronic counter measure devices and a nuclear explosive. When an enemy vessel approached the decided limit, the mine exploded. The nuclear bomb pumped X-rays through rods, directing the deadly radiation at the computer-selected target.

Instead of normal mines, however, the mass driver would use its magnetic coils to accelerate the steel-jacketed, precisely sized ice-chunks.

As the crew readied its mass driver Commodore Blackstone stood with Toll Seven in the command center of the *Vladimir Lenin*. As before, they stood around the holographic module. This time it showed several of the convoy spaceships, squat vessels drifting at the outer edge of the Battlefleet. Those spaceships were nearest Mars. At a quiet order from Blackstone, passed along by the communication's officer, the squat vessels began to spew aerosols into space. It was a thin shield placed between Mars, its moons, the space-defense platforms, and the bulk of the Battlefleet. The aerosol density was miniscule, little more than a mist. A laser would burn through in a nanosecond. An enemy missile wouldn't even know the aerosol screen existed.

The aerosol screen was a precaution. Ever since the Doom Star had vacated the Mars System and as the SU warships began to congregate, the Rebel sensor probes and satellites aimed on this side of Mars had been destroyed. That left the radar stations on the two moons and on the space platforms in near-Mars orbit. Those sites possessed teleoptic equipment. The Martians and the SU Battlefleet closely watched each other through powerful telescopes. The aerosols spewing from the squat convoy vessels now put a temporary screen between those teleoptic systems and Social Unity's painfully gathered

150

warships.

The aerosol screen wouldn't last long. But then, it didn't have too. Already, SU warships and cyborg battle pods began to change positions into a different formation. The aerosol screen was not meant to mask this change. Instead, once the aerosols drifted apart and the fleet moved beyond the screen, the Martians would no doubt redouble their efforts studying the Battlefleet. The new formation would hopefully satisfy their curiosity. The Martians would hopefully debate for several days what it meant. By that time, the true reason for the aerosol screen would have made itself known.

"The aerosol screen is up, sir," the communications officer told Blackstone.

The Commodore took a deep breath and glanced at Toll Seven. The cyborg impassively watched the holograph.

Blackstone adjusted the module. It now showed the mine-spewing warship, the *Kim Philby*. It was hard to accept the plan. It seemed impossible.

Blackstone heard himself ask, "You're certain we're not sending your cyborgs to a futile death?"

It was difficult to tell, but Toll Seven seemed amused. "Supreme Commander Hawthorne approved the tactic. He must understand as I do that it will work flawlessly."

Could cyborgs know pride? "Very well," Blackstone muttered. He spoke to the communications officer. "Order the initiation of Operation Icebreaker."

Aboard the *Kim Philby*, its captain received Blackstone's order. She sat at the edge of her chair, with her clenched fist near her chin. "Are the coordinates perfect?"

"The cyborgs seem to think so, sir," the First Gunner answered.

"This will never work," the captain said. She was a tall woman, known as a perfectionist. "Begin."

"Fire one," the First Gunner said.

The fusion engines kicked in as power flowed through the mass driver's magnetic coils. The first steel-jacketed ice-chunk shot out of the cannon at almost two kilometers per second. It headed for a precise location at something near three times the speed of a fired bullet. After a mere two seconds, or after traveling a little less than four kilometers, the steel jacket exploded off the ice like a saboted gyroc round. That accelerated the ice-coated pod, pushing it even closer to two kilometers per second.

One after another, the *Kim Philby* shot the steel-jacketed ice-pods. The steel was obviously needed for the magnetic coils to "grab" the pod and give it velocity. But that was all the steel was needed for.

After a short travel time the first ice-pod reached the limit of the Battlefleet's farthest ship. The pod then sped through the screening aerosol mist. Some aerosol mist pitted some of the ice-pods, but not enough to deflect the trajectory or destroy the cyborgs embedded deep within.

Because no explosive power had been used to expel the ice-coated pods, Martian detection equipment had nothing to pick up. Steel bounced radar, so the steel jackets had been shed before the pods reached the aerosol screen. Radar had a much harder time detecting ice. Ice was cool, so there would be no heat signature to give the approaching pods away. Ice was also a common element found in space in the form of ice comets, ice asteroids and even ice rings and ice moons. Teleoptic scopes could pick up pods. Thus, the ice was black and it would not bounce light well. So teleoptic scopes would have a nearly impossible time sighting the chunks. Compared against the backdrop behind them—the vastness of space—the individual pods were less than pinpricks.

In other words, the ice-coated pods were part of an elaborate stealth attack. The first barrage targeted Phobos, the deadliest component of the Martian space defense. A second barrage would soon blast at Deimos. Given the speed of two kilometers per second and a distance of something over 350,000 kilometers, the pods would reach Phobos in 42.69 hours, almost two full Earth days.

Supreme Commander Hawthorne's operational plan called for the quick capture of the two moons. He also wanted to capture them without paying a heavy price in SU warships. Social Unity needed those warships for the true fight, the Doom Stars that would surely come in time.

Toll Seven's refinement was the ice-coated pods and the

scanty numbers sent at each target. The slender number of cyborgs meant fewer pods. Fewer pods meant a greater chance of stealth success. Could, however, forty-five cyborgs capture heavily armored Phobos?

As Commodore Blackstone stared at the holographic map, watching the *Kim Philby* fire the barrage, he had his doubts. He had grave doubts. Blackstone had also come to believe that killing cyborgs might be more important than killing Highborn. He wondered about that, however. He had stopped taking Commissar Kursk's drugs. It had lowered his rage. It had made him think more about his ex-wife. It had also made him many times more afraid of Toll Seven. And the worst thing about that was that the cyborg surely knew it.

-13-

The clone Lisa Aster sensed her opportunity two hours before the second barrage of cyborgs was fired at Deimos.

Through General Fromm's manipulation, Lisa found herself working a lifter alone in the second ice-coating ship. She moved stiff cyborgs to the battlesuits.

Her plan was simplicity itself. So Lisa wondered why she felt so nervous. This would be safer than waiting on the ceiling for deceleration to begin, the little game she'd played with herself during the journey to Mars.

Lisa braked the lifter and jumped off. She hurried around the magnetic forks. The cyborgs lay in a line on her lift. They looked like mannequins. If one of them had twitched just then, Lisa would have screamed. Fortunately, they stayed as stiff, cold and still as the dead. She took a spy-monitor from her belt and hesitated. Lisa didn't want to touch their dead flesh, or their cool metallic parts. These things couldn't be alive.

Lisa swallowed hard and told herself she was the Blanche-Aster now. She was here because the cyborgs had destroyed one of her sisters. The cyborgs had likely caused Mother's death.

Resolved, Lisa reached behind a cyborg's head and attached the spy-monitor to the base of the neck. The monitor was made of chameleon-skin, and it would look like just like the cyborg's armored flesh. Lisa shivered as her fingers touched cyborg skin. It was warm, and that seemed horrible. She backed away, staring at the dead-seeming thing. It was warm. It was actually alive, if frozen now.

Feeling eyes on her, Lisa whirled around, and she yelped in fear.

Massive Toll Seven stared at her.

"What did you do?" Toll Seven asked in his strange voice.

"There… there was something on a cyborg's face," Lisa said. "I wiped it off."

"Give the something to me," Toll Seven said.

The clone Lisa Aster began to tremble. That made her angry. She had been the Madam Blanche-Aster's bodyguard. The cyborgs had done something to Rita Tan. Rita had done something to Mother. So this cyborg here was part of the cabal that had slain Mother Blanche-Aster.

Lisa put her hand on the hilt of a hidden vibroblade. "I have to get these cyborgs to the battlesuits."

"You will give me the thing you took off the cyborg."

It dawned on Lisa that there was no way Toll Seven should be here. It meant that somehow her role had been compromised. The only one who knew her objective was General Fromm. Had the cyborg already gotten to Fromm? With a sick feeling, Lisa wondered if the cyborgs were superior to Highborn. If that were true, then the cyborgs should be able to outthink mere Homo sapiens.

"Show me this thing," Toll Seven said ominously.

"Yes," Lisa said. She meekly approached the big cyborg. He waited with his metal hand open. Lisa stepped closer yet. With her thumb, she switched on the vibroblade as she drew it.

The vibroblade was a deadly close-combat device. It vibrated a thousand times a second, making the motion invisible to the human eye. It allowed the blade to slice metal with ease. It should have the capacity to cut armored cyborg flesh.

Lisa slashed at the hand before her, sheering off three fingers as zapping-sounds and sparks emitted from the shorn digits. The sheered finger-parts hit the deck like lead shot. Lisa stabbed, and the tip sank into the armored body. Then Toll Seven chopped. Lisa moaned as her wrist snapped. She staggered away. The cyborg drew the knife from his chest, and he crushed the hilt so the blade quit vibrating.

"Stay away from me!" Lisa shouted. She groped left-handed for a communicator.

Toll Seven lifted his good hand and pointed a finger at her. Something flew out of the tip. Then something sharp hit Lisa in the chest. She stared down and saw it was a dart. She looked back up at Toll Seven. She wanted to ask what it had been. Then Lisa's legs crumpled and she was falling. She opened her mouth as waves of nullity washed over her.

The last thing she remembered was Toll Seven lifting her and carrying her. She knew not where.

***

For five days Marten and Omi had trained ten carefully selected security personnel.

In that gym five days ago Marten had spoken with each assassin in turn, asking random questions. He'd stared into their eyes, searching for indefinable qualities. It had been more than a gut feeling. If anything, he'd searched for a core of stubbornness and a sense of calling, of duty, if you will. All the men had killed before. Some had shot PHC police in the back. Some had stepped up and stared PHC officers down as their needler sprayed its deadly slivers. Others had beaten traitors to death with their fists, held fast by other enforcers. None of the chosen team members were pleasant. With more than a few, Marten had Omi engage them in hand-to-hand combat. None of them could match the Korean's skills or withstand his Earth-powered strength.

During those short bouts Marten had searched each man's reaction to his defeat. Only two security men had the fortitude to drag themselves back up each time. One had snarled and charged fiercely, only to land on his back a second, third and a fourth time. The other one had picked himself up slowly, glaring at Omi and then ploddingly circled the Korean yet again, trying to pierce Omi's deadly martial arts. Those two, Gutierrez and Rojas, were now squad leaders.

Ten men, plus Omi and he, were enough to fill three skimmers. Three skimmers loaded with long-range gyroc rifles could hit hard and fast and do some real damage to the strike-craft parked on an airfield.

The first three days Marten used his Highborn training, speaking HB battle maxims, and showing each man a critical

156

trick. On the fourth day, he took out the open-topped skimmers and practiced raids. On the fifth day, they bounded out of the skimmers in their environmental suits and hit the red Martian sand. Each man fired his gyroc rifle at distant targets that Marten had set up on the previous day.

The gyroc rifle was an interesting weapon. It fired a .75 caliber spin-stabilized rocket shell. After leaving the rifle barrel the rocket ignited, giving the bullet the majority of its speed. The rifle acted like a recoilless weapon, which meant that even though it fired high-caliber bullets, it was of light construction and didn't slam the shooter each time and thus wear him out. The various rounds meant that gyrocs were highly versatile.

The Armor Piercing Explosive round (APEX) had a big motor and a heavy projectile. There were shrapnel rounds that acted like a line-of-sight mortar, a smart rocket that could fly around objects, and sabot rounds where the outer shell burned off to add deadly velocity against hardened targets.

Marten watched the men, shouted corrections into their helmet's headphones, and cursed their stupidity. He raged at their Martian weakness and the impossibility of achieving anything with morons like them. He used the techniques used on him in the Free Earth Corps boot camp by the HB.

Later, back at the barracks at the base of Olympus Mons, Marten showered and played cards with Omi in their room. It was an old deck from Highborn days, the edges worn and frayed. They played at a small table, their equipment sprawled on their bunks.

"What do you think?" Marten asked Omi.

"Gutierrez is deranged."

Five days ago, Gutierrez had charged Omi each time during the hand-to-hand testing. The big Martian still had bruises around his eyes from Omi's blows.

"Gutierrez reminds me of the kamikaze troops we faced during the Japan Campaign," Marten said.

"Seeing that PHC ran this planet for so long," Omi said, "I'm surprised he's still alive."

Marten drew a card, examined his hand and slowly pulled another card. In disgust, he threw his hand down. "I'm over by one."

Omi put the discards under the deck and flicked himself two cards from the top and Marten two.

"There will come a time when we need someone like Gutierrez," Marten said as he examined his cards.

"You don't care if he dies?"

"If he fights under my command," Marten said, "I'm going to do my best to bring him back alive. I'm just saying that it's good to have at least one madman along. That makes him a treasure compared to the rest, a treasure I plan to hoard."

"Gutierrez is a walking dead-man, and he doesn't even know it," Omi said softly.

"I don't agree. Sometimes it's the madman who makes it through everything."

"There's only one Marten Kluge," Omi said dryly.

"I'm nothing like Gutierrez."

"No," Omi said, "of course not."

Marten scowled.

Omi drew a card and spread out his hand. "Twenty-one," he said.

Marten's scowl intensified. He grabbed the deck to reshuffle. Halfway through the shuffle someone rapped against the door.

The two men exchanged glances. Marten reached to his bed and grabbed a gun. Omi stood up, moved onto his bed and sat down amidst his sprawled equipment.

The knock came again, harder.

"Enter," Marten said as he shuffled cards.

The door opened as Major Diaz entered. Behind him followed Secretary-General Chavez.

"This is a surprise," Marten said.

Diaz scowled, and he opened his mouth.

"No, no," Chavez said. "Their customs are different than ours."

Marten raised an eyebrow.

"Usually, people stand as a superior enters a room," Chavez explained.

"Ah," Marten said.

There was a pause.

"...may I?" Chavez asked as he touched Omi's vacated

chair.

Marten nodded, and he wondered how long Major Diaz would stand there, upset and glaring at him.

Chavez sank into the chair as if standing had wearied him. His eyes were haunted today and more red-rimmed than during their meeting five days ago. Marten was glad the Secretary-General didn't pull out any stimsticks. He hated the mildly narcotic smoke.

"I will be brief, Mr. Kluge," Chavez said. "My intention was that you train all fifty of Major Diaz's men. I only learned about this oversight an hour ago. I decided a face-to-face encounter would be more productive. I flew here exclusively to speak with you."

"I'm honored," Marten said.

Major Diaz moved a step closer. He seemed angry.

"You have a problem?" Marten asked the major.

Chavez cleared his throat. "Mr. Kluge, we all have a problem. The SU Battlefleet has engaged in odd behavior. My chief military officers suggest that something fateful will happen this week. If that is true, I can no longer allow Social Unity the possession of the planetary aircraft. I'd hoped to send a demolition team. I realize fifty men can achieve little compared to our planetary scale. Yet fifty men can achieve much more than ten can."

"So that's what has you worried," Marten said, thinking fast. "Maybe I should have explained myself better to Major Diaz. I need to train those most able to absorb what I'm trying to teach. Then, when I take on the rest of Major Diaz's men, the trained ten will help teach the rest."

Secretary-General Chavez looked up at Major Diaz. Diaz's scowl had lessened so he almost seemed abashed.

"You said the Battlefleet is moving," Marten said. "Does that mean my shuttle is in danger?"

"Your shuttle?" Chavez asked. "Mr. Kluge, there is a war going on, or about to erupt. Your shuttle hardly matters in the equation of planetary freedom."

Marten's kept his features the same, but his heart-rate increased. He didn't agree with the Secretary-General.

"I cannot allow Social Unity to choose the time of its

attack," Chavez was saying. "The Planetary Union must strike first. Unfortunately, our space assets are minimal. Thus, we must strike where we can. I wish you to hit four of the seven airfields and destroy all the aircraft you can."

"Ten men—"

"Not ten men," Chavez said stiffly, "but fifty. You will take the rest of Major Diaz's soldiers—"

"I'm sorry, sir. But they're not soldiers."

Chavez leaned back, the closest to glaring at Marten that the Secretary-General had ever been. The force behind his eyes was considerable. His stare also said that he had ordered the death of many enemies. Quietly, Chavez said, "They're the most loyal fighters Mars has."

"That's fine," Marten said. "But they're not soldiers. They're killers, gunmen, assassins. A soldier is something different."

"I don't follow you, Mr. Kluge. Soldiers kill. Major Diaz's men have all killed the hated enemy. Therefore, they are soldiers. Perhaps they lack your training. But that's why I hired you. Now that we have an emergency, we cannot afford the luxury of taking our time. We must strike with what we have and hope to forestall a combined attack."

Marten thought about that and finally nodded.

"You will leave tonight," Chavez said. "The skimmers are loaded, and the men are waiting. By tomorrow night I wish you to strike the first airfield."

"I'll have to inspect the skimmers," Marten said. "And we don't dare skim straight there. We will use some subtlety in order to achieve surprise."

"You'll do exactly what the Secretary-General orders you to do!" Major Diaz snapped.

Marten stared at Chavez. "You hired my expertise, sir. That means I have to do things my way. Attack tomorrow? I'll do what is militarily wise. First, I'm going to make sure we have the needed equipment to ensure success. Your men are killers, but they're not soldiers. The two soldiers you have need to make sure that this operation is run properly, like a real military operation."

Chavez forced himself to his feet as he wearily waved a

160

hand. "Yes, yes, inspect the skimmers. And make certain my supply officers give you everything you need. I feel the weight of oppression, as if something terrible is about to happen to Mars. I hope you can understand my position. I need you to attack tomorrow, or if not then, in two days time."

Marten suddenly felt sorry for the Secretary-General. The man used what he had. Chavez and his Martian Union were cornered. The fact that the ruler of a planet personally came to speak with two Highborn-trained soldiers showed that Chavez fully understood his grim situation.

Marten stood up, and he saluted crisply.

Secretary-General Chavez asked, "What was that for, Mr. Kluge?"

"You have earned my respect, sir."

"Ah," said Chavez. "Thank you." He turned to Major Diaz. "Make sure you follow his orders, Juan. He is a soldier, and he knows what he is doing. However it is done, we must destroy those attack-craft."

**

Three hours later a convoy of open-topped skimmers flew across the Tharsis Bulge, an enormous volcanic plateau. Olympus Mons dominated the west behind them as they traveled eastward paralleling the equator. Before them in the hazy distance towered the Tharsis Montes. It was a chain of spectacular volcanoes: Arsia Mons, Pavonis Mons and Ascraeus Mons. The skimmers used the plains between the volcanoes, which was a barren desert of blown red sand. Over the years the Martian wind had created huge dunes similar to those in the Western Desert of Egyptian Sector on Earth.

The silver skimmer in the lead wobbled. It sank lower toward the dunes. Its engine whined. The two suited men in back half-rose as if they would leap out just before the skimmer crashed. Then the skimmer stabilized. A great puff of sand blew upward, and the silver skimmer rose back up to twenty meters above the desert floor. The two men settled back in their seats. The soldier on the left leaned forward until his helmet touched the seat in front of him. Maybe he was asking himself why he'd agreed to this mission. Maybe he was already tired.

161

The moon Phobos shone brightly in the night sky. Despite being a fraction of the size of Luna, to Marten and the others Phobos appeared as half the size of Earth's moon. It was because Phobos was so much closer to Mars than Luna was to Earth.

It had been a long time since Marten had seen a moon in a night sky from a planetary surface. The months of training on the Sun-Works Factory and then later the death-like existence in the Storm Assault Missile—

Marten shook his head. Like everyone else, he wore an environmental suit. It was plugged into the skimmer and was presently heated and energized by the craft's rotary engine. The skimmer whined as it flew twenty feet above the Martian sands. Those sands were too fine and found their way into everything, even Marten's suit. The dust gave his suit an odd smell. It was a sterile desert, a dry and sterile world. To the north he noted a vast low dome, one of the farms that dotted Mars.

Marten commanded twenty skimmers with fifty-some raiders. Marten wasn't under any illusions. Major Diaz could order any of the men to do anything, and they would obey. So Marten realized he was only in nominal control. He had a plan for that. If Diaz gave him real trouble, he would kill the man. Afterward he would have to cow the men so they wouldn't mutiny. Marten hoped it didn't come to that. His other problem was quite different. Despite Chavez's disinterest concerning the *Mayflower*, Marten was very interested in its fate. Was the SU Battlefleet about to move? If not now, when would it? He had to leave the Mars System before the space fighting started.

Marten sighed. He was tired. He needed sleep. He hated sleeping in this suit, however. With the skimmer whining and trembling, it reminded him too much of the Storm Assault Missile. That brought back horrible memories.

Despite those memories he slid lower in his seat until his pack jammed against his back. He had to twist half sideways before he was comfortable. That put pressure on his right shoulder, and over time it would irritate an old shoulder-pull. Even so, he shut his eyes. Major Diaz said he knew a path down the eight-kilometer canyon. Twenty skimmers with fifty security personnel and about as many gyroc rifles, and three plasma cannons—that's all Marten had to take out four airfields and seventy fighters. If everyone did what they were supposed to and obeyed his orders instantly, they could likely do some serious damage. But they would take losses. Even the ten he'd trained for several days—

"It's amateur hour," Omi whispered to him. "We're a mob."

Marten silently agreed. The chief factor for success would be surprise. If they lost surprise it would all be over. Therefore it would at least be two days before he made his first attack.

Marten opened his eyes again. He stared up at Phobos shining half the size of Luna. The moon looked like a cyclops staring down at him with its single eye. What was happening up there? Was the *Mayflower* safe? Had anyone tried to break into his shuttle?

What a way to buy fuel. He was risking his neck, unsure if the Martians were genuine or if they would have the ability to pay when the time came.

-14-

The moon Phobos was a fortress, the best circling Mars. Six months ago the Highborn had taken it with battleoids. Otherwise, it would have given the Doom Star trouble. It had merculite missiles and heavy laser batteries dug deep into the moon's surface like gigantic pillboxes. Before the Highborn had left six months ago they'd given the moon to the Planetary Union, along with the other surviving orbital stations.

The key to Phobos was the giant fusion plants that powered the lasers. Those fusion plants were deep in the moon that was about 27 kilometers in diameter. A Doom Star was an over a kilometer in diameter sphere, a gigantic space vessel. The Martian moon had greater mass than any Doom Star, although it was not as lavishly armored; Phobos' armor was its mass.

The name Phobos meant "fear." In ancient times, Fear had been a companion of Mars, the Roman god of war. Deimos meant "panic," another of Mars' companions.

The range of a laser depended on several factors. One of them was the size of the focusing systems. All beams of light lost coherence over distance. A common flashlight lost its brilliance because of diffusion or the spreading of its light. A laser beam was no different. Its light was more tightly focused, and that was the source of its dreadful power. Therefore, a long-range beam needed to start with a large diameter focusing system. The larger the diameter, the bigger the beam one could use. The bigger the beam, the longer it took for the beam's light to diffuse into uselessness. The second dynamic for long-range beams was power. Power needed a source. A small orbital fighter lacked a power plant to supply it with a battle-worthy laser. That's why orbitals used cannons and missiles. A SU Battleship was big. That size allowed it massive fusion engines. Those engines supplied its laser batteries with enough power for long-range beams.

One of the reasons the Doom Stars were so deadly was that their lasers could fire farther than any SU warship. The experimental beamship *Bangladesh* had trumped the Doom Stars in range and therefore had been superior in many ways.

The heavy lasers embedded on Phobos were of Doom Star range and power. That made Phobos a dangerous fortress to tackle. Unfortunately, the Highborn battleoids had not been able to storm Phobos six months ago fast enough. Knowing they were losing the moon, the SU defenders had destroyed many of the key components for the heavy lasers. Day and night, Martian Unionists labored intensely to fix the lasers. Two lasers were operational, and a third was weeks away from being ready.

If those two lasers had been ready when the SU Battlefleet began to gather at far orbit, Chavez likely would have ordered strikes against the individual spaceships. Those two laser cannons were ready now, and the fusion plants were online. They targeted SU Battleships over 350,000 kilometers away, but held their fire.

Almost two days ago an aerosol cloud had begun forming before the massed Social Unity Fleet. The commander of Phobos had considered firing then. A stern order from Chavez had halted the thought from turning into action. The moon station was still under high alert, however. The SU Battlefleet had taken an unusual formation, but otherwise had remained inactive since the building and dissipation of the light aerosol cloud. Martian military planners were still arguing over the cloud's significance.

***

The forty-five black ice-chunks drifting at two kilometers per second neared Mars and neared Phobos.

That the black ice had remained hidden was due to the vast volume of space. That volume was unlike anything on a planet. Even something like the mighty Pacific Ocean on Earth shrank into insignificance compared to the lonely expanse of outer space. If any of the ice-coated pods had been orbitals using chemical fuel, spotting them would have been simple. Space was huge, but space was also cold. An orbital's chemical-fuel rocket would have blazed its presence with its heat signature. The ice-coated pods were cold as the immense volume of vacuum around them. The inner pods gave a miniscule heat signature which was masked by the surrounding ice.

So even though a planet-bound human would expect someone to spot the forty-five ice-chunks barreling straight at Phobos, the probability of that was low. Teleoptic scopes were like a person's eyes. To see an object they had to be looking in that direction. Just as it would take many people standing all around the moon to watch every quadrant of space, so it would take many teleoptic scopes pointing everywhere to do likewise. Radar would have a better chance picking up the icy chunks once they were near Phobos, as radar could more easily cover broad sections of space.

That radar-probability had entered Supreme Commander Hawthorne's original plan and Toll Seven's adjustments to it. Therefore, two critical elements now affected the success of the cyborg assault. First, the arrival of the ice-embedded pods near Mars was timed with Phobos' orbit around the planet. The moon circled Mars three times during the Martian day or once every 7.3 hours. The pods used Mars as a shield and reached Phobos just as it came around the curvature of the planet. The radar stations on Phobos thus had less time than otherwise to spot the approaching ice. Deimos could still catch the pods by radar, or one of the laser or orbital platforms in close-Mars orbit could. Yet Toll Seven had suggested that those stations would be less likely to radar-spot the ice as Phobos would, since the ice-coated pods came at the moon and not at those platforms. Still, the probability existed. And to lessen that probability Toll Seven, with Commodore Blackstone's agreement, had decided to add one more factor. They would inundate Martian space defense with data, giving the Martians something else to worry about other than faint radar signals.

***

Commodore Blackstone's gut churned. He had slept

poorly, knowing that the next wake cycle would either begin the end of everything he knew or begin the end of Highborn arrogance. Because of the cyborgs, there was also the possibility it would do both.

Blackstone now stood in the cramped command center of the *Vladimir Lenin*. Commissar Kursk and General Fromm stood with him around the holographic map-module. For once, Toll Seven was absent. The cyborg remained in his command pod, he said overseeing the moving of the pods to the safest location in the Battlefleet. It seemed like a strange reason, but perhaps it made logical sense to a cyborg. Whatever the reason, Blackstone appreciated Toll Seven's absence and would have liked to make it permanent.

"It's time," Commissar Kursk said. With Toll Seven's absence she had regained some of her composure. She even wore lipstick, and her stance was more aggressive, more like the commissar Blackstone remembered.

Blackstone stared at the holograph, his thoughts weighted by his responsibility.

Months of lonely waiting out here, months of dodging the Doom Star a half-a-year ago, and then weeks of gathering the Battlefleet now came down to this moment. The sneak attack on Mars orbital defense had begun nearly two days ago. Before that the warships had received much needed material. The supply convoy from Earth had brought new coils, missiles, foodstuffs, cloths, laser parts and sundry other items that humans needed to survive in cramped quarters in outer space. Each of the warships had come in ragged. Months of running from Doom Stars or floating uselessly in deep space had badly affected morale. These last few weeks had changed much of that, but not all. The Battlefleet wasn't as sharp as it could be. If he lost too many warships in the coming hours and days, it would mean disaster.

Commodore Blackstone's gut churned, his mind shying away from that brutal thought. If he lost too many warships, Social Unity would never get another chance to make a new fleet. He could lose the future of Inner Planets here in the next few hours. If he won, the gamble for survival continued.

"Toll Seven is on line three, sir," the communications

officer said.

Blackstone continued to stare at the holograph, switching views so he could study the many spaceships that made up his fleet. This was it. This was the moment of decision.

"Commodore Blackstone," the communications officer said. "Toll Seven is insistent."

Blackstone felt warm flesh touch his wrist. He looked up into Commissar Kursk's brown eyes. They stared with worry, while the brim of her cap was low over her eyes. The curve of her cheekbones—the commissar was quite beautiful. She still held his wrist as she touched his skin. His wife's touch had felt like that. Blackstone glanced at the commissar's hand. What if he twined his fingers with hers? What if they lay on his bed together, naked?

"Commodore Blackstone, are you well?" Kursk asked.

Blackstone squeezed his eyes shut and then snapped them open. "It's time," he said, his voice hoarse. "Open a channel to all ships," he told the communications officer. "It's time we began the Mars Attack."

***

Burn-scarred Commander Zapata, the orbital launch officer and the Martian with an eye-patch, had been busy the past two hours. The strange SU Battlefleet maneuver almost two days ago still bothered him. It had been bothering him ever since the klaxons had wailed that day.

Then Zapata had ordered a layer of prismatic crystals sprayed from the containers between the SU Battlefleet and his satellite. He had given the order to protect his station from sudden laser-strikes. Then he had launched probes to keep an eye on the Battlefleet. The layer of prismatic crystals had blocked his teleoptic scopes from watching the SU warships. The probes had therefore radioed their data back to him. He had been certain then that the layer of aerosols laid by the Battlefleet had been a prelude to a sneak attack.

Now, almost two days later, he had been proven wrong. They had all been wrong. Most of the strategists now believed it had been a maneuver to upset them and to make them waste prismatic crystals and aerosol gels. The new SU Battlefleet disposition had also started endless debates.

Commander Zapata hadn't accepted any of those explanations. He had ordered a radar and teleoptic sweep on the Battlefleet. Those sweeps had discovered nothing other than the new formation.

"There has to be something more," he said.

He stood on his command bridge. It was more spacious than Commodore Blackstone's command center. Space was a premium on the *Vladimir Lenin*. On the orbital launch station, they had extra room.

Zapata stared up at a main screen. Other officers and personnel behind consoles faced the same way, but most of them studied their smaller vidscreens.

"The Battlefleet is accelerating!" someone shouted.

That created a babble of noise.

"Put it on the main screen," Zapata ordered.

With powerful teleoptic scopes at full magnification the commander was able to view the SU Battlefleet. Over one hundred spaceships engaged their engines. It created a bright burn behind each vessel. The majority of those vessels were the convoy supply ships from Earth. The huge battleships and missile-cruisers led the way.

"Where are they headed?" Zapata shouted. He wanted to speak in a quiet, confident voice. He was too excited for that, too scared.

"For Mars, sir!"

The babble of noise intensified.

"Sir," someone else shouted. "I'm picking up strange readings."

"From the Battlefleet?" Zapata asked.

"No, sir. It's in near orbit."

"Show me."

On the main screen came the blackness of space, with a vast number of stars.

"Is this a joke?" Zapata shouted angrily.

"I'll freeze it, sir, and color it orange where the stars are blotted out."

Zapata gaped at the new image, with over two dozen small orange globs on the screen. "What am I looking at? What are those? How big are they?"

"They're not much bigger than orbitals, sir. The computer suggests they're all made of ice."

"Ice?" Zapata asked.

"That's why our radar never picked them up."

Commander Zapata took a step back. His good eye grew wide. "Where are those ice-orbitals headed?"

There was a tapping of computer keys. "It looks like for Phobos, sir."

"Orbitals," Zapata whispered. "Orbitals—those aren't orbitals!" he shouted. He remembered Marten Kluge and the stern Korean. Those two had storm assaulted the *Bangladesh*. Could those ice-orbitals contain the SU version of storm assault troops?

"Get me Phobos!" he shouted.

"What about the Battlefleet, sir?"

"Get me Phobos!" Zapata screamed. "Get them online now!"

-15-

The black ice-chunks neared Phobos. They were less than ten thousand kilometers away from target. From Phobos speared an incredibly powerful laser. That giant laser completely encompassed an ice chunk. The ice vanished in a puff of steam. The exposed pod slagged and then disappeared. The cyborg in the pod no longer existed. The beam switched to a new target, to a new comet of black ice, and began the fatal sequence all over again.

***

OD12 was jolted awake. It took her a nanosecond to realize she was in a battlesuit, in a pod, surrounded by black ice. She stirred, and the internal computer ticked off the seconds as it urged her to greater speed.

OD12 moved her battlesuit fingers. She pressed a switch. That switch caused her pod's outer shell to overheat. The heat caused the ice around the pod to soften. Then explosives blew off the ice. Several seconds later the pod decelerated hard. OD12 easily endured that, having greater tolerance to high Gs than even a Highborn possessed. A second after deceleration quit the pod exploded. It sent metallic shards hurtling in precise directions. Toll Seven and Web-Mind had configured those directions to ensure the safety of the attacking cyborgs. It wouldn't do to kill your own cyborgs with your own shrapnel. The metal shards were meant to bounce radar and provide the Mars Rebels with many easy targets of opportunity, useless targets. Those shards acted as chaff to hide the attackers.

OD12 now hung alone in space, encased in her battlesuit and with a hydrogen thruster-pack to supply her motive power. She used side jets to correct her position, using huge Mars below her as a reference point. Phobos was much smaller and pockmarked. It was ugly and dark compared to the beautiful Red Planet.

The internal computer still ran its censor program. *Warning!* It shouted at her.

Within her helmet, OD12's elongated head twitched. Couldn't she even enjoy a planet's beauty for a few seconds? She might die soon.

This is your second warning! The third warning will begin the override sequence.

Apparently, enjoying a planet's beauty was bad for a cyborg. It fulfilled no useful function for a combat machine. OD12 made a quick calculation. She decided in the next second that inhaling the beauty of Mars was best left to another life. There was no room for frivolities in this existence. Besides, she had a mission to complete and a bastard of a computer censor to please.

Salient information now flooded her as thirty-seven cyborgs counted off. Eight cyborgs didn't, maybe couldn't. A frightful beam stabbed through the darkness of space. OD12's visor blackened to protect her costly eyes. That beam was close, a mere one hundred meters to her left. It slagged pod-shrapnel and then, like a conjurer, made the shrapnel disappear. Information from Toll Seven's Web-Mind fed her mind. The laser had destroyed eight pods during their frozen ice-cycle. The attack had been prematurely spotted.

The terrible beam switched off and then stabbed again, this time to her right by one hundred and twenty meters. It originated from the approaching moon. OD12 focused on the moon, using her helmet's imager. She had been through a hundred such sequences in the simulator. She knew exactly what to do, and she did it much faster than a human could. Faster even than Highborn.

The moon hardly fit the description of one. It lacked a pleasing, perfectly spheroid shape, but looked more like an asteroid. Phobos was an ellipsoid, with three axes about 27, 21 and 19 kilometers long. It had craters and most resembled the lunar highlands. The surface was very dark, and was one of the blackest objects in the Solar System. Phobos reflected 2 percent of the light shined on it. Luna reflected 7 percent.

There was a massive pillbox on the dark moon. It was in the Stickney crater, the largest on the moon and 10 kilometers in diameter. Out of the pillbox protruded a huge focusing system. From that focusing system shined the dreadful laser. OD12 yearned to launch smart missiles at it. It was possible that all the cyborgs wanted to. Unfortunately, that was against the mission's parameters. Their attack was supposed to capture the moon for Social Unity. They were to capture it intact, with as many functioning weapon systems as possible left in working order.

OD12 was close now. They all were—the cyborgs in their battlesuits hung in space like lethal fruit. OD12 and many other cyborgs rotated using small side jets. She applied hydrogen-thrust from her pack, braking. A nearby ECM pod crackled interference waves, hopefully throwing off enemy tracking radar.

The giant beam burned into space again, and another cyborg stopped broadcasting.

OD12 glanced over her shoulder. The moon loomed before her. She applied more thrust. Then she rotated again and detached from the thruster pack. It automatically burned hydrogen spray, flying elsewhere.

A missile rose from the moon. It tracked the thruster-pack, zeroed in on it, and exploded on impact. Since there was no atmosphere, it was a silent hit. And because there was no atmosphere, there was nothing to carry the shock wave. There was heat, but not enough to bother OD12 in her battlesuit. There was radiation, but it was negligible, since the missile had not been nuclear-tipped.

OD12 now readied herself for moon-impact. Her analyzers said it would be a hard landing, barely within the tolerable limits of her graphite-bone legs. The moon expanded with startling speed until it was everything to her. She couldn't see the beautiful Red Planet anymore, just this dark, pitted surface. She wished for another thruster-pack. She was coming down too hard. The surfaced rushed nearer. She clenched her teeth together so she wouldn't accidentally bite off her tongue. Retro-rockets on her legs fired a last burst to slow her just another fraction. Then she hit the moon hard.

OD12 had trained a hundred times for this in the simulator. If she hit too stiffly, it might bounce her off the tiny asteroid-like moon. If that happened, it would send her spinning away from Phobos with no way to return. The moon's escape velocity was minuscule. She would drift around Mars and eventually fall onto the planet. Long before that, however, she would have run out of battery power and air.

OD12 crumpled and rolled and rolled. Dust floated up and seemed to hang there. Then the particles slowly began to fall.

The internal computer blanketed her pain sensors. Pain would only interfere now. OD12 rose and tested her legs. She might have grinned in ordinary times. But she was a cyborg. It took something fantastic to awaken the deep "I" of her old self, fantastic things like a beautiful planet hanging right there below her feet. Now she was on this dark, ugly moon with a mission to perform. So instead of grinning at her impossible achievement, she began to move over the moon's surface.

It took most people a lifetime to learn how to move fast on an asteroid that had a minuscule escape velocity. The subjective years in the Web-Mind simulator had given OD12 those "years" of training. She was an expert, likely one of the greatest in the Solar System. Her only equals in asteroid-gliding were the other cyborgs in the attack team. Thirty-six of them had made it. That was less than Toll Seven had computed they would need to storm and capture the moon intact.

The internal computer listened to emergency instructions messaged from the Web-Mind on Toll Seven's command pod. The internal computer computed and injected enhancement drugs into OD12's system. The agenda had been set, and Web-Mind had decided to risk possible burnout to heighten cyborg functions.

Thirty-six machine-enhanced humanoids in battlesuits converged on the first bunker in the Stickney crater. The Martian Planetary Union was about to experience the first Inner System battle with the nightmare called cyborgs.

-16-

Lisa awoke for the last time as the clone of Madam Blanche-Aster.

There were odd humming noises around her, and the light was an eerie dark green. A harsh chemical odor made Lisa scrunch her noise. She wanted to spit, as a rusted taste was on her tongue.

Lisa frowned. The last thing she remembered was Toll Seven pointing a finger at her. The cyborg had shot her with a dart.

Lisa tried to shake the sluggishness from her. She had to get up and warn somebody that the cyborgs were dangerous. She had chopped off the cyborg's fingers, and he hadn't seemed to care.

It was then Lisa realized she was immobilized and quite nude. There was a strap around her forehead, and others securing her torso, arms and legs. All she could see by rolling her eyes was an ominous humming machine. It had a human-sized chute. Fear surged through her as her stomach painfully tightened. She lay on some kind of belt that led into the human-sized chute. Her feet would go in first. The belt or conveyer would take her into—was it a medical machine?

Where am I?

As if to answer her silent question, Toll Seven floated before her. Lisa glanced at his hands. They were whole, his shorn fingers fixed.

"Where am I?" Lisa whispered.

"In the cyborg command pod," Toll Seven said. He pushed

himself to the floor, and there was a tearing-cloth sound as he attached his feet to a Velcro-carpeted floor.

"You have to let me go," Lisa said. "I'm sure to be reported missing."

"General Fromm has already reported you as a suicide."

Lisa's heart beat faster. "Fromm is your spy?"

It seemed as if the cyborg wanted to smile, but something held him back. "General Fromm has learned the uses of Web-Mind. He is a Webbie."

"What is a Webbie?"

"I had considered it for you," Toll Seven said. "But the Martian Unionists have fought back more efficiently than Web-Mind had computed. Web-Mind has recomputed the casualty rates and indicated an immediate need for cyborg reinforcements."

"From Neptune?" Lisa asked.

"Fear pheromones are leaking from you," Toll Seven said. "But I had computed you capable of rational thought even under dire stress."

"Do you know who I am?"

"You are a clone of Madam Director Blanche-Aster."

"Madam Blanche-Aster is dead," Lisa said.

"We know."

It wasn't *I know*, but *we know*. "How could you know?" Lisa asked.

"By direct communication with Chief Yezhov of Political Harmony Corps," Toll Seven said.

"I am the Blanche-Aster now."

"There are other clones."

"But none are as highly ranked as me."

"Ah," Toll Seven said. "You are bargaining in the hope of forgoing your transformation."

"I can help you," Lisa pleaded.

"The Rita-Tan solution failed."

Those fear pheromones Toll Seven had talked about poured off Lisa now. She struggled, but the straps binding her head, torso, arms and legs were too snug and too strong. She was trapped on this nightmare conveyor, and she was about to enter the ominous machine.

Lisa's mouth was bone dry. "What does this thing do?" she asked hoarsely.

"It converts human flesh into a cyborg soldier."

Lisa struggled harder and was soon panting. "I can kill James Hawthorne for you!" she said.

"Our cyborg-reinforcement need is more pressing."

"I'll become like those things you shot at Phobos?"

"No."

Lisa's eyes boggled as hope retuned. "No. What do you mean?"

"You will not be as efficient as those soldiers. This is a micro-converter. Once we land on Mars, I will construct a true converter and the process of complete conversation will begin."

"Do to me what you did to General Fromm," Lisa begged.

"The risks increase with each Webbie."

"Have mercy," Lisa said, while trying to control her terror.

"Mercy is illogical."

Lisa tried to thrash. She twitched and heaved against the straps. Toll Seven's metallic hand touched her naked shoulder.

"Cease these useless efforts," he said. "You will tear a muscle, and that will make conversion less useful."

"Let me go!" Lisa screamed.

"Such emotional flesh," Toll Seven said. "It is a wonder humans ever made it off their mud-ball world." Toll Seven stepped back, becoming harder to see in the dark green light. He seemed to make a minute gesture.

The conveyor lurched. Lisa Aster the clone began screaming. The scream became piercingly loud. She struggled as her feet entered the human-sized portal. She tried to lift her head so see what would happen next, but the straps were too tight.

She should have tried to kill Supreme Commander James Hawthorne back on Earth. She should never have agreed to this journey. Stupid General Fromm had allowed Toll Seven to change him. The cyborgs were invincible. They had no mercy. They had no flaws whatsoever. They would shred the Martians, Social Unity, and then shred the arrogant Highborn.

A cold spray spewed against Lisa's feet and then her legs.

It made them numb.

Lisa's screams became hoarse as her head disappeared into the whirring machine.

***

Marten and Omi ate cold soybean sandwiches in an EVA tent. They had been skimming for forty-eight hours in a southeastern direction. After passing Pavonis Mons they'd entered jumbled terrain composed of huge blocks and deepening channels. One of those dangerous channels had led into the Noctis Labyrinthus, the most western of the Valles Marineris Rift System.

The Valles Marineris was the largest canyon in the Solar System and stretched for nearly a quarter of Mars' circumference. It wasn't a single vast canyon, but was made up of many different merging formations. Nearest the Tharsis Bulge was the present canyon. Traveling east, one would reach eight different canyon systems before it ended at the basin of the Chryse Planitia. The Valles Marineris was a vast tectonic crack in the Martian crust, formed as the Tharsis region had risen in the west. Over the centuries carbon dioxide fluid and gas had eroded even more of the canyon.

In the tent, Marten's hair was oily and his face dirty. Surprisingly, Omi seemed fitter. Being on a planet again, even one with only one-third Earth's gravity, had accelerated Omi's health more than his many hours on the *Mayflower's* workout unit had.

After finishing the sandwiches both ex-shock troopers donned their environmental helmets and turned their heaters up full blast. Only then did they zip open the EVA tent. The warm, oxygen-rich air left in a cloudy rush.

They were in shadow beside a towering cliff eight kilometers high. There were ice crystals on the rocks and patches of carbon-dioxide snow on the ground. Those patches were less than a quarter-inch thick. It was cold down here at the bottom of the Valles Marineris Canyon. But it wasn't as cold as the Martian South Pole, which sometimes hit -193 degrees Fahrenheit in winter. It was cold enough. Because they were eight kilometers down from the regular Martian surface there was enough atmospheric pressure for it to rain or snow.

Major Diaz had led them down the eight kilometers. It had been six hours of harrowing maneuvering. One skimmer had flipped and killed all four passengers.

Omi folded the tent as other raiders opened theirs, the oxygen-rich air escaping like cloudy genies. EVA-suited men began trudging to the parked skimmers. This was the last leg of the journey. Forty kilometers away was the first airstrip. None of them knew anything about the cyborg assault on the two moons.

"Look!" Diaz shouted into their helmet receivers.

Marten looked up. In the distance and leaving lines of vapor streaked four jets.

"Where are they headed?" Diaz radioed.

Marten watched the specks in the pink sky. Unlike Earth, which scattered the blue part of sunlight better than the other colors and thus made a blue sky, Mars had a reddish tinge. The reason was all the reddish dust in the air. The SU jets climbed to get out of the vast canyon. If those jets turned and burned down for them it would be a mad scramble for the anti-air rockets. Marten mentally kicked himself for not having several of them rocket-armed at all times. He gave the order now.

The jets kept streaking higher, however, until they disappeared over the distant edge of the canyon. Were they headed for Olympus Mons?

As Marten strode for his skimmer he began issuing commands. Soon they were going to find out if a mob of security personnel could pull off a commando raid. Maybe the thing to do was only take Omi with him and hit the airfield alone. He doubted Major Diaz would agree to that. No, Diaz would be sure they were turning traitor against the Planetary Union. That would bring about a gunfight Marten didn't want to explain to the men or later to Secretary-General Chavez.

***

An hour later Marten lay on a rock using an imager on the airfield. There were two machine-sweepers on the runway, clearing it of dust and any thin layers of carbon dioxide ice. The airfield had a tower, four hangers, what might have been a barracks, and then several long buildings behind that. Around the airstrip were low bunkers, likely automated weapon

179

systems.

Marten slid off the rock and jogged back to the parked skimmers. He had the squad leaders gather around him. Using a holopad he dumped the imager's pictures into it and outlined the plan of attack.

"Any questions?" Marten asked later.

There were a few. By the quaver in the voices, Marten knew the squad leaders were scared. It was the right emotion. None of them had likely ever made a raid like this. Most had nerved themselves up in the past in the underground city streets they had grown up in. Then they would have walked up to PHC police and needled them to death. Hopefully they were tough enough so they wouldn't panic and freeze today. Marten was more worried they'd panic and shoot their own by mistake.

The men climbed into the skimmers as Omi and Marten strode back to the rock. Both of them dragged mobile missiles. They were TAC-84s, the latest in raiding tech and left behind by the Highborn. Without them, Marten would never have agreed to the raid.

Marten set his up with practiced ease, his training from the Free Earth Corps days returning as if it had been yesterday. An excited feeling ran through him, competing against the fear. Highborn training was the best in the Solar System, and Marten had taken two doses of it, once for FEC and the second time as a shock trooper. He unfolded the tripod legs and then swiveled the launch tube, using the comp-scope until he had the nearest bunker in sight. The missile launcher was like a giant gyroc rifle. It was easy enough to shoot these that one of the men could have done it. But in battle, what should have been easy quickly became difficult.

Marten looked up at Omi. Omi swiveled his launcher and looked over at him. Marten waved his finger to the left.

Omi glanced at his launcher and then at Marten's launcher. He nodded, likely seeing now that they had both targeted the same bunker.

Marten waited for Omi to adjust, wondering how many of his men were going to die today. It would have been safer having his men crawl to the airfield. But they weren't real soldiers, and he didn't know what they would do once under

180

fire. Too many might jump up and run away. He'd decided to keep them together in the skimmers. Hit the enemy hard and hit fast, so fast that none of his men would think about jumping out of the skimmer. If Social Unity had posted tough military personnel here, however…

Omi gave him the thumbs up.

Marten returned the gesture. He sighted the first bunker, pressed the firing stud and watched the first TAC-84 leap out of the launch tube. It ignited immediately and whooshed at the target. Beside him, Omi's missile roared a second later.

They targeted two other low bunkers each and let fly before the first missile hit with a terrific explosion. Concrete flew into the air, and the concussion wave soon reached them. On Earth the concussion would have been greater because of the greater density of the air.

"Hit the barracks," Marten said over the radio.

Omi and he swiveled their launchers and let missiles zoom at the buildings in the distance.

Then Major Diaz's voice roared over their headphones. Seconds later, the first skimmers zipped past them.

Marten glanced at Omi.

Omi shrugged, and said over the radio, "He's eager."

Marten turned, expecting to see their skimmer parked behind them. There was nothing but Martian ice crystals and shadows. In exasperation, Marten realized their driver had become too excited and had followed Major Diaz in his skimmer charge.

"They're clumping together," Omi said.

The fools, they were supposed to spread out, each team hitting their selected areas. Instead, as Major Diaz war-whooped over the radio, the other skimmers followed his like an old-time cavalry charge.

Omi crouched over his TAC-84. Marten did likewise. SU-suited soldiers appeared in the distance. They climbed out of hidden portals. There must have been underground barracks they'd failed to spot. That was just great.

Marten judged the skimmers, the SU personnel and took the risk. He sent another missile at the enemy. Then he deactivated his missile launcher.

"Shut it down," Marten said.

"It's a long run to the airfield," Omi said.

"Yeah," Marten said. "So we'd better start. Set your gyroc for sniper-fire."

In moments the two ex-shock troopers trudged across the cold Martian sand. With their gyroc rifles ready they headed for the airfield.

Thirty seconds later, Marten cursed. The SU soldiers flung themselves behind concrete slabs, on the runway and behind corners. They began firing at the charging skimmers and immediately gained results.

A skimmer flipped as its driver lurched back hard in his seat, his helmet exploding. The three other occupants went flying. Upon landing, two lay still. The last lifted up and then slumped down again as bullets riddled his body. The skimmer exploded in a ball of fire.

Marten hurled himself onto the cold sand, steadied his gyroc rifle and used the scope. Three enemy soldiers far in the distance set up a plasma cannon. Marten fired. The gyroc round ignited and sped at the enemy. It missed, however.

Omi lay a little ahead of Marten, firing as well.

Another skimmer exploded as a heated ball of plasma hit it.

"Land! Land!" Marten shouted into his radio unit.

Someone in that cavalry-like charge finally began to listen. A skimmer dropped with a hard landing, plowing up cold dust and white carbon dioxide. Soon four troopers spilled out. They began peppering the enemy with gyroc fire.

As the enemy plasma team swiveled their cannon Marten held his breath and slowly squeezed the trigger. Three second later another explosion released a heated ball of plasma. This one cooked the three SU soldiers, shriveling them as if they'd been insects.

Two reckless skimmers raced almost on top of the enemy. They landed. The security teams jumped out and charged, pumping shots. It was suicide. It was crazy. But maybe their recklessness favored them today. About a quarter of the security teams flopped onto the cold ground. The rest ran up to prone enemy and shot them at pointblank range.

With Omi and Marten acting as snipers the short battle

turned hard against the surviving SU soldiers. There had only been a few of them to begin with.

The victory was costly, however. And the terrible casualties left the Rebel Unionists in an ugly mood. The last Social Unity personnel tried to surrender. Major Diaz personally shot each of them in the back of the EVA helmet.

Later Marten walked through the wreckage of the hangers and counted fifteen jets. He set demolition charges on any that looked in good shape.

The living were elated at their victory. The wounded with torn EVA suits had already died from exposure. Counting himself, there were thirty-one effectives left.

"These EVA suits are crap," Marten told Omi.

The grim Korean grunted agreement.

Major Diaz poked into the barracks ruins with a gyroc pistol ready. He was likely hunting for SU survivors. Five of the men were with him.

Marten collected everyone else and went down a hidden portal. As he'd suspected, it was an underground barracks. He found three men in a communications room. They were white with terror and begged for their lives.

Marten whispered to Omi, "If Diaz tries to shoot them, take him out."

"Kill him?" Omi asked.

"Fast," Marten said. He turned to the three shaking men. They were pale, wore PHC patches, and had sweat-soaked tunics.

Before Marten could ask his first question the PHC captain said, "You know the Battlefleet has attacked, right?"

Marten stared at the man. The PHC captain had gray sideburns, curly gray hair and looked as if he was ready to start crying.

"It-It's on all the channels," the captain stammered. "They stormed Phobos and Deimos."

The door opened, and Major Diaz entered the room. His brown eyes blazed. "Good," he crooned. "There are more." He lifted his gun.

"Do it," Omi said, "and you're dead."

There were six other Unionists in the room. They looked

183

up, surprised. Omi had a needler pressed against Diaz's back.

Major Diaz scowled at Marten, who sat on a chair.

"Put away your gun, Major," Marten said.

"I see vermin in the room," Diaz said coldly. "I crush vermin to remove the infestation from Mars."

"You took out the airfield," Marten said. "Now we gain intelligence. You do know about that, right?"

Diaz laughed. "Then we kill them?"

"No," Marten said. "There's been enough killing today."

Major Diaz had a crazed look. "There you are wrong." He lifted his gyroc, aiming at the PHC captain.

Omi clutched Diaz's elbow and made a sharp motion. Major Diaz cried out as the gyroc dropped from his hand and hit the floor with a crack.

"Take him outside," Marten said. "Let him cool down."

Omi put a hand on Diaz's shoulder. The major tried to shake it off. Omi rabbit-punched Diaz in the solar plexus and Diaz groaned, going limp. Omi turned him around and pushed him into the next room.

"Stay here," Marten told two of Unionist raiding party who had risen to follow Omi and Diaz.

They glanced at Marten, and they must have seen something in his face that frightened them. They hurriedly sat down.

"Finish your story," Marten told the visibly trembling PHC captain.

"Y-You're not going to shoot me?" the captain whispered.

"I'm no murderer," Marten said.

The captain gulped as a tear leaked from an eye. In a quavering voice, he told Marten what had come in over communications.

Marten knew the truth when he heard it. He told Squad Leader Rojas. "Watch these three, but let them live. That's an order."

"I understand," Rojas said.

Marten motioned the other Unionists into the next room, leaving Rojas with the three enemy communications men.

Diaz glared at him. This was a central command room with vidscreens and a small cooler to the side. Many of the other

Unionist raiders were piled in the room, their manner ugly and angry as they stared at Omi.

"You have dared lay hands on me," Diaz pronounced. "You have shamed me in front of Social Unity swine. I will have my revenge, I promise you."

"You had your fun," Marten said, "blowing holes in men who wanted to surrender."

"It is a war to the death!" Diaz shouted. "They sought to make us slaves. Now they pay the price for their arrogance."

"The Battlefleet has moved," Marten said.

Major Diaz shook his head as if to shake off a fly.

"Space commandos have stormed Phobos and Deimos," Marten said.

"PHC lies!" Diaz spat.

"Not this time."

Diaz's eyes narrowed. "Are you suggesting we scamper home with the mission only a quarter completed?"

Marten took his time answering. They were under a communications blackout so no eavesdropping equipment could pinpoint them. Social Unity would know about them now. Marten debated radioing Chavez, and he saw how the other Unionists listened intently. Several fingered their weapons as if thinking about turning them on him. Marten debated with himself on how to do this. Diaz was a man of rage. So shouting and raging at him likely wouldn't work. Likely, nothing would work with Diaz but determination and the upper hand. Marten realized he had to win the other Unionists to him. They had to realize he was right, and that Diaz had horribly compromised the mission.

Marten let a sneer slide onto his face. He spoke contemptuously. "Scamper home, Major? I wish to abort the mission before you kill the rest of the men the Secretary-General gave into my keeping."

Diaz's head swayed. "I only killed Social Unity swine."

Marten sneered. "You were like a teenager with his first woman. You did everything in a rush. What might have been beautiful, you spoiled by finishing before her clothes were even half off."

Livid, Diaz shot to his feet.

185

"I was still firing missiles when you led a madman's charge at the airfield," Marten said. "You pulled everyone with you. You led unarmored skimmers straight into enemy fire. I lost a third of my men because of that. Did you count them, Major? Five skimmers lost out of twenty and thirty-one effectives left. We barely have a little over half our raiding force intact. Do you think I can hit each airfield in turn while losing almost half my men? Do you think I'm going to return to Secretary-General Chavez with handful of men left?"

"I killed no one—"

"Bah!" Marten said. "A third of our force was wiped out because you hunted for glory."

Major Diaz blinked in shock. "I want to kill the enemy."

"Good," Marten said. "So do I. But this isn't an assassin's mission where we nerve ourselves up to face the cops, blow them away and run. This is a military strike. You do it by the numbers, not through heroics. You charged this base like a white knight on a mythical horse. The men followed you, forgetting everything I taught them. Because of that, a third of them are dead. Can you understand that? They are dead, and we are too weakened to continue the mission."

"Next time—"

"There won't be a next time, Major. I've lost faith that you and your men want to learn how to fight like soldiers." Marten began to stride back and forth, gesturing angrily. He had to drive this lesson home. "Not only do you act like a heroic fool, but you butcher those who could have given me important information. You even tried to kill those communications officers. We could have used those soldiers you killed to help us gain entrance onto the next airfield. I can appreciate that you're a fighter Diaz. I like your hot-blooded courage. What I can't abide is that you lose all sense while your bloodlust consumes your better intelligence. A good soldier has to stay cool-headed. That's how he keeps his men alive for the next fight."

One of the Unionists actually nodded. That gave Marten hope.

Major Diaz stared at the floor. He wore a puzzled look. Then he nodded the slightest bit and glanced at the men, glanced at Omi and finally at Marten. He opened his mouth, let it hang open and then shut it. Without another word, he headed for the outer door. He moved without his customary arrogance.

Omi watched the major as if he expected Diaz to whirl around and open fire.

Marten didn't think Diaz would. Maybe there was hope for the man, although Diaz's hate ran deep. For the moment, the major would think about this day.

After the door closed, Omi glanced at Marten. His look said: *Now what?*

Marten crossed his arms, staring at the door as if he thought deeply about Major Diaz. He did it for the benefit of those watching. What he really wondered was what he should do next. And he wondered about the orbital launch station where the *Mayflower* was docked. If the SU Battlefleet was attacking the moons, what had they done to his precious shuttle?

The news was horrible and sent a shudder of fear through the surviving space defense forces of the Planetary Union.

The last defenders of Phobos had broadcast strange images of battle-suited invaders. Those SU invaders had moved with insect-like speed and used inhuman cunning. To see them glide over the moon's surface without bounding into space, no Martian could have done likewise. Nothing had stopped the space invaders, and their reactions had been brutally efficient as bunkers, missile-sites, laser batteries and shuttle hangers had all fallen before them. The last broadcast had shown invaders blasting surrendering Martians. The poor sods had crumpled and lain so utterly still. Then a helmeted invader had turned to a camera. For a moment the metallic face inside the helmet had stared at the broadcast unit. That image had been frozen and sent everywhere throughout the Planetary Union. Then the thing had lifted its weapon. There had been a flash, and nothing more had broadcast out of Phobos.

Shortly thereafter, Deimos had also gone offline.

Now Commander Zapata stood in his command center. He was ashen-faced and trembling. He watched the main vidscreen as harsh laser beams chewed through the prismatic crystal field around his orbital station. More crystals flowed from the supply tanks, trying to rebuild the field faster than the enemy lasers could chew through it. Soon however, the station's tanks would run dry. Then nothing could save them.

Those laser beams originated from big SU battleships. Those warships accelerated hard for near-Mars orbit.

The prismatic crystals were the orbital launch station's primary defense against such killing beams. The crystals were highly reflective and contained all the colors of the rainbow. Their purpose was to bounce or reflect the laser's light and dissipate its strength. If deep enough, a prismatic crystal field could completely absorb a laser.

The intense strength of these battle-beams slagged the crystals by the bucketful. That stole the reflective power and meant the full force of the beam soon hit them. In space-battle terms, the lasers did a *burn through.*

Zapata shouted questions at the few people still at their screens.

"Eighty percent of the crystal supplies are gone, commander."

To stop his hands from trembling Zapata gripped a monitor as he stared at the main screen.

"Emergency deployment," he whispered.

Computer keys told him someone carried out his command. He swallowed hard as sweat prickled his back. Most of the station personnel were abandoning the station. The last of the orbital fighters were even now catapulted from the hangers. He could have ordered them to burn for Phobos. Maybe a strafing run over the moon would kill some of those metallic horrors. Somehow, he doubted it. Besides, the Planetary Union needed those orbitals. Mars couldn't give up just like that. It had taken so many grueling years gaining their precious freedom. To return to serfdom so easily—who were those metallic soldiers? What were they? Where had Social Unity found them?

Zapata made a sound deep in his throat. All those years of hiding, of gunning down PHC police, making secret plans.... He couldn't throw it all away now on a gesture.

His hands hurt he was gripping a monitor so hard. He had elected to remain behind and run a last ditch defense. They had to save the orbitals and anyone else they could. He had to scrape something together out of this disastrous defeat.

He thought about the shuttle, the one the ex-shock troopers had used. Several days ago he'd ordered its codes broken. Engineers had entered the shuttle, refueled the tanks and stocked it with supplies. He wondered who else knew about it.

Surely a few of those fleeing would have entered the Highborn shuttle and tried for somewhere.

"Burn through," someone whispered.

Commander Zapata looked up with his one good eye. The power of Social Unity was too much. After everything the Highborn had done to Inner Planets, how was it possible that the SU military still possessed so many warships? He shook his badly scarred head. At least Mars had tasted a few months of freedom. It had been a good feeling. For the first time in twelve years a Martian had been able to hold his head up again. Despite their arrogance, he wished the Highborn had stayed on Mars. Social Unity would have never dared attack if a Doom Star had orbited the planet. Zapata frowned. Could the genetic super-soldiers have known this would happen? After a moment's thought, he shrugged. They couldn't have known. No one could have.

On the main screen incredibly powerful lasers burned holes through the drifting field of prismatic crystals. Those lasers now speared toward the station. The armored hull could withstand the hellish beams for a few seconds. More lasers now burned through the crystals.

Zapata turned to those who had remained at their screens. He saluted them. "For the Mars Planetary Union!" he shouted.

Chairs scraped back as one by one the others stood. They glanced at the large screen. Tears ran down one man's face. They saluted, and shouted, "For the Mars Planetary Union, sir!"

Seconds later the powerful lasers punched ten-meter wide holes through the orbiting structure. Terrific explosions began and fires roared. Then the vacuum of space stole the oxygen needed to let fires burn. Long before however the personnel aboard the command center were dead, charred into horribly shriveled things that barely resembled humans.

Parts of the gutted station tore free, or had been shredded free and drifted. Among those sections was the *Mayflower*. No one had entered the shuttle. The engineers who had broken in had failed to let the others know it could be used an escape vehicle. No beam had touched it and ignited the fuel in its tanks. Instead, the former Highborn shuttle floated high above

Mars, another piece of debris formed by the deadly Inner Planets civil war.

-18-

As the cyborgs stormed Phobos and Deimos, and as the SU Battlefleet destroyed the rest of the Martian space defense, the Highborn were on the move. Nearly 249 million kilometers away the Highborn Praetor circled the Sun.

The nine-foot tall Highborn lay on an acceleration couch and endured debilitating G-forces. The Sun was vast, with a diameter of 1,392,000 kilometers. If the Earth were the size of a dime, the Sun would be two meters in size; the Sun had 109 times the diameter of the Earth. The distance from the Earth to the Moon was approximately 350,000 kilometers. Thus orbiting one full circuit around the Sun would roughly be like Luna orbiting twice its normal distance from Earth. The *Bangladesh* had orbited the Sun much nearer than the Praetor did now. His ship lacked the special shielding that had allowed the experimental beamship to survive the Sun's terrible x-rays and radiation at so close a range.

The Praetor and his Highborn crew had endured the Gs for some time as the *Thutmosis III* built up speed. Highborn could endure greater Gs than a Homo sapien, who blacked out at a sustained 6 or 7 Gs.

The former SU missile-ship had undergone radical transformation at the Sun-Works Factory. First, the massive particle shields had been removed. Then it had received a new low radar signature hull and a new coat of anti-teleoptic paint. Massive detachable tanks and huge warfare pods had also been added. The tanks contained propellant for the fusion engines. The warfare pods held specially designed drones and missiles.

The Praetor lay on the couch, enduring and mentally cursing himself as a fool to have trusted Grand Admiral Cassius. If the Praetor were to design a clever punishment module, he would use the *Thutmosis III*. Instead of having the freedom and energy to plot to unseat the Grand Admiral the Praetor had lost weight under the emergency acceleration. He was no longer near the center of power, the Doom Stars in Earth orbit, but tucked away near the Sun. If the constant acceleration didn't kill him, the Sun's radiation would. In his opinion they flew much too near the nuclear ball of matter. And the warship's velocity . . .if this went on much longer, the Praetor's ship would reach speeds for a trip to Alpha Centauri.

The Praetor had studied the files about the *Bangladesh*. The SU beamship had reached respectable speeds, but the acceleration of the *Thutmosis III* dwarfed what the SU ship had achieved.

As he lay on the acceleration couch the Praetor made a grotesque grin. The acceleration deformed his features and made bowel moments a horror. But if a Homo sapien could do a thing, a Highborn could do it twice as well, even three or four times better. The *Bangladesh's* attack plan had been clever, and it had employed its fantastically-ranged beam to good effect. The new Highborn strategy for drones and missiles would be even cleverer.

Yet it would only be clever if Social Unity moved as the Grand Admiral had predicted. If not, then soon the *Thutmosis III* would have to begin deceleration. The Praetor made a grotesquely wry face. The Grand Admiral had never been specific about how the *Thutmosis III* was to stop its terrific velocity. The only reasonable method would use Jupiter or Saturn's gravity to brake the *Thutmosis III*. Would the lords of Jupiter or Saturn allow that?

Like all Highborn, the Praetor was well aware of his superiority. The Grand Admiral might assume that those of Jupiter or Saturn would fear Highborn too much to harm a lone ship. Unfortunately, he'd learned one thing as the governor of the Sun-Works Factory: Premen were strangely resistant to rational behavior. Some preferred death to the logical submission to their betters.

The Praetor slowly shifted upon his acceleration couch. He had learned through his crew that anything but slow moves could cause muscle tears. Already several Highborn lay in mortal agony on their couches. Groin, gut and sexual organ tears were the worst. Pulled hamstrings and triceps were also bad, but not necessarily fatal.

For the upcoming battle the *Thutmosis III* was the Highborn secret weapon. It would win them the war for Inner Planets. Of that, Grand Admiral Cassius had been certain. The Praetor had studied the plan in detail. He had even received reports that the SU Battlefleet Mars had finally made its stab at the planetary defenses. The Grand Admiral had correctly predicted each of those moves. Soon, the Doom Stars would accelerate for Mars. Then the fateful clash between the space fleets would determine who controlled the high ground between the planets. Whoever controlled space could quarantine the separate planets.

Were the premen truly foolish enough to think they could destroy Doom Stars? Would they actually remain at Mars to do battle? That seemed incredible to the Praetor. Yet the Grand Admiral was certain the premen would possess a secret weapon of their own, and that the premen would be brash enough to think their secret weapon could give them victory over their superiors.

The Praetor grinned harshly. The *Thutmosis III* was the weapon that would trump anything the premen could cobble together. It would shatter the preman surprise. His drones and missiles would hit their fleet at precisely the worst time for them. It would cause the premen to panic. They would then make even more foolish tactical decisions than otherwise and face annihilation.

"Good," the Praetor whispered. He yearned to burn premen hopes into ashes. He'd suffered for too long aboard this death-ship. The Highborn under his command had suffered as well. But their suffering would end the Inner Planets War. Yes, after such an annihilating blow, the hope would drain from the lower order. Many would drop their weapons and meekly seek the good graces of their genetic superiors. Premen would cower in fear, and they would finally realize that a New Order had come to the Solar System.

"Then," the Praetor whispered. Then he would have achieved his dream. He would have won military glory in the most stunning victory of the war. That would catapult him into every Highborn's thoughts. The Praetor had patiently videoed every aspect of his ordeal. He would replay the files and show the others what he had endured to bring them unqualified success. He already had a following. That following would grow, and in time, he would topple Grand Admiral Cassius from his high seat of supreme power.

As he pondered such lovely thoughts the Praetor of the *Thutmosis III* missile-ship groaned as his stomach cramped. He feared a muscle tear. He panted, but slowly the pain faded. He tried to shift to a more comfortable position. He could not take many more days of this.

The screen before him crackled. It was fuzzy, and it told him better than anything else could that his ship was too near the Sun.

"Praetor."

"Here," the Praetor whispered. Through screen static, he barely made out Grand Admiral Cassius's features.

"The premen of Social Unity have finally made their move," the Grand Admiral said in a distorted voice.

The Praetor wanted to groan with relief. Instead, he glared at the Grand Admiral's fuzzy image.

"In two days you will begin the breakout from Sun orbit," the Grand Admiral said. "The exact data and angle of your attack are already entering your tactical computer."

"Yes," the Praetor whispered.

"I admire your fortitude, Praetor. Your ship will bring us ultimate victory. I personally salute your courage and your daring."

The Praetor managed a terse nod, and almost tore a neck muscle doing it.

"Grand Admiral Cassius out." The fuzzy image faded away.

Two more days, the Praetor thought. Two more days, and the *Thutmosis III* would break out of Sun orbit and shut off its mighty engines. Then the stealth ship would zoom at terrific

velocity for Mars. The final battle for Inner Planets was about
to begin.

SU jets jumped Marten's skimmers at the worst possible moment. He had time to wonder how long they had been under observation. Then Marten screamed at Omi to take the controls as he turned and grabbed the rocket-launcher between the frozen knees of the raider sitting behind him.

They climbed out of the Noctis Labyrinthus Canyon using the skimmer's VTOL jets. Each skimmer did it in stages. The rotary engines whined so long and loud that Marten's teeth began to ache, and it made the metal craft shake as if it was about to burst apart from stress.

One moment, Marten watched the skimmer ahead of him. The dark craft wobbled as it rose higher and higher, its engines screaming to gain enough lift as the skimmer climbed beside a wall of red rock. Then a missile streaked out of the pink sky. It streaked and exploded, and the skimmer that had wobbled was now hot shards of metal and bloody body chunks flying in all directions. Some of those chunks smeared against the red rock wall, leaving gore and hot streaks of gashed basalt.

At the same moment something higher up flashed into view and out of view at almost the same instant. Marten recognized it as a jet. He knew because of the afterburners that glowed orange long him for him know they were all about to die.

Omi leaned over and grabbed the controls.

"Move!" Marten roared.

The security men in the back leaned away from Marten. The man's face behind the visor showed petrified shock.

Marten lifted the anti-air rocket launcher. It was a heavy

weapon like an ancient bazooka. With a grunt, Marten hefted it onto his shoulder, flicked tracking with his thumb so the launcher beeped and a green light winked. He peered through the scope in time to see another jet fire a missile. That missile streaked like lethal death just as the first one had.

With a thud, Omi landed the skimmer. That violently jostled Marten and almost threw him out of the craft. Then the enemy missile slammed into the rock face with a shattering explosion. Marten heard rock shards whiz past his helmeted head.

High above the SU jet's afterburners engaged, and it flashed out of view.

With his teeth tightly clenched so his jaws hurt, Marten scanned the pink sky. The first jet had re-appeared. It must have made a wide circle. Yes. It was still turning. It was going to strike again.

"Bastard," Marten whispered under his breath. He hefted the rocket-launcher onto his shoulder.

"Run for cover!" someone shouted into Marten's headphones. He was vaguely aware that one of his men dove out of the skimmer. Didn't the fool realize that if they lost the skimmer, he'd never make it anywhere alive in time before his suit ran out of power?

Beside him Omi lifted another anti-air launcher. "The jet jocks should have fired a flock of missiles each and called it a day," Omi said through his speakers.

The Korean's coolness helped Marten's tripping heart. Could the air jocks up there be as green as his men were? It seemed unlikely. But it did seem to Marten that it would have been smarter for the pilots to stay out farther and use their heavier missiles to advantage instead of coming in so close.

Marten tracked the first jet as it swung back around. The launcher beeped again, which meant it had gained radar-lock. Marten thanked God he held Highborn tech and not some imitation Martian crap. Marten held himself stiffly and pulled the oversized trigger. This wasn't a gyroc weapon. The blast almost knocked him over backward. It was a Highborn weapon and was meant for a nine-foot giant in battleoid armor.

The rocket whooshed fast and climbed with astonishing

speed. A second rocket whooshed. It was Omi firing.

The pilots must have recognized their danger. Without firing another missile, the first jet nosed up and the afterburners roared orange flames and made a thunderous sound. Anti-radar chaff drifted from the jet in a silvery clump behind the steeply climbing craft. Neither the chaff nor the steep climb helped. The anti-air missile hit the jet squarely, exploding with an impressive display of pyrotechnics. Omi's missile did the same thing with the second jet.

Marten heard himself wheezing, the noise loud in his helmeted ears. He scanned the Martian sky as he trembled. If there were another jet it would likely kill them all. Slowly it dawned on him that the two aircraft were it. No more appeared.

Omi put his hand on Marten's shoulder. Marten whirled around with a snarl. Then he grinned sheepishly and nodded as he settled down.

"Major Diaz?" Marten asked over the radio. There was nothing but static. Were his troubles with Diaz over? Was the man dead? "Major!" he shouted.

"Here," Diaz answered in a choked voice.

"Glad to still have you among the living, Major," Marten said. "Rojas."

"Here, sir," Rojas said.

Gutierrez was also alive, with his entire skimmer crew. Lopez and Barajas were dead, and their skimmers destroyed. There were no survivors from either vehicle.

Thirteen skimmers were left out of the original twenty. They had destroyed two more jets, but at too high of a cost.

"Listen up, people," Marten said over their headphones. "We're going to use over-watch from now on."

Marten waited for Diaz or one of the others to ask him why they hadn't been using over-watch before this. But none of them did. Omi and he had killed the two jets and likely saved the remainder of the raiding party. Maybe it was finally starting to sink in with them that they weren't soldiers and this was a real shooting war, not a guerrilla raid on underground city streets.

Too soon, their skimmer whined and shook so violently the metal rattled like a child's toy. They rose higher and higher, using the VTOL jets to reach the next plateau.

Marten's throat was dry like rust and tasted just as bad. He was sick of the planet's sandy smell and the gigantically oversized geographical formations. He wanted to get back to the *Mayflower* and head for Jupiter. Jets, sand, kilometers deep canyons, he yearned for the quiet of outer space.

What a way to buy fuel. He snarled as the VTOL jets whined down and they flew over the ground by a normal few feet. If Social Unity had done something to his hard-won shuttle…then he was going to find a way to make them pay in a manner that they would never forget.

-20-

As Marten and the remnants of his commando team skimmed for Olympus Mons, the SU Battlefleet had already braked to match orbits with Phobos, Deimos and the edge of the Martian atmosphere.

Commodore Blackstone sat in his wardroom, staring at a still-shot of his ex-wife. The vidscreen showed a young woman with long auburn hair in a three-piece bathing suit. Through bio-sculpture, she had maintained her youthful looks. Through vigorous exercise, she had maintained her shape. To realize now that she hadn't done it for him but in order to keep catching new lovers drove Blackstone near despair.

There was a soft knock at his door.

Blackstone's hand shot out as he pressed his keyboard, switching the screen to a tactical display of the Mars System.

"Enter," he said.

The door opened and General Fromm stepped in and saluted.

"No need for that," Blackstone said quietly. "We're not on the bridge."

General Fromm nodded stiffly and then managed an odd smile.

"Is there something troubling you?" Blackstone asked.

Fromm cocked his head, blinking at him. The general seemed distant, as if he'd lost his train of thought.

"If you could make it brief, General," Blackstone said. "I'm rather busy." He gestured at his vidscreen. "I'm planning the next maneuver."

"Ah..." Fromm said. "Yes. That's why I'm here, sir."

"Oh?"

"It's about the prisoners on Phobos."

"There are prisoners?" Blackstone asked. This was the first he'd heard about them.

"Strange, I know," Fromm said. "The cyborgs are so rigorous that it would seem they'd kill everyone. Apparently, they are keen to digest every iota of intelligence they can from the enemy. Toll Seven wishes for my people to interrogate the prisoners."

Blackstone frowned. Wasn't that Commissar Kursk's task? "It surprises me the cyborg doesn't want to do it himself."

"My thinking exactly," Fromm said. He touched his neck and rubbed a heavy bandage there.

Blackstone was surprised he hadn't noticed the bandage before now. It was flesh colored. He wanted Fromm out of here so he could decide whether to send his ex-wife a message regarding his possible return to Earth. Although Blackstone found it irksome, he forced himself to show interest in the general and his request.

"What happened to you?" Blackstone asked.

Fromm's hand shot away from the bandage as if it was suddenly hot.

"Ah..."

"Is it a deep injury?" Blackstone asked.

"I jabbed myself," Fromm said.

Blackstone couldn't really care less. He did note that Fromm spoke in an odd manner, and Blackstone decided it must be the stress of battle. "Is it healing?" he asked, wishing he'd never brought up the injury.

"Yes," Fromm said. "It's healing very well, sir. Perfectly."

Blackstone indifferently waved his hand. "Yes, take care of the interrogations. But be sure to notify Commissar Kursk about it." He frowned. "Why did Toll Seven ask you? The more I think about it—you realize that interrogations are the commissar's prerogative?"

Fromm stiffened, and he saluted. Then he opened his mouth as if to explain, but said nothing.

Blackstone wondered if Supreme Commander Hawthorne

had become a martinet concerning military protocol. Is that why Fromm acted so oddly? Had Fromm gained these strange mannerisms during his time on Hawthorne's staff?

"Perhaps the cyborg realizes the commissar is overworked," Blackstone said, answering his own question. He showed his teeth in a feral grin. "If Toll Seven had asked for the prisoners to interrogate, I'd have said no."

General Fromm cocked his head, and his eyes became glassy before he asked, "Is there a reason why you would have refused Toll Seven?"

Blackstone laughed without mirth. "I don't trust the cyborgs. I hope you don't either."

"No, no," Fromm said, "not at all."

"Say, whatever happened to that aide of yours?" Blackstone asked. "She used to dog your heels. Now I never see her."

"The clone?"

"That's right. The Aster clone."

Fromm blinked several times. "She's hard at work monitoring the cyborgs."

"The Supreme Commander asked about her in his last lightguide message," Blackstone said. "If she discovers anything unusual, I want to know about it immediately."

"Yes, sir," Fromm said.

Blackstone drummed his fingers on his desk. "Was there anything else?"

"No, sir," Fromm said. "With your permission, sir, I shall communicate your decision to Toll Seven."

Blackstone waved him away, and he switched the tactical display back to a still-shot of his ex-wife. He was hardly aware as the door closed and General Fromm took his leave.

***

Nine minutes later, Fromm secured the door to his cubicle. He double-checked it. Then he sat down on a chair and peeled the thick, flesh-colored bandage from his neck. A deep jack was embedded there.

Stout General Fromm licked his lips, feeling an odd sense of sexual arousal as he uncoiled a warm flexible tube. It was synthi-flesh. He wormed the tube into the jack in his neck. He shivered with delight as the pseudo-nerve endings linked with nerves in his neck. It always began as pleasure sensations as the insert sent pulses to the needed brain centers. Drool trickled from his slack mouth. He moaned in pleasure and shifted in short sudden movements.

Then the deeper functions occurred. Mentally, he entered Web-Mind, the unit of the Neptune whole that resided in Toll Seven's command pod. The general reported directly to Web-Mind about his talk with Commodore Blackstone. With his Web-heightened memories he relayed the conversation perfectly.

Afterward, Web-Mind took General Fromm's consciousness into his favorite simulation. During the episode Web-Mind continued reprogramming the chaotic mass of the general's neurons, gaining yet another level of control over the bio-form's thoughts.

***

The unpleasant task of beginning the conversion process fell to OD12 and three other cyborgs. The Phobos prisoners were a mix of male and female bio-forms.

Twenty-seven naked humanoids drifted toward the far wall of the storage room as OD12 and three other cyborgs entered. The prisoners were male and female bio-forms. The cyborgs had already shaved off every hair on their bodies. The prisoners had bruises and scabs, but each was now as hairless as a newborn.

The bio-forms babbled frightened questions. And they stared at OD12 with wide-eyed horror.

That troubled her. And what troubled OD12 even more was that her internal computer didn't notice her unease. During the battle for Phobos a bullet or a shard from an explosion had struck her armored chest with terrific force. Adrenalin had already flown through her system. That adrenalin had accelerated many bio-functions in her, but for too long a period without rest. At the time OD12 hadn't noticed either problem. Replaying it later in her computer memories she'd noticed that a glitch or an electronic burn had surged through her internal computer several microseconds after the impact. Certain data had been lost. OD12 suspected now that the censor program had been damaged. Her computer had repeatedly given her a message to report the incident to Web-Mind. She ignored it, and the computer ignored her disobedience.

Because of that, OD12 pushed aside the override controls over her emotions. She had done so with a sustained effort of will.

She now studied the horror on the faces of the naked prisoners. They babbled questions concerning their fate. Some wept. Some begged for mercy. Two of them scowled horribly.

OD12 shrugged. She heard servos whine and knew two of the other cyborgs had noticed the shrug. Would their internal computers consider that an anomaly, something foreign to proper cyborg behavior? In that instant OD12 realized she would have to hide her freedom of thought. She must mimic the others perfectly or she would return to Toll Seven's pod for repairs.

No thank you, she told herself. *I like my damage just fine.*

In another life she would have chuckled. She knew, however, that if she chuckled, the other cyborgs might destroy her.

"That one," AZ9 said. His voice box was scratchy due to battle damage.

OD12 swallowed down a sigh. With mechanical detachment she strode at the chosen bio-form. The male screamed and he tried to struggle, using a wrestling hold against her arms.

By using magnetic footing to walk upright and anchor herself OD12 plucked him out of the herd. His wrestling grapples only minimally interfered with her task. She moved away from the protesting bio-forms. She twisted him around as if he were a baby. His hysterical strength was useless against her cyborg muscles. She bent his arms behind him and clicked handcuffs over his wrists. Next she cuffed his ankles, turned on magnetic power and attached him to the metal floor. She put a neural inhibitor on his neck, and all his struggles ceased as if he'd become catatonic. Lastly, she brought up a jack-gun. It was a heavy, bulky piece of equipment. She placed it at the base of his neck, and the jack-gun began to vibrate.

OD12 looked up and noticed that the herd of bio-forms

watched her in fascinated horror. A few babbled whispered questions.

After three minutes the unit made a loud noise. OD12 removed the jack-gun from the male's neck. He now possessed a gleaming jack in his neck, ready to receive a plug into Web-Mind. But that was for later.

AZ9 pointed out the next bio-form.

Dutifully, OD12 went into the herd to get the female. Now all the bio-forms tried to fight. It didn't matter. They were naked, lacked gravity and possessed minimal strength. Still, it was an ugly process. It wounded OD12 to hear their whispered words concerning what they thought she was.

She wanted to tell them she used to be just like them. She would have told them their screams didn't matter. They would become cyborgs or Webbies, and the memories of their horror would be overridden. It might not be for the best, but it was inevitable, as escape was impossible.

OD12 understood that, because life was rigged. The only freedom was what she possessed now, a little self-awareness. It saddened her to realize the self-awareness wouldn't last. It meant.... It meant she had to figure out a way to enjoy it as much as she could while it did last.

She pressed the jack-gun against another neck and the machine began to vibrate and dig into the captured female's flesh.

21

After passing Pavonis Mons and with Olympus Mons towering in the distance Marten saw SU jets once more.

The commandos skimmed eight meters above huge red dunes, with the sand below drifting in ominous swirls. All day Marten had fought against an increasingly strong headwind. Omi now tapped his shoulder and pointed into the reddish sky.

At first, Marten thought Omi meant the wispy ice clouds kilometers high. Then Marten noticed slow-moving specks.

"Can the jets climb that high?" Marten asked over the comm-link.

"Did you see that flare?" Omi asked.

"Flare?"

"It was near one of those jets, might have been one of them."

Marten made a shrewd guess. "Martian orbitals must have jumped the jets."

During the next few minutes there were four more flares. Likely it was aircraft dying a violent death.

Marten hoped that meant some Martian space defenses still existed. The thought of being trapped on Mars for good made him queasy. He had been trapped in Australian Sector for years. He wondered sometimes if he ever should have escaped from the Sun-Works Factory the day his parents died. He'd yearned for freedom all those years in Australian Sector. He'd resisted Social Unity, just as the Martians had resisted here. The Storm Assault Missile had changed him. He no longer resisted because he no longer accepted either Social Unity or the Highborn as even nominally in charge of his life. Until he found a free society, a free government, he was his own government, his own self-run State.

Marten squinted up at the wispy ice clouds. He searched for specks, but the jets and orbitals had either perished or left for somewhere else. The Planetary Union was the closest thing to freedom there was in Inner Planets. Yet they followed Unionist doctrine. It talked a good game, but essentially meant the union leaders made the decisions. It leaned heavily on original Social Unity doctrine. The great difference was power. Social Unity wielded it, and the Planetary Union wanted it. Because the Unionists fought like a wounded beast it granted its individual members greater autonomy than otherwise.

To pass the long hours riding the skimmer Marten had spoken to Squad Leader Rojas about the Planetary Union. It's how he'd discovered the majority of his information concerning Martian ideals.

Rojas's major credo, and apparently the Planetary Union's as well, was—*Mars was for the Martians*. That was reasonable. But Marten no longer found socialist theories acceptable in any form. As far as he could tell, socialism always led to a police state, with a heavy emphasis on thought control.

Marten wanted a free state, where free people united to achieve goals they genuinely desired. Instead of Thought Police, individual people would work toward individual goals. His mother had taught him about such systems. They had existed in the past and might possibly exist farther out in the Solar System. Yet his mother had also taught him another truth. People were not inherently good. Each human possessed an evil streak, and a propensity toward bad actions. Each person needed a code of conduct that corralled that propensity toward bad actions. For his mother it had been God and the ancient book called the Bible.

Do not steal was one of the ancient maxims. Social Unity stole a man's labor and stole his freedom. Social Unity theory spoke about equality, using it so the State could plunder the production of the individual.

Marten shook his head. He refused to let anyone plunder him anymore. His stint in the Storm Assault Missile had torn the last veils from his eyes. He had no allegiance to Social Unity or the Highborn. Both systems sought to enslave him. So the Sovereign State of Marten Kluge—the germ to an ancient method of governance—was going to leave Mars before the Planetary Union tried to usurp his freedom and mold him in its likeness.

The great question was how to achieve his dream. If the SU Battlefleet had moved into near orbit it meant they had likely captured his shuttle. If they held his shuttle, how was he going to tear it out of their grasp? Perhaps just as importantly, how was he going to get into space again to try to wrest his shuttle back into his rightful control?

***

Twelve hours later, Omi drove the skimmer into a low garage at the base of Olympus Mons. Marten had the men line up in an oxygen zone. They actually looked strange without their EVA helmets on. Most had matted hair and dark circles around their eyes.

Marten spoke tersely to them, commending some and giving others Highborn axioms concerning combat. Then he dismissed the men and told them to get some sleep.

As the men filed away Major Diaz strode up and saluted. The major looked as dangerous as ever and his hair, incredibly, was swept back hard into perfect form. Diaz had lost weight, but none of the harshness to his features.

"I will report to the Secretary-General," Diaz said. "I will tell him you are a crafty soldier. I will tell him your courage and quick action saved the commandos from almost certain destruction. I refer to the jets, of course."

Marten waited for the kicker. He didn't have long to wait.

"However, I demand satisfaction from your lieutenant," Diaz said.

"In what form?" Marten asked.

"A duel," Diaz said.

"Are you tired of living?"

Major Diaz stiffened. "Without honor, a man is an animal."

"I ordered Omi to disarm you," Marten said. "Therefore, your desire for satisfaction should lie with me."

"I have no desire to kill a soldier who could teach the

209

commandos useful skills," Diaz said.

"That's something, at least. Major, why not wait for satisfaction until we find out if Martian space defense still stands? If it doesn't, the Planetary Union is going to need each one of us. I know that I want you with me when Social Unity launches drop-troops."

"The weight of honor compels me—"

"Major Diaz," Marten said. "Honor compels you to save your planet. Mars is for the Martians, remember? Honor means that you must forgo your personal desires until the emergency ends. We are free and wish to remain so. As much as I dislike your murder of prisoners, I recognize your combat ability. You are what the Highborn refer to as a *natural soldier*. You're a killer. Omi is also a killer. I've been trained to mimic one. Killers are always rare and always feared by the vast majority of people. It is strategic and tactical stupidity for the killers of one side to eliminate its best warriors. So despite our personal dislike for each other, we need to work together for at least a little while longer."

Diaz's lips had compressed tighter throughout Marten's speech. Now both his hands gripped his belt. Diaz glanced at Omi, who seemed to watch the major indifferently.

"Your words are compelling," Diaz said. "I hadn't realized you possessed honor as well. This changes the issue. ...I will agree to your suggestion if you will cede me one concession."

"What?" Marten asked.

"You must show Secretary-General Chavez Martian dignity."

In surprise, Marten lifted an eyebrow. "You mean I should stand up when he enters a room?"

"Yes."

"...agreed," Marten said, and he held out his hand.

Diaz and he shook. Then the major turned around and hurried away for the door the rest of the men had used.

"You never know," Marten told Omi.

Omi remained silent.

"Come on," Marten said. "I need a shower, and then I want at least an hour's sleep."

***

Marten had his shower, but not the hour nap. He and Omi were summoned to join Secretary-General Chavez in the Olympus Mons command center.

They rode the magnetic lift, and Marten's ears popped twice as he hastily swallowed time after time.

The command room was surprisingly cramped, with a handful of officers clumped around two monitors. A glass partition showed technicians in white lab-coats watching a room-length monitor-board. The board possessed a hundred multicolored lights and displays, a bewildering amount.

Diaz stood in a corner. The major was pale and his eyes staring, as if he'd learned dreadful news. Secretary-General Chavez stood behind the officers around the two monitors. He stared at an unseen point as he sucked heavily on a stimstick. Mildly narcotic red smoke hung in a haze above him like a broken halo.

Marten and Omi moved quietly. The guards outside hadn't even questioned them about their sidearms. Each of them wore long-barreled slug-throwers with explosive bullets. Each carried extra clips. These were deadly close-combat guns. Until now, Marten hadn't used them. Something about the immediate summons had troubled him. A laser pack and rifle would have been more powerful. But Marten didn't own one, and he doubted the guards would have let him shoulder such a weapon.

Omi had asked about the choice.

"Do you notice how empty this place feels?" Marten had asked.

"Now that you mention it," Omi had replied, "yes."

"There's a reason for that," Marten had said. "And I don't think it's a good reason. So we wear the long-barrels."

In the cramped command center no one seemed to notice the difference in armament. The officers were too intent on the monitors. Diaz looked pale enough to faint, and Chavez was lost somewhere in his thoughts.

After two minutes of inattention Marten discreetly cleared his throat.

Major Diaz's head swiveled around. Marten expected a glare. Instead, Diaz looked lost, bewildered.

Chavez took a deep pull on his stimstick. He exhaled through his nostrils as he slowly turned around. Just as slowly, the distant stare departed as he focused on Marten.

"The shock troopers," Chavez said. The Secretary-General coughed until he took another deep drag on his stimstick. He left it between his lips as his arm swung down to his side, as if it was too heavy to hold onto the smoldering stick anymore. "Major Diaz said you eliminated an airfield and its jets."

"At heavy cost, sir," Marten said.

Chavez took another drag as he shook his head. "Frankly, the way events proceed, that was fantastic success. I can only hope to achieve a like result today."

"Your men have fixed the proton beam?" Marten asked.

"Not entirely," Chavez said. With the barest flick of his wrist he indicated the officers, and then the worried-looking technicians in the other room. "They're petrified. So am I, I suppose. Even Major Diaz shows the strain. Juan," he told Diaz, "I told you to flee to New Tijuana. Take the shock troopers with you. Someone must survive this day."

"I stay," Diaz whispered.

"Stubborn fool," Chavez said without any rancor.

"Why are you here if the proton beam doesn't work?" Marten asked.

"'Not entirely' means it works after a fashion," Chavez said. He smiled tiredly. "You don't understand which is entirely understandable. The Battlefleet is arriving at near orbit. Nothing up there belongs to us. It is all theirs. They captured our moons before the main weapons could inflict damage. We have images of incredible space marines, robots, or some deranged form of android. They used stealth tactics and took the moons by surprise. It means they obliterated our satellites with hardly a fight. What kind of domination will they inflict on us if we couldn't even kill a few of them? They will become even more unbearably proud than before. No. We must damage them. We must make them realize they fought a battle. That is why I am here. That is why I have decided to use a half-working proton beam."

"The battle is over?" Marten asked in dismay.

Chavez slowly shook his head. "It will never be over. The

Martians shall always fight. The Planetary Union has given millions of needlers to the workers. Social Unity will face a bloodbath as they attempt to rule us. It will bring fierce retribution. Of this, I am certain. But it is better to die a fighting Martian than to submit to invaders from another planet. Mars is for the Martians."

Marten stared at the officers. All the Martian satellites had been destroyed? That meant the *Mayflower*—

"We're trapped on Mars," Omi whispered into his ear.

"I'm sorry we could not return you to your shuttle, Mr. Kluge. Commander Zapata took the liberty of cracking your code. He fueled your shuttle." Chavez made a vague gesture. "It must be space debris now, likely destroyed. I am sorry."

Marten frowned. Zapata had filled the tanks with propellant?

"You must join your commandos and head for New Tijuana," Chavez said. "If the deep-core mine should erupt or the dynamos overheat, Olympus Mons could receive a new and impressive crater."

"You're going to beam the Battlefleet," Marten said, finally understanding.

"For the future of the Planetary Union, we shall try," Chavez said.

"When is zero-hour?" Marten asked.

A rail-thin officer looked up. "It's as ready as its ever going to be, sir," he told Chavez.

"You have a target?" Chavez asked. There was new life in his voice. He had apparently already forgotten about Marten and Omi.

"A battleship, sir."

"Their flagship?" Chavez asked with savage hope.

"Can't tell that, sir," the officer answered. "But it is one of their heavies."

Secretary-General Chavez removed the stub of the stimstick from his lips and flicked it into a corner. He took two steps closer to the monitor. At a word from the officer others hurried out of the way. Chavez raised his hands. They were clenched tightly into fists. "Kill it!" he rasped. "Show them we still have teeth."

213

A different officer seated at the other monitor began to enter the firing code.

"We must leave," Omi whispered, tugging Marten's arm.

Marten shook his head. He stepped closer to the monitor Chavez viewed. It showed a computer image of an SU battleship. It was near Phobos, which was a little more than 9,000 kilometers away.

A loud and fierce whine began from somewhere in the volcano. It was the dynamos as they converted the deep-core mine heat into proton-beam power. The whine increased as the dynamos pumped the power into the cannon poking out of the giant crater at the top of Olympus Mons. That crater was over 60 kilometers in diameter. The cannon targeted the SU battleship.

Twenty seconds after Secretary-General Chavez gave the order, a deadly-white beam of proton particles lanced upward into the reddish heavens.

22

Several SU warships circled Phobos.

The *Kim Philby* had already collected half the Rebel prisoners. Now that the battle was over, General Fromm planned to use the mine-ship as their supposed *interrogation center*. Toll Seven had exported enough equipment to it so three of Fromm's fellow converts could set up a Web-link. If anybody should ask about the strange equipment the answer would be that it was a new interrogation technique hot from Earth.

The *Alger Hiss* supply ship presently maneuvered for docking. In its cargo-holds were tons of laser coils, merculite missiles, and other items meant to make the moon bristle with functioning weaponry. Now that Social Unity owned Phobos again, there was no time to waste to make it battle-ready for the Highborn.

The Battleship *Ho Chi Minh* protected the others. If the Planetary Union should foolishly attempt to send its last orbitals in a kamikaze raid the *Ho Chi Minh* would obliterate every fighter. The Battleship's captain, however, had not taken any undue chances. The heavy particle-shields were all in place. The shields were 600-meters of asteroid rock surrounding the war-vessel. Before any laser or projectile could touch the Battleship's armored skin it would first have to pierce the 600 meters of rock.

The proton beam from Olympus Mons stabbed into near orbit. The thin Martian atmosphere created some friction, but not enough to dissipate the beam's awful power. The deep-core mine functioned. The Olympus Mons equipment and the jury-rigged emergency coils held for the moment.

The proton beam hit the number six particle-shield of the *Ho Chi Minh*. As amazing as it would seem, the attack caught the Battlefleet cold. They had destroyed all orbital defenses. They knew the proton beam was offline because of the damage it had sustained when the Highborn battleoids had stormed into it six months ago. SU officers also sneered at Martian technical ability, and they had been quite sure the Martians would have not been able to fix the deep-core link in time. Besides, if the proton beam had been online, it should have fired when the Battlefleet first matched orbits with the moons.

It fired now, however. The proton beam smashed into the particle shield, into the asteroid rock.

The proton beam operated differently than the conventional methods of smashing through particle shields. A heavy laser burned through, slagging rock as it chewed deeper and deeper. It also created clouds of dust and hot gas that slowly began dissipating a laser's strength until the gas and dust *drifted* elsewhere or settled. Nuclear-tipped missiles blasted their way in, but by necessity, most of the blast blew in other directions, wasting much of its potential. The proton beam worked on a different principle than either a laser or a nuclear warhead.

A laser was focused light. The proton beam was made up of massed protons, elements of matter, in a deadly and coherent stream. It meant that a proton beam was slower than a laser, but not by much. And at this close of a range—around 9,000 kilometers—that difference was negligible. Unlike a nuclear-tipped missile, where much of the blast was wasted as it blew elsewhere, none of the beam striking the particle shield was wasted. The entire power of the beam smashed against the particle shield. It chewed through fast. Dust, gas, they made no difference. That deadly proton beam stabbed like a rapier.

At long ranges, a beam could only stay on target for a few seconds, usually less. That meant heavy lasers needed to burn away huge sections of a particle shield before those lasers could reach the actual ship underneath the rock. The same was true with nuclear-tipped missiles. The particle shield's length became nearly as important as its depth.

The proton beam made a mockery of the particle shield's length as it bored through the 600 meters of asteroid rock.

The *Ho Chi Minh* had only one true defense against the terrible proton beam, and that was aerosol gels with lead additives. Because the attack caught them cold the aerosols did not begin spraying until the proton beam punched through the particle shield and smashed against the armored hull. By then it was far too late.

The proton beam cut through the layered hull and beamed through the battleship. It hit living quarters, food supplies, missed the bridge by fifty meters, and cut into the coils that supplied power from the fusion core. Air pressure rushed out into the vacuum of space. Klaxons rang. Bulkheads crashed down to minimize damage. Battle-control teams raced to don equipment. Then explosions started. One of those explosions ruptured a coil. It built an overload in the fifth fusion reactor.

By that time the proton beam had chewed through the particle shield in another area. As the damage-control teams sealed their magnetic clamps on their exoskeleton-suits the proton beam smashed through new living quarters, the food processors, a warhead storage area, and then it hit the fusion core itself.

Several of the warheads in storage exploded, pumping heat, radiation and x-rays into the guts of the ship. Ninety-five percent of ship personnel died then. The damage-control parties had greater protection in their suits. Unfortunately for them, most already began to cook like meat in a pot. They died horribly, screaming in agony. A few managed to undo the magnetic clamps and die through vacuum exposure.

The *Ho Chi Minh* did not explode in a ball of fire. In space battles, few such mighty ships died like that. The proton beam had done its task, but the people in Olympus Mons didn't know it yet. So the technicians continued to aim the deadly beam at the dead battleship, repeatedly punching proton holes through the particle shield and into the vessel.

***

Seven minutes after Secretary-General Chavez gave the order the first sections of the enemy battleship began to break apart.

"We killed it, sir!" an officer shouted in glee.

There were wild cheers. Three officers tossed their caps, hitting the ceiling with them. Marten cheered as heartily as the others did.

"Target another ship," Chavez ordered.

"Yes, sir," the targeting officer said. He tapped keys. As the mighty cannon began to move to target a different vessel, something gave between the deep-core mine and the dynamos. The targeting officer barely hit the shutdown key in time. Maybe he'd forgotten something. Maybe he'd overloaded the makeshift coils.

An ominous silence occurred as the dynamos no longer whined with their loud noise. The rooms no longer trembled.

"What's wrong?" Chavez shouted.

A technician in the other room looked through the glass partition. Her face was whiter than Major Diaz's face.

"Somebody tell me what's wrong?" Chavez shouted.

"The coils have melted," the targeting officer whispered.

"Fix them!" Chavez shouted.

The targeting officer began to type keys.

Speakers on the wall crackled into life. "The coils have fused."

"Fix them!" Chavez repeated.

Though the glass partition, the tech nodded. "Yes, sir, we will, in about six weeks."

Stunned silence filled the room. The euphoria of seconds earlier had departed.

"How is this possible?" Chavez asked in a choked voice.

No one answered.

"No," Chavez whispered. "No. We had them."

Major Diaz stepped smartly forward. "If the proton beam is ruined, we must flee. We must all flee."

Marten thought that a wise suggestion.

Secretary-General Chavez looked up ashen-faced. "What's the point of fleeing?"

"The point is the Highborn," Major Diaz said. "They didn't let Social Unity have Mars before. Why will they let Social Unity have Mars now?"

"Must we always rely on others?" Chavez asked

218

dispiritedly.

"No," Marten said, stepping near. "You hit them, sir. You killed a battleship. Now keep your Planetary Union alive by staying alive."

"...I can no longer hide," Chavez said.

Marten laughed harshly. "Is that how you gained your freedom the first time?" He slapped his chest. "I've fought for my freedom all my life. I refused to surrender. You must now refuse to surrender. You did what you could. Now hide among your people and lead the struggle against Social Unity. Keep these vital technicians alive for the next time you rise out of the ashes of defeat. As long as you fight, you haven't lost. But once you surrender your will, sir, everything is over. Do you have the courage to keep on fighting, Mr. Secretary-General?"

Chavez blinked at Marten. Many of the officers stood open-mouthed, looking at the ex-shock trooper.

"They'll send drop-troops to take you alive," Marten told those in the room. "You have to be gone by then. You tried to go down fighting, but the proton beam self-destructed in the middle of your victory. They won't laugh at you now, not with a battleship killed. They'll fear you. Keep them afraid by keeping out of their clutches to fight another grueling guerilla campaign. Never surrender, never, never, never."

"...yes," Chavez said slowly. "There is wisdom in your words."

"Even better," Major Diaz said, "there is fire in his belly."

"Let's go!" Marten shouted. "We likely don't have much time."

***

Marten was more right than he knew. The destruction of the *Ho Chi Minh* sent a shock wave through the Battlefleet. The warship's sudden death caused Blackstone to scream orders.

The *Kim Philby* accelerated at full speed for the planet. Toll Seven had a battle pod nearby and quickly launched it toward Mars. Three other ships maneuvered for a combat drop on Olympus Mons. Even in his anguish, Commodore Blackstone realized they needed that proton beam against the Highborn. With the *Ho Chi Minh's* destruction they needed that beam more than ever. He could have ordered a saturation nuking of the giant volcano. Instead he screamed orders for the volcano's capture, and he screamed to pump out lead aerogels to they didn't lose more ships to that beam.

SU drop-troops and cyborgs donned battlesuits and then climbed into their drop shells. Machines and drop specialists used electric trolleys to roll the drop-shells into firing position. Usually a mass combat-drop from space took days of careful calculations. Precise entry points into the atmosphere were prefigured. Orbital spin, gravity, atmospheric density, wind velocity and other factors were each studied in detail. Today there was no time for that. The selected ships roared for the entry point and then they braked, hard.

The *Kim Philby* was the first to reach the upper atmosphere. It was a mine-laying ship but could second as a drop-assault vessel. At high speed it entered an insertion orbit. Then, like an old-fashioned soldier with a bolt-action rifle, the ship loaded its tube, fired, worked the bolt, chambered another shell and fired. One after another the drop-shells slammed into the thin atmosphere and screamed down at the immensely vast, waiting volcano below.

* * *

OD12 blinked in growing perplexity. She lay in a battlesuit, in a drop-shell, surrounded by combat equipment. That shell was on a conveyer. The conveyer jerked and from somewhere OD12 heard a *BANG!* And her shell trembled.

She knew from a thousand simulations that the *BANG* was from the ship firing a drop-shell at a planet. The shudder came from the same source. What had her perplexed was her luck. Until now, it had all been bad. She would not have been a cyborg unless her luck was horrible. After inserting jacks into the prisoners she had been certain that a new, awful worsening of her fate would soon begin.

It had been difficult these last few hours standing in a roomful of cyborgs. They had all stood motionless and expressionless. None had shown boredom, because likely none of them had been bored. Likely, none of them had possessed stray thoughts. They waited for instructions. Essentially, they had all been dead. No emotions, no boredom, no worry, no

220

questions—they were good cyborgs waiting for Toll Seven. OD12 had stood among them, realizing that she was not a good cyborg. She was a *bad* cyborg, a bored cyborg, full of questions and changing emotions. She had known elation, joy, a chaffing of spirit, depression, and then a growing sense of dread of what would happen next.

She had not wanted to enter Web-Mind. It would immediately know that her internal computer was damaged. Web-Mind would demand a new censor program. It might even demand she be deleted.

That had not happened. Instead she had floated into the *Kim Philby* and waited longer. Then klaxons had wailed, and she and other cyborgs had run to don battlesuits for an attack on Mars.

BANG!

In her drop-shell OD12 jerked nearer the firing tube.

BANG!

Her stomach churned, which should have been impossible. She was a cyborg. *No. I am Osadar Di. I am alive and I am going to escape Web-Mind.*

A metallic clack occurred; the sound was loud and very near. She felt herself lifted and shoved somewhere, and realized she was in the firing tube now. Seconds ticked by.

BANG!

The acceleration was brutal and badly jarred her. She lost her breath. She tried to think. Then weightlessness struck, and everything seemed so peaceful. She knew that she was over the Red Planet.

The beautiful Red Planet, the one I love.

OD12—*no, I am Osadar Di.* Within the drop-shell, Osadar Di grinned. It was hard with her plastic-featured face, but she did it.

She dropped toward Mars, toward Olympus Mons. They were supposed to kill or capture everyone on the volcano and in it. Compared to the attack on the moon, this was going to be a mass drop, with every available cyborg and SU drop-soldier. The volcano had greater mass and size than both the Martian moons combined.

Because she was tougher than humans, her drop-shell fell

221

fast. In a heavy atmosphere like Earth, her shell would have deployed successive chutes to slow her descent. But that made little sense in the thin Martian atmosphere because of lesser friction. Yet there was friction. Her shell pushed the thin Martian air ahead of it. That caused heat. The heat transferred to the shell and might have soon cooked Osadar Di.

The drop-shells were made, however, to shed skin as they heated. The hot skin joined the atmosphere instead of transferring its heat to the deeper skins and eventually to Osadar Di. Inside the shell Osadar felt the skins shedding. It caused her drop-shell to wobble. If it wobbled too much and flipped over, she would be in trouble. Either the pilot of the *Kim Philby* had known what he was doing or more blind luck had helped Osadar. Her shell wobbled. The wobbling increased, and then slowly began to stabilize.

At that point the last skin blew away and Osadar was freefalling toward the giant volcano. She had reached Martian terminal velocity, and that was too fast. She plunged through ice-crystal clouds and saw the vast base of Olympus Mons. She also saw the crater, her objective. Her computer told her she was going to miss the crater by twenty kilometers and land on the volcano's side.

Instead of chutes Osadar Di wore a modified jetpack similar to those worn by Free Earth Corps Hawk Teams. It took constant practice to use jetpacks correctly. Until this moment, Osadar had never used a real jetpack. However she had practiced this type of drop over a hundred times in the Web-Mind simulator. She knew what to do, and she did so now.

She blasted the jetpack to slow her descent. In another life she had been a first-rate pilot. So not only had she trained in the simulator doing this, but in her old life she'd loved this type of work. With the surfacing of her memories and emotions, the love emerged and gave her artistry.

As Olympus Mons raced up toward her, Osadar glanced around. Other cyborgs used their jetpacks. One, however, must have had a wobbling shell that had flipped. That cyborg plunged headfirst toward Mars.

Osadar wondered why the cyborg didn't shift and assume a flying position to work himself upright. Then she wondered if something had happened to his internal computer. Had he regained enough of his old self that he now committed suicide? It was a sad thought, sobering and completely understandable. Not that she would commit suicide. As rotten as life was, she planned to live it to the very end, come what may.

Osadar blasted jetpack air again, using more thrust. The plunging cyborg now used his jetpack, but he used it to speed his descent, not slow it.

That brought a strange elation to Osadar. The Web-Mind could make more than one mistake. Or it was possible for the universe to sustain more than one glitch that went against the cold minds from Neptune. Did it follow therefore that it was possible to defeat Web-Mind and its cyborg soldiers? Osadar found that doubtful. Maybe she should simply be happy with her rebellion and call it a victory.

She thrust again, and had managed to shift nearer the crater.

She would not call it victory, this continued self-awareness. She would strive against Web-Mind's goals. Yes, she would use this piece of good luck, and she would extract every ounce of pleasure from it that she could. Therefore, she must plot to remain free of Web-Mind. The question was how.

Yes… how?

Osadar Di's longish metallic-plastic head twitched within her helmet. She had no more time for conjecture. The suicidal cyborg hit with a splat, becoming a smear on Olympus Mons.

Osadar judged this to a nicety as she examined the vast cannon aimed at the pink sky. At precisely the right moment, she hit the thrust button and held it down. She passed the crater wall until she hit hard, but not as hard as against Phobos. She made a perfect two-point landing. Then she shed the jetpack and lifted a laser carbine. A metallic line from it snaked to a heavy laser-pack on her back. She charged with other landing cyborgs for the entrance to the proton cannon's turret.

23

The cyborgs dropped hard, using jetpacks, shedding them upon landing, bounding for the vast structure that housed the proton-beam cannon.

The human drop-troops used incredibly huge, multiple chutes, which only had minimal effect. They also used jetpacks at the end, although they lacked the cyborgs' skill. Too many of them broke legs, arms, necks or their ribs. Too many of them tore their suits. Their breathers still worked, at least most of the time. But because the Martian atmosphere lacked an ozone layer, their skin would severely burn if exposed to direct sunlight for very long.

The cyborgs moved with insect-like speed. Once inside the volcano, they worked down through the vast network of elevators, levels, rooms and chambers. If a Mars Rebel fired a shot before the cyborgs captured him or her, red laser-beams cut them down. If the Rebel seemed to be in the act of sabotage, he died even faster.

Much lower down in Olympus Mons, Marten, Omi, Major Diaz and Secretary-General Chavez rode a magnetic lift for the skimmer garage. Other military officers rode with them. It was quiet in the lift as each exhausted man was absorbed with his personal sorrow.

They would have been gone long ago, but running the proton beam earlier had burned out more than just a few coils. In many places, the lifts didn't work. In other places, the lack of working lights meant stygian darkness. Olympus Mons was vast. The men had raced through kilometers of empty corridors before finding this operational lift.

The lift now slowed, and the doors swished opened. "Go!" shouted Marten.

The others were exhausted from running. They walked quickly, but none of them ran for their lives.

Omi traded glances with Marten. Then the bullet-headed Korean sidled near. "If we wait too long to escape, we're dead," Omi whispered.

The garage was huge, with a twenty-foot ceiling. It had long ago been blasted out of the volcano, with volcanic pillars instead of concrete stanchions as supports. Crates, equipment, spare parts and tunnel machinery were everywhere. At the far end near the outer doors, almost out of sight, were parked skimmers and other EVA vehicles. The lights were low, and the air was cold.

"We must hurry," Marten told the others.

The thin Martians trotted for five minutes and then slowed back to a fast walk. They had been moving for some time. Most breathed heavily, and despite the cold, sweat soaked their garments.

Far behind them, the lift doors opened.

Omi hissed. Marten turned, and his eyes grew huge.

Able to cover ground many times faster than a human and with extreme stamina, three cyborgs made incredible bounding leaps for the Martians. The three lacked helmets. Their polished metal faces, combined with shiny black plastic and fleshy components, horrified Marten.

"What are those?" Omi whispered.

Marten yanked Omi behind a huge crate. "This way," he whispered. He crawled along the volcanic floor, using crates, machinery and more crates to try to ambush those things.

None of the Martians had looked back. They were too absorbed with their fatigue. Then something must have alerted them. Diaz shouted a warning.

The cyborgs moved fast, and they brought up their arms in a blur. Chugging sounds emitted from their short-barreled tanglers. Glistening black eggs sped at the humans. Sticky tangle-threads webbed individual officers. Shouting hoarsely, the officers thudded hard onto the hanger bay's floor. Two hit their heads, and they were knocked unconscious.

The cyborgs shot another volley of the glistening black tangle-eggs. From hiding, Marten and Omi opened fire. For three seconds their explosive bullets shredded uniforms, metal, plastic and flesh, but the cyborgs kept coming.

"What are they?" Omi shouted.

"Keep firing!" Marten hissed.

Then tangle-eggs caught Marten and Omi, and it was over. One of the cyborgs landed by them, kicked away their long-barrels, and scanned the vast garage.

"Who are you?" Omi asked.

"Silence," the cyborg said.

It dragged Marten and Omi to the others, where two more cyborgs stood.

The computer-like voice reminded Marten of Blake, the Bioram Taw2 that had run his old Tunnel Crawler Six in Sydney, Australian Sector. Marten knew that Blake would have been a cold-hearted killer if given a chance. Maybe it was the same with these horrors.

The cyborgs exchanged glances. One of them bounded away, leaving two of them behind.

The nearest cyborg stood motionless. The second cyborg scanned the garage. It seemed to be searching for something. That cyborg almost seemed agitated. Then it crouched beside the Martian officers.

The first cyborg now watched the second one. "The specimens are secure," the first cyborg said.

"Why are they so emaciated?" the second cyborg asked.

The first cyborg froze. Then its longish head cocked to the left. "Your question... it indicates—" The first cyborg aimed its tangler at the second cyborg. "There is a seventy-eight percent probability that your query stems from emotive reasons. You must immediately head to the rendezvous point and ask for a diagnostic check."

"Yes," the second cyborg said, standing. Then it drew a laser carbine, ducked as a tangle-egg popped from the first cyborg's weapon, and opened fire with the laser.

In moments the first cyborg slumped to the volcanic floor. Blue sparks emitted from its component parts, as if it were a broken machine.

The surviving cyborg aimed the laser carbine at the nearest tangled Martian.

"Wait!" Marten shouted.

The cyborg hesitated. Then it stepped beside Marten, aiming the carbine at him.

"You shot one of your own," Marten said.

"Now I will shoot all of you," the cyborg said.

"You have emotions," Marten said, remembering his talks with the Tunnel Crawler in Sydney. "I understand that. We understand. Leave the others and join us."

"Join?" the cyborg asked. "You would have joined us as cyborgs. But my secret dies with all of you."

Marten licked his lips. Blake the Bio-ram Taw2 had always wanted to be human again. "Help us, and we'll help you become human."

The cyborg stood perfectly still.

"Stay here," Marten said, "and they will find your defect of emotion and expunge it."

"...none can escape," the cyborg said.

"If you free us," Marten said, "we'll flee in skimmers for one of the Martian cities. That way, you can keep your emotions longer."

The cyborg lowered its carbine. Then it unhooked a canister from its belt. It bent before Marten and said, "Turn your head."

Marten did. He heard a hiss, felt mist gently falling on him. Immediately, the tangle-threads lost their binding power. Marten sat up as he tore the threads from him as if they were spider webs.

The cyborg bent before Omi and sprayed more anti-tangle mist.

"Who—" Marten had to moisten his dry mouth. "Do you have a name?"

The cyborg turned its head toward him. It stared at him with such machine indifference that it chilled Marten's blood.

"I am Osadar Di," it said.

"That's a female name," Marten said. "You're a female?"

"I am a woman, yes."

"A woman?" Marten heard himself asking.

"They changed me," the cyborg said in its dreadful voice. "I did not ask them to do it. They kidnapped me from Ice Hauler 49." Maybe the cyborg recognized Marten's incomprehension. "That was in the Neptune System."

Neptune? These horrors are from Neptune? "What about that one?" Marten asked, indicating the dead cyborg.

"All were turned into machines against their will," the cyborg Osadar Di said.

"Kill it," Major Diaz whispered from the floor.

Marten glanced at the major trussed in tangle webs. He ignored the advice. Soon other cyborgs would undoubtedly descend into the garage. The idea of—who had made these things? Marten had never heard of cyborgs. These were not bionic soldiers, but living machines melded with human flesh and brains. It was inhuman. Were they madmen out in the Neptune System?

"Right," Marten said. "You're one of us now. Let's shake on it."

Marten dared to hold out his hand. And he kept himself from wincing in horror as he heard servos whine as the cyborg lifted her hand. They shook, and Marten was chilled again. Could the cyborg have torn off his arm if it—if she—had wanted to?

The cyborg continued spraying the tangled officers. Soon they all raced for the skimmers.

Doom Stars

-1-

Heydrich Hansen seethed with hatred against his fellow neutraloids and against the Highborn. He had a special hatred for Nadia Pravda who had grossly tricked him. But deep in his heart, he hated Marten Kluge the most. Oh, yes, he remembered that awful shock trooper. Everything had gone sour at the Sun-Works Factory the day Marten Kluge and Kang had showed up in his bailiwick at the Pleasure Palace.

Heydrich Hansen wore a strange harness around his blue-tattooed skin. He used to be thin, with sparse hair and slyly, cruel features. He had stark muscles now, with almost no body-fat. They were sinewy muscles, as hard as iron when he flexed, which was often. His blue-tattooed face had become harsher and thinner, and his eyes often bulged with the fierceness of his emotions.

He craved specialty foods and ate with animal gusto. Sometimes, secretions in his new body gave him abnormal speed and strength. Sometimes, post-hypnotic commands drove him to raging bloodlust. Then he killed normal humans for practice.

Now was one of those times. Hansen prowled through narrow corridors aboard the *Julius Caesar,* a Doom Star headed for Mars. He gripped a stun gun and bore a shock rod on his hip. Other neutraloids moved through other corridors. A headset like a sweatband was around his forehead. He could speak into a mike and had an implant in his right ear. They were supposed to coordinate their efforts and drive the ordinary humans into the main exercise chamber.

Unlike his old existence, Hansen now moved with silky grace. The Doom Star presently accelerated at one-G. It traveled to Mars, he had overheard. This was a Highborn fleet action. Hansen didn't care anything about that. Ever since they had gelded him, tattooed his entire body, and surgically put wonder-glands into him, his thoughts had metamorphosed. He raged with primitive desires that involved crushing, slashing, kicking, biting and stabbing.

He snarled, baring his teeth at a camera in the corner. The Training Master watched them. The Training Master graded their worth.

Hansen trembled with suppressed rage. He wanted to blow the camera away. He wanted to kill the Training Master, spread out his intestines, and urinate over them. Something pounded in his head then—it was the post-hypnotic commands.

"I know," he hissed in a soft, high-pitched voice. "I know. Kill the damn humans."

Hansen groaned as punishment shocks zapped him. He yearned to rip off the harness. He had done that once, and he had faced horrible punishments afterward. His free hand flexed with his yearning. Then he endured the *zap, zap, zapping* that made him twitch with agony.

"You must capture the humans, Neutraloid Hansen," he heard from the implant in his ear. "Not kill, but capture. There is a subtle difference."

"Yes, Master," snarled Hansen, as he hunched his blue-tattooed shoulders. He knew the Training Master mocked him. All Highborn did. Learning to answer to the Highborn had taken weeks of grueling punishment and practice. Learning not to tiptoe at night and strangle fellow neutraloids, to awaken in the morning to hideous punishment shocks... that, too, had taken time.

Hansen chuckled evilly as he hunched his head. He hadn't really learned not to strangle neutraloids. Those he had choked to death were Ervil and the others, the ones who had hated him worse than he had hated them. He had simply endured the Highborn shocks, the whippings and the slaps in the face until his old friend Ervil and the others were all dead. Only then had Hansen felt safe enough to sleep at night. The newer neutraloids feared him because they had seen and had learned that Heydrich Hansen always got his revenge.

He'd heard one of the Masters say once that newer neutraloids were better because they could control their emotions to a higher degree. The Masters worked to *improve* their surgically enhanced, hypnotically trained and always castrated berserkers.

Hansen stiffened and sniffed the air. A human was ahead of him. Hansen began to tremble in anticipation of killing the human. His head hurt with a stabbing pain between the eyes. He was supposed to call now and report to the others. Hansen was supposed to *coordinate* his actions.

"Human," he whispered softly into his mike.

"What?" another neutraloid asked, the sound coming from the ear-implant.

"Human!" Hansen shouted into his mike. He roared with rage, sprinting down the corridor. Ahead, a thin man leaped up with a yelp from behind a bulkhead. The human had a gun. With a shaking arm, the human aimed at Hansen. Hansen hurled his stun gun at the human. Wide-eyed, the human watched the gun. He watched it hit the deck with a clatter and slide. The human blinked stupidly, and then he must have remembered Hansen. He looked up, aimed and fired. The bullet grazed Hansen's ribs with a fiery pain. Shouting in a strangely high-pitched voice, Hansen closed the final distance. He didn't pull out his shock rod. He simply leaped on the human, knocking him to the floor. Then he grabbed the man's head.

"No, no!" the human pleaded.

"Die!" Hansen screamed, and he twisted with all his newfound strength, snapping the neck. Then he laughed with joyous mockery as the dying human jerked and thrashed under him.

Immediately, punishment shocks zapped from the straps Hansen wore. They zapped with numbing strength, toppling Hansen, soon rendering him unconscious.

Hansen awoke strapped to a table. The rest of the neutraloids stood there, glowering at him, muttering and shuffling their feet. Hansen turned his head. On the opposite side of the table towered the Lot 6 Highborn, the Training Master.

"You failed to use your stun gun, Neutraloid Hansen," the Training Master said.

"It was a stinking human," Hansen replied.

"Wrong answer," the Highborn said, and he brushed Hansen with a shock rod.

The pain made Hansen's muscles leap up starkly as he squealed with agony, jerking against the restraints.

"You failed to use your stun gun, Hansen," the Training Master repeated.

"…I'm sorry, Master. I forgot."

The shock rod brushed Hansen again. "Lying won't help you, Neutraloid."

"…master, the bloodlust came over me. I don't know how to stop from using my hands."

The Highborn studied him and finally addressed the others. "Listen closely. Hansen is foolish. He must learn control. If he fails to learn control, he will learn pain. Like this." And the Highborn brushed his body seven times, even shocking the mutilated genital area.

Hansen's voice was hoarse from screaming as he writhed on the training table.

"Soon we will be at Mars," the Highborn said calmly. "Then you will face armed soldiers. You must use weapons, or you will die. You will not throw them away or forget them. That is bad, very bad. Learn the lessons now, yes?"

"Yes," the others muttered sullenly.

The Highborn smiled at them. Then he smiled down at Hansen. "You are worse than premen. You are animals. But even animals must serve the New Order. Next time you fail, Hansen, I will personally cut out your intestines and make a noose to choke you to death. Do you understand?"

"Yes, Master," Hansen wheedled, trying desperately to sound contrite. But in his heart, in his raging soul, he yearned to kill the Highborn, all of them, and piss on their corpses.

2

From the files of Grand Admiral Cassius: Selected memorandums and notes. From: August 7 to August 11, 2351.

August 7

The Julius Caesar's *Training Master, Recommendation to Admiral Cassius:*

After months of intensive training, I have reached what I must concede as now unalterable opinions concerning the Neutraloids. The creatures possess commendable berserker qualities, and their reaction times and strength compare favorably to the premen. However, they lack sustained self-control. Only a few among them—what I've come to consider as Neutraloid geniuses—have the minimal ability to operate guns or use vibroknives. No amount of hypnotic commands has changed this inability. Higher technical equipment operation is beyond their present capabilities.

There has been talk of lessening the hate-conditioning. But I doubt that will alter the situation. Such conditioning gives them their only redeeming quality: berserker rage against the universe. On a primitive planet, such creatures would have innate terror value. On the technological battlefield, however, they are a liability.

Therefore, it is my stated view that for the present Mars Campaign, that each Doom Star's complement of Neutraloids should be destroyed.

August 7

From Grand Admiral Cassius:

Training Master, *Julius Caesar*, I am dissatisfied with your recommendation. I scanned the attached report on your training methods. Let me remind you of the obvious. The Neutraloids are clay in your hands. They are beasts. Beasts react to both pleasure and pain. Heighten them in the necessary quantities until the achieved result is obtained.

August 8

From Training Master, Julius Caesar:

All Highborn stand in awe of your military achievements, Grand Admiral. The lesser races quiver at the mention of your name. Your strategic and tactical insights are like rare wine, consumed at the risk of intoxication.

However, regarding the Neutraloids, they are a risk to ship personnel. Fear of us only minimally restrains their hatred, their feral desire to kill us. The greatest battle of the war approaches. I consider the possibility of their running loose, in the unforeseen event of a Doom Star sustaining hits, as an unneeded danger. Respectfully, Grand Admiral, my recommendation stands.

August 8

From Grand Admiral Cassius:

Your literary skills left me cold, Training Master. Your fawning praise only served to emphasize your inability to obey my orders.

All that said, your recommendation is noted and recorded. Cage your beasts so they do not run loose during battle. In the unlikely event of serious Doom Star damage, you have permission to kill the beasts.

Let me point out, however, that their strategic and tactical value does not lie as shipboard marines. The Praetor's desire to replace premen shock-troopers with Neutraloids is an unqualified failure. You have already pointed out, Training Master, that their use as terror troops is their sole strength. On your recommendation, their combat role has changed. In the remaining time left you, retrain your animals as terror troops. They will be inserted as needed into underground Martian cities, to help create panic so the Rebel populace will gratefully accept Highborn security forces to restore order.

August 8

From Training Master, Julius Caesar:

Please allow me to say, Grand Admiral, that this is a precise decision. It is the perfect use of gravely flawed creatures. I have already reevaluated my training tactics. As terror troops, especially against poorly armed premen, the Neutraloids will excel. I can almost pity the Martians.

August 9

Top Secret Memorandum: The Grand Admiral's Strategic Assessment for the Mars Campaign:

The critical battle for the Inner Planets is about to take place. I refer to the finding, fixing, and the annihilation of the Social Unity Space Fleet. As long as Social Unity possesses a credible Battlefleet, we must garrison each planet with strong space forces. That weakens us at the critical points of military conflict.

In order to put overwhelming strength at the critical point, I deemed it necessary to coax Social Unity to fix its space forces at one locale. Then I ensured their hardened resolve to defend their conquest. The premen will need this resolve as they see the *Julius Caesar, Hannibal Barca* and the *Napoleon Bonaparte* majestically head for Mars, the place of their recent conquest.

Some have questioned this overwhelming display of force, the use of *three* Doom Stars to annihilate the premen Battlefleet.

Firstly, let me add that more than three Doom Stars head to Mars to inflict this punishing defeat. Concerning that, the individual admirals will soon learn the extended details.

Secondly, too often in wars past, commanders have tried to maintain strength in all areas of conflict in order to hold onto all territorial gains. That is a strategic error of the first order. One of the most *fundamental* rules of war is that battles entail risk. A corresponding maxim is that one can never be too strong at the point of decision. The Mars Campaign will be our point of decision. Therefore, we cannot be too strong in our head-to-head fleet battle.

Thirdly, this gathering of Highborn strength into one point means a lessening of Highborn strength in other important areas. I have ordered the Doom Star from Venus and the last Doom Star remaining at the Sun-Works Factory to immediately head for the Earth System. The space platforms around Venus will continue to harass the enemy. The defenses of the Sun Works are in good repair, especially in lieu of the fact that the SU Battlefleet is orbiting Mars. The critical junctions at this point are firstly to maintain control of the Earth System, secondly the Sun-Works Factory and lastly Venus. To gain massive strength for Mars, we are accepting a possibly dangerous lowering of strength at Venus first and then the Sun-Works Factory second. That is a risk. But it is a risk we must accept in order to gain the crushing victory needed at the point of maximum gain.

Fourthly, as superior as Highborn innately are to the inferior premen, I urge none to think this victory is preordained. Nothing in this universe is free. Few things die willingly. We are two million supermen among thirty-eight billion, seething, hating and fearing subhumans. They possess courage, stamina and cunning. They will fight. They will have obtained a secret weapon, and they will have devised clever tactical dispositions.

Fifthly and lastly, we are the Highborn. We are born to conquer and born to rule. It is our burden to bring order and rationality to the Solar System. This is the critical fight for that rule. Once the Inner Planets are ours, we shall expand throughout the Solar System, and in time seed the stars. This test of our valor, our resolve, guile and brilliance will go down as the most glorious feat of arms in the annals of military history.

Because of that, I have decided to lead the fight in person. The Second Battle of Far-Mars orbit saw my elevation to supreme command among the Highborn. Social Unity and the Martian Planetary Union have fought the Third Battle of Mars Orbit. In a few weeks' time will begin the last battle for Mars Orbit. I expect nothing but the best from all of you, which means the best that anyone can give in this chaotic Solar System.

August 10
From the Praetor:
I have two questions, Grand Admiral. When will you order the breakout? We sicken and die at this miserable orbit around the Sun. I have read your memorandum and seen the tactical displays you broadcast. Three Doom Stars accelerate at a leisurely pace for Mars. We groan here. We suffer intensely, while the rest of you float in lazy serenity. That is intolerable.

My second question is this: do you deliberately conceal the use of the *Thutmosis III*? Do you deliberately attempt to conceal our glory? We die here in order to achieve massive victory for the Highborn. It is only right that you broadcast our role. This is insufferable, Grand Admiral. If I did not know you better, I would consider this treachery against a possible rival for high command.

August 10
From the Grand Admiral:
My dear Praetor, your paranoid ranting shows me that you and your gallant crew are under fierce stress. A lesser Highborn could not have endured what you have. I endure these slurs against my character out of sympathy for your plight, and for your willingness to have put yourself in harm's way for the good of our united greatness.

I have kept your role secret out of dire need. Social Unity spies are clever and numerous. Premen nature dictates their slyness. Spies are sly. Therefore they excel at the nefarious game.

Rest assured that my records and diary have within them a constant stream of wonderment regarding your suffering.

Let me add this, and I hope its importance sinks in, Praetor. A surprise always has greater effect when it is sprung suddenly and completely. That few know about your hazardous duty and the deadliness of the *Thutmosis III* will only help them remember your deeds when they suddenly appear. It will galvanize the Highborn. Your name will sprout from every lip.

Highborn will ask questions, wanting to know more about you.

I applaud you, Praetor. Please, keep your paranoia in check a few more hours. Then I shall order the breakout. Then you will fly for Mars at terrific velocity and inflict in the next few weeks, punishing, even horrific damage to the enemy.

All Hail the Praetor!

August 11
From the Praetor:
We sicken and die and you spout platitudes. Order us out now. End this bitter existence.

Let me also add this: I have recorded our conversations and will hold you to every golden promise.

August 11
From the Grand Admiral:
I have glorious news, my dearest Praetor. Begin breakout procedure now, and head for a flyby of Mars.

I, too, have recorded these messages and I, too, will gladly play them for all to see what noble deeds you have performed. From every Highborn everywhere, I wish you the greatest luck. Kill the enemy, Praetor, and win the laurels you so richly deserve.

3

Several weeks after the victory of the SU versus the Rebels in near-Mars orbit, Commodore Blackstone yearned to rub his tired eyes. He floated at the end of a docking tube. He wore a vacc-suit as a precaution, with a bubble helmet. He had just completed a whirlwind tour of Deimos, Phobos and each of the major warships of the Battlefleet. A bit of good luck had occurred as another straggling battleship had joined them a week ago, replacing the lost *Ho Chi Minh*. Unfortunately, the straggling ship was in a terrible state of repair.

He now had eleven battlewagons of the *Zhukov*-class, big ships with immense firepower and the heaviest particle-shields of any known spacecraft, including Doom Stars. Until the construction of the first Doom Star, the *Zhukov*-class battlewagon had been the largest and deadliest spacecraft in the Solar System. Once, there had been many more than a mere eleven of them. The First Battle of Deep Mars Orbit in 2337 against the Mars Planetary Union and the Jupiter Confederation had seen the death of too many SU battleships. Twelve years later, at the beginning of what had originally been known as the *Highborn Rebellion*, had seen the worst slaughter of battleships. Then the Doom Stars had turned on fellow fleet vessels, destroying them before fleet personnel knew they were in a war to the death.

Blackstone shook his head. Past glories were best forgotten. Eleven *Zhukov*-class battleships were still a powerful concentration of fleet units. They were the heart of his Battlefleet. *En masse*, and while their particle-shields held, they could dare match Doom Stars in a slugfest. To complement the battlewagons, he had nine missile-ships. Each of them was equally as large as a battleship. But missile-ships by nature were raiding vessels, not stand-up spacecraft to smash through the guts of an enemy fleet. Heavy lasers beamed at the speed of light, approximately 300,000 kilometers per second. Missiles and drones traveled at a tiny fraction of that speed. Thus a missile-ship usually launched drones and missiles and then hurried elsewhere, monitoring the battle from a safe distance.

The Highborn had been particularly adept at luring the remaining SU missile-ships into traps and obliterating them. It was the reason the Battlefleet only had nine.

The ECM vessels, the troop transports, the orbital launch ships, the minelayers, the stealth ships and the recon vessels and probes added another twenty-eight spacecraft to the Battlefleet. Hawthorne's Earth convoy added another forty-nine. Each of the transports became decoy vessels as the supplies in their cargo-holds poured into the warships and onto the two moons.

Within his bubble helmet, Commodore Blackstone grinned tightly. Phobos and Deimos were going to be the first grim surprise for the Highborn. General Fromm's people worked overtime, massing the moons with point-defense emplacements, merculite missiles and repairing every heavy-laser cannon. There were also extra laser cannons being added, a new one every three days.

These past weeks since the victory over Martian space defenses, General Fromm's people had swarmed the moons. Social Unity lacked Doom Stars. Yet as big as a Doom Star was, even two tiny moons like Phobos and Deimos dwarfed them. Fromm's sweating and harried technicians slept three hours a cycle. They were hyped with stimulant so they worked like automatons. Unfortunately, the moons had precise and known orbits, which weakened their combat uses. But they had much greater mass then the Doom Stars and could theoretically absorb much more punishment. If given enough time, they would become bristling fortresses.

From his original plan, Supreme Commander Hawthorne's

meant to use the moons to break the Doom Stars. Blackstone would cluster the Battlefleet around the fortress moons. If the Doom Stars went after the Battlefleet first, the moons would pound the enemy craft. If the Doom Stars tried to take out the moons first, the Battlefleet would maneuver and overwhelm each Doom Star one at a time.

Within his helmet, Commodore Blackstone's grin slipped. The problem with the grand plan was it required time to set up.

The Highborn likely had communication with the Mars Rebels. The past few weeks had surely proven that. As the Battlefleet had mopped up Martian space resistance, it was now known that the gargantuan warships had circled the Earth many times, building up velocity. Even as the drop-troops and cyborgs had captured Olympus Mons, three Doom Stars had broken out of Earth's orbit and accelerated toward the Red Planet.

Radar and teleoptic scopes had discovered that the Doom Stars no longer accelerated, but used their velocity to travel the 100-million kilometers between Mars and Earth that presently separated the two. The enemy had traveled three weeks, and at present speeds could pass Mars in a flyby in four more weeks. It was more than possible, however, that the Highborn planned to decelerate hard to match orbits with Mars. In that case, the Highborn million-kilometer ranged lasers would need another four and a half weeks before they could reach the SU space defenses.

Blackstone thought carefully. If the Highborn planned a flyby, wouldn't the Doom Stars continue to accelerate to reach here even faster? A flyby seemed unlikely, however, for the simple reason that it would take the Highborn much too long to decelerate later and head back for Mars or Earth. If the Doom Stars sped past the Red Planet in a flyby, it might behoove Social Unity to stab with every spaceship it had for Earth and drive off whatever Doom Star defended the mother planet.

Blackstone's gloved fingers twitched with his impatience for the hatch to pressurize.

Would the Highborn begin to decelerate soon? Would it be four weeks, or four and a half weeks, until the battle started? This battle would likely decide the fate of the Solar System.

Would it be a slugfest as Supreme Commander Hawthorne and Toll Seven envisioned, or would the Highborn attempt something completely different that would confound everyone?

Blackstone chewed the inside of his cheek. Three Doom Stars filled with Highborn—even with two bristling moons and nearly four-fifths of the remaining SU war-fleet at his disposal, and with a planetary proton beam—

They had to get the proton beam online! That beam was amazingly deadly. The brutal and astonishingly quick death of the *Ho Chi Minh* had proved the planetary proton-beam's worth.

Eleven battlewagons, two fortress moons, a massive support fleet and sundry other vessels could still lose to three Doom Stars. That's what made the proton beam so important. Yet they could only use it at near orbit. Its range was so pathetically short in space combat terms. That's why they would need Toll Seven's battle pods and stealth packs. Their planned use was a revolutionary tactic, and the cyborgs were perhaps the only troops able to pull it off.

Blackstone shook his head. Much depended on the Highborn. Would they use their long-range lasers and slowly devour everything in Mars orbit? At present, Social Unity lacked a million-kilometer weapon. Therefore, the Doom Stars standing off seemed like the wisest enemy strategy. It seemed like it at first blush, but it wasn't. The Earth convoy fleet had brought enough prismatic crystals to absorb extended laser fire, and the plants on Mars churned out more and more defensive crystals. If the Highborn remained at long laser range, it would give them extra time to fix the moons and bring online their own million-kilometer ranged lasers.

The Highborn were impossibly clever concerning tactics and strategy. That meant the three Doom Stars might bear into close orbit, using prismatic crystals and aerosol-gel screens to shield them. Three Doom Stars massed together, all pouring laser fire at one target at a time, chewing through everything fast and annihilating ship after ship—

Sweat prickled Blackstone's face. He hoped Supreme Commander Hawthorne knew what he was doing. Was this all simply a mad gamble? Were the Highborn invincible? It made

Blackstone's stomach churn just thinking about it.

Commodore Blackstone finally heard hisses from the other side of the hatch. A green light flashed. With a gloved hand, he touched the switch. The hatch opened, and he climbed through into a pressure chamber with his security detail following. They waited, and soon the inner hatch slid open. Blackstone led the way into a larger chamber with vacc-suit racks and emergency breathing masks dangling from hooks.

He noticed Commissar Kursk. She stood with her arms crossed, and tapped the toe of her jackbooted foot.

As Blackstone unclasped his helmet, he wondered idly what it would be like to pull off her cap and muss up her hair. Then he would grab her face and force a passionate kiss on her. It was the least he could do before he died in battle. A man deserved a woman before he risked his life for victory.

"Ah, breathable air," Blackstone said. He pitched the helmet to one of his security detail. Then he rubbed his eyes. That felt so good. He was so tired. His ex-wife used to rub his shoulders at times like this. Would Commissar Kursk consent to rub his shoulders?

"Where have you been?" she snapped. She sounded angrier than usual. Now that he looked, he noticed she glowered.

Blackstone sighed. He needed a nap, not an angry PHC Commissar. "Will you walk me to my quarters?" he asked.

"I need to speak to you now."

"This is hardly the place. I'm tired. I've been shuttling back and forth for the past four days and now I need—"

"Did you grant Toll Seven the use of Olympus Mons for his continued interrogations?" Kursk asked.

Blackstone stared at her. Why did it always have to be about Toll Seven? Irritated, he shrugged.

"The proton beam is a primary weapon," Kursk said. "Now you've installed the cyborgs there and have effectively given them control of it. What if the cyborgs decide to blackmail us at the critical moment?"

Blackstone became cross. "We are all part of Social Unity. That's why they won't. They need us." He wondered if that was true. Did the cyborgs need anybody? "I desperately need a nap, Commissar. I'm exhausted. So what I'm going to do

244

now—"

"If you're wise, you'll head straight to Olympus Mons with a regiment of drop-troops," she said.

Couldn't she even let him finish a sentence? "I'm not drop trained," he said tonelessly.

"Use fast shuttles," she said.

Blackstone glanced at his security chief. The man stonily stared into space. Blackstone rubbed his neck. He hated these vacc-suits. He hated living in a battleship for months on end. Three weeks ago, they had won a brisk battle and now three Doom Stars headed for Mars. He didn't have time for the commissar's imaginary worries.

"I'm taking a nap," he said. "Write a report if you think it's so important."

She took a step closer, and now worry replaced her anger. "Toll Seven has become too secretive. He's doing something down there that—"

"Did you send operatives to Olympus Mons? I know you were talking about it."

"...I did."

"And?" he prompted.

Commissar Kursk licked her lips.

Blackstone found it stimulating. He wished she would do that under more pleasing circumstances. Perhaps it was time to arrange that.

"My operatives have reported that everything is well," she said.

A dull headache throbbed into existence so Blackstone rubbed his eyes again. Kursk was unhinged concerning the cyborgs. He hated them, too. But the Battlefleet had to use what fate had given them. He attempted a smile as he said, "Don't tell me you think Toll Seven has suborned your best operatives."

"Maybe I shouldn't think that," she said, "But I do. They're reports... there was something odd about them that I can't quite decipher."

"Do you want to go down to Mars yourself?" he asked.

Fear put lines on her face. Blackstone wondered about her age, if she was older than he suspected.

"...I'd only go down with a full regiment of your best combat troops," she said.

Commodore Blackstone raised his eyebrows. "The cyborgs are our best hope for victory against the Highborn. So I hardly think that now is the time to anger Toll Seven. I'm going to take a nap. Once I'm awake, talk to me again. Until then, I can't even think straight."

Blackstone floated past her, and the security detail followed. He heard her garments rustle as she turned, probably to watch him. He felt her eyes on him and wished it were her hands running over his skin. He grinned. It felt good to have put her in her place. Maybe he needed to do it more often.

***

Down on Mars within Olympus Mons, Toll Seven oversaw the secret installation of a mass cyborg-converter. Most of the equipment had come down the past weeks in heavy orbital shuttles under General Fromm's command. During the massive shuttle flights between the warships and the cargo-carrying vessels from Earth, the converter equipment had been carefully ferried from several battle pods and to the *Alger Hiss*. The entirety of that crew was finally jacked into Web-Mind. Their chaotic minds had been systematically reprogrammed to the extent free bio-forms could retain such programming.

Toll Seven paced along the length of the converter. It was in a vast garage, deep inside the volcano, near the bottom. Heaters labored to raise the temperature to an even 90 degrees Fahrenheit. Conversion demanded a warm environment. Cyborgs worked like ants over the garage-sized machine, using drills, sonic screwdrivers, laser-welders, and micro computing-cubes. It created a bedlam of electronic whirls, air-compressor hisses, clacks and metallic clangs.

Toll Seven had already rerouted the magnetic lifts that led to this garage. No one could enter the area without a complex code-sequence given at cyborg speeds.

The working cyborgs never looked up to watch him or each other. Each was controlled by preprogramming inserted by Web-Mind. They moved fast and with cyborg precision, and still this was taking too long.

Toll Seven used a visual-imaging handscanner, checking

the calibration of delicate machinery. He needed more cyborgs, and he needed them now. Drop assaulting the volcano had damaged far too many prime units. He hadn't even recovered all of them yet. OD12 was still missing and so was KR3. Reviewing Web-Mind, he suspected that KR3 might have committed self-destruction. It was irritating to realize, but such anomalies happened.

Toll Seven used inner nanonics to dump chemicals into his brain's irritation centers. The bio-chemicals struggled to dampen his unhappiness. He needed clean concentration more than ever. The great enemy came: the Highborn, the genetic super-soldiers. They moved three of the hated Doom Stars toward Mars. The giant spacecraft were the ultimate in warship design and construction. Web-Mind had calculated for two, but had accepted the possibility of three.

This was the delicate moment. Web-Mind still needed Social Unity, or more precisely, Social Unity's fleet. It wasn't possible to suborn the rest of the Battlefleet in time. The Highborn came on too quickly, and he hadn't brought enough neck-jacks, nor set up a facility yet to make new ones. It would have been so much easier if they could have reached the Earth System and landed amongst the Homo sapiens. With PHC eager for help, it would have been simplicity to set up a processing center in one of the vast cities. In several months, hundreds of thousands and maybe even millions of cyborgs could have emerged from that city and swarmed the Eden planet.

This was the critical juncture. He had a foothold on Mars, but he lacked a large populace to convert. He would have to visit the Olympus Mons prisoners again and weed out the culls, those too damaged to convert. Once the Highborn threat had been dealt with, however, then it would be time to assist Social Unity re-conquering the Martian underground cities. Web-Mind would choose a city and begin turning the masses into cyborgs.

Toll Seven studied the handscanner. He turned around and took several steps back. He adjusted the scanner. The skin-chopper with its many blades that removed human epidermis— ah, he saw the problem. He had misplaced a decimal in his configurations. He adjusted and reread the scanner. Then he continued down the line.

He needed cyborgs down here, and he needed them in space, ready to implement the stealth-attack tactic that would win them the Battle for Mars. If only there was some manner to speed up converter construction—but there wasn't now. Later—

His inner nanonics dumped more chemicals, keeping stress out of his system. He needed to send a message to Earth soon, to Chief Yezhov of Political Harmony Corps. That particular Homo sapien had been invaluable with his warning. The original ploy to assassinate James Hawthorne had not only failed, but had also alerted the general to the real danger. If not for Yezhov's timely lightguide message—

Toll Seven halted, and his silver eyeballs swiveled in their plastic sockets. Reminiscing would not improve his efficiency. He must concentrate and extract every ounce of effort from himself during these critical weeks.

Against the Highborn—

Toll Seven longed to plug into Web-Mind and reconfigure the statistics one more time. He would have to use the half-cyborgs, the ones converted in his command pod. It was yet another risk in this daring stab for Solar System-wide conquest. With three Doom Stars approaching, the odds were 62.34 percent in cyborg favor.

Those odds would fall fifteen points, however, if the bio-forms of the Battlefleet discovered that key Homo sapiens had been jacked into the Web-Mind. If only he could capture Commissar Kursk, or even better, Commodore Blackstone. The time might come, but so far, they had each proved too cautious by training or by instinct. They would soon make an error, however, for that was the way of free bio-forms. Once he gained control over those two, the odds for space-battle victory would increase another 3.22 percentage points.

4

Marten Kluge felt trapped and was depressed, as if he had never escaped out of the punishment tube in Sydney, Australian Sector. It felt as if the blue water still gushed over his head as he pumped and pumped the red handle.

He had lived as a meaningless cipher in an underground megalopolis on Earth. Now he lived again in a sprawling subterranean city, but this time on Mars. Only this time the city was a titanic slum compared to Sydney.

A little over three weeks ago, they had skimmed from Olympus Mons and had made it to New Tijuana, 343 kilometers away. That was much too near the giant volcano, too near the terrifying nest of cyborgs.

Marten tightened his back muscles so they wouldn't quiver. He and Omi were in an underground firing-range, practicing with genuine Gauss needlers. Others of his commando troop practiced here. Secretary-General Chavez had given him permanent command of them.

Marten hefted what Major Diaz had called *a combat needler*. It was bulky, but light. He suspected it would prove useless against cyborgs or battle-armored drop-troops. Marten settled a pair of goggles over his eyes, lifted the needler and sighted the human-shaped target one hundred feet away. He fired a burst, listening to the cracks of noise and listening to all the other cracks from the other compartmentalized lanes. The hit area glowed red, showing dots on the target's forehead.

"Let me try," Omi said.

With his thumb, Marten flicked the safety, set down the

weapon and stepped back. Omi picked it up and fired burst after burst. The glows showed in the head, the chest and in the genital area. When the needler clicked empty, Omi slammed in another clip and methodically emptied it, too. He picked up a third clip.

"That will do for now," Marten said, putting a hand on Omi's shoulder.

Omi whirled around, and there was something dangerous in his dark eyes. That something settled down as Omi seemed to realize who touched him and where he was.

"It's getting to you, too, eh?" Marten asked.

Omi took a deeper breath than normal and gave a minimal shrug. "Is this why we escaped the Highborn?"

"Meaning?"

"To die on Mars?" Omi asked. "It's only a matter of time before they unleash those cyborgs on us."

"Right," Marten said. It was as if Omi's words had flipped a switch in him. Marten knew what he had to do. He'd been playing the long shot for a long time now. Until they were free of the Inner Planets, there was no sense in trying to play it safe.

"You've finally thought of something," Omi said.

"What gives you that idea?"

Omi made a softly deprecating noise. "I've seen that look on your face before. You're psyching up to charge through a wall. But whatever you're planning, I'm in."

"Good," Marten said. "I'm going to have a word with Major Diaz. Then we're off to see Chavez."

***

Major Diaz continued running the commando troop through the target-practicing drills. In the lobby, Marten and Omi donned bulky spylo-jackets and hurried onto the cold street.

There were on the tenth city-level of New Tijuana. Instead of high-arching levels with bright sunlamps and well-modulated temperatures like Sydney, the Martian city had a claustrophobically low ceiling a mere twenty feet high. Many of the glass buildings reached that height, making it seem even more cramped. Instead of sunlamps on the ceiling to simulate sunlight, streetlamps provided dim lighting. Worst of all, both men could see their breath as the cold seeped into their bones.

Martian children ran screaming past. They wore sythi-woolen caps, spylo jackets and ragged shoes. They chased a bouncing ball, and theirs were the only bright faces. The adults all looked haggard, were amazingly thin and moved with slouched shoulders. They all shuffled out of Marten's way and avoided making eye-contact, treating him as if he were some escaped beast.

Omi had complained before that wherever he went, he felt eyes staring into his back like needles.

The Red Planet was closer to Luna's density than to Earth's density. What it came down to was that Mars lacked a large molten core like Earth's. It also lacked the richness in metallic ores. Although it was a shorter distance to drill a deep-core mine here, the type of planetary mantle and other factors had mandated against planet-deep drilling. The Social Unity government had never granted the necessary funds for such work, too. Thus the Martian cities used nuclear fusion plants to power everything. That meant they needed sufficient fissionable ores to feed the hungry reactors. That meant mines, and in the past, it had meant importing massively from the Jupiter Confederation. Mars also lacked sufficient water. The Jupiter cartels and the Martian Water Corporation had combined to scour the Jupiter System for ice asteroids and to import from Saturn. Saturn's rings contained a treasure in movable ice, one that had been mined for decades.

These and other factors had contributed to Martian squalor, at least in Earth terms. Marten felt constricted in New Tijuana and at times found it difficult to breathe. Until reaching New Tijuana, Marten and Omi had received a false impression about Mars. As Marten had said, "We only saw the best, the military people and the defense facilities."

With fusion plants instead of deep-core mines, and the need to import water and the struggling food domes, the Martian economy wavered on permanent disaster. Likely, the constant rebellion had heavily contributed to that. Too many glass buildings in New Tijuana had blast holes that had never been repaired.

"I'd hate to see the slums here," Omi had said their first

day down.

"Mars is the slum of Inner Planets," had been Marten's observation.

The two ex-shock troopers now showed their special passes to the elevator police and rode a lift up two levels. Then the lift stopped, and police in black-visored helmets asked them to step out. Levels One through Seven were the best lit and the best heated. They contained the government buildings and the homes for the highest ranked in the Planetary Union.

Only after placing a call through to the Secretary-General's office did the police grudgingly let them enter the prized levels.

Marten might have grumbled to Omi about it, but both of them knew the lifts were monitored. They knew because Major Diaz had warned them about it. Soon the two hurried down a cleaner street. And here, all the broken streetlamps and buildings had been fixed. In time, Marten and Omi waited in a plush office, each half-sunken in a soft chair.

A little over three weeks ago, they had fled from Olympus Mons with the cyborg in their skimmer. None of them had trusted her, if such a thing could be called female. Marten had used several opportunities to talk with Osadar Di. The one fact that had stuck in his mind was that originally she had been from the Jupiter System. She had been a pilot that had escaped to Saturn, and then to Neptune. She used to be human. Someone named Toll Seven had captured her and her ice-hauler crew, and on a Neptune habitat, she had been turned into a cyborg. It was a horrifying tale.

As Marten sat waiting for Chavez, he realized that Osadar Di had been trapped worse than he ever had been. No one had ever ripped his humanity from him. Yet the more Marten thought about it, the more he wondered if that was so. She wasn't like Blake, the Bioram Taw2. Blake's mind had been sliced and rearranged. It sounded as if Toll Seven had left Osadar her original mind, reprogramming it in certain ways and vastly changing her form. But if she had her brain, wasn't she still Osadar Di, still the human from the Jupiter System? It was hard to decide. The interesting point was this: She knew the Jupiter System. She had lived there before escaping to the Neptune System where the cyborgs had caught and

252

transformed her. He knew nothing about Jupiter, or almost nothing. If he was ever going to find Nadia Pravda there, he could use a native Jovian. But if he was ever going to reach his shuttle, the *Mayflower*—

Marten's head twitched. He didn't even want to think about that right now. It was his secret. He hadn't even told Omi.

There was a truth about secrets. If you told them to someone, others soon learned about them. The only way to keep a secret was to keep it secret. And that meant to tell no one. Marten knew that, and he was the only one who needed to know about the secret—for now. Besides, he couldn't make a stab for the *Mayflower* just yet. Mars orbit swarmed with a Social Unity Battlefleet. The fact there hadn't been any space bombardments, city invasions or food-dome invasions meant the rumor must be true. Major Diaz had told him about the rumor a day ago. The Highborn were heading to Mars with three Doom Stars.

As Marten sat waiting, he brooded. Three Doom Stars would keep the Battlefleet busy.

His mood shifted, and Marten lurched to his feet. He hated slouching in the soft chair. He began to pace. A plush carpet covered the floor and strange, no, bizarre paintings hung on the walls. He could feel Omi's eyes on him. Marten wondered if hidden cameras recorded his actions.

Marten needed Osadar Di. He needed the cyborg, because what he planned was madness. Getting the cyborg out of Unionist hands would be hard, however, if not impossible. The Unionist scientists had taken Osadar Di, and according to Major Diaz, had run her through a battery of tests and asked her thousands of questions. Also according to Diaz, the cyborg had become stubborn and now remained silent.

Would Chavez continue to feel grateful that the cyborg had saved his life? Marten was grateful. Maybe as importantly, he sympathized with Osadar's extraordinary resolve to gain freedom. Despite the metallic quality of her voice, the few times he'd talked with her, he'd felt connected. He'd understood her. Marten suppressed a shudder. If Osadar Di hadn't killed the other cyborgs, would Omi and he now be cyborgs? The thought was terrifying. Whatever else happened,

Marten knew he had to get off Mars. He had to get out of the Inner Planets. Cyborgs versus Highborn versus Social Unity—the Inner Planets might become cinders before such a war ended.

When faced against overwhelming odds, one either had to fight for honor or run away. It was time to run away to live to fight another day. But to do that, he was going to have fight better than he ever had in his life. He could have used Kang, Vip and Lance. He would have loved to see Stick or Turbo again and hear their voices.

The door opened. Marten whirled around. A stunningly beautiful woman stood there. Her hair was done up in an appealing style, and her lips were glossy. She wore a wraparound dress, the hem all the way to the floor, even hiding her feet.

"The Secretary-General will see you now," she said. "But he can only give you five minutes. So it will have to be brief."

"I understand," Marten said.

She gave him a quick study, nodded pertly and said, "If you would follow me, please…"

***

"That's insanity," Chavez said, "pure insanity."

Marten and Omi sat in low chairs before the Secretary-General's huge desk. Red smoke drifted through the room. The walls held a hundred plaques, photos, and more of the bizarre paintings of swirls and thick ink. Chavez leaned back in his swivel chair, a stimstick dangling from his lips. Several bronze busts of old Unionist leaders rested on his desk. Outside the door to the spacious office waited a five-man security team.

Chavez took a deep drag on his stimstick. "We have one cyborg. One! The scientists need it for study."

"She saved our lives," Marten said quietly, trying to keep calm.

"Did she?" Chavez asked.

"Do you remember being tangled?" Marten asked.

Chavez snapped forward and placed his elbows on the desk. He mashed the stimstick in an ashtray, and from his greater height looked down at Marten sitting on a lower chair.

It reminded Marten too much of Hall Leader Quirn, and

that made his stomach queasy.

"The scientists have postulated an interesting theory," Chavez said. "Did the cyborgs plant a spy among us? Did this *Osadar Di* destroy the other machines in order to win my gratitude?"

"They're not just machines, sir, but living things."

"They *were* living things," Chavez said.

"They still have brains."

Chavez frowned. "I'm not here to argue with you, Mr. Kluge. Your five minutes were up some time ago. I appreciate all that you've done for us, but—"

"Tell me this," Marten said. "Why would Social Unity put a cyborg spy in your midst?"

Chavez's frown deepened. "The answer is obvious."

"Mr. Secretary-General, from what I've seen of your military, you have nothing that can stand against the cyborgs or a full military attack. The only reason you won your freedom before was that the Highborn defeated Social Unity for you."

"That is quite enough, Mr. Kluge."

Marten stood up. He hated sitting in that low chair. He hated looking up at the skinny Secretary-General.

"Where are your military weapons?" Marten asked. "My commando team has Gauss needlers. Those are a joke."

Looking stricken, Chavez sank back in his chair. "The enemy has already defeated and retaken our military equipment. I refer to the space stations, the orbitals and the proton beam. All we have left are the needlers, a few gyroc rifles and some plasma cannons. It stings our pride, but the truth is the Highborn freed us the first time, as you said. Now we're depending on them again to free us."

"That's what I'm trying to change," Marten said.

Chavez stared at him. "Your plan is suicide."

"Freedom only comes at the price of blood," Marten said. "The Highborn paid last time, I know. You've fought a guerilla war against PHC for years. And that meant you had pride because many of your noblest fighters had fallen. The pride allowed you to man the space defenses and fire the proton beam. Just like last time, you can't solely rely on the Highborn. You must hurt Social Unity. You must help the Highborn, and

255

thereby stake your claim to freedom. Otherwise, sir, the Highborn might decide to remain as your masters."

"That would be intolerable," Chavez said. "We would fight for a thousand years to prevent that."

"Then you must show the Highborn and Social Unity that you still have fight left. As importantly, you must show them that you can still hurt your enemies."

Chavez folded his thin hands on the huge desk, and something seemed to leak out of him. His eyes became bleak, and there was that Martian slouch to his skinny shoulders.

"What happens if Social Unity begins to beam our food-domes? What happens if they unleash the cyborgs on us?" Chavez wearily shook his head. "We must wait for the Highborn to appear."

Marten stepped up to the huge desk and planted his knuckled fists on it. He leaned toward Chavez so that the Secretary-General leaned back in his swivel chair.

"I can understand that," Marten said. "At the same time, you can still allow me to train the commandos. And now I'll have time to train them in unit tactics. If they'll fight as a team, they'll be five times as deadly."

"You're talking about pitting men in EVA suits and gyroc rifles against cyborgs."

"Yes!" Marten said.

"That's suicide," Chavez whispered.

"Not if we learn what the cyborgs can and cannot do."

"That's what the scientists are finding out."

"In the lab," Marten sneered. "What we need to know is in the field where it counts. Even better, Mr. Secretary-General, you will be honoring the woman who saved your life. Despite what your scientists tell you, unless Osadar Di had showed up, you and I would be cyborgs now."

With a trembling hand, Chavez opened a drawer, tore open a new pack and popped another stimstick between his lips. He took a deep drag, inhaling it into a red glow. He began to cough and blew out a stream of smoke.

"The men fear her," Chavez whispered.

"That's another reason I need her for training," Marten said. "I need to accustom my commandos to them."

"Why do you want to throw away your life?" Chavez asked.

Marten straightened. He turned away. Mars was doomed one way or another. Was that something you could tell a man? Could he lie to Chavez? Marten sneered at himself, glanced at Omi and faced Secretary-General Chavez.

"I'll tell you why, sir," Marten said. "Then you can decide whether to let me attempt this. Mars is doomed. But I think you already know that."

"Doomed?" Chavez whispered.

"You saw the cyborgs. You've seen the Highborn. The time of man... maybe our era is over."

"You believe that?"

"I don't know," Marten said. "Maybe. Does that mean I'm going to accept it? No. But it means I know when to run."

"There is no place to run," Chavez said.

"Not for an entire planet, no," Marten said as he began to pace before the huge desk. "Look. I'm going to be honest. I'm not going to lie to you. I wanted to bypass Mars. But I couldn't. I needed fuel. We bought fuel with our service. Now I want to get to my shuttle and head to Jupiter."

"Your shuttle has been destroyed," Chavez said.

Marten stared Chavez in the eye. "You can give me diplomatic power. I'm willing to represent you. I'll go to the Jupiter System, and see if I can drum up support. If terror of the cyborgs can't unite humanity, nothing can. We need a fleet of freemen to face... these *aliens*."

"Your shuttle was destroyed," Chavez said.

"No," Marten said. "I sent it a coded signal a week ago and received one back, just one single beep. My shuttle is up there, floating like debris. You said Zapata filled the tanks with propellants. I plan to reach my shuttle and head to Jupiter."

"How can you reach your shuttle?" Chavez asked.

"I'll need an orbital fighter."

"You can fly one?"

"Osadar Di can," Marten said.

Chavez blinked at him. "And you think there are orbitals at Olympus Mons?"

Marten nodded.

"You want me to loan you Martian commandos so you can flee and stay alive?" Chavez asked in disbelief.

"You buy my service by providing me a service," Marten countered. "I hit the enemy for you when the Highborn attack. I show the Highborn and the cyborgs that the Planetary Union can still strike. Your men provide me with my one chance of returning to my spaceship. In return, I train your men to the best of my Highborn-training. That training is more valuable to your Union than plutonium."

"We attempt to take out the proton beam and help the Highborn," Chavez said thoughtfully.

"You give them something they can really appreciate."

Chavez swiveled around and stared at one of the bizarre paintings. He slowly shook his head. "We must fight like men if we hope to be treated like men."

"That's part of it," Marten said. "The other is that you kill your oppressors."

"Or run away," Chavez said.

"Give me diplomatic credentials and it might turn my going away into drumming up human reinforcements and allies."

"Does that ease your conscience, Mr. Kluge?"

"Maybe," Marten said. "It also gives me a worthy goal."

"I don't understand."

"I saw the cyborgs. I've been a slave to the Highborn, and I've worked like an ant for Social Unity. I want to make the Solar System a place where people like me can thrive. That means I need a side, and a side that can win. Maybe that means I'm a seed that begins to link the free human outposts into a grand alliance to save all of us."

"That sounds like megalomania," Chavez said.

"That's better than waiting to die."

A wintry grin spread across the Secretary-General's narrow face. "Diplomatic credentials, eh? Yes. I agree. It is a gesture, if nothing else. It says that I believe Martians will always fight to be free."

"I'll need the cyborg."

"You'll need more than that, Mr. Kluge, much more."

5

Two weeks after Marten's meeting with Secretary-General Chavez, and many millions of kilometers away, the Praetor's pink eyes glowed with fierce hatred. His sharply angled face was taut with the unholy zeal that filled him. His thick dark hair was cut short to his scalp so that it seemed like fur. He sat in his command chair, a giant of a Highborn, fourth-ranked in the competitive world of super-soldiers. At other consoles sat other Highborn. Like him, they were strapped in. Like him, they had regained their health during their weightless period of flight.

Five weeks ago, the terrible acceleration around the Sun had ceased. For weeks, they had hurtled through the empty voids of space. The Grand Admiral's Doom Stars had a much shorter distance to travel to reach Mars, 100 million kilometers. From the Sun, it was almost 250 million kilometers to Mars, since the Red Planet was at aphelion, at its farthest orbital distance.

Out of all the planets in the Solar System, Mars had the third most elliptical orbit, a 9 percent variation. At perihelion, at its closest point, Mars was approximately 208 million kilometers away from the Sun. It was a difference of 46 million kilometers between the two extremes. For comparison, Earth had a difference of 5 million kilometers between perihelion and aphelion.

For five weeks, the *Thutmosis III* had sped at over two and a half times the speed of the Grand Admiral's Doom Stars. That calculated out to over five million kilometers per Earth day.

In several hours, the *Thutmosis III* would catch the Grand Admiral and pass the Doom Stars.

The Praetor slipped VR goggles over his eyes and slipped on twitch gloves. He used outer video cameras and carefully examined his stealth-ship. It was as black as the voids it hurtled through, with heat shields and an anti-radar coating. For weeks now, Highborn had hunched over their consoles, listening for radar and other detection pings sent by the enemy. To spot the *Thutmosis III* with teleoptic scopes should be nearly impossible until the stealth-ship was right on top of Mars. And that was something the Praetor had no intention of doing. The engines were silent so there was no telltale engine burn. Since leaving the Sun's orbit, they'd moved on velocity alone. Since no enemy probes or vessels had been anywhere near the Sun, it was impossible that Social Unity even knew the *Thutmosis III* had circled Sol to build up speed.

Until they fired missiles, or fired the engines or lasers, it was unlikely Social Unity would ever realize the stealth ship was there.

The Praetor twitched his fingers, using his VR goggles to peer through the ship's teleoptic sights. Mars was brighter now than any other object in the scopes except for the Sun, which was presently at the Praetor's rear view. At Mars waited the last SU fleet worthy of the name. In a little over two weeks, as the Doom Stars neared to within 1-million kilometers, huge prismatic-crystal fields would begin to spew into existence at Mars, along with aerosol-gel clouds. Those fields and clouds were supposed to protect whatever needed protection from heavy lasers or possible Highborn proton beams.

The Praetor's lips peeled back to reveal strong white teeth. The false smile concealed his nervousness. Because of its stealth-mission, the *Thutmosis III* would not send any radio or lightguide signals until the very last minute. Despite its impressive size, the stealth-ship was less than a tiny mote in the voids of space. As an almost microscopic speck, it still held life, energy and missiles. Compared to the planets, the stealth-ship was next to nothing. Compared to the SU warships, its stealth-missiles and drones would hopefully be thunderclaps out of the blackness. Yet because of the nature of his mission, the Praetor now had to wait for the next critical move.

If the Grand Admiral had miscalculated—

The Praetor let out a hiss, sounding like an angry snake. The Grand Admiral had calculated it to a nicety. The Doom Stars' engines burned brightly and massively ahead of the *Thutmosis III*. The gargantuan warships poured out energy and began hard deceleration. That should conceal his actions.

Immediately, the Praetor spoke loudly but calmly to his command crew. It would not do at this recorded moment to show emotion. He must present the picture of the perfect soldier. From his command chair, with the VR goggles firmly in place, he struck a martial pose and gave the order.

The Praetor hid his smile as the command crew began to move with practiced ease. The Praetor used the VR goggles to watch through a recording device to see how they all looked. He and the crew had literally gone through a hundred and seventeen dry runs of this procedure. They were Highborn, the greatest soldiers in the Solar System. They, however, would not rely just on their excellence, but on dedicated training.

Huge stealth-missiles and drones were now magnetically ejected from the ship's tubes. For the next twenty minutes, every warhead must exit the ship. Time passed, and everything went off perfectly. The Praetor gave another calm order. Highborn ran their big hands over various controls. Magnetic coils cooled down, and firing tubes closed.

Each of the stealth drones and missiles were cold black objects, difficult to detect until the last moment. They would reach the Mars System as the Doom Stars reached the one-million kilometer range. Because of the angle of the approaches, as the stealth weapons reached the Mars System, the *Thutmosis III* would already be flying past Mars, no longer toward it. The Praetor's ship would thus be able to use its teleoptic scopes to see *behind* whatever prismatic-crystal fields and aerosol-gel clouds the enemy had. It could lightguide and radio-message that targeting data to the Doom Stars. Just as importantly, the *Thutmosis III* could send targeting data to readjust the flight of its drones and the stealth-missiles so they struck the most militarily worthy objects.

It was the Grand Admiral's surprise stroke, and it would likely open the Last Battle for Mars.

Pride surged through the Praetor. They had much to do in the coming two-and-a-half weeks. For now, however, each Highborn of his command had done splendidly.

"We have them," the Praetor said, using, he thought, the perfect pitch in which to say it. He spoke toward a video-recorder, knowing that his words were something that future Highborn would likely replay in files for generations to come.

6

The new cyborg LA31, once known as Lisa Aster, climbed into a stealth capsule. She was different from the tall cyborgs with the skeletal limbs. She still had a fleshy human face, although with a steel dome in place of her former bone-skull. Bionic parts had replaced her arms and legs, and her spine had been reinforced with graphite rods. A Neptune-made cyborg could likely defeat any four emergency-made cyborgs from Toll Seven's command pod. Still, these models fulfilled a needed function, at this, the most critical hour of the Inner Planets assault.

LA31 had undergone speed programming. She had less hardware governing her emotions or actions than Neptune-made cyborgs. Thus, as she settled into the stealth-capsule, a prearranged command forced her to jack a plug into the slot for her brain. Immediately, a lightguide laser linked her to the controlling Web-Mind. Toll Seven and the Web-Mind had decided that it—the Web-Mind—should remain in the command pod instead of coming down in sections and being rebuilt inside of Olympus Mons. That would happen later as Mars received its Web-Mind Master.

LA31 jacked the plug into the slot for her brain. She frowned for a moment. She'd had a mother once, someone very important. She shrugged. She couldn't remember who that had been, although she did recall that she'd been a clone.

LA31 went rigid as a training reprimand surged through her. The plug into Web-Mind caused chemical reactions in her bio-form brain. Her face contorted and tears leaked from her eyes. Unknown to her, she had received a harsh emergency brain overlay. It sought to expunge old memories and lay down new ones, false ones generated by Web-Mind.

LA31 groaned and her throat became unbearably dry. Pain made her head throb, and it almost caused her to open her eyes. Another impulse-surge went through the prong in her jack. It caused soothing chemical reactions in her brain, along the nerve endings.

LA31 twitched once. Then she relaxed. She would sleep now as an SU stealth-ship carefully maneuvered her capsule into position. Her capsule contained a modified vacc-suit, hand weapons and an abundance of ammo. The capsule's outer skin was asteroid rock. Soon, the capsule would float alone near Mars, as if the Red Planet had long-ago captured a piece of space flotsam. There were more like her, and they would be sprinkled at strategically and psychologically reasonable locals. They were the secret cyborg weapon, the one that was supposed to defeat the Highborn.

LA31 knew nothing about that. She sighed, remembering a happier time as a cyborg dropping on Triton, a moon of Neptune. It was a false memory. Most of her old ones had been chemically raped away. Like a mental vulture, Web-Mind watched for any resurgence of them, ready to expunge the last of the personality of the clone Lisa Aster.

7

The next week rapidly passed as Marten Kluge trained the commandos on the sands of Mars. Osadar Di practiced with them. She demoralized the men with her amazing bounding leaps like a Highborn battleoid, her uncanny reaction time and precision, and her long-range shooting.

Near the end of the week, Marten spoke to her in an EVA tent. It was larger than the survival tents they'd used for the raid into Valles Marineris. He preferred the tents to remaining in New Tijuana. Marten hated the black-visored police there, the similar city strictures as practiced on Earth, and the possibility that Chavez could change his mind at any moment and imprison them.

Marten sat on a folding chair, with a folding table between them. On the table was a rollout computer-sheet. It showed Olympus Mons, its various entrance points and the orbital hangers.

Osadar Di stood, with her head near the tent's ceiling. It was still hard for Marten to look at her. It was like looking at a living mannequin, or at a statue that had supernaturally come to life. Her face was so immobile. Her arms and legs were more like metal rods, with bigger motorized joints that moved them. It was unholy, a cruel joke against the living and a mockery of humanity. Marten had to tell himself constantly that inside this mostly mechanical machine was a living being, a person just like himself, with hopes and dreams.

"Osadar," he said, lifting his gaze from the map, forcing himself to stare into her strange eyes. "There's something I haven't told you."

There was no change of expression on her face. He had no idea what she was thinking.

"Go on," she said in her metallic voice.

Marten kept himself from flinching and kept his eyes from darting away. "Mars is doomed," he said.

"We're all doomed," Osadar said. Her voice was like a heavy bell, a gong of certain defeat.

"I don't believe that," Marten said.

"What you believe makes no difference."

"...if you think we can't win," Marten said, stung, "why do you help us?"

"Shooting gyroc rounds out here is better than those fools asking me a thousand questions in the labs. Do you know they kept me in a sealed vault, only speaking to me via a screen?"

"It doesn't surprise me," Marten said.

"Do you think I belong in a vault?" she asked.

"I know you terrify my men."

"Do I terrify you?" she asked.

"Yes," Marten admitted, "but I'm trying to learn to control that."

She nodded, and she tapped a metal finger on the map. "What you propose with this attack, it's a suicide mission."

"Do you want to escape Mars?" Marten asked.

Her longish head moved fast, faster than a human could twitch, and she nodded yes.

Marten broke eye contact, and he felt relief doing so. On the computer-map, he indicated an orbital hanger high up on Olympus Mons. "The commando raid's secondary objective is to reach here. Here we will take an orbital and you, hopefully, will fly us into space."

"The SU Battlefleet will target and eliminate any stray orbitals," Osadar said.

"I'm hoping they will be too busy right then," Marten said.

"How can one orbital affect the battle for—" A grim smile moved her plastic lips. "You wish me to ram the orbital into Toll Seven's command pod?"

Marten shivered. Osadar Di usually seemed emotionless like a computer. For the first time, Marten felt her hatred, her intense desire to hurt Toll Seven and likely Web-Mind. That expressed hatred coming from an emotionless machine was unnerving.

"There is a better way to hurt the cyborgs," he said.

"How?"

The single word had sounded metallic and emotionless. But Marten wasn't fooled. A lifetime of pain, of hope, of bitterness, seemed rolled into that one question.

Marten began to tell Osadar his plan and his hope. He also had a new idea. It had sprouted a week ago as he'd accepted the diplomatic credentials Chavez had handed him. Marten had shoved the credentials into a special pouch in his suit. He now told Osadar about his new idea.

When he'd finished talking, she said, "Your plan is impossible."

"Maybe, maybe not," he said.

"No. It is impossible."

Marten slammed a fist against the computer-map, almost breaking the fold-up table. He glared at her, glared into her strange eyes. For those seconds he forgot that she was a cyborg. He forgot to be squeamish or afraid of her bizarreness.

"What does impossible have to do with anything?" he shouted. "We fight until we're dead! Nothing is impossible until you shrivel up and quit. Then it is impossible. If you want out, tell me. I'll pilot the damn orbital myself, or I'll die trying."

"If Toll Seven or any other cyborg captures you—"

"Are you in or out?" Marten asked.

Osadar Di broke eye contact as she stared at the roll-up computer-map. "A madman to lead us and a damned thing to pilot his orbital fighter, we are doomed before we begin. It is the law of the universe, an inexorable truth."

"Your gaining freedom from Web-Mind was also against all the odds."

Osadar turned away. "You have a beautiful dream, Marten Kluge. To find the Neptune habitat and burn it—I can conceive of nothing more worthy to do with my miserable existence. Yes, I am in."

"You won't regret this," Marten said.

Osadar regarded him. She had the saddest smile Marten had ever seen. It hurt his heart to witness it. "I hope *you* don't live to regret it," she said. "For it is very likely that sooner or later you will become a cyborg like me."

Osadar turned away abruptly and hesitated. Then in silence, she began to don her EVA gear. It was time to get moving.

-8-

A little over a week after Marten's talk with Osadar, the three Doom Stars sailed majestically into far orbit around Mars. Their average velocity for the last seven weeks had been approximately two million kilometers per Earth day.

That velocity had lessened since the hard braking. The three Doom Stars now serenely moved into their firing-range, one million kilometers. For the next three days, all the SU warships, the moons and orbital platforms would be in range of the heavy lasers without being able to fire back with anything but missiles.

One million kilometers was an immense distance. Light traveled at 300,000 kilometers per second. It would take a fired beam more than three full seconds to travel to the target. In those three seconds, the target could have shifted minutely enough to upset targeting. Thus, the targeting personnel, equipment and computers needed to know where the target would be in a little over three seconds after the shot. That, however, was nothing compared to the need for precise accuracy. To hit with the beam at one million kilometers was comparable to a sniper hitting a penny on Olympus Mons from orbit.

The Highborn possessed such molecular accuracy, another factor that made them so deadly. Like ill omens of destruction, the three Doom Stars with their heavy laser-ports eerily glided through the stellar void and toward the bright disc of Mars.

The *Julius Caesar*, the *Hannibal Barca* and the *Napoleon Bonaparte* were spheroid vessels and contained massive fusion reactors. Those reactors produced the incredible power needed for the unbeatable heavy lasers. Each Doom Star also carried its own complement of orbital fighters, drop-troops and drones. The heavy lasers were their primary armament, however.

On the bridge of the *Julius Caesar*, Grand Admiral Cassius waited in his command chair. Around him and on various levels were the modules of his battle staff. There were a hundred monitors, screens, VR-wearing personnel, and thousands of lights on a hundred boards. Techs poured over computer-enhanced teleoptic scans, and radar specialists studied the graphics. Before the Grand Admiral was a ten–foot holographic globe of Mars, with the two moons in correct alignment and the already spotted SU warships as green dots. Incoming data constantly shifted the information on the holo-globe. The Grand Admiral watched impassively as prismatic-crystal fields sprayed into existence as out of thin air. They appeared as three-dimensional blankets before the clusters of SU warships. Phobos spayed no fields, as the moon was presently behind Mars. Deimos also remained bare of covering crystals or aerosol gels.

Grand Admiral Cassius studied the holographic globe. The normal practice in such a situation would be for his three Doom Stars to attempt a burn through. It would be a mathematical formula of pouring enough laser energy against the constantly replenished prismatic-crystal fields. Once through, the lasers would have to probe for the warships behind the PC-Fields. Those warships would naturally be moving, hoping to confound Highborn targeting computers.

Such was the normal tactic, but the Grand Admiral refrained from giving the order. He had won the Second Battle of Deep Mars Orbit in 2339 practicing just that scheme. Then, he had destroyed the Mars fleet and the armada of the Jupiter Confederation. The premen would naturally expect him to use the same tactic as before. It was reasonable of them to think so, for premen invariably followed the tried and true. Historically, it was also natural for any previous victor to fight the new war with the old war's winning methods.

Grand Admiral Cassius sat back in his chair so it creaked. He tapped a forefinger against his gray temple. How good was the premen's equipment? The likely answer was very good. Soon now, they would spot the *Thutmosis III's* stealth-missiles and drones.

The deadly waiting game was nearly over. The battle could begin at any moment. The fleets had made their dispositions. It was soon time to hand the premen a terrible surprise. They thought they could face three mighty Doom Stars. It was monumental arrogance on their part, and animal desperation. The power of the Highborn was about to crush their last aspirations.

Cassius smiled. This was why he had been born. This was his purpose: to conquer, to defeat and to subjugate those weaker and softer than himself. It was the law of life that the strong should devour the weak. It was a good law, a reasonable thing, and the way he would reorder the Solar System once he gained mastery of it.

Emperor Cassius. That had a noble ring. Since he was the greatest sentient in the Solar System, he then should mold those under him. Grand Admiral Cassius lowered his hand and stared steely-eyed at the holographic globe. In truth, it was his burden to rule, to govern those too stupid to order their lives correctly. If humanity—and he meant Highborn with that word—were to expand throughout the galaxy, then this Mother System, this womb, must be reordered along rational lines.

The Grand Admiral forced himself to relax. He had many hours yet of waiting. He wanted the premen to sweat and to fear. He wanted them to worry about him, to wonder why the Doom Stars hadn't fired yet. That was the great premen weakness, the inability to wait without their animal-like nervousness. Only a superior Highborn could control himself properly.

"Soon," Grand Admiral Cassius whispered. "Very soon now..."

-9-

"What's wrong with them?" Commodore Blackstone shouted. "Why aren't the Doom Stars firing?"

Heads turned on the *Vladimir Lenin's* cramped command bridge. Commissar Kursk frowned. Only General Fromm remained unmoved at the outburst.

Blackstone, Kursk and Fromm stood around the raised holographic map-module. Red light bathed the bridge, and a constant stream of chatter on headphones and speakers combined with the tap of keyboards.

The Commodore gripped the map-module as he stared at the enhanced image of the Doom Stars. Beside the images of the mighty ships were green numbers that constantly changed as their range closed. Blackstone tried to quell the raging uncertainty in his heart. This waiting for the battle to open was the worst feeling. Presently, the Doom Stars held all the advantages. Why then didn't they begin a burn through? He had ships waiting behind the prismatic-crystal field, ships ready to dump an immense quantity of crystals to add to the field. Other ships were lined up behind those, ready to rush to the field and increase it for days. That the Highborn didn't attempt the obvious meant they had another plan. That terrified Blackstone.

If he lost the battle—

"Sir," the communications officer said, "tracking has spotted approaching anomalies."

"What? What?" Blackstone asked, knowing that he spoke too loudly and too quickly. He strove to control himself. He wanted to control himself. Everything rested on his command decisions. He had the power today to lose everything for Social Unity. If he lost, his ex-wife would become a slave to the Highborn.

Then Blackstone was blinking at new images on the map-module, a flock of images. "What am I seeing?" he shouted.

The targeting officer swiveled around. The bridge's red glow made his sharp features seem devilish. "Sir, those are missiles."

"What's propelling them?" Blackstone asked. "Where's their exhaust?"

"High velocity moves them, sir. They must have been fired... weeks ago."

"Why didn't anyone spot it until now?" Blackstone asked.

"The *Bangladesh*," General Fromm said.

Blackstone glared at Fromm. How could the stout Earth General sound so calm? The man's fleshy features were smooth. His voice was unruffled. Blackstone envied and hated Fromm.

"The *Bangladesh*," Fromm repeated. "The Highborn must have fired the missiles from the Sun, or had them gain velocity there. That's what we did with the *Bangladesh*. It appears they've stolen our method and turned it against us."

"The missiles are headed for the PC-Fields," the targeting officer said.

Blackstone slammed an open hand against the map-module as a cold wave of logic quelled his raging heart. He saw the Highborn plan, or this part of it, at least. They would blast a hole through the prismatic-crystal field and only *then* fire their hated heavy lasers. But he had a reaction team, a squadron of battlewagons. If they could move in time—

"Communications, get me the *Fidel Castro*. And *hurry!*" Blackstone added, his voice having the power of a lash.

***

The *Thutmosis III* had passed Mars by ten million kilometers. That no enemy missiles burned at high gravities after them showed the Praetor and his crew that the premen had failed to spot the giant stealth-ship. A sense of calm filled the vessel. The great danger was over. Now every resource and effort was bent on one task, using the teleoptic scopes to locate everything behind Mars and behind the prismatic-crystal fields. There were obvious gaps in their knowledge, the areas hidden by Mars for one. What they already knew was vital.

The Praetor watched the enemy through his VR-goggles. Excitement caused him to rise from his chair. SU battleships and... missile-ships engaged their engines.

"Are their ships using full burn?" the Praetor asked.

Computers analyzed the intensity of the various ship exhausts, and they analyzed the brightness of the expelled propellants.

"They're using emergency speeds," a Highborn answered. "They must have spotted our incoming missiles. The computer gives it an eighty-seven percent probability that they're sending those ships around their own PC-Fields so they can try to laser our missiles."

The Praetor gave a sharp, sardonic bark. That was the danger of creating a prismatic-crystal field too soon in a battle. It stopped the enemy from hitting your ships, but it also stopped you from firing lasers at the enemy.

"Ready the lightguide system," the Praetor ordered. "Then relay our information to the Grand Admiral."

The Grand Admiral had long ago shot probes in a lateral direction. Otherwise, Social Unity's PC-Fields would have blocked a lightguide message beam as effectively as it would a battle-beam. Now, the *Thutmosis III's* lightguide laser would hit the communication probe, which would relay the message to the *Julius Caesar*.

The Praetor sat down, although he kept his spine stiff and his pose that of a conqueror. The premen moved predictably. They were such simple creatures, really. How they could ever hope to win against their genetic superiors was beyond him. It was like a child groping to fight an adult. They so yearned to ape Highborn combat efficiency. Inevitably, utter failure was the result.

The Praetor let out his breath as the message was beamed to the *Julius Caesar's* probe. If the premen had good equipment, they might spot the lightguide beam, but fail to crack its contents. That meant the premen could theoretically spot the *Thutmosis III*. It was unlikely, however, as the lightguide beam had been sent in a short burst. If the pathetic premen hadn't spotted them yet, it was unlikely they would when they had so many other things to worry about.

***

The Praetor was correct concerning the SU Battlefleet. Every ship, every piece of detection equipment was aimed toward the Doom Stars and the stellar voids in that general direction. It was a massive volume of space. That the *Thutmosis III's* stealth-missiles and drones had only been spotted now was not incredible or surprising. A cold dark object fashioned to give almost no radar signature was a maddeningly difficult thing to find. Radar and teleoptic technicians were trained to search for any telltale clue, but until very near, the stealth-missiles simply hadn't given those clues.

But the radar and teleoptic technicians on the Phobos moon scanned in the opposite direction. Phobos was presently on the other side of Mars as the Battlefleet and thus couldn't track the Doom Stars. The commander of Phobos didn't expect to find anything. The commander merely wanted his crews busy because busy people had less time to think themselves into useless nervousness.

One radar specialist, a Corporal Bess O'Connor, noticed a blip on her screen, a flash and then nothing. She ran a diagnostic on it and keyed for a computer suggestion. The computer flashed a single message: *Lightguide beam.*

Even though a lightguide beam out there seemed impossible, Corporal Bess O'Connor logged the blip at the computer's suggestion and passed it along the chain of command. Others in teleoptics received it and that caused a flurry of excitement. Teleoptics backtracked and used percentage probability analyzers. As they did so, they caught a flash of the second lightguide beam sent from the *Thutmosis III*.

That created an emergency and triggered several command decisions. First, even though the black-ops enemy vessel moved at extreme speeds away from Mars, the Phobos commander ordered a missile launch. Several minutes later, huge hunter-seeker missiles lofted from Phobos and charged

275

into the void after the last known location of the enemy. With them lofted several specialized missiles whose sole purpose was to find and fixate upon this craft and relay the information to the deadly killer missiles. The second command involved three cargo ships. Those three cargo ships engaged emergency thrusters, hurrying into position. Once there, they would begin spraying a fine mist of aerosol gels. That mist was meant to blind the stealth enemy from observing anything more of military importance around Mars.

***

Grand Admiral Cassius closed his eyes, quietly exuding in his brilliance. He loved chess. He loved any competitive game, but especially enjoyed those that involved long-term strategy and careful moves. The moves that now brought him this joy had been planned nearly a year ago.

He had received the Praetor's lightguide messages, which had given them the precise locations of everything they on the Doom Stars couldn't see because of the prismatic-crystal fields. Now the desperate premen used battleships to kill the *Thutmosis III's* missiles. It was the obvious thing to do. The better strategy would have been to let the missiles hit the PC-Fields as the enemy fleet raced to get behind Mars. Nevertheless, Cassius had given the present action a seventy percent probability. Running for cover behind Mars would have meant leaving the moons to heavy laser attacks. It was only reasonable that the premen would have stocked the moons with weaponry, hoping to use the moons as heavy platforms. What it truly did was leave the moons hostage to the Doom Stars and force the enemy commander to shield them. No prismatic-crystal field guarded Deimos yet. Cassius was certain it was in order to try to fool him into thinking Deimos was harmless. Unfortunately for the premen, he wasn't fooled in the slightest.

"Enemy vessels have left the protection of the prismatic-crystal field," a Highborn officer said.

"Begin firing," Cassius ordered.

***

The lasers of the battlewagon *Fidel Castro* speared into the

276

starry darkness. Nearby sister-ships did likewise. From farther away, missile-ships launched anti-missiles. Mars was behind them. A vast prismatic-crystal field like a nebula cloud-system glittered strangely in the vacuum blackness closer to them, but still to their rear.

The commander of the *Fidel Castro* felt naked and alone out here. His battleship was the oldest in the fleet, but it was still a deadly vessel. The 600-meter thick particle-shields were in place. And the battleship changed positions constantly, jinking, engaging engines, shutting them down and swerving to a different heading. They did all that to avoid the heavy lasers of the Doom Stars one-million kilometers away. All the while, the battleship's lasers burned the incoming missiles and drones.

Then, out of the voids, incredibly huge lasers stabbed with hellish fury. Those heavy lasers were three times the diameter of the *Fidel Castro's* lasers. In them had been pumped five times the killing power. Because the Doom Stars possessed such massive fusion engines, they could afford to pay the energy costs to fuel these lasers.

Nine giant lasers hit the *Fidel Castro* in unison. It was a display of incredible targeting skill. Three Doom Stars from nearly one-million kilometers away sent nine beams into the SU battleship's guts. They sliced off huge chunks of the particle-shield. Then the *Fidel Castro*, which was always moving, changed heading enough that the nine beams stabbed around it. The commander and crew hoped they had time to escape. The Highborn probability computers, or maybe the genetically enhanced gunners, guessed right again. Six beams chewed off more of the particle-shield. For eight minutes and twenty seconds, the uneven game played out. Then the heavy lasers struck past the ruined particle-shields and slammed into the battleship's hull.

Titanium and steel burned in nanoseconds. Clouds of heated gas and molten droplets shed from the hull. In another minute, it was over, as the *Fidel Castro* floated in space, a dead and irradiated hulk.

The forty-year-old battleship had tried to defend the prismatic-crystal field and destroy enough of the incoming missiles. The question was, had it been enough?

Eighty percent of the *Thutmosis III's* stealth-missiles and drones perished under a flurry of SU laser beams and anti-missile missiles. They were winks of bright light in the darkness, sometimes a red glow that died like a shooting star.

Twenty percent of the missiles in layered waves hit the prismatic-crystal field. The nuclear explosions blew vast holes in the field. They opened it up and exposed a portion of the SU Battlefleet behind it. They exposed SU ships to the heavy lasers of the *Julius Caesar*, the *Hannibal Barca* and the *Napoleon Bonaparte*.

The attacked showed to great effect the deadliness of long-rage beams. Blackstone shouted himself hoarse. Ships churned out more prismatic-crystals. But many ships perished under the Doom Star lasers.

"Head behind Mars!" Blackstone shouted. "Hide behind Deimos!"

All around him, battleships, missile-ships, ECM vessels and minelayers engaged their engines and slammed their crews with six-Gs of acceleration. Like terrible searchlights, the giant lasers stabbed and killed. They moved so much faster than the sluggish spacecraft. Sometimes they seared chunks of particle-shields off huge battleships. More often, the lasers struck thinner-skinned vessels, cutting some in half so living beings tumbled like space-scum into the black vacuum.

Commodore Blackstone's plan to absorb energy by taking days of heavy laser fire was destroyed. Yet by sending the *Fidel Castro* and other ships to their deaths to kill the majority of the enemy missiles, he had saved the majority of the SU Battlefleet. At least, he'd saved it from annihilation here at the opening of the battle.

Like thieves frightened by policemen, the SU Battlefleet scattered for safety. All the while, the terrible beams from the voids fired. The untouchable Doom Stars lived up to their names. The master plan to envelop the Doom Stars had fallen apart days before it could be implemented.

Commodore Blackstone gripped the map-module as he listened to the list of ships destroyed and those that had taken heavy damage. The *Fidel Castro* and two other battleships were gone, along with two missile-ships. Those were appalling losses when he had absolutely nothing to show for it.

"We have eight battleships left," Blackstone said tonelessly, "and seven missile-ships. That's unspeakable. We didn't even touch them."

General Fromm looked up from the map-module. He had never changed expression throughout the disaster. "You are incorrect in saying we have achieved nothing."

Blackstone stared open-mouthed at the stout Earth General. He finally managed to ask, "What are you talking about?"

"The Highborn have played one of their surprises," Fromm said in his maddeningly calm voice. "We still have our surprises."

"But three priceless battleships—"

Fromm shook his round head. "The Highborn have a limited number of surprises. Now they approach Mars where our surprises wait. They have damaged us, but we still possess a Battlefleet." Fromm's fat fingers indicated the list of other destroyed vessels displayed on the holographic module. "Twenty other vessels destroyed. The greater majority of these are the decoy ships."

"Which were still full of personnel," Blackstone half sobbed.

"Battle entails losses, Commodore," Fromm said without any change of inflection. "The decoy vessels have served a useful purpose. They fulfilled two purposes, in fact. They perished, so battle-worthy craft could live to fight again. And they have no doubt given the Highborn a higher sense of accomplishment than they should have. That will heighten one of their greatest weaknesses."

"Highborn don't have weaknesses," Blackstone said. "This attack should have proved that to you."

"They are arrogant," General Fromm said. "They are insufferably arrogant. That, in the end, shall be their undoing."

Commodore Blackstone glanced at Commissar Kursk. She stared at the list of destroyed ships. The *Vladimir Lenin* along with most of the Battlefleet was now behind Mars in relation to the oncoming Doom Stars. Supreme Commander Hawthorne's grand plan—Blackstone sneered. They should have kept the fleet in small pieces between the Inner Planets, harrying the Highborn where they were weakest. To try to match the nine-foot super-soldiers in a head-on battle, it was suicide for Social Unity.

Vaguely, Blackstone wondered why Toll Seven wasn't here aboard the *Vladimir Lenin*. He could have used the cyborg's advice. He wondered what the strange cyborg thought about the disaster. The cyborg surprise would be all-important now. Without the stealth capsules...

10

Toll Seven sat alone in his command pod with Web-Mind all around him.

Web-Mind was the greatest technological marvel in the Solar System. It was a mass bio-computer merged with metric tons of neural processors. Hundreds of bio-forms had died to supply Web-Mind with the needed brain mass. Each kilo of brain tissue had been personality scrubbed and carefully rearranged on wafer-thin sheets and surrounded by computing gel. Other machinery kept the temperature at a perfect 98.7 degrees Fahrenheit. Tubes fed the tissues the needed nutrients. Sensors monitored bio-health. Sub-computers did a hundred other necessary chores to keep Web-Mind functioning perfectly. The bio-brain-mass could outthink any known entity and track many thousands of enslaved bio-forms. The Web-Mind on the Neptune Habitat was supreme, but the one in Toll Seven's command pod had been given override authority here. That meant it could adjust the master plan to suit emergency needs. It had more than enough brain mass to engineer victory at Mars System. Its future function would be to act as syndic for all Inner Planets.

Toll Seven wore a wireless headband linking him to Web-Mind. Well before the Doom Stars had reached the one-million kilometer range, he had slipped the command pod to a safer location near the atmosphere of Mars. He had initiated shutdown procedures and implemented stealth-sheathing to the outer hull. Then he had cooled the pod's hull so his vessel imitated space debris. The safety of Web-Mind superseded all other considerations. In the coming days of heavy battle, there would be no real safe place in the Mars System. Web-Mind had considered slipping out of the system and awaiting the battle's outcome. But it had decided that camouflaging as space debris was safer than engaging engines for an extended burn to reach a suitable distance.

Toll Seven scanned his pre-battle arrangements. The Neptune-made cyborgs were scattered throughout the Mars System. Most waited in single stealth-capsules as did the newly converted half-cyborg, Lisa Aster. Others guarded Olympus Mons, ready to take over the proton beam and the point-defense systems there. Perhaps as importantly, critical Webbies were stationed throughout the Battlefleet, ready to assume command positions. They would gain those positions through surprise assassinations.

Toll Seven's head rotated like a robot's head. His silver eyes swiveled in their black plastic sockets as he read the message on the monitor before him. The green letters scrolled past at impossible speeds. Toll Seven's fingers blurred as he typed the reply. Web-Mind concurred.

General Fromm had asked a last question via Web-link. Toll Seven answered. Web-Mind then informed him that General Fromm had unplugged from the link and was returning to his place on the *Vladimir Lenin's* bridge.

Several days would pass now as the Doom Stars approached. Likely the genetic super-soldiers would continue to fire their heavy lasers at targets of opportunity.

A strange reaction surged through Web-Mind. It caused Toll Seven to stiffen because he was linked via the wireless headband. He felt Web-Mind's emotions and sensed that soothing chemicals poured along the wafer-thin bio-sheets. The great bio-brain entity knew a moment of uncertainty. Was it possible that its secret plan would fail in the face of the Highborn? Web-Mind wished for continued existence. Its location above Mars as camouflaged debris—

Then the soothing chemicals softened the unease, and Web-Mind began to reconfigure its strategies and coming tactics. No single entity could outthink it. The Master Plan would surge ahead, and the Mars Gravitational System would fall to Web-

Mind. It was inevitable. If only this waiting period could be sped up.

"The wait will unhinge the Highborn more than it can possibly disturb us," Toll Seven interjected.

Both Web-Mind and Toll Seven understood the truth of that. Still, the wait for unperceived possibilities to interfere with the smooth application of the Master Plan was difficult. Only time and events would bring an end to that.

11

The Doom Stars bore toward Mars as the heavy lasers swept Deimos with brutal destruction. Belatedly, the commander there began pumping chaff and prismatic-crystals before the moon. Then all the moon's missiles were launched at the Doom Stars.

With contemptuous ease, the Doom Stars targeted and destroyed them. The heavy lasers swept through the thin PC-Fields and continued their systemic obliteration of anything that appeared dangerous on Deimos.

Deimos was the smaller moon, with the greater orbit. Phobos was larger, although not by much. It was closer to Mars and orbited the planet three times a Martian day or every 7.3 hours. At Commodore Blackstone's orders, supply ships added their prismatic-crystals to what Phobos poured into a field before itself. The PC-Field was of small width but great thickness, and absorbed the heavy lasers for several hours a day. Then it orbited back around Mars and was safe for another cycle from the terrible lasers.

To the Highborn, Mars began to take on greater size. When the Doom Stars were approximately 250,000 kilometers from the Red Planet, Grand Admiral Cassius opened a channel with admirals of the *Hannibal Barca* and the *Napoleon Bonaparte*.

"In twenty-four hours at the earliest," Cassius said, "our ships will be in range of the battleships. We must assume they will form a fighting circle and attempt to attack en masse against one Doom Star."

"Which side of Mars do you think they will choose to

appear around?" asked Admiral Brutus of the *Hannibal Barca*."

"I am a fighting man, not a magician," Grand Admiral Cassius said. "But it would be logical to assume they will try to shield themselves behind Phobos as it orbits into view."

"I would think the other side," Admiral Brutus said. "They will expect us to believe they will use Phobos as a shield and then do the opposite for a surprise effect."

"That hardly amounts to a tactical surprise," Grand Admiral Cassius said.

"I expect their surprise to be similar to the 10 May Attack, and to their recent breakout from Earth," Admiral Brutus said.

"A mass assault?" asked Cassius. "Yes. I agree. They will use full laser batteries and launch masses of missiles at short range. They will hope to crash through with tonnage instead of with guile. Yet they will have a true surprise for us."

"You still insist upon that, Grand Admiral?"

"Logic dictates it."

"As you say—"

"The premen are rash and prone to wild panics," Cassius said. "But their highest officers have a modicum of ability. They will not have used their last fleet to lure us unless they believed they could win. That mandates a surprise."

"The moons—" Brutus tried to say.

"Surely constituted part of their surprise," Cassius said. "Their fierce defense of Phobos shows that, as does their former military formation. Remember, gentlemen, both moons show a continual face toward Mars. We have not damaged the Mars-facing side of Deimos."

"I thought the asteroid-busters—"

"Admiral Gaius, Admiral Brutus," Cassius said, "I am implementing Attack Plan 27. I gather that each of you gentlemen is familiar with the outlines of it…"

Grand Admiral Cassius continued to speak as the majestic Doom Stars moved toward Mars. Then the admirals began to debate the finer points of Attack Plan 27. The great victory over the final premen space-fleet of Inner Planets was about to enter the annihilation phase.

285

-12-

A naked Commissar Kursk knelt behind an equally naked Commodore Blackstone. He sat up. She rubbed his shoulders and occasionally ran her fingers across the back of his bald head.

"We can't win," Blackstone whispered.

"Hush," Kursk whispered, leaning against him as she draped her arms around his neck.

"They swatted us like flies. Three battleships and two missile-ships—destroyed *like that*." Blackstone snapped his fingers. "Twenty other vessels are dead."

"They had greater range," Kursk whispered in his ear. "Now they are closing in. Now our weapons can come into play. If you can lure them near the proton beam—"

"These are Highborn," Blackstone said.

Kursk tightened her grip around him as her breasts flattened against his back. "I forbid you to fear," she whispered.

He clutched one of her wrists. "Is this technique in your PHC training manual?"

"As a matter of fact…" she said, and she nibbled on his ear.

Blackstone had responded earlier. Now this felt too much like the last request of a dead man. Instead of a meal, he had taken the Commissar. He had wanted to take her for so long. Now… now he felt as if he'd betrayed his ex-wife. The Highborn were superior. The cyborgs, Toll Seven's plan would fail.

Blackstone tightened his grip on Commissar Kursk's wrist

just the same. In his gut, he knew that death waited. But he was a fighting man, a fighting officer. He had to show a brave front. If nothing else, he had to die well. He could show his crew how to do that. Yes, he would not shout and rave as last time. This time, he was going to kill at least one Doom Star. To kill all the Doom Stars seemed impossible, but at least they could take down one of those damned super-ships.

He turned around, catching Commissar Kursk by surprise. His decision to die well gave him a resumed appetite.

"Where were we," he murmured as he kissed her.

Amazingly, she giggled. It seemed like an unnatural sound considering the nearness of the Doom Stars. But maybe that was the sound of life. If they could kill one Doom Star, maybe that meant that someday in the future man would rise again against the nine-foot supermen. Blackstone didn't know. Instead, he pushed the Commissar onto her back as his hands roved over her thighs, and he tried to enjoy a final moment of love before oblivion claimed him forever.

-13-

Marten Kluge stood alone on the windswept sands of Mars. Behind him over a large dune were the EVA tents, skimmers and plasma cannons.

It was night, with the stars bright in the cloudless sky. Phobos sailed serenely through the blackness, to him, half the size of Luna as seen on Earth. It was hard to believe that outside Mars' atmosphere waited the SU Battlefleet. Beyond them came the Doom Stars full of arrogant Highborn, which meant arrogant Training Masters, battleoids and super-soldiers with unnatural vitality and the lust to kill.

Something alerted Marten then. He turned and watched an EVA-suited Omi trudge toward him. He knew the Korean's stride. Omi shouldered a gyroc rifle and had a grenade-launching carbine dangling from his hip.

Marten pointed in the far distance at the giant volcano of Olympus Mons. It dominated the dark landscape. The majestic mountain was uniquely Martian, a thing of towering awe and splendorous beauty. This was a strange, dead world, similar to the ocean on Earth with its life underground.

"Tomorrow," Omi said over his comm-unit.

"You have word on the Doom Stars?"

"Major Diaz did," Omi said, "from Chavez. He wants to talk to you."

Marten shrugged. Everything seemed peaceful tonight. Olympus Mons, the red sands, it was beautiful. The wind never stopped blowing. He wondered if he would miss Mars.

Omi and he stood side-by-side in silence, staring up at the

288

stars.

"It's up there," Marten said, breaking the calm. Both of them knew he meant the *Mayflower*.

"Did you try another signal?" Omi asked.

"I'm not pushing my luck more than I need to," Marten said.

"Since when did you decide that?"

"We can't stay on Mars," Marten said.

"Never said we should," Omi replied. "I'm just saying that your supply of luck ran out a long time ago. You're living on borrowed time."

"That's the trick."

"I don't know what that means," Omi said.

"I've already borrowed more luck than I can ever hope to repay," Marten said. "Knowing that, I've decided to push it and borrow even more. The bank is open as far as I'm concerned."

"What's a bank?" Omi asked.

"It's like a loan shark."

"Got it," Omi said. "You're not worried about an enforcer like me coming along and demanding repayment because you're too high on DD."

"What did Chavez want?" Marten asked.

"More diplomatic jargon," Omi said. "None of it made any sense to me. I think what he really wants is the commandos back in New Tijuana."

Marten turned toward Omi and stared at his friend's visor. All he saw was a dark reflection of himself, with his own EVA helmet and suit.

"It's time we moved closer to Olympus Mons," Marten said.

"As he listened to Chavez over the radio, Major Diaz looked pretty thoughtful," Omi said. "He might not agree with you."

"Yeah," Marten said. "We'll see." And he began trudging through the red sands back to camp.

"Help us!" a colonel screamed. "Can anybody hear me? They're pounding us with missiles and beaming everywhere. Commodore Blackstone! Captain Vargas! Please, somebody answer. Somebody—"

A boom sounded over the comm-link. There were the noises of things crashing and then came hissing static. It was a terrible and accusing sound.

"Shut it off," Blackstone whispered.

Belatedly, the *Vladimir Lenin's* communications officer snapped forward and broke the link with Deimos. The Mars-facing side of the tiny moon had been under Highborn attack for the past half-hour.

Commodore Blackstone's hands were greasy with sweat. His dry mouth tasted like bile. As if he were attending a funeral, he wore his black uniform with its row of medals. He also wore his officer's cap at its regulation angle. On the map-module where he rested his hands was the image of the great mass of Mars, the curvature of it. The flock of specks was the SU Battlefleet. For the past three days, the fleet had remained behind Mars in relation to the terrible Doom Stars. Now the Doom Stars had braked again, and they were in near orbit, hunting for the Battlefleet.

The grim silence on the bridge was like a psychic weight.

"There was nothing you could have done," Commissar Kursk whispered.

Blackstone savagely wiped his eyes. This entire plan had been madness. Now he had let the personnel on Deimos die because otherwise his one chance to hurt the Highborn—

Blackstone's head snapped up. Listening to those pleas had broken a dam in him. Maybe it had begun long ago when his ex-wife had first filed for divorce. He had bottled up so much pain and so much anguish. That anguish and pain now poured out in a torrent from his heart. He wanted to hurt somebody. He wanted to hurt them badly.

"It's time to make them pay," Blackstone said hoarsely.

General Fromm watched him.

Blackstone made a sharp gesture. "The Highborn have come to step on our necks. It's time to make them understand that we're men. It's time to bring them down by destroying the Doom Stars."

The bridge officers had all turned to stare. Commissar Kursk nodded belated agreement.

The communications officer asked, "Do you think we can win, sir?"

"Yes!" Commodore Blackstone said, although he didn't believe that. His crisp tone caused several officers to straighten. What Blackstone did believe was that he was going to hurt them now. He was done with waiting. With the help of the cyborg stealth-attacks, the Highborn were going to know that they had been in a battle.

The communications officer turned toward her comm-board. "What are your orders, sir?"

Commodore Blackstone studied the map-module. Then he began to issue curt commands.

-15-

The SU warships subtlety changed their dispositions. In his command pod and linked to the Battlefleet-net, Toll Seven heard Blackstone's orders. Soon, Toll Seven began to issue his own commands, to mesh the cyborg plan with the reinvigorated bio-forms.

A thousand kilometers away in her stealth-capsule, LA31 opened her eyes. In other stealth-capsules scattered throughout the Mars System, other cyborgs readied themselves for the desperate battle to come.

A wait of three hours then occurred as the Doom Stars and the SU Battlefleet maneuvered for position. The super-ships were between the orbits of ruined Deimos and Phobos, which would soon appear from around Mars and face an obviously brutal strike from the Highborn. Deimos orbited 23,500 kilometers away from the center of Mars. Phobos orbited 9,400 kilometers away. The three Doom Stars had reached a 17,000-kilometer distance from Mars.

To kill an enemy fleet that was determined to use a planet as a shield meant that the hunting ships had to come into close orbit. The reason was simple. The angles and distances were all on the side of the fleet closest to the planet. If the Doom Stars had stayed even 100,000 kilometers out, they would have had to travel a much greater distance to get onto the other side of the planet as compared to the fleet just above the planet's atmosphere. Supreme Commander Hawthorne had understood that as he'd made his plans many months ago. His strategy had counted on it. Toll Seven and Web-Mind had concurred. For each side, this was the most dangerous phase of the battle. At these ranges, beams almost struck immediately, and missiles streaked the distances in a matter of minutes.

The commander of Phobos sprayed a prismatic-crystal field before the moon. Then every laser-port, missile battery and point-defense systems went on high alert. Behind the moon as it moved in its orbit followed the bulk of the decoy fleet. Behind the decoy-vessels flew the SU orbitals, over five hundred fighters. They had little chance against massive lasers and point-defense systems. It was a suicide run, and most of the pilots knew it. But here at this hour every piece of equipment would enter the cauldron of battle to try to eke out a few more percentage points for its side. The presence of the orbitals provided one other benefit, a hopeful overloading of the Highborn targeting computers.

The cyborg stealth-capsules waited for that time as they floated in the system like space debris.

As Commodore Blackstone gave the orders, relayed by the *Vladimir Lenin's* communications officers, the SU Battlefleet accelerated behind Phobos for its death-ride.

***

Although Grand Admiral Cassius was a Highborn with a heroic ethos, and although he had personally taken command in the field for the final stroke against Social Unity, he used a medieval Mongol general's strategy in terms of himself. He remained in the *Julius Caesar*, which was the last Doom Star in the three-ship fleet. He remained at the safest spot in order that his fleet would continue to have the benefit of his presence.

Admiral Brutus in the *Hannibal Barca* led them, with Admiral Gaius in the *Napoleon Bonaparte* behind at an oblique angle, using the formation that the Theban Strategos Epaminondas had used against the Spartans in the Battle of Leuctra July, 371 B.C.

The Grand Admiral sat before the holographic globe as the Doom Stars headed to meet Phobos. Deimos had fired more missiles and lasers than Cassius would have thought possible. Clearly, the premen were readier for him than he would have believed. The premen either had taken Deimos intact or had brought more supplies than he had counted on. Could the Planetary Union have thrown in their lot with Social Unity?

Cassius shook his large head. The Planetary Union bosses hated Social Unity. Premen naturally and foolishly divided at the worst possible moments. It was another mark of their inferiority.

Grand Admiral Cassius allowed himself a smirk. Whatever the case with Deimos, in the end, it hadn't mattered. He'd heard the final broadcasts. The cowardly premen hadn't even known how to die well. It was a portent of good fortune.

"The moon has appeared!" a Highborn tracking-officer shouted.

"I can see that well enough," the Grand Admiral said, allowing just a hint of displeasure to enter his voice. That should calm any undue excitement from his command crew.

"It has a PC-Shield," the tracking officer said, his voice under control now.

Grand Admiral Cassius pressed a comm-button on his chair. It was a direct link to Admirals Brutus and Gaius. Beside the holographic globe of Mars now appeared two faces. Admiral Brutus had a low forehead for a Highborn, with a large nose and fiercely dark eyes. A stark red scar like a half-moon had been burned years ago onto his right cheek. Brutus wore his admiral's hat at a jaunty angle. On it was pinned a Galactic Spiral for extreme courage in battle.

Cassius spoke to the two holographic faces. "As I'm sure you gentlemen are aware, the prismatic-crystal field this time is a trick."

"A trick, Grand Admiral?" asked Brutus.

Sometimes Cassius wondered how Brutus had ever made it to Third. It clearly wasn't for cleverness.

"An elementary trick," Cassius said. "Behind the field await their ships, ready to attack once we burn through."

"Have you received another burst of information from the *Thutmosis III*?" Admiral Brutus asked with a concentrated frown.

"If you'll remember, the Praetor sent us a lightguide-message saying the premen were wise enough to form an aerosol-gel cloud, blocking his view. No, gentlemen, my knowledge comes from analyzing premen tactics and personalities. Their hope now will rest on tonnage. That indicates a mass attack."

"We'll slaughter them," Admiral Brutus predicted.

"Undoubtedly true," Grand Admiral Cassius said. "But we must be ready for the true surprise. It must come now or it will never help them."

"What surprise?" Admiral Brutus asked.

"An astute question," Cassius said dryly. "Make sure you report any unusual activities. Happy hunting, gentlemen. Grand Admiral Cassius out."

The two faces wavered for a moment and then folded in on themselves and disappeared. It left the Mars holographic image hanging by itself.

The Grand Admiral leaned back in his chair, studying the holographic globe. Then he uttered a low-toned command. "Begin emergency engine sequences," he said.

Several Highborn glanced down at him from their higher levels.

Cassius smiled grimly. "In the next few hours, we're going to need all the energy we can lay our hands on. We must wipe the Mars System clean of all enemy vessels. This is the hour when Social Unity dies, when its last hope is killed."

Highborn officers turned back to their boards as the needed commands were relayed.

Grand Admiral Cassius leaned forward with his balled fists resting on the arms of his command chair.

-16-

Three mighty Doom Stars bore down on Phobos as the moon swung around Mars. The Doom Stars were composed of an unbelievable tonnage of steel, titanium and asteroid particle shielding.

Phobos was asteroid-shaped and had three axes, about 27, 21 and 19 kilometers in length. Although a tiny moon in Solar System terms, it dwarfed the three super-ships. On it bristled a mass of point-defense systems, missile launch sites and laser ports. In front of Phobos floated a prismatic-crystal field.

Highborn heavy lasers remorselessly chewed through the field. The prismatic crystals reflected the laser-light and dissipated its strength. The power of the lasers slagged and destroyed the crystals, slowly digging deeper and deeper into the field. Then the lasers burned through and hit Phobos, burning moon-dust, melting some of it into glass. That action opened what many would come to call the third phase of the Third Battle for Mars.

As the prismatic-crystal field disappeared under the hellish fury of the Highborn lasers, the SU Battlefleet engaged its engines. Just behind Phobos was the decoy fleet, and it charged at the Doom Stars. Behind them followed the orbitals, and finally came the heart of the SU Battlefleet, the eight *Zhukov*-class battlewagons and the seven missile-ships.

"Launch Operation Trojan Hearse," Grand Admiral Cassius thundered.

In seconds, three huge missiles launched from each of the three Doom Stars. Every weapon aboard the *Hannibal Barca*, the *Napoleon Bonaparte* and the *Julius Caesar* was now dedicated toward destroying whatever tried to hinder the flight of these nine asteroid-busters. The spaceship-sized missiles accelerated hard for Phobos, flashing through a maelstrom of lasers, shells, anti-missiles and the final wisps of the prismatic-crystal field.

Six of the nine giant missiles died before reaching the moon. An orbital fighter rammed one, the pilot thinking it a new Highborn spacecraft. The nuclear explosion sent X-rays and EMP blasts through the vacuum. Most of the SU vessels washed by the X-rays were hardened against that, although twenty orbital fighters perished in a wave of EMP. Then the moon's point-defense cannons smashed through the seventh missile's hull and made a clean kill, this time without igniting the gargantuan warhead.

The eighth and ninth mega-missiles slammed into the moon in an interesting manner. Seconds before impact, a heavy plasma cannon in the missile's nose sent a gout of super-heated plasma ahead of itself. The plasma ate dust and moon-rock, and the missile slammed deeper and bored in an incredible distance. Everyone on Phobos felt the impact like a quake. Only then did the nova-warhead explode. It was like a miniature sun and caused a cataclysmic reaction. Gigantic cracks like the end of the world splintered through the entire moon, tearing buildings apart and destroying merculite-missile launch-sites and point-defense emplacements. Then the second asteroid-buster exploded.

The *Gotterdammerung* moment came for the Martian moon. The nova-warhead lived up to its name as Phobos blew apart into fourteen large chunks and millions of tiny particles of rock and dust. Several of the larger chunks tumbled toward the Red Planet. In a matter of days, several of those would slam against the planet and create unbelievable misery for hundreds of millions of Martians below.

***

From the safety of the cyborg command-pod, Toll Seven and Web-Mind observed this incredible display of military might. This was more than they had anticipated. The genetic super-soldiers had amassed fierce weaponry in the Doom Stars and its newest ordnance created on the Sun-Works Factory.

Yet the moon's destruction played to their secret plan. It filled space with matter; with dust, rocks and chunks. The SU Battlefleet, under the terse orders of Commodore Blackstone, roared through the debris like army ants yearning for vengeance. Missiles, lasers, sabot-rounds and orbital cannons blazed at the three super-ships in the distance.

Like ancient gods, the Doom Stars hung in the heavens and beamed with abandon, attempting to kill the last hope of Social Unity.

At the same time, the countless asteroid-appearing capsules scattered throughout the Mars System split open. Out of them like space-insects appeared vacc-suited humanoids. These vacc-suited cyborgs leaped from their capsules and engaged their hydrogen-thruster packs. They jetted for the Doom Stars. Each individually was an insignificant particle as compared to the orbitals, missiles and laser-beaming battleships. Time would tell if, united on the skin of a Doom Star, whether they would prove a battle-winning tactic or not.

On Mars it was early morning as Marten Kluge with five skimmers of commandos glided over the red dunes. The others had returned to New Tijuana, although Major Diaz and Rojas had remained with him.

The volcanic base of Olympus Mons was before them. In the high altitudes, near the peak where ice-crystal clouds drifted, several orbitals boomed as they broke the sound barrier and screamed toward space to join the fight. Perhaps even more ominous, a heavy whine emanated from the volcano.

"The proton beam is online," Omi crackled over the headphones.

"That's the injured dynamos revving with power," Marten said. He sat in front beside Osadar. The cyborg was the best pilot among them and the best driver, and thus she drove.

As if she knew Marten was thinking about her, Osadar swiveled her helmet toward him.

"Over there!" Marten pointed. About five kilometers away, the blast doors were shut. He had studied those doors before, and for days, he'd studied the specs of Olympus Mons that Chavez had emailed him from New Tijuana.

Marten's stomach churned. The skimmers were frail craft and there were only a few of them. As everyone had been telling him lately, this was a matter of luck. He shook his head. It was more than luck. This was the hour of decision. Logically, eyes were on the main event in space. When your enemy was distracted, that was the time to strike.

"Check your rifles," he said over the comm-unit. Then he

felt a hand on his shoulder. Marten turned back to Omi.

Instead of saying anything, Omi patted his shoulder a second time. Then his best friend returned to his portable plasma cannon. It was a dirty job and a risky task, but Marten couldn't trust anyone else to do it right. Omi and he had survived many battles together. Dear God, let his good friend survive this fight, too.

Afterward, Marten watched the doors as the skimmers roared toward destiny. His palms became sweaty and the churning worsened in his gut. They were going to face cyborgs. He hated them. He—

"We're almost in range," Osadar said.

"Omi," Marten said.

"I'm on it." The Korean charged the plasma cannon. On the other skimmers, chosen commandos did likewise.

Marten clenched his teeth as Osadar grounded the skimmer. One by one in a line, the others parked on the rock before the huge blast doors.

"Let's do this," Marten said. "Crack it open."

The cannon whined with energy and then a gout of superheated plasma discharged. Steam hissed from it, and the ball struck the blast doors, eating away at it as if the stuff were acid. Another plasma globule struck and another.

"Get ready," Marten said.

Air rushed out the breeched blast doors. It was a wave of heat. Marten had time to wonder about that. Then Osadar applied power. They lifted, and they leapt for the new entrance.

"Do we try to drive through that?" Major Diaz radioed.

"Roger," Marten said, as his eyes gleamed.

"But—"

"It's time to pray and then to kill if we have to." Brave words, Marten thought, as his stomach tightened.

Osadar flipped on the skimmer's lights. With perfect piloting skill, she took them through and into the giant underground garage. It was different than before, cleared out, with a new giant machine churning near the elevators.

"What is that?" Diaz radioed.

"A cyborg converter," Osadar whispered. "Marten, there will be—"

"Look out!" a commando roared. Gyroc fire sent shells screaming into the gloom.

Then Marten saw them: cyborgs. The creatures bounded at them with incredible speed. They were almost impossible to kill. A rocket-shell struck one, and exploded, tearing off plastic and flesh, knocking it to the garage floor. It didn't stay down, but got up and kept coming.

How many were down here?

Omi fired the recharged plasma cannon. It lit up the garage, and it caught a cyborg, burning half it, dropping the smoldering thing to the floor.

Finding his rifle in hand, Marten realized he laid down suppressing fire. He shred the flesh and uniform off one. Then it leapt, and might have landed among them. Osadar jumped up, meeting it over the skimmer's hood. They crashed, and the two cyborgs fought, one with its fists and Osadar with a blade.

Another cyborg sailed over Marten, smashing against the plasma cannon. Something broke in it. Superheated substance boiled out, burning the cyborg so its head simply melted into slag. Omi roared with pain, snatching his suited hand away.

Finding himself out of the skimmer, Marten aimed with deadly precision, firing three shells into the next skimmer. Each explosion caused a killing cyborg's head back, back and then something broke within the armored brainpan. The creature died, but not before it killed everyone in the skimmer.

The fight was short and savage, with six unarmed cyborgs demolishing most of them in less than half a minute. Without Osadar and the plasma cannons, none of them would have survived.

"Count off," Marten said.

They had a pitiful few: Osadar, Omi, Rojas and himself. The rest were dead, including Major Diaz. The man should have returned to New Tijuana with the other commandos.

"What do we do now?" Osadar asked.

Marten swallowed in a dry throat. If any of the cyborgs had borne arms, none of them would be alive. Was he crazy to have come here?

"I want to see that convertor," Marten said. "Then we stick with the plan and find a way up to the orbital hanger."

-18-

In the middle of a deadly space battle, where bright beams lased, huge ships passed like mini-planets and missiles zoomed and exploded with dazzling pyrotechnics, the creature formerly known as Lisa Aster rotated her cyborg body. A Doom Star with its pitted particle-shield was her entire world. She applied thrust from her nearly empty hydrogen-pack, braking. At the last moment, she rotated back and readied her legs. The asteroid-like particle-shield rushed at her. Then she crashed against a Doom Star, smashing her head against rock.

She awoke seconds or minutes later. She was never sure afterward. She clung tenaciously like a mechanical spider to the pitted surface. The surface shook and trembled constantly as beams, missiles and cannon-rounds struck. It was badly chewed up and had craters and deep laser holes, although it was still intact. Dust, rocks and boulder-sized chunks floated before the immensely thick shield.

LA31 cocked her dented helmet with its short antenna. The radio-pulse was low-key and garbled. Radiation, EMP blasts, jamming waves; the vacuum here was thick with invisibly harmful elements. LA31 felt sick and wanted to vomit. Worse, she felt weak. Programming kept her going, and enhancement drugs surged through her system like blood. She began to crawl like an insect across the pitted surface.

If there had been an independent observer between the two fleets, between the flashing lasers and streaking missiles, they might have seen hundreds of shifting motes on the particle-shields of the *Hannibal Barca*. Like a broken nest of spider bantlings, the mechanical-seeming motes crawled fast and headed for the seams between the giant blocks of particle-shielding. Lasers indifferently burned many of them into blackened crisps. Missiles blew off even more, along with asteroid-chunks and dust from the abused particle-shield. Yet for every three killed, one made it between the seams and crawled quickly for the hull below.

It was a cyborg infestation. LA31 was one of the lucky ones. She no longer felt lucky, as she had already vomited a black bile. She felt sicker than ever. Drugs, Web-Mind-programming and cyborg enhancements barely kept her functioning. She wanted to curl up and die. Instead, with fifty-three other cyborgs, she used magnetic clamps and clanged along the hull and to a main heavy laser-port.

There, with breach bombs, the cyborgs gained entrance to the Doom Star. Like cockroaches, they scurried into the hull, behind the walls and corridors that made up the vast spacecraft. They had the super-ship's specs imprinted in their memories. They had one goal, one destination—the giant fusion engines in the center of the unbeatable vessel.

***

"Sir..." a Highborn officer said aboard the *Hannibal Barca*.

"What?" Admiral Brutus shouted. On the holographic display before him, his number three particle-shield had almost crumbled into nothing. A suicidal SU missile-ship was too close, launching an unbelievable number of missiles from its tubes. Admiral Brutus had killed SU ship after SU ship, yet still these rabid premen attacked. He would kill every mother-birthing one of them.

"Sir!" another officer shouted. "We've been boarded."

"What?" Admiral Brutus roared, his features turning crimson with rage.

"Take a look, sir," the Highborn tech said.

Before Admiral Brutus appeared a holographic image of strange bionic soldiers scurrying through emergency hatches and repair corridors. Their vacc-suit emblems were nothing issued by the Highborn.

Admiral Brutus snarled orders to his security teams. They

would take care of these intruders. Then he concentrated on the SU missile-ship that still dared to rush a Doom Star.

***

Blue-tattooed Neutraloid Heydrich Hansen paced endlessly in his confinement chamber. He gnashed his teeth in hatred and felt every tremor that washed through the Doom Star. He wanted out of confinement. He wanted to kill. He wanted to rend. He wanted to destroy and feel hot blood gushing over his hands.

Then a terrific blow shook the vessel and threw Hansen to the metal floor. Lights flickered and then went out so darkness filled his world.

With a roar of almost feline excitement, Hansen leapt to his feet and tore at the door. In the blackness, he opened it, snarling with joy. At the same moment, emergency lighting came on and the electronic locks snapped back into place. It didn't matter for Neutraloid Heydrich Hansen. He was out of confinement. He was free. Now he needed weapons and he needed reinforcements. That meant freeing more neutraloids. He cackled with berserk laughter and floated toward the next door.

***

"Begin ship-shielding maneuver," Grand Admiral Cassius ordered. He sank into his chair as the *Julius Caesar's* engines engaged hard.

With grim concentration, Cassius studied the battlefield on his holographic display. Radiation, EMP blasts, X-rays, enemy jamming and debris meant his holographic image was fuzzy in places. He lacked full intelligence. But that had always been the nature of the battlefield. Making the right decision with only partial information had been a commander's lot for untold millennia. They had destroyed countless enemy vessels. Finally Cassius had come to realize that many of those kills had been shells, decoys. The heart of the enemy fleet remained: the *Zhukov*-class battleships. Even a Doom Star needed time to take out the most modern of them.

Those SU battleships concentrated on the *Hannibal Barca*. Admiral Brutus's Doom Star had taken damage. Now it was time to relieve the *Hannibal Barca*, to shield it with the relatively intact *Julius Caesar*.

"A few more minutes, old friend," Grand Admiral Cassius muttered. "More speed!" he ordered, keeping any worry out of his voice. In another twenty seconds, Cassius was pushed even deeper into his chair as the warship sped for war and glory.

"You're fighting hard, premen," Cassius muttered. "But it's not going to be enough to give you victory over me."

***

Aboard the *Vladimir Lenin*, Blackstone wanted to shout himself hoarse. The fight had come down to two giants grappling for a death-hold, to break the other giant's back.

His orbital fighters were nearly all destroyed. They had never had a chance against the Doom Stars. It had been a grim order to give and still sickened him. The bulk of the decoy fleet was space wreckage. Now he faced off against the battered *Hannibal Barca*. He had maneuvered the battlewagons so the first Doom Star shielded his battleships from the other Doom Stars. It might have been a clever tactic, but Blackstone felt too sick at Social Unity's losses to feel elated.

"We're beaming into the Doom Star's hull!" the targeting officer shouted.

"It's so huge," Commissar Kursk said. "A super-ship like that will take time to die."

"It's rotating!" the targeting officer shouted. "Damn! They're swinging the entire ship to bring an untouched shield into our line of fire."

Blackstone wondered if he dared to order a charge. It would likely mean the final destruction of the last battleships of his fleet. If he bored in now and kept chewing the particle-shields, he might actually kill a Doom Star. But the cost, the entire SU Battlefleet, that seemed too high a price.

As he hesitated, General Fromm's eyes narrowed. "We must accelerate," Fromm said in his strangely calm voice.

"…no," Blackstone whispered. "We can kill the *Hannibal Barca* from here."

The Earth General cocked his head strangely. Then a small dark object appeared in his hands. It was a needler. General Fromm aimed it at Blackstone.

"You will order full acceleration toward the Doom Star," Fromm said.

"He has a needler!" someone shouted.

Fromm drew a solar grenade from his garments. "One flick of my thumb," he said, "and I can destroy the command center of the Battlefleet. If you want to live, you must do as I order."

"Why are you doing this?" Blackstone asked.

"Do not attempt any subterfuge tactics," Fromm said. "You will obey me or—"

There was a strange sound, and then General Fromm crumpled, sliding in an almost boneless fashion from the map-module and onto the floor. Commissar Kursk rushed around the module. She had a stun gun in her hand. She had shot Fromm at full power. The tall Commissar knelt beside the Earth General as Blackstone stumbled to that side of the module. He watched in shock as Kursk picked up Fromm's needler. She pressed the tip of the needler against Fromm's head, shooting twenty needles into his cranium, making it a bloody mass of mush and bone. She dropped the needler and snatched the solar grenade, carefully examining it.

Her face pale, Kursk looked up and met Blackstone's eyes.

"You killed General Fromm," was all Blackstone could say.

"I'm taking this elsewhere," Kursk said, hefting the still live solar grenade.

Blackstone was too stunned to respond.

"Commodore!" Kursk snapped in her best PHC voice. "You have a battle to run. See to it and let me worry about security."

A moment later Blackstone nodded and turned back to the map-module.

19

The *Hannibal Barca* was vast beyond any other class of spacecraft. It contained thousands of decks, chambers, corridors, storage bays, launching tubes, laser coils, reactor space, sleeping quarters, exercise areas, weapons lockers, toilet cubicles, hatches and repair space-ways in a complex maze. The cyborgs propelled themselves through the maze like a metallic infestation. Their memories were flawless. Their execution of attack proved fast, lethal and bewildering.

Out of hatch ATR-19 shot cyborg after cyborg. During the weightless periods, they magnetized their palms and pressed them against the metal walls to propel themselves like swimmers. When ship acceleration produced pseudo-gravity, the cyborgs magnetized their boots and ran in a *clank, clank, clank* charge.

The first Highborn to witness them was Third Rank Marco in a damage-control suit. He swiveled toward a strange sound, gawked at the cyborgs for a full second. Then he snatched up his laser-welder, roared a battle cry, and died in a fusillade of red laser-light. Each cyborg in turn, including LA31, leaped over his smoldering corpse as they invaded deeper into the *Hannibal Barca*, seeking the massive fusion cores.

A minute later, interior ship-cameras recorded the slaughter of a Highborn reaction-team.

On the command deck, Admiral Brutus roared, "What are those?"

The admiral received his answer two-and-a-half minutes later. In gymnasium F-7, three Highborn in battleoid-armor

307

opened up with .55-caliber rotating hand-cannons. A cyborg staggered backward before dodging behind a bulkhead. Depleted uranium slugs had slammed against its armored torso, but failed to kill it. Return laser-fire reflected off the shiny battleoid skin.

"The things aren't human. They're some kind of battle machine!" the Highborn officer shouted into his microphone. "I don't think they feel pain, and they're faster than greased death."

As if to prove the officer's point, three cyborgs sheathed their laser-carbines and charged with vibroknives. A single cyborg blew backward from more hand-cannon fire. The three Highborn had targeted its head. The .55-caliber Gatling guns were an integral part of a Highborn's battleoid-arm. The two surviving cyborgs were wasp-fast. Graphite-enhanced muscles drove the vibroknives as the blades whined at high-performance. And in a shocking display of knife-fighting techniques, the cyborgs opened the three battleoid-suits and butchered the giants inside.

Now that they were meeting real resistance, the cyborgs broke into triad teams. They ceased the single concentrated thrust and attacked in a wave-assault. The next ten minutes saw savage fighting as cyborgs clashed with more battleoid-armored Highborn. To the astonishment of Admiral Brutus, it took three Highborn dead to produce a cyborg kill.

"Are they better than us?" Brutus shouted, as he pounded the arm of his command chair.

Three Highborn dead versus one cyborg killed, the honor went to the cyborgs, but the victory pushed toward the Highborn. As remorseless as the cyborgs were, the Highborn kept setting up ambushes, taking the losses and killing the alien things.

LA31's triad reached deeper into the Doom Star than any other cyborg team. Because of that, she neared the mighty fusion cores. The cores produced a constant sound and caused the ship's walls and corridors to vibrate with power.

Five Highborn waited for her in a narrow corridor, it being painted with yellow and black stripes, with red warning signs. They had set up a plasma cannon. One Highborn watched a monitor-board, which showed the cyborgs advancing toward them. Two Highborn knelt beside and readied the plasma cannon. Another battleoid soldier stood behind it, eager to fire the dangerous weapon. The last Highborn stood back with his rotating hand-cannon ready, playing lookout.

"Eight seconds," the monitor-board watching Highborn said.

"I'm ready," the plasma gunner said.

***

LA31 led the other two cyborgs against the waiting Highborn. They floated fast as they pushed off the walls and attacked from around the corridor.

A Highborn in battleoid-armor shouted. Another pointed. Then superheated plasma roiled toward LA31. She pushed off against a deck plate, moving even faster. The plasma caught the cyborg behind her, killing it in a wash of superheated mass. Bits of plasma scorched the back of LA31's legs, eating into her. It caused a microsecond of intense pain. Then her internal computer shut it off.

Two Highborn swiveled the big gun. Another aimed his hand-cannon. It rotated wildly as flames spewed. The shells *spanged* off LA31's shoulder-guards, and the impacts slowed her. Then her left arm refused to respond to her will.

Before the .55 caliber shells could halt or kill her, LA31 and the other cyborg were among the Highborn. The battle was lethally quick. The second to last Highborn, with battleoid-armored strength, twisted the head off the other cyborg. Then LA31 used her vibroblade to deadly effect, slaughtering the last two giants.

LA31 might have smiled, but she felt sick, and her emotions had died some time ago. Remorselessly, she continued her lonely charge toward the fusion cores.

***

A lone Highborn waited in LA31's path. He was the last of the battleoid-armored super-soldiers to stand between her and the fusion cores. He watched a monitor and knew she was injured. He could kill this thing. He promised Admiral Brutus that over his comm-link.

But the last battleoid-armored Highborn was unaware that another factor was about to enter the situation.

Neutraloid Heydrich Hansen lurked nearby. With Hansen were seven other neutraloids. They had floated past many dropped guns and knives, taking several. The floating globules of blood and the Highborn corpses had unhinged them. The teeth-gnashing, blue-tattooed berserks wanted to kill the Masters. They wanted the joy of *feeling* the Masters gasping their last breath as the giants shuddered in death-agony.

Hansen raised a hand for silence. He heard the lone Highborn ahead of them in the corridor. "We must kill him," he said in his strangely high-pitched voice.

The others whined with eagerness.

Hansen smiled savagely as he remembered the training table. Then he hissed with rage and floated around the corridor and behind the last Highborn defending the fusion cores from LA31.

The Highborn must have heard something. He turned, with his servos whining. Then he brought up his arm as the hand-cannon boomed.

Neutraloids screamed. Neutraloids lost fist-sized pieces of flesh as the .55 caliber bullets shredded them. Yet they kept coming, and three of them gripped vibroknives, finally have learned to hang onto them.

The neutraloids grappled with the armored giant. The Highborn squeezed the head of one, killing it. Then vibroknives entered his armor, and one smashed into his guts. He staggered, and crashed onto the deck plates.

The remaining neutraloids howled with glee. Then the three grinned down at the fallen Highborn.

"Fools," the Highborn said.

One of the neutraloid slapped his chest. "I am Heydrich Hanson." He might have said more, but he roared with high-pitched rage. So did the others. Instead of talking, they tore the giant out of his armor and began to beat him to death.

20

"It's too late, Commodore," the targeting officer said. "If the Doom Star hadn't rotated to a relatively undamaged particle-shield, we would have killed it. Unless the cyborgs are going to do something…"

Blackstone stared down at the map-module. On the holographic display, two huge Doom Stars appeared like vast planets. They moved into position above and below the most damaged Doom Star. Blackstone gripped the map-module's steel-gleaming sides and willed the first Doom Star to die. What had happened to the cyborgs and their stealth attacks? He had five battleships left and one missile-ship. He couldn't lose an entire SU Battlefleet and not even kill a single Doom Star. Were the Highborn that much better than regular humans and cyborgs?

Blackstone's gut churned with the knowledge of defeat. He had been given the solemn task of halting the Highborn, and he had failed miserably and totally. The Solar System belonged to the Highborn. The genetic super-soldiers would rule. The question now was how to die. Should he charge with the remnants of his fleet? Or should he take these last vessels and run to try to fight another day?

"Sir," the communications officer whispered. "I've decrypted a strange message."

"What is it?" Blackstone asked listlessly.

"The Highborn are broadcasting it openly, sir," the communications officer said. "I think you should see this."

"Put it on the map-module," Blackstone said.

The images of the space battle wavered and Blackstone frowned. It looked like a cyborg in a fusion reactor area. The cyborg used a laser, beaming into delicate equipment.

"Who is broadcasting this again?" Blackstone asked.

"The Highborn, sir."

Blackstone continued to blink at the startling image.

***

"Kill it!" Admiral Brutus roared. "Destroy it! The machine is in a fusion core!"

Ten Highborn reaction-teams in battleoid armor clanked through the corridors, each knowing life and death for an entire Doom Star depended on reaching that thing soon enough.

***

Even cyborgs couldn't take lethal doses of radiation for long. LA31 could hardly see anymore. Her pain sensors—

It stopped mattering then as the fusion core overloaded. In another three seconds, the former Lisa Aster ceased to exist.

***

From his command bridge, Grand Admiral Cassius watched in horror as the *Hannibal Barca* went nova.

The vast bulk of the super-ship absorbed some of the radiation, X-rays and EMP blasts. Then the incredible mass and tonnage exploded outward like a vast grenade. Its bulkheads, cargos, particle-shields, coils, walls and hull became projectiles.

The *Napoleon Bonaparte* and the *Julius Caesar* took the brunt of those projectiles. The heavy SU battlewagons received a lesser wave. The majority of the former *Hannibal Barca* sped out into space and toward Mars in the near distance as a million particles of debris.

***

The *Vladimir Lenin* shuddered as its particle-shields took the heavy impacts of the exploded Doom Star. Blackstone was pitched off his feet, and he hit his shoulder hard against the map-module. He lay stunned for seconds and in throbbing pain. Then someone was helping him up.

Blackstone stared at the image of the map-module. There were two Doom Stars where seconds earlier there had been three. The SU Battlefleet had destroyed a Doom Star. The other two must have taken heavy damage from the blast.

"Awaiting orders, Commodore," the targeting officer said.

Blackstone blinked at the map-module. What was the correct decision now? One third of the Highborn fleet was dead. The other two Doom Stars were hurt, perhaps critically. The question was: could he finish them off?

He listened several seconds to battle reports. The SU Battlefleet was almost gone. He had four battleships left and no missile-ships. The last one hadn't survived the Doom Star's destruction. Four battleships could not defeat two Doom Stars, not even badly wounded ones.

"It's time to run," Blackstone said.

"Run where, sir?" the targeting officer asked. "We can't outrun a Doom Star's long-range lasers."

Then it hit Blackstone, and he realized this could be his most brilliant move of the battle. "We run for Mars. We head for the outer edge of the atmosphere."

"Sir?" the targeting officer asked.

"We run toward the proton beam," Blackstone said.

21

Marten, Omi, Osadar and Rojas rode a magnetic lift. Everyone else who had broken through the blast doors was dead.

Marten was grim-faced and thoughtful. Omi cradled a burned hand, his face white and strained with the pain. Osadar seemed impassive. Rojas stared wordlessly at a spot in the elevator.

The Martian finally turned his head. "Did you see those things on the converter?"

Marten had been the one to shoot those things. None of the melds had possessed skin, only exposed musculature. The cyborgs that had attacked the skimmers must have been on converter duty. That's why none of the creatures had been armed. Even so, they had almost ended the orbital attempt as it started.

"People turned into cyborgs," Omi whispered.

"Is that what awaits Mars?" Rojas asked in a choked voice.

"Yes," Osadar said.

Rojas shivered and squeezed his eyes closed as sweat oozed onto his forehead.

Marten checked the lift monitor. It had taken too long to get this thing working. Was it already too late?

"We're almost there," he said. "Let's get ready." He flicked off the safety of his gyroc rifle as his thighs tensed for running.

The whine of the lift slowed, stopped and the doors swished open. And each of them opened fire even before they saw the cyborg waiting for them. Marten hammered a shell against its chest, blowing away parts. It cut down Rojas with carbine fire before Osadar leaped out and shoved a vibroblade into an eye.

"Don't stand around and gawk!" Marten shouted. "Follow me!"

He dragged Rojas with him. Then they ran for the hanger as the sounds in the volcano became unbearably loud.

"The dynamos are pumping the proton beam with power!" Rojas screamed into Marten's ear.

Marten skidded to a halt and dropped to his knees. Then he fired his gyroc rifle in quick succession and took out a PHC security team that stood before a door.

"What if there aren't any orbitals left?" Rojas asked.

"Then we're screwed!" Marten roared.

Osadar swiveled her head to stare at him.

"Come on!" Marten shouted over the rising whine of the dynamos. "Let's find out the worst."

***

Aboard the *Julius Caesar*, Grand Admiral Cassius was white-faced with fury. But he did not shout any orders or rave at fate. Instead, he chased the SU battleships around the curvature of Mars, seeking to bring his heavy lasers on them.

The premen had destroyed a Doom Star. The animals had managed to kill one-fifth of Highborn space power. That the SU Battlefleet had almost ceased to exist was something, but to Cassius it wasn't enough. He must annihilate all of it. Four battleships and a few other sundry vessels could still be enough to form the nucleus of another fleet. Other SU warships hadn't made it to Mars. If those warships joined the four battleships—

"That won't happen," Cassius whispered, "because soon these last battleships will be just more space debris."

***

In their haste to kill the battleships, the Doom Stars edged nearer Mars. They edged to within range of the deadly proton beam on Olympus Mons. As the Doom Stars accelerated around the curvature of Mars, the huge volcano became visible on the planet below.

The white proton beam stabbed into space. It stabbed at the

Napoleon Bonaparte. And as the beam had sliced through the particle shield of the *Ho Chi Minh* several weeks ago, it now sliced through the particle shield of the battle-worn Doom Star.

***

Marten Kluge strapped into an orbital crash seat. Beside him, blood trickled out of Rojas's mouth. He wasn't sure the Martian would make it.

"The craft is low on fuel," Osadar declared. She was flipping switches and turning on orbital systems.

"That's doesn't matter!" Marten shouted. "Lift off. We don't have any more time."

Osadar pressed another switch, and a motor whined. She shut it down and turned to Marten.

"Risk everything," he said. "It's now or never."

Osadar reengaged. The whine resumed and then roared with sudden power. "This will be rough," she said.

Marten almost yelled again to tell her to go, go, go. He felt the lurch then as the orbital rose off its pad. Would they be in time?

With a gush of power, Osadar aimed the orbital at the half-opened launch portal.

***

Highborn reactions were much faster than Homo sapien reactions. As the *Napoleon Bonaparte* began to take terrible damage from the proton beam, Grand Admiral Cassius ordered the launching of a Hellburner.

While the Hellburner was launched and fell toward the cone of the Solar System's largest mountain, the *Napoleon Bonaparte* took critical hits. Admiral Gaius did everything he could think of, but the proton beam proved superior to his actions.

The Hellburner shrugged off the point-defense cannons of Olympus Mons. And it maneuvered too sharply for the proton beam to target it. As the giant bomb neared, a lone orbital roared out of a hanger bay in the highest third of the mountain. The orbital engaged afterburners almost immediately as it shot toward the heavens. The Hellburner slammed into Olympus Mons and ignited. It made sunlight because it *was* sunlight. A

316

Bethe solar-phoenix reaction began. It would burn for hours and harm those within a five-hundred-kilometer radius. It killed the proton beam. It killed the cyborgs in and on Olympus Mons and it destroyed the cyborg converter deep in the mountain.

The Hellburner pushed up a massive mushroom cloud that climbed into the Martian atmosphere. It had destroyed many, but also saved what was left of the *Napoleon Bonaparte*.

The Third Battle for Mars was nearly over.

-22-

Three humanoids in vacc-suits drifted between the abandoned orbital fighter and the *Mayflower*. The former Highborn shuttle orbited Mars. Tall Osadar Di was in the lead, with a towline attached between her and Marten. Another line connected Marten to Omi.

Soon Osadar reached the shuttle, and she engaged her magnetic clamps. She stuck to the side of the shuttle and pulled Marten in. He soon magnetized himself beside her and drew in Omi. Once everyone was secured to the shuttle, Marten unclipped a handscanner and typed in the needed codes. They waited as the *Mayflower's* computer decided if the codes matched. Then the outer lock that Training Master Lycon had shot out of many months ago opened for them. Marten, Omi and Osadar floated in. Squad Leader Rojas had died during the hard liftoff from the mountain.

Far to the west of them down on Mars, Olympus Mons glowed brightly.

Hissing occurred as the airlock filled with a breathable atmosphere. Soon, the inner hatch slid open. Leaving his helmet on, Marten floated for the pilot's chair. Osadar and Omi floated after him. It was time to leave Mars, to slip away if they could.

***

Grand Admiral Cassius came to a painful conclusion. He needed to get the *Napoleon Bonaparte* to the Sun-Works Factory as fast as possible. It would take at least a full year,

318

maybe more, to repair the mighty super-ship.

The numbers of sick and dying Highborn aboard the radiated Doom Star were horrifying. Combined with the dead of the *Hannibal Barca*... the Third Battle for Mars had been a disaster.

Yes, he had destroyed the bulk of the SU Battlefleet. Intelligence reports indicated that twelve battleships had arrived at Mars. Those battleships were the heart of the SU Fleet. One third of those vessels remained. He wasn't sure how heavy their damage was. The fact Social Unity still had one third of their most crucial warships left was galling.

The new factor made his decision obvious. That factor was the cyborgs. They were a new element in the war for Solar System Supremacy. The tactic of swarming a Doom Star with stealth cyborgs—

Grand Admiral Cassius slowly eased out of near-Mars orbit. The *Napoleon Bonaparte* was a crippled warship. Even worse was the Highborn dead. Cassius refused to accept he had lost the battle. He had done better than a draw. Yes, the premen had killed one third of his fleet. But he had destroyed close to ninety percent of their force. The galling truth, however, was that he was retreating.

Could Social Unity hang onto Mars with what it had? What about the cyborgs? Where had they come from?

Grand Admiral Cassius felt something strange then. In a lesser being, it would have been fear. He refused to accept that this feeling was fear. Maybe it was trepidation about the future.

"This is a setback," he whispered. He would not lie to himself. The premen had hurt the Highborn. Yet the essence of the Highborn was to fight through to victory.

What about the cyborgs? The machine men troubled him. They were an unknown factor. He consoled himself with one thought. Working hard to keep their presence hidden, the cyborgs had played their bid to destroy three Doom Stars. Instead, one Doom Star was dead and another badly hurt. Yet now the Highborn realized they had another enemy to contend with. Next time he would be ready for the cyborgs.

The war with them had just begun.

***

319

Commodore Blackstone and his four battleships hid behind Mars as probes watched the two Doom Stars leave near-Mars orbit.

"Did we win?" Commissar Kursk asked.

Blackstone stared stonily at his vidscreen. They were in his wardroom. On another display in his screen, he was reading the report of what the medical officers had found implanted in General Fromm's neck.

"The cyborgs did this to Fromm," Blackstone said.

"What did you say?" Kursk asked.

"Here," Blackstone said, shifting aside. "You'd better read this."

***

In the hidden command-pod from the Neptune System, in its close-Mars orbit, Toll Seven and Web-Mind debated their next move. Almost all the Neptune cyborgs were gone. Everything on Olympus Mons was lost. General Fromm had failed to report in. What had happened aboard the *Vladimir Lenin*? Their allied bio-forms had been strangely silent. The bio-forms should have tried to communicate with him by now.

It was then Web-Mind alerted Toll Seven.

Toll Seven turned on a screen. There was a bright image on it that showed an engine was burning. Before Toll Seven could ask, Web-Mind had computed the shuttle's flight-path. It seemed to be headed for Jupiter. Cyborg Osadar Di had been from the Jupiter System. Web-Mind therefore gave it a thirty-three percent probability that Osadar Di was aboard that shuttle. They could not allow her to escape. She knew too much.

Toll Seven acknowledged Web-Mind's probabilities and he recognized the danger. He opened a comm-link and hailed the *Vladimir Lenin*. Then he sent them the shuttle's coordinates and asked that they destroy the vessel.

***

Seconds later, at Blackstone's urgent command, lasers burned into space. They used Toll Seven's radio-message, triangulating from the four battleships. Those lasers pierced the camouflaged hull of Toll Seven's command-pod, killing the

Neptune cyborg and Web-Mind.

"What will you tell Supreme Commander Hawthorne?" Kursk asked on the *Vladimir Lenin's* bridge.

Blackstone gave her a wintry grin, and said, "Mission completed."

***

Aboard the *Mayflower*, Marten and Osadar noticed the lasers. Omi was in the medical unit, receiving treatment for his burned hand.

"I wonder who they're firing at?" asked Marten.

Osadar remained silent. Perhaps she was waiting for fate to screw her further.

"Get ready," Marten said. "We're going to increase thrust and pretend we're a missile." After alerting Omi, Marten applied greater power. And the former Highborn shuttle left Mars orbit.

Marten Kluge grinned at Osadar. "We did it," he said. "We finally escaped Inner Planets."

"For how long?" she asked.

"For now," he said.

"And tomorrow?"

Marten shrugged. "Tomorrow will take care of itself. Today, we've done the impossible and won." He felt the diplomatic credentials in his hidden pocket. He thought about the Martian commandos who had died to make his dream possible. He owed them a blood-debt. He would try to repay. He wasn't sure how, but he knew that he was going to help the Planetary Union gain its freedom and keep it.

The End

12053450R00182

Printed in Great Britain
by Amazon.co.uk, Ltd.,
Marston Gate.